KU-042-203

George du Maurier

TRILBY

Edited by
LEONEE ORMOND
King's College, London

EVERYMAN
J. M. DENT · LONDON
CHARLES E. TUTTLE
VERMONT

Introduction © J. M. Dent, 1992
Other critical apparatus © J. M. Dent, 1994

All rights reserved

First published in Everyman in 1931
This edition, 1994

J. M. Dent
Orion Publishing Group
Orion House
5 Upper St Martin's Lane,
London WC2H 9EA
and
Charles E. Tuttle Co. Inc.
28 South Main Street,
Rutland, Vermont 05701, USA

Typeset by CentraCet Limited, Cambridge
Printed in Great Britain by
The Guernsey Press Co. Ltd, Guernsey, C. I.

This book if bound as a paperback is subject to
the condition that it may not be issued on loan or otherwise
except in its original binding.

British Library Cataloguing-in-Publication Data
is available upon request.

ISBN 0 460 87447 0

CONTENTS

LIST OF ILLUSTRATIONS

NOTE ON THE AUTHOR AND EDITOR

GEORGE DU MAURIER was born in Paris in 1834 to a French father and an English mother. He died in London in 1896. *Trilby* (1894), like his other novels, *Peter Ibbetson* of 1891 and *The Martian* of 1896, reflects his Anglo-French background. Du Maurier intended to be a painter, and began his training in Paris and Antwerp. The loss of his left eye forced a change of direction and he became an illustrator of books and a social cartoonist. He worked for the comic magazine *Punch* from 1860 until his death. In his early days in London Du Maurier tried his hand at writing short stories, but when his Latin Quarter story was rejected by his idol, Thackeray, he abandoned the project. It was his anxiety about the effect of eye-strain on his *Punch* work which turned Du Maurier back to fiction and transformed him into a successful novelist in his late fifties.

Du Maurier was a man of great personal charm with a strong streak of melancholy. He adored his five children, the youngest of whom was the actor-manager Gerald Du Maurier. Gerald's daughter, Daphne, inherited her grandfather's gift for narrative as well as his fascination with the paranormal. Each of George Du Maurier's novels mingles the supernatural and the autobiographical in a remarkable way. *Trilby*'s popularity, which disturbed and dis-oriented the author, resulted from his successful evocation of student life in the Latin Quarter as well as from his sensational plot. Du Maurier died not long after, worn out by the strain of having written a best-seller.

LEONEE ORMOND is Reader in English at King's College, University of London. Her particular interests are nineteenth- and early twentieth-century literature and Victorian painting and book illus-tration. She has written on a wide range of authors and artists including Browning, Dickens, George Eliot, Kipling, Shaw, G. F. Watts and Linley Sambourne. A biography of George Du Maurier was published in 1969 and books on Lord Leighton (with her husband, Richard Ormond), J. M. Barrie and Tennyson came out in 1974, 1987 and 1993.

CHRONOLOGY OF DU MAURIER'S LIFE

Year *Age* *Life*

1834		6 March, George Louis Palmella Busson Du Maurier born Paris, son of a Frenchman, Louis-Mathurin Du Maurier, and an Englishwoman, Ellen Clarke Winter, taken to England to stay with maternal grandmother, Mary Anne Clarke, formerly the mistress of the Duke of York
1835	1	Family moves to Brussels
1836	2	9 February, brother, Alexander Eugène, born
1837	3	Autumn/winter, family moves to London
1839	5	Spring, sister, Isabella Louise, born Family moves to Boulogne, where they live with Mary Anne Clarke
1842	8	Family moves to Passy on the edge of Paris; George at school there
1847	13	Family moves to rue du Bac, Paris; George and Eugène enter Pension Froussard in the Avenue Bois de Boulogne

CHRONOLOGY OF HIS TIMES

Year	Artistic Events	Historical Events
1830		Louis Philippe takes French throne Belgium achieves independence
1831	Victor Hugo, *Notre Dame de Paris*	
1832		First Reform Bill
1833		Abolition of slavery
1834		New Poor Law
1835	Théophile Gautier, *Mademoiselle de Maupin*	
1837	Chopin, *Impromptu in A flat*	Queen Victoria comes to the throne
1838	Dickens, *Oliver Twist*	
1840	Nicolo Paganini dies	Queen Victoria marries Prince Albert
1841	*Punch* founded	
1842	Tennyson, *Poems*	Chartist riots
1843	Dickens, *Martin Chuzzlewit*	
1844	Disraeli, *Coningsby*	
1846		Repeal of the Corn Laws
1847	Emily Brontë, *Wuthering Heights* Tennyson, *The Princess* Charlotte Brontë, *Jane Eyre*	Lionel Nathan de Rothschild elected MP, but not able to take his seat because Jewish

Year	Age	Life
1848	14	February, witnesses fighting during the revolution in Paris
1851	17	Fails the Baccalaureat, joins his father in London Entered as a student in the Birkbeck Chemistry Laboratory of University College
1852	18	Death of Mary Ann Clarke improves the family's financial position Established as an analytical chemist in Barge Yard, Bucklersbury, but does very little work
1856	22	8 June, death of Louis-Mathurin Du Maurier Returns to Paris and enrols as a student at studio of Charles Gleyre; meets, among others, Thomas Armstrong, Thomas Reynolds Lamont, Edward Poynter, James McNeill Whistler
1857	23	Summer, enters Antwerp Academy of Fine Arts Autumn, suddenly loses the sight of his left eye Moves to Malines (Mechelen) with his mother
1859	25	May, to Düsseldorf with his mother to consult oculist; is told that he will not go blind Shares a studio with Edouard Hunziker and makes friendships in the artistic community

Year	Artistic Events	Historical Events
1848	Thackeray, *Vanity Fair* Pre-Raphaelite Brotherhood founded Elizabeth Gaskell, *Mary Barton*	European Revolutions Louis Philippe exiled Louis Napoleon becomes President of France
1849	Murger, *Scènes de la vie de Bohème* Thackeray, *Pendennis*	
1850	Tennyson, *In Memoriam* Thackeray, *Rebecca and Rowena* Dickens *David Copperfield*	
1851		Great Exhibition Louis Napoleon's Coup d'Etat
1852	Thackeray, *Henry Esmond* Dumas, Play of *La Dame aux Camélias*	Second Empire under Napoleon III
1853	Dickens, *Bleak House* Verdi, *La Traviata* and *Il Trovatore*	
1854	John Leech, *Pictures of Life and Character*	Crimean War (to 1856)
1855	Tennyson, *Maud* Browning, *Men and Women* Thackeray, *The Newcomes*	
1856	J. D. Ingres, *La Source*	
1857	Moxon illustrated Tennyson Baudelaire, *Fleurs du Mal*	Indian Mutiny (to 1858)
1858	Adam, *Noël*	Lionel de Rothschild takes his seat in the Commons
1859	Tennyson, *Idylls of the King* begins publication Dickens, *Tale of Two Cities* Darwin, *Origin of Species* Gounod, *Faust*	

Year	Age	Life
1860	26	Early May, meets his sister's friend Emma Wightwick, having previously seen her as a schoolgirl Late May, to London with the Wightwicks, intending to be an illustrator Lives in studios at 8 Berners St and 70 and 85 Newman St; 29 September, first drawing in *Once a Week* 6 October, first drawing in *Punch* Wightwick drapery business founders, causing a temporary coolness towards Emma
1861	27	May, engaged to Emma Wightwick June, moves to 91 Newman St 21 September, short story 'Recollections of an English Gold Mine' published in *Once a Week*; October, first drawing in *Good Words*; submits a short story about student life in Paris to *The Cornhill* and it is rejected
1862	28	August, first drawing in *London Society*, a new magazine
1863	29	3 January, marries Emma Wightwick; settles at 46 Great Russell St (later no. 91) April, first drawing in *The Cornhill*; June/July, in Bonn and Düsseldorf; August/September and November/December, illustrations for 'Santa' and 'The Notting Hill Mystery' in *Once a Week*, possibly his finest drawings; To 1867, drawings for eight volumes of novels and stories by Elizabeth Gaskell
1864	30	1 January, Beatrix Isabel Du Maurier born; August/September, first visit to Whitby October, death of John Leech; replaces Leech as social cartoonist for *Punch*
1865	31	13 May, Guy Louis Du Maurier born
1866	32	*A Legend of Camelot*, an extended parody of the Pre-Raphaelites in verse and drawings, appears in *Punch*; May, takes part of Box in first performance of *Cox and Box* by Francis Burnand and Arthur Sullivan November, Sylvia Jocelyn Du Maurier born
1867	33	August, in Paris for the International Exhibition
1868	34	March, moves to 12 Earls Court Terrace, Kensington; August, Marie Louise (May) Du Maurier born Illustrates Thackeray's *Henry Esmond*
1869	35	June, moves to 4 Holly Mount, Hampstead and September, to Gangmoor House, Hampstead

Year	Artistic Events	Historical Events
1860		Garibaldi in Sicily and Naples
1861	George Eliot, *Silas Marner* J. L. Gérôme, *Phryne Before her Judges*	American Civil War (to 1865)
1862	Elizabeth Gaskell, *Sylvia's Lovers*	
1864	Death of John Leech Elizabeth Gaskell, *Wives and Daughters*	
1865	Dickens, *Our Mutual Friend*	Assassination of Lincoln
1866	Swinburne, *Poems and Ballads*	
1867	Zola, *Thérèse Raquin*	Second Reform Act
1868		Disraeli Prime Minister

Year	Age	Life
1870	36	February, death of Ellen du Maurier; summer, moves to 27 Church Row, Hampstead September to November 1871, illustrates George Meredith's *Harry Richmond* in *The Cornhill*
1871	37	September, revisits Boulogne
1872	38	January, serious problems with his remaining eye; begins to draw on a larger scale
1873	39	26 March, Gerald Du Maurier born To 1882, the aesthetic cartoons, satirising the cult of beauty, begin to appear in *Punch*
1874	40	Early in year, moves to New Grove House, Hampstead
1875	41	July to May 1876, illustrates *The Hand of Ethelberta* by Thomas Hardy
1877	43	Family holiday in France, at first in Normandy and then at Auteuil, near Paris; sees effects of Franco-Prussian war
1880	46	June to November, illustrates *Washington Square* by Henry James in *The Cornhill*; beginning of his friendship with James December to December 1881, illustrates *A Laodicean* by Thomas Hardy in *Harper's Magazine*, the beginning of his association with *Harper's*
1881	47	Begins to paint watercolour portraits and watercolour paintings from his own cartoons and illustrations; March, Associate of the Royal Society of Painters in Watercolours; exhibits there until 1894-5
1882	48	Summer, returns to Whitby; continues to go there in later years
1884	50	July, Beatrix marries Charles Hoyer Millar; summer, Guy based in India with the Royal Fusiliers Summer, exhibition of drawings at the Fine Art Society June and December, publishes two poems, both translations from French, in the *English Illustrated Magazine*
1885	51	Autumn, holiday in Scotland with John Millais
1886	52	Spring, takes a house in Gloucester Gardens, Bayswater; continues to do this in different Bayswater houses until 1890 May, briefly in Paris; September, in Paris, Barbizon and Fontainebleau

Year	Artistic Events	Historical Events
1870	Dickens, *Edwin Drood*	Franco-Prussian War (to 1871)
1871		Paris Commune
1872	George Eliot, *Middlemarch* Frederick Walker, *The Fishmonger's Shop*	
1873	Pater, *The Renaissance*	
1874	Trollope, *The Way We Live Now*	Disraeli Prime Minister (to 1880)
1876	George Eliot, *Daniel Deronda*	
1877	Opening of the Grosvenor Gallery	
1878	Frederic Leighton President of the Royal Academy Whistler versus Ruskin libel case	
1881	Henry James, *Portrait of a Lady* Gilbert and Sullivan, *Patience*	Death of Disraeli Anti-Semitic programs lead to deaths of many Jews in Russia
1884		Third Reform Act passed
1885		Freud observes hypnosis in Paris
1886	R. L. Stevenson, *Jekyll and Hyde* Henry James, *Princess Casamassima* Emile Zola, *L'Oeuvre*	Gladstone's Irish Home Rule bill is defeated

Year	Age	Life
1887	53	May, *Punch* visit to Paris
1889	55	24 March, offers Henry James the plot for *Trilby*; begins writing *Peter Ibbetson* May, *Punch* visit to Paris
1890	56	August and September, two articles on illustration in *The Magazine of Art* Winter, death of Du Maurier's brother and sister
1891	57	June to November. *Peter Ibbetson* published in *Harper's* Mid-December to January 1892, no *Punch* cartoons because of near blindness. Winter, gives a series of lectures on book illustration in England and Scotland; later published as *Social Pictorial Satire* (1898)
1892	58	January, begins work on *Trilby*. August, Sylvia marries Arthur Llewellyn Davies. November, *Harper's* offer terms for *Trilby*, giving the novelist a year to complete it
1893	59	Stanhope Terrace for winter
1894	60	January to July, *Trilby* in *Harper's*; great success; March, Joe Sibley passage appears. 19 May, *Pall Mall Gazette* publishes an interview in which Du Maurier admits that Joe Sibley is in part drawn from Whistler; May, Whistler threatens injunction; 1 June, Du Maurier agrees to remove Joe Sibley passage from book edition and to submit new passages; September, Harper and Whistler agree to stop the sale of the March number and to remove offending passages and illustrations. October, play of *Trilby* by Paul Potter opens in Manchester and moves to the Haymarket
1895	61	June, leaves Hampstead for 17 Oxford Square
1896	62	July, last visit to Whitby; 8 October, dies October to July 1897, *The Martian* published in *Harper's*
1897		March, Fine Art Society exhibition of drawings

Year	Artistic Events	Historical Events
1887		Victoria's Golden Jubilee
1888	Kipling, *Plain Tales from the Hills*	
1891	Hardy, *Tess of the D'Urbervilles* Wilde, *The Picture of Dorian Gray* Death of Henri Litolff	
1892	Wilde, *Lady Windermere's Fan*	
1893	Pinero, *The Second Mrs Tanqueray*	Gladstone's second Home Rule bill defeated in the Lords
1894	*Yellow Book* starts publication	The Dreyfus case in France (until 1899)
1896	Death of John Millais Edward Poynter becomes President of the Royal Academy	

INTRODUCTION

On Sunday afternoons in the 1880s, two men, one large and one small, could be seen walking together on Hampstead Heath. The more portentous but younger figure was that of Henry James, already known as the author of a range of novels and stories. His slighter companion was the French-born social cartoonist of *Punch*, George Du Maurier. As they strolled, the pair often discussed the differences between literature and the visual arts, presumably recalling how, in their youth, each had essayed the other's art. The young Du Maurier had published an autobiographical short story about his brief career as a research chemist. At the same time, he had submitted another, set in the Paris Latin Quarter, to the *Cornhill Magazine*, then under the editorship of Du Maurier's hero, William Makepeace Thackeray. This story was rejected, however, and, with the exception of short pieces accompanying his drawings in *Punch*, he had given up the idea of writing fiction. Now the friendship with James revived his interest: 'If I were a writer', he told him, 'it seems to me that I should have no difficulty about plots. I have in my head now plots for fifty stories. I'm always working them out for my own amusement.'[1]

As an example, Du Maurier outlined the plot of a story he had in mind:

> the history of the servant girl with a wonderful rich full voice but no musical genius who is mesmerized and made to sing by a little foreign Jew who has mesmeric power, infinite feeling, and no organ (save as an accompanist – on some instrument, violin) of his own.[2]

James wrote this down a year or two after the conversation. Du Maurier had again offered him the story, and James in turn encouraged the artist to write it himself. To James the outline appeared 'curious, picturesque and distinctly usable'. He hesitated to use it, not because it was fantastic, but from a fear that his own 'want of musical knowledge would hinder *me* somewhat in handling it'.[2]

Following this second conversation (24 March 1889), Du Maurier went home and began to write, working until first light the next morning. But the result was not the tale of the mesmeric musician, *Trilby*, but a story drawing upon memories of Du Maurier's childhood on the outskirts of Paris, *Peter Ibbetson*. Like all three Du Maurier novels, *Peter Ibbetson* combines a supernatural plot with a romantic memoir of the novelist's own youth. The hero, Peter, discovers that he can 'dream true', that he can lead another life in his sleep.

It was not until three years later, early in 1892, that Du Maurier again turned to the 'servant girl' plot. Initially, he had conceived of a story told by 'a poorish artist' who encounters the girl as a landlady's 'stupid, handsome daughter'.[2] When the narrator meets her again, years later, she is travelling with a Jewish musician and has become a magnificent singer. Only when her companion dies does the story-teller realize that 'she had had the glorious voice, but no talent – he had had the sacred fire, the rare musical organization, and had played into her and through her. The *end*, as regards her, [is] miserably pathetic.'[3]

Retaining the musician plot, Du Maurier decided on an important change in his plan – he made Paris his setting. The original tale began in London's artists' quarter, north of Oxford Street, a place well known to Du Maurier from the early 1860s. Now he drew upon an earlier part of his life, the time of his training at Charles Gleyre's studio in Paris (1856–7). Like the rejected short story of the 1860s, *Trilby* begins in a studio shared by three British artists, Taffy, the Laird and Little Billee. In the short story, Du Maurier made it clear that this was his own Paris studio in the rue Notre Dame des Champs, and that the three painters were Thomas Armstrong, Thomas Reynolds Lamont and himself. By the 1890s, he had so effectively blurred the portraits that other possibilities have sometimes been suggested as the originals of Taffy and Little Billee. The greatest difference between the short story and the novel, however, is that the former contains no Trilby. There is a commonplace art students' model, Aldegonde, but she possesses none of the Irish charm of the later Trilby O'Ferrall. Trilby is a 'grisette', a young girl from the working classes, but, most unusually, she is Irish, not French, the freckled and open-faced daughter of a disgraced clergyman and a Scotswoman.

The Paris setting of *Trilby* was one element in its popular success. Du Maurier introduces numerous details which only an insider could have known. There are episodes in Carrel's (Gleyre's) atelier, with its initiation rituals. The artists' studio is fully described with its plaster casts and reproductions, views over the rooftops and down the long streets. Celebrations of food and wine abound, as they had in the earlier short story, there are walks by the Seine and visits to the Morgue. At Christmas the artists attend midnight Mass at the Madeleine and then comes a party for their friends. These descriptions are bathed in nostalgia, as though the narrator cannot wait to share each experience with the willing reader. He writes of them in a breathless and intimate tone, sometimes using direct (and un-idiomatic) translations from the French.

Setting his novel in the Quartier Latin allowed Du Maurier to hint at an atmosphere of sexuality which certain British critics and readers found offensive. With the encouragement of Henry James, Du Maurier had become well read in contemporary French fiction. The bilingual artist was one of the few people with whom James could talk of Zola and Maupassant, and the subject frequently came up on their walks together. Du Maurier was occasionally shocked by French novels, but he enjoyed the idea that *Trilby* was a 'naughty' book, telling James that his 'Nouveau roman n'est pas pour les petites filles' (new novel is not for little girls).[4] In the 1890s, the 'fallen woman' was a fashionable literary topic, with novels like Hardy's *Tess of the D'Urbervilles*, and with the production of Oscar Wilde's *Lady Windermere's Fan* and A.W. Pinero's *The Second Mrs Tanqueray*. Du Maurier, however, was no Maupassant, and he approaches the subject of Trilby's past with considerable tact. Little Billee senses a 'thin slimy layer of sorrow and shame' under her cheerful exterior, and the narrator sadly concurs:

> My poor heroine . . . had all the virtues but one; but the virtue she lacked (the very one of all that plays the title-role, and gives its generic name to all the rest of that goodly company) was of such a kind that I have found it impossible so to tell her history as to make it quite fit and proper reading for the ubiquitous young person so dear to us all.

For one of the high points of the drama, Du Maurier turned to another French novelist, Alexandre Dumas the younger, whose *La Dame aux Camélias* was adapted for both drama and opera. When Durien, a sculptor, takes Trilby to the theatre, they see Mme Boche play Marguerite Gautier at the Porte St Martin. Trilby weeps when, on the appeal of his father, Dumas' heroine leaves her lover, Armand. Not long afterwards, perhaps with some memory of the play in her mind, Trilby performs the same act of tragic generosity. Like Marguerite, she is eventually rediscovered, only to die with her hand in Little Billee's. Du Maurier's novel, however, is not really a 'shocking' book. Trilby and Little Billee, unlike Marguerite and Armand, are never lovers.

Du Maurier was remarkably talented in all three major arts. As a popular amateur tenor, he performed many of the songs which make Trilby so famous, including the French nursery rhymes 'Au clair de la lune' and 'Malbrouck s'en va-t'en guerre', as well as 'Ben Bolt', a nineteenth-century American song by Nelson Kneass to words by Thomas Dunn English. Before the romantic movement, the practice of music was not greatly respected. Composers, instrumentalists and singers often 'belonged' to princely courts. The nineteenth century, however, witnessed the rise to fame of a series of great performers, some also composers. Beethoven, Chopin and Liszt were brilliant pianists, and, among singers, Adelina Patti, Marietta Alboni and Jenny Lind, all mentioned in *Trilby*, had towering European reputations. The creation of the near diabolical Svengali may have been inspired by the career of the Italian violinist and composer Nicolo Paganini, who is said to have mesmerized his audiences with his extraordinary virtuosity. Svengali plays the penny whistle and the piano, but Du Maurier's original intention had been to make him a violinist.

Svengali is the musical genius of Du Maurier's novel, Trilby merely his means of expression, the perfect voice box which he can manipulate. The inspiration for this idea of possession is undoubtedly that of the Gothic novel, deriving from the popular fiction of the late eighteenth and early nineteenth centuries. Gothic became a strategy for articulating the unconscious, for expressing, through fantastic tales, those aspects of the human psyche which many Augustan writers preferred to omit or suppress. In several famous Gothic tales the divided self is projected as two separate beings, the subconscious becoming a Doppelgänger or alter ego. Mary Shelley's Victor Frankenstein constructs his 'other' from fragments of dead bodies, R. L. Stevenson's Dr Jekyll chemically projects a second self, and *Trilby* shares with these works the idea of 'using' another being. Svengali, like Victor Frankenstein, is obsessed with finding an outlet for his own genius. Svengali, however, is a more villainous figure, a caricature of the worst aspects of the brilliant artist – dirty, rude, bullying, greedy and ungrateful. Like Dr Jekyll, who leads a double life though the evil Hyde, Svengali cannot find a way of expressing one side of his nature – he cannot sing. In order to do so, he violates the rules of basic human morality and takes over another person, both sexually and hypnotically.

From the stories of the early nineteenth century German writer, E. T. A. Hoffmann, comes another relevant theme, that of the magician who makes an amazingly lifelike female doll (Coppelia) which can entrance an audience, until her mechanism runs down. In *Trilby*, Svengali's mesmeric power performs the same function as the magician's unholy arts: he creates an instrument through which he can exercise power and revenge by confusing and deceiving a gullible public.

Mesmerism, as developed by Franz Anton Mesmer in the early nineteenth century, both fascinated and frightened the Victorians. Felix Moscheles, writing after the publication of *Trilby*, claimed that Du Maurier and he had tried to hypnotize a young girl in Belgium in the 1850s, although with little success. In the 1860s, Du Maurier had himself illustrated two 'sensational' stories whose outcome depended upon the revelation of hypnotism, 'The Notting Hill Mystery' and 'The Poisoned Mind'. The latter shares with *Trilby* its theme of the jealous hypnotist – here a scientist, forcing the woman to perform experiments of which she is quite unconscious.

Such tales presuppose that genius is a transferable commodity. Trilby has good lungs and a large mouth, so, hypnotized by Svengali, she can sing divinely. Earlier in Du Maurier's novel, we hear of the musician's other pupil, Honorine, whose sweet but weak singing voice is ruined by over-tuition. Although tonedeaf, Trilby is physically able to carry out the task under the spell of Svengali.

The influence of Gothic fiction, often combined with ideas of hypnotic possession, was continuously felt through the nineteenth century, indeed it is still active in the popular fiction of our own day. Charles Dickens, to whom Du Maurier pays tribute in *Trilby*, shows a fascination with the divided self in some of his later novels, like *Our Mutual Friend* and *Great Expectations*. Most relevant for *Trilby* is his last, incomplete book, *Edwin Drood*, where a cathedral organist, John Jasper, leads a second life as an opium addict. Jasper provides an instructive parallel with Svengali. Both are musicians who become fixated upon a young girl; both give singing lessons. Trilby's reactions to Svengali are close to those attributed to Dickens's heroine, Rosa Bud, as she senses the power of Jasper's will:

> The song went on ... As Jasper watched the pretty lips, and ever and again hinted the one note, as though it were a low whisper from himself, the voice became a little less steady, until all at once the singer broke into a burst of tears, and shrieked out, with her hands over her eyes: 'I can't bear this! I am frightened! Take me away!' (*Edwin Drood*)

> So he would playfully try to mesmerize her with his glance, and sidle up nearer and nearer to her, making passes and counter-passes, with stern command in his eyes, till she would shake and shiver and almost sicken with fear, and all but fear the spell come over her, as in a nightmare, and rouse herself with a great effort and escape. (*Trilby*)

Du Maurier followed Hoffmann and Dickens in making the manipulator male and the victim female. Jekyll and Hyde, Frankenstein and his creation – all are male pairings. But Svengali is sexually attracted to Trilby. He begins by curing her migraines through hypnosis and so acquiring a psychological power over her. Only while she remains within the circle of the English artists in Paris is she safe from him. There are unpleasant racial overtones in these passages. Svengali is constantly under attack as a Jew, while the British are presented as clean-living paragons. One of them, Taffy, is capable of controlling Svengali by brute force, and it is he who brings about Svengali's death from heart failure at the end of the novel. There are parallels here with Bram Stoker's *Dracula*, another man of sinister and Central European origins, practising diabolic arts on British womanhood. *Trilby* works on two levels, however – the realistic and the fantastic. Svengali may be the novel's villain, but it is

Little Billee's family, not the wicked musician, who destroy Trilby. Even the narrator is ambivalent about the idea of a marriage between a respectable young man and an artist's model.

Svengali's rival for Trilby is not the giant and athletic Taffy, who loves her in silence, but the young artist, William Bagot, Little Billee. (For the nickname of his hero, Du Maurier went to one of Thackeray's ballads.) When Dickens dubbed his heroines Little Nell or Little Dorrit, he was implying not only their small size but their childlike innocence. Here, too, Du Maurier makes Little Billee the least worldly character in the novel. He is not only considerably shorter than Trilby, but far less experienced sexually. Trilby, on the other hand, 'would have made a singularly handsome boy', and first appears dressed in a soldier's greatcoat.

One crisis in the novel comes when Little Billee sees her posing 'in the altogether' and is overwhelmed with distress, as though forced to recognize her womanhood for the first time. Elsewhere, the narrator reminds us that a woman posing for a life-class is without sex, but here this proves untrue. As Little Billee rushes from the room, Trilby loses her innocence. Having never been embarrassed by modelling before, she gives it up forthwith, and becomes a laundress. The influence of the British artists draws her away from Bohemia into bourgeois respectability, as she cooks and darns in the studio. Svengali, it must be admitted, offers her a more exciting life.

Svengali and Little Billee are both geniuses, and each uses Trilby to further his own art. Little Billee's first response is to draw her perfect foot on the wall, and, posing as a French peasant girl, she becomes the inspiration for his masterpiece, *The Pitcher Goes to the Well*. By the end of the novel, the painting hangs in the National Gallery in London, while a watercolour of Trilby darning the young men's clothes has been sold for a large sum at Christie's. By sitting as a model for many of the artists of Paris, Trilby has already been appropriated as an object before Svengali ever sees her. Although Du Maurier never analyses the issue, Svengali's sexual interest in Trilby, like Little Billee's and Durien's, becomes closely entangled with her value to them as a commodity. Bernard Shaw's famous version of the Pygmalion myth draws attention to the same division of interests between the vivisective male artist and the woman whom he can train to display his gifts. Ironically, one of the several real life sources suggested for *Trilby* is the relationship between Shaw's mother and her singing teacher, George Vandeleur Lee.

Trilby was serialized in *Harper's Magazine* from January to July 1894 and then published in book form. The illustrations, by Du Maurier himself, are coarser than his best work, a result of failing eyesight. The novel soon became an international bestseller of the kind that authors dream of. Henry James, who had indirectly provoked the book's appearance, was unable to understand its popularity. It is to his credit that he scarcely grudged Du Maurier the overwhelming success which always eluded James himself. The heroine's name (taken by Du Maurier from a work by Charles Nodier) was given to clothes, sweets, music – even to a town in America. A dramatization by Paul Potter ran to packed houses at Her Majesty's Theatre. On the stage, Trilby wore a soft felt hat, not mentioned in the novel, and the trilby is now the one permanent survivor of an 1890s craze. For Du Maurier, success was a poisoned chalice. Fame exhausted him, and he felt, like many writers, that his book was being travestied by its admirers. Worse still, his old Paris friend, James Whistler, objected to the portrait of himself as Joe Sibley, 'the idle apprentice', and moved through the preliminary stages of a lawsuit. Whistler's letters on the subject reveal an appalling vindictiveness, unworthy of a great artist. Only a humiliating climb-down by Du Maurier, with the removal of the offending passages and of a number of illustrations, kept Whistler out of the courts. Du Maurier lived less than two years after the publication of *Trilby*. When writing his last novel, *The Martian*, he wryly told a friend that he would call it 'soured by success'.[5]

References

1 J. L. and J. B. Gilder, *Trilbyana: The Rise and Progesss of a Popular Novel* (New York, 1895), p. 11.

2 *The Complete Notebooks of Henry James*, ed. Leon Edel and Lyall H. Powers (1987), p. 51.

3 *Ibid*, p. 52.

4 Leonee Ormond, *George Du Maurier* (1969), p. 442.

5 Henry Lucy, *Sixty years in the Wilderness* (1909), p. 394.

NOTE ON THE TEXT

Trilby was originally published in seven monthly instalments in *Harper's Magazine*, fully illustrated by Du Maurier himself. The March instalment, Part Third, contained an account of a character called Joe Sibley, who was clearly based upon Du Maurier's friend from Paris days, the American painter James McNeill Whistler. Whistler threatened to sue for libel and the text was therefore altered for the book editions, with a character called Anthony replacing Joe Sibley. A similar but much less extensive change was made in Part Fifth, where a character called Macey Sparks, obviously based upon Du Maurier's old friend Henry Stacy Marks, was also removed. While the excision of the offending passages was fairly effectively performed in the letterpress, more than one illustration still clearly showed Whistler in the background. The deleted passages are printed in the appendix to this edition.

Trilby was first published in book form by Osgood McIlvaine in a three-volume edition with no illustrations. The one-volume illustrated edition was published in the following year, 1895. An 1894 illustrated edition had appeared in New York, published by Harper's. The book edition contained certain passages which had been thought unsuitable for *Harper's Magazine*. These included discussions of nudity and a few references to the more racy aspects of Paris student life. The text printed here is that of the book edition.

TRILBY

'It was Trilby!'

Part First

Mimi Pinson est une blonde,
  Une blonde que l'on connait;
Elle n'a qu'une robe au monde,
Landérirette! et qu'un bonnet!*

It was a fine, sunny, showery day in April.

The big studio window was open at the top, and let in a pleasant breeze from the north-west. Things were beginning to look shipshape at last. The big piano, a semi-grand by Broadwood,* had arrived from England by 'the Little Quickness' (*la Petite Vitesse*, as the goods trains are called in France), and lay, freshly tuned, alongside the eastern wall; on the wall opposite was a panoply of foils, masks, and boxing-gloves.

A trapeze, a knotted rope, and two parallel cords, supporting each a ring, depended from a huge beam in the ceiling. The walls were of the usual dull red, relieved by plaster casts of arms and legs and hands and feet; and Dante's mask,* and Michael Angelo's alto-rilievo of Leda and the swan,* and a centaur and Lapith from the Elgin Marbles* – on none of these had the dust as yet had time to settle.

There were also studies in oil from the nude; copies of Titian, Rembrandt, Velasquez, Rubens, Tintoret,* Leonardo da Vinci – none of the school of Botticelli,* Mantegna,* and Co. – a firm whose merits had not as yet been revealed to the many.

Along the walls, at a great height, ran a broad shelf, on which were other casts in plaster, terra-cotta, imitation bronze: a little Theseus,* a little Venus of Milo,* a little discobolus;* a little flayed man* threatening high heaven (an act that seemed almost pardonable under the circumstances!); a lion and a boar by Barye;* an anatomical figure of a horse, with only one leg left and no ears; a horse's head* from the pediment of the Parthenon, earless also; and the bust of Clytie,* with her beautiful low brow, her sweet wan gaze, and the ineffable forward shrug of her dear shoulders that makes her bosom as a nest, a rest, a pillow, a refuge – the likeness of a thing to be loved and desired for ever, and sought for and wrought for and fought for by generation after generation of the sons of men.

Near the stove hung a gridiron, a frying-pan, a toasting-fork, and a pair of bellows. In an adjoining glazed corner cupboard were plates and glasses, black-handled knives, pewter spooons, and three-pronged steel forks; a salad-bowl, vinegar cruets, an oil-flask, two mustard-pots (English and French), and such like things – all scrupulously clean. On the floor, which had been stained and waxed at considerable cost, lay two cheetah-skins and a large Persian praying-rug. One half of it, however (under the trapeze and at the end farthest from the window, beyond the model-throne), was covered with coarse matting, that one might fence or box without slipping down and splitting one's self in two, or fall without breaking any bones.

Two other windows of the usual French size and pattern, with shutters to them and heavy curtains of baize, opened east and west to let in dawn or sunset, as the case might be, or haply keep them out. And there were alcoves, recesses, irregularities, odd little nooks and corners, to be filled up as time wore on with endless personal nick-nacks, bibelots, private properties and acquisitions – things that make a place genial, homelike, and good to remember, and sweet to muse upon (with fond regret) in after years.

And an immense divan spread itself in width and length and delightful thickness just beneath the big north window, the business window – a divan so immense that three well-fed, well-contented Englishmen could all lie lazily smoking their pipes on it at once without being in each other's way, and very often did!

At present one of these Englishmen – a Yorkshireman, by the way, called Taffy* (and also the Man of Blood, because he was supposed to be distantly related to a baronet) – was more energetically engaged. Bare-armed and in his shirt and trousers, he was twirling a pair of Indian clubs round his head. His face was flushed, and he was perspiring freely and looked fierce. He was a very big young man, fair, with kind but choleric blue eyes, and the muscles of his brawny arm were strong as iron bands.

For three years he had borne Her Majesty's commission, and had been through the Crimean campaign without a scratch. He would have been one of the famous six hundred in the famous charge at Balaklava* but for a sprained ankle (caught playing leapfrog in the trenches), which kept him in hospital on that momentous day. So that he lost his chance of glory or the grave, and this humiliating misadvanture had sickened him of soldier-

Taffy, alias Talbot Wynne

ing for life, and he never quite got over it. Then, feeling within himself an irresistible vocation for art, he had sold out; and here he was in Paris, hard at work, as we see.

He was good-looking, with straight features; but I regret to say that, besides his heavy plunger's moustache, he wore an immense pair of drooping auburn whiskers, of the kind that used to be called Piccadilly weepers,* and were afterwards affected by Mr Sothern in Lord Dundreary.* It was a fashion to do so then for such of our gilded youth as could afford the time (and the hair); the bigger and fairer the whiskers, the more beautiful was thought the youth! It seems incredible in these days, when even Her Majesty's Household Brigade go about with smooth cheeks and lips, like priests or play-actors.

> What's become of all the gold
> Used to hang and brush their bosoms . . .?*

Another inmate of this blissful abode – Sandy, the Laird of Cockpen,* as he was called – sat in similarly simple attire at his

The Laird of Cockpen

easel, painting at a lifelike little picture of a Spanish toreador
serenading a lady of high degree (in broad daylight). He had
never been to Spain, but he had a complete toreador's kit – a
bargain which he had picked up for a mere song in the Boulevard
du Temple* – and he had hired the guitar. His pipe was in his
mouth – reversed; for it had gone out, and the ashes were spilled
all over his trousers where holes were often burned in this way.

Quite gratuitously, and with a pleasing Scotch accent, he
began to declaim:

> A street there is in Paris famous
>   For which no rhyme our language yields;
> Roo Nerve day Petty Shong its name is –
>   The New Street of the Little Fields . . .*

And then, in his keen appreciation of the immortal stanza, he
chuckled audibly, with a face so blithe and merry and well
pleased that it did one good to look at him.

He also had entered life by another door. His parents (good,
pious people in Dundee) had intended that he should be a
solicitor, as his father and grandfather had been before him.

The third he was 'Little Billee'

And here he was in Paris famous, painting toreadors, and
spouting the 'Ballad of the Bouillabaisse', as he would often do
out of sheer lightness of heart – much oftener, indeed, than he
would say his prayers.

Kneeling on the divan, with his elbow on the window-sill,
was a third and much younger youth. The third he was 'Little
Billee'.* He had pulled down the green baize blind, and was
looking over the roofs and chimney-pots of Paris and all about
with all his eyes, munching the while a roll and a savoury
saveloy, in which there was evidence of much garlic. He ate with
great relish, for he was very hungry; he had been all the morning
at Carrel's studio,* drawing from the life.

Little Billee was small and slender, about twenty or twenty-
one, and had a straight white forehead veined with blue, large
dark blue eyes, delicate, regular features, and coal-black hair.
He was also very graceful and well built, with very small hands
and feet, and much better dressed than his friends, who went
out of their way to outdo the denizens of the Quartier Latin* in
careless eccentricity of garb, and succeeded. And in his winning

and handsome face there was just a faint suggestion of some possible very remote Jewish ancestor – just a tinge of that strong, sturdy, irrepressible, indomitable, indelible blood which is of such priceless value in diluted homœopathic doses, like the dry white Spanish wine called montijo, which is not meant to be taken pure; but without a judicious admixture of which no sherry can go round the world and keep its flavour intact; or like the famous bulldog strain, which is not beautiful in itself, and yet just for lacking a little of the same no greyhound can ever hope to be a champion. So, at least, I have been told by wine-merchants and dog-fanciers – the most veracious persons that can be. Fortunately for the world, and especially for ourselves, most of us have in our veins at least a minim of that precious fluid, whether we know it or show it or not. *Tant pis pour les autres!**

As Little Billee munched he also gazed at the busy place below – the Place St Anatole des Arts* – at the old houses opposite, some of which were being pulled down, no doubt lest they should fall of their own sweet will. In the gaps between he would see discoloured, old, cracked, dingy walls, with mysterious windows and rusty iron balconies of great antiquity – sights that set him dreaming dreams of mediæval French love and wickedness and crime, bygone mysteries of Paris!

One gap went right through the block, and gave him a glimpse of the river, the 'Cité,' and the ominous old Morgue;* a little to the right rose the gray towers of Notre Dame de Paris into the checkered April sky. Indeed, the top of nearly all Paris lay before him, with a little stretch of the imagination on his part; and he gazed with a sense of novelty, an interest and a pleasure for which he could not have found any expression in mere language.

Paris! Paris!! Paris!!!

The very name had always been one to conjure with, whether he thought of it as a mere sound on the lips and in the ear, or as a magical written or printed word for the eye. And here was the thing itself at last, and he, he himself, *ipsissimus*,* in the very heart of it, to live there and learn there as long as he liked, and make himself the great artist he longed to be.

Then, his meal finished, he lit a pipe, and flung himself on the divan and sighed deeply, out of the over-full contentment of his heart.

He felt he had never known happiness like this, never even

It did one good to look at him

dreamed its possibility. And yet his life had been a happy one.
He was young and tender, was Little Billee; he had never been
to any school, and was innocent of the world and its wicked
ways; innocent of French especially, and the ways of Paris and
its Latin Quarter. He had been brought up and educated at
home, had spent his boyhood in London with his mother and
sister, who now lived in Devonshire on somewhat straitened
means. His father, who was dead, had been a clerk in the
Treasury.

He and his two friends, Taffy and the Laird, had taken this
studio together. The Laird slept there, in a small bedroom off
the studio. Taffy had a bedroom at the Hôtel de Seine,* in the
street of that name. Little Billee lodged at the Hôtel Corneille,*
in the Place de l'Odéon.*

He looked at his two friends, and wondered if any one, living
or dead, had ever had such a glorious pair of chums as these.

Whatever they did, whatever they said, was simply perfect in
his eyes; they were his guides and philosophers as well as his
chums. On the other hand, Taffy and the Laird were as fond of
the boy as they could be.

His absolute belief in all they said and did touched them none
the less that they were conscious of its being somewhat in excess
of their deserts. His almost girlish purity of mind amused and
charmed them, and they did all they could to preserve it, even in
the Quartier Latin, where purity is apt to go bad if it be kept
too long.

They loved him for his affectionate disposition, his lively and
caressing ways; and they admired him far more than he ever
knew, for they recognised in him a quickness, a keenness, a
delicacy of perception, in matters of form and colour, a mysterious facility and felicity of execution, a sense of all that was
sweet and beautiful in nature, and a ready power of expressing
it, that had not been vouchsafed to them in any such generous
profusion, and which, as they ungrudgingly admitted to themselves and each other, amounted to true genius.

And when one within the immediate circle of our intimates is
gifted in this abnormal fashion, we either hate or love him for
it, in proportion to the greatness of his gift; according to the
way we are built.

So Taffy and the Laird loved Little Billee – loved him very
much indeed. Not but what Little Billee had his faults. For

instance, he didn't interest himself very warmly in other people's pictures. He didn't seem to care for the Laird's guitar-playing toreador, nor for his serenaded lady – at all events, he never said anything about them, either in praise or blame. He looked at Taffy's realisms (for Taffy was a realist*) in silence, and nothing tries true friendship so much as silence of this kind.

But then, to make up for it, when they all three went to the Louvre,* he didn't seem to trouble much about Titian either, or Rembrandt, or Velasquez, Rubens, Veronese, or Leonardo. He looked at the people who looked at the pictures, instead of at the pictures themselves; especially at the people who copied them, the sometimes charming young lady painters – and these seemed to him even more charming than they really were – and he looked a great deal out of the Louvre windows, where there was much to be seen: more Paris, for instance – Paris, of which he could never have enough.

But when, surfeited with classical beauty, they all three went and dined together, and Taffy and the Laird said beautiful things about the old masters, and quarrelled about them, he listened with deference and rapt attention and reverentially agreed with all they said; and afterwards made the most delightfully funny little pen-and-ink sketches of them, saying all these beautiful things (which he sent to his mother and sister at home); so lifelike, so real, that you could almost hear the beautiful things they said; so beautifully drawn that you felt the old masters couldn't have drawn them better themselves; and so irresistibly droll that you felt that the old masters could not have drawn them at all – any more than Milton could have described the quarrel between Sairey Gamp and Betsy Prig;* no one, in short, but Little Billee.

Little Billee took up the 'Ballad of the Bouillabaisse' where the Laird had left it off, and speculated on the future of himself and his friends, when he should have got to forty years – an almost impossibly remote future.

These speculations were interrupted by a loud knock at the door, and two men came in.

First, a tall bony individual of any age between thirty and forty-five, of Jewish aspect, well-featured but sinister. He was very shabby and dirty, and wore a red *béret* and a large velveteen cloak, with a big metal clasp at the collar. His thick, heavy, languid, lustreless black hair fell down behind his ears on to his

Among the old Masters

svargale

shoulders, in that musician-like way that is so offensive to the
normal Englishman. He had bold, brilliant black eyes, with long
heavy lids, a thin, sallow face, and a beard of burnt-up black,
which grew almost from his under eyelids; and over it his
moustache, a shade lighter, fell in two long spiral twists. He
went by the name of Svengali,* and spoke fluent French with a
German accent and humorous German twists and idioms, and
his voice was very thin and mean and harsh, and often broke
into a disagreeable falsetto.

His companion was a little swarthy young man – a gypsy, *gecko*
possibly – much pitted with the smallpox, and also very shabby.
He had large, soft, affectionate brown eyes, like a King Charles
spaniel. He had small, nervous, veiny hands, with nails bitten
down to the quick, and carried a fiddle and a fiddlestick under
his arm, without a case, as though he had been playing in the
street.

'Ponchour, mes enfants,' said Svengali. 'Che vous amène mon
ami Checko, qui choue du fiolon gomme un anche!'*

Little Billee, who adored all 'sweet musicianers,' jumped up
and made Gecko as warmly welcome as he could in his early
French.

'Ha! le biâno!' exclaimed Svengali, flinging his red *béret* on it,
and his cloak on the ground. 'Ch'espère qu'il est pon, et pien
t'accord!'*

And sitting down on the music-stool, he ran up and down the
scales with that easy power, that smooth even crispness of
touch, which reveal the master.

Then he fell to playing Chopin's impromptu in A flat,* so
beautifully that Little Billee's heart went nigh to bursting with
suppressed emotion and delight. He had never heard any music
of Chopin's before, nothing but British provincial home-made
music – melodies with variations, 'Annie Laurie,' 'The Last Rose
of Summer,' 'The Blue Bells of Scotland';* innocent little
motherly and sisterly tinklings, invented to set the company at
their ease on festive evenings, and make all-round conversation
possible for shy people, who fear the unaccompanied sound of
their own voices, and whose genial chatter always leaves off
directly the music ceases.

He never forgot that impromptu, which he was destined to
hear again one day in strange circumstances.

Then Svengali and Gecko made music together, divinely.

Little fragmentary things, sometimes consisting of but a few bars, but these bars of *such* beauty and meaning! Scraps, snatches, short melodies, meant to fetch, to charm immediately, or to melt or sadden or madden just for a moment, and that knew just when to leave off – czardas,* gypsy dances, Hungarian love-plaints, things little known out of eastern Europe in the fifties of this century, till the Laird and Taffy were almost as wild in their enthusiasm as Little Billee – a silent enthusiasm too deep for speech. And when these two great artists left off to smoke, the three Britishers were too much moved even for that, and there was a stillness . . .

Suddenly there came a loud knuckle-rapping at the outer door, and a portentous voice of great volume, and that might almost have belonged to any sex (even an angel's), uttered the British milkman's yodel, 'Milk below!' and before any one could say 'Entrez,' a strange figure appeared, framed by the gloom of the little antechamber.

It was the figure of a very tall and fully-developed young female, clad in the gray overcoat of a French infantry soldier, continued netherwards by a short striped petticoat, beneath which were visible her bare white ankles and insteps, and slim, straight, rosy heels, clean cut and smooth as the back of a razor; her toes lost themselves in a huge pair of male slippers, which made her drag her feet as she walked.

She bore herself with easy, unembarrassed grace, like a person whose nerves and muscles are well in tune, whose spirits are high, who has lived much in the atmosphere of French studios, and feels at home in it.

This strange medley of garments was surmounted by a small bare head with short, thick, wavy brown hair, and a very healthy young face, which could scarcely be called quite beautiful at first sight, since the eyes were too wide apart, the mouth too large, the chin too massive, the complexion a mass of freckles. Besides, you can never tell how beautiful (or how ugly) a face may be till you have tried to draw it.

But a small portion of her neck, down by the collar-bone, which just showed itself between the unbuttoned lapels of her military coat collar, was of a delicate privet-like whiteness that is never to be found on any French neck, and very few English ones. Also, she had a very fine brow, broad and low, with thick level eyebrows much darker than her hair, a broad, bony, high

'Wistful and sweet'

bridge to her short nose, and her full, broad cheeks were beautifully modelled. She would have made a singularly handsome boy.

As the creature looked round at the assembled company and flashed her big white teeth at them in an all-embracing smile of uncommon width and quite irresistible sweetness, simplicity, and friendly trust, one saw at a glance that she was out of the common clever, simple, humorous, honest, brave, and kind, and accustomed to be genially welcomed wherever she went. Then suddenly closing the door behind her, dropping her smile, and looking wistful and sweet, with her head on one side and her arms akimbo, 'Ye're all English, now, aren't ye?' she exclaimed. 'I heard the music, and thought I'd just come in for a bit, and pass the time of day: you don't mind? Trilby,* that's my name – Trilby O'Ferrall.'

She said this in English, with an accent half Scotch and certain French intonations, and in a voice so rich and deep and full as almost to suggest an incipient *tenore robusto*;* and one felt instinctively that it was a real pity she wasn't a boy, she would have made such a jolly one.

'We're delighted, on the contrary,' said Little Billee, and advanced a chair for her.

But she said, 'Oh, don't mind me; go on with the music,' and sat herself down cross-legged on the model-throne near the piano.

As they still looked at her, curious and half embarrassed, she pulled a paper parcel containing food out of one of the coat-pockets, and exclaimed:

'I'll just take a bite, if you don't object; I'm a model, you know, and it's just rung twelve – "the rest." I'm posing for Durien* the sculptor, on the next floor. I pose to him for the altogether.'

'The altogether?' asked Little Billee.

'Yes – *l'ensemble*, you know – head, hands, and feet – everything – especially feet. That's my foot,' she said, kicking off her big slipper and stretching out the limb. 'It's the handsomest foot in all Paris. There's only one in all Paris to match it, and here it is,' and she laughed heartily (like a merry peal of bells), and stuck out the other.

And in truth they were astonishingly beautiful feet, such as one only sees in pictures and statues – a true inspiration of shape and colour, all made up of delicate lengths and subtly-modulated curves and noble straightnesses and happy little dimpled arrangements in innocent young pink and white.

So that Little Billee, who had the quick, prehensile, æsthetic eye, and knew by the grace of Heaven what the shapes and sizes and colours of almost every bit of man, woman, or child should be (and so seldom are), was quite bewildered to find that a real, bare, live human foot could be such a charming object to look at, and felt that such a base or pedestal lent quite an antique and Olympian* dignity to a figure that seemed just then rather grotesque in its mixed attire of military overcoat and female petticoat, and nothing else!

Poor Trilby!

The shape of those lovely slender feet* (that were neither large nor small), facsimiled in dusty pale plaster of Paris, survives on the shelves and walls of many a studio throughout the world, and many a sculptor yet unborn has yet to marvel at their strange perfection, in studious despair.

For when Dame Nature takes it into her head to do her very best, and bestow her minutest attention on a mere detail, as happens now and then – once in a blue moon, perhaps – she makes it uphill work for poor human art to keep pace with her.

It is a wondrous thing, the human foot – like the human hand; even more so, perhaps; but, unlike the hand, with which we are so familiar, it is seldom a thing of beauty in civilised adults who go about in leather boots or shoes.

So that it is hidden away in disgrace, a thing to be thrust out of sight and forgotten. It can sometimes be very ugly indeed – the ugliest thing there is, even in the fairest and highest and most gifted of her sex; and then it is of an ugliness to chill and kill romance, and scatter love's young dream, and almost break the heart.

And all for the sake of a high heel and a ridiculously-pointed toe – mean things, at the best!

Conversely, when Mother Nature has taken extra pains in the building of it, and proper care or happy chance has kept it free of lamentable deformations, indurations, and discolorations – all those gruesome boot-begotten abominations which have made it so generally unpopular – the sudden sight of it, uncovered, comes as a very rare and singularly pleasing surprise to the eye that has learned how to see!

The 'Rosamonde' of Schubert

Nothing else that Mother Nature has to show, not even the human face divine, has more subtle power to suggest high physical distinction, happy evolution, and supreme development; the lordship of man over beast, the lordship of man over man, the lordship of woman over all!

*En voilà de l'éloquence – à propos de bottes!**

Trilby had respected Mother Nature's special gift to herself – had never worn a leather boot or shoe, had always taken as much care of her feet as many a fine lady takes of her hands. It was her one coquetry, the only real vanity she had.

Gecko, his fiddle in one hand and his bow in the other, stared at her in open-mouthed admiration and delight, as she ate her sandwich of soldier's bread and *fromage à la crème** quite unconcerned.

When she had finished she licked the tips of her fingers clean of cheese, and produced a small tobacco-pouch from another military pocket, made herself a cigarette, and lit it and smoked it, inhaling the smoke in large whiffs, filling her lungs with it, and sending it back through her nostrils, with a look of great beatitude.

Svengali played Schubert's 'Rosemonde,'* and flashed a pair of languishing black eyes at her with intent to kill.

But she didn't even look his way. She looked at Little Billee, at big Taffy, at the Laird, at the casts and studies, at the sky, the chimney-pots over the way, the towers of Notre Dame, just visible from where she sat.

Only when he finished she exclaimed: 'Maïe, aïe! c'est rudement bien tapé, c'te musique-là! Seulement, c'est pas gai, vous savez! Comment q'ça s'appelle?'*

'It is called the "Rosemonde" of Schubert, matemoiselle,' replied Svengali. (I will translate.)

'And what's that – Rosemonde?' said she.

'Rosemonde was a princess of Cyprus, matemoiselle, and Cyprus is an island.'

'Ah, and Schubert, then – where's that?'

'Schubert is not an island, matemoiselle. Schubert was a compatriot of mine, and made music, and played the piano, just like me.'

'Ah, Schubert was a *monsieur*, then. Don't know him; never heard his name.'

'That is a pity, matemoiselle. He had some talent. You like
this better, perhaps,' and he strummed,

Messieurs les étudiants,
S'en vont à la chaumière
Pour y danser le cancan,*

striking wrong notes, and banging out a bass in a different key
– a hideously grotesque performance.

'Yes, I like that better. It's gayer, you know. Is that also
composed by a compatriot of yours?' asked the lady.

'Heaven forbid, matemoiselle.'

And the laugh was against Svengali.

But the real fun of it all (if there was any) lay in the fact that
she was perfectly sincere.

'Are you fond of music?' asked Little Billee.

'Oh, ain't I just!' she replied. 'My father sang like a bird. He
was a gentleman and a scholar, my father was. His name was
Patrick Michael O' Ferrall, Fellow of Trinity, Cambridge. He
used to sing "Ben Bolt." Do you know "Ben Bolt"?'

'Oh yes, I know it well,' said Little Billee. 'It's a very pretty
song.'

'I can sing it,' said Miss O'Ferrall. 'Shall I?'

'Oh certainly, if you will be so kind.'

Miss O'Ferrall threw away the end of her cigarette, put her
hands on her knees as she sat cross-legged on the model-throne,
and sticking her elbows well out, she looked up to the ceiling
with a tender, sentimental smile, and sang the touching song,

> Oh, don't you remember sweet Alice, Ben Bolt?
> Sweet Alice, with hair so brown? etc., etc.*

As some things are too sad and too deep for tears, so some
things are too grotesque and too funny for laughter. Of such a
kind was Miss O'Ferrall's performance of 'Ben Bolt.'

From that capacious mouth and through that high-bridged
bony nose there rolled a volume of breathy sound, not loud, but
so immense that it seemed to come from all round, to be
reverberated from every surface in the studio. She followed more
or less the shape of the tune, going up when it rose and down
when it fell, but with such immense intervals between the notes
as were never dreamed of in any mortal melody. It was as
though she could never once have deviated into tune, never once

have hit upon a true note, even by a fluke – in fact, as though she were absolutely tone-deaf, and without ear, although she stuck to the time correctly enough.

She finished her song amid an embarrassing silence. The audience didn't quite know whether it were meant for fun or seriously. One wondered if she were not paying out Svengali for his impertinent performance of 'Messieurs les étudiants.' If so, it was a capital piece of impromptu tit-for-tat admirably acted, and a very ugly gleam yellowed the tawny black of Svengali's big eyes. He was so fond of making fun of others that he particularly resented being made fun of himself – couldn't endure that any one should ever have the laugh of *him*.

At length Little Billee said: 'Thank you so much. It's a capital song.'

'Yes,' said Miss O'Ferrall. 'It's the only song I know, unfortunately. My father used to sing it, just like that, when he felt jolly after hot rum-and-water. It used to make people cry; he used to cry over it himself. *I* never do. Some people think I can't sing a bit. All I can say is that I've often had to sing it six or seven times running in *lots* of studios. I vary it, you know – not the words, but the tune. You must remember that I've only taken to it lately. Do you know Litolff?* Well, he's a great composer, and he came to Durien's the other day, and I sang "Ben Bolt," and what do you think he said? Why, he said Madame Alboni* couldn't go nearly so high or so low as I did, and that her voice wasn't half so big. He gave me his word of honour. He said I breathed as natural and straight as a baby and all I want is to get my voice a little more under control. That's what *he* said.'

'Qu'est-ce qu'elle dit?'* asked Svengali. And she said it all over again to him in French – quite French French – of the most colloquial kind. Her accent was not that of the Comédie Française,* nor yet that of the Faubourg St Germain,* nor yet that of the shop, or the pavement. It was quaint and expressive – 'funny without being vulgar.'

'Barpleu!* he was right, Litolff,' said Svengali. 'I assure you, matemoiselle, that I have never heard a voice that can equal yours; you have a talent quite exceptional.'

She blushed with pleasure, and the others thought him a 'beastly cad' for poking fun at the poor girl in such a way. And they thought Monsieur Litolff another.

She then got up and shook the crumbs off her coat, and slipped her feet into Durien's slippers, saying, in English: 'Well, I've got to go back. Life ain't all beer and skittles,* and more's the pity; but what's the odds, so long as you're happy?'

On her way out she stopped before Taffy's picture – a chiffonnier* with his lantern, bending over a dust-heap. For Taffy was, or thought himself, a passionate realist in those days. He has changed, and now paints nothing but King Arthurs and Guineveres and Lancelots and Elaines, and floating Ladies of Shalott.*

'That chiffonnier's basket isn't hitched high enough,' she remarked. 'How could he tap his pick against the rim and make the rag fall into it if it's hitched only half-way up his back? And he's got the wrong sabots,* and the wrong lantern; it's *all* wrong.'

'Dear me!' said Taffy, turning very red; 'you seem to know a lot about it. It's a pity you don't paint, yourself.'

'Ah! now you're cross!' said Miss O'Ferrall. 'Oh, maïe aïe!'

She went to the door and paused, looking round benignly. 'What nice teeth you've all three got! That's because you're Englishmen, I suppose, and clean them twice a day. I do too. Trilby O'Ferrall, that's my name, 48 Rue des Pousse-Cailloux!* – pose pour l'ensemble, quand ça l'amuse! va-t-en ville, et fait tout ce qui concerne son état! Don't forget. Thanks all, and good-bye.'

'En v'là une orichinale,'* said Svengali.

'I think she's lovely,' said Little Billee, the young and tender. 'Oh heavens, what angel's feet! It makes me sick to think she sits for the figure. I'm sure she's quite a lady.'

And in five minutes or so, with the point of an old compass, he scratched in white on the dark red wall a three-quarter profile outline of Trilby's left foot, which was perhaps the more perfect poem of the two.

Slight as it was, this little piece of impromptu etching, in its sense of beauty, in its quick seizing of a peculiar individuality, its subtle rendering of a strongly-received impression, was already the work of a master. It was Trilby's foot and nobody else's, nor could have been, and nobody else but Little Billee could have drawn it in just that inspired way.

'Qu'est-ce que c'est, "Ben Bolt"?'* inquired Gecko.

Upon which Little Billee was made by Taffy to sit down to

Trilby's Left Foot

the piano and sing it. He sang it very nicely with his pleasant little throaty English baritone.

It was solely in order that Little Billee should have opportunities of practising this graceful accomplishment of his, for his own and his friends' delectation, that the piano had been sent over from London, at great cost to Taffy and the Laird. It had belonged to Taffy's mother, who was dead.

Before he had finished the second verse, Svengali exclaimed: 'Mais c'est tout-à-fait chentil! Allons, Gecko, chouez-nous ça!'*

And he put his big hands on the piano, over Little Billee's, pushed him off the music-stool with his great gaunt body, and, sitting on it himself, he played a masterly prelude. It was impressive to hear the complicated richness and volume of the sounds he evoked after Little Billee's gentle 'tink-a-tink.'

And Gecko, cuddling lovingly his violin and closing his upturned eyes, played that simple melody as it had probably never been played before – such passion, such pathos, such a tone! – and they turned it and twisted it, and went from one key to another, playing into each other's hands, Svengali taking the lead; and fugued and canoned and counterpointed and battle-dored and shuttlecocked it, high and low, soft and loud, in minor, in pizzicato, and in sordino – adagio, andante, allegretto, scherzo* – and exhausted all its possibilities of beauty; till their susceptible audience of three was all but crazed with delight and wonder; and the masterful Ben Bolt, and his over-tender Alice, and his too submissive friend, and his old schoolmaster so kind and so true, and his long-dead schoolmates, and the rustic porch and the mill, and the slab of granite so gray,

> And the dear little nook
> By the clear running brook,*

were all magnified into a strange, almost holy poetic dignity and splendour quite undreamed of by whoever wrote the words and music of that unsophisticated little song, which has touched so many simple British hearts that don't know any better – and among them, once, that of the present scribe – long, long ago!

'Sacrepleu! il choue pien, le Checko, hein?' said Svengali, when they had brought this wonderful double improvisation to a climax and a close. 'C'est mon élèfe! che le fais chanter sur son fiolon, c'est comme si c'était *moi* qui chantais! ach! si ch'afais pour teux sous de voix, che serais le bremier chanteur du monte!* I cannot sing!' he continued. (I will translate him into English, without attempting to translate his accent, which is a mere matter of judiciously transposing p's and b's, and t's and d's, and f's and v's, and g's and k's, and turning the soft French j into sch, and a pretty language into an ugly one.)

'I cannot sing myself, I cannot play the violin, but I can teach – hein, Gecko? And I have a pupil – hein, Gecko? – la betite Honorine;' and here he leered all round with a leer that was not engaging. 'The world shall hear of la betite Honorine* some day – hein, Gecko? Listen all – this is how I teach la betite Honorine! Gecko, play me a little accompaniment in pizzicato.'

And he pulled out of his pocket a kind of little flexible flageolet* (of his own invention, it seems), which he screwed together and put to his lips, and on this humble instrument he played 'Ben Bolt,' while Gecko accompanied him, using his fiddle as a guitar, his adoring eyes fixed in reverence on his master.

And it would be impossible to render in any words the deftness, the distinction, the grace, power, pathos, and passion with which this truly phenomenal artist executed the poor old twopenny tune on his elastic penny whistle – for it was little more – such thrilling, vibrating, piercing tenderness, now loud and full, a shrill scream of anguish, now soft as a whisper, a mere melodic breath, more human almost than the human voice itself, a perfection unattainable even by Gecko, a master, on an instrument which is the acknowledged king of all!

So that the tear, which had been so close to the brink of Little Billee's eye while Gecko was playing, now rose and trembled under his eyelid and spilled itself down his nose; and he had to dissemble and surreptitiously mop it up with his little finger as he leaned his chin on his hand, and cough a little husky, unnatural cough – *pour se donner une contenance!**

He had never heard such music as this, never dreamed such music was possible. He was conscious, while it lasted, that he saw deeper into the beauty, the sadness of things, the very heart of them, and their pathetic evanescence, as with a new inner eye – even into eternity itself, beyond the veil – a vague cosmic vision that faded when the music was over, but left an unfading reminiscence of its having been, and a passionate desire to express the like some day through the plastic medium of his own beautiful art.

The Flexible Flageolet

When Svengali ended, he leered again on his dumbstruck audience, and said: 'That is how I teach la betite Honorine to sing; that is how I teach Gecko to play; that is how I teach *"il bel canto!"** It was lost, the *bel canto* – but I found it, in a dream – I, and nobody else – I – Svengali – I – I – I! But that is enough of music; let us play at something else – ; let us play at this!' he cried, jumping up and seizing a foil and bending it against the wall ... 'Come along, Little Pillee, and I will show you something more you don't know ...'

So Little Billee took off his coat and waistcoat, donned mask and glove and fencing-shoes, and they had an 'assault of arms,' as it is nobly called in French, and in which poor Little Billee came off very badly. The German Pole fenced wildly, but well.

Then it was the Laird's turn, and he came off badly too; so then Taffy took up the foil, and redeemed the honour of Great Britain, as became a British hussar* and a Man of Blood. For Taffy, by long and assiduous practice in the best school in Paris (and also by virtue of his native aptitudes), was a match for any *maître d'armes** in the whole French army, and Svengali got 'what for.'

And when it was time to give up play and settle down to work, others dropped in – French, English, Swiss, German, American, Greek; curtains were drawn and shutters opened; the studio was flooded with light – and the afternoon was healthily spent in athletic and gymnastic exercises till dinner-time.

But Little Billee, who had had enough of fencing and gymnastics for the day, amused himself by filling up with black and white and red-chalk strokes the outline of Trilby's foot on the wall, lest he should forget his fresh vision of it, which was still to him as the thing itself – an absolute reality, born of a mere glance, a mere chance – a happy caprice!

Durien came in and looked over his shoulder, and exclaimed: 'Tiens! le pied de Trilby! vous avez fait ça d'après nature?'

'Nong!'

'De mémoire, alors?'

'Wee!'

'Je vous en fais mon compliment! Vous avez eu la main heureuse. Je voudrais bien avoir fait ça, moi! C'est un petit chef-d'œuvre que vous avez fait là – tout bonnement, mon cher! Mais vous élaborez trop. De grâce, n'y touchez plus!'*

And Little Billee was pleased, and touched it no more; for Durien was a great sculptor and sincerity itself.

And then – well, I happen to forget what sort of day this particular day turned into at about six of the clock.

If it was decently fine, the most of them went off to dine at the Restaurant de la Couronne, kept by the Père Trin (in the Rue de Monsieur),* who gave you of his best to eat and drink for twenty sols Parisis, or one franc in the coin of the empire. Good distending soups, omelets that were only too savoury, lentils, red and white beans, meat so dressed and sauced and seasoned that you didn't know whether it was beef or mutton – flesh, fowl, or good red herring – or even bad, for that matter – nor very greatly cared.

And just the same lettuce, radishes, and cheese of Gruyère or Brie as you got at the Trois Frères Provençaux* (but not the same butter!). And to wash it all down, generous wine in wooden *brocs** – that stained a lovely æsthetic blue everything it was spilled over.

And you hobnobbed with models, male and female, students of law and medicine, painters and sculptors, workmen and *blanchisseuses** and grisettes,* and found them very good company, and most improving to your French, if your French was of the usual British kind, and even to some of your manners, if these were very British indeed. And the evening was innocently wound up with billiards, cards, or dominoes at the Café du Luxembourg opposite; or at the Théâtre du Luxembourg, in the Rue de Madame,* to see funny farces with screamingly droll Englishmen in them; or, still better, at the Jardin Bullier (la Closerie des Lilas),* to see the students dance the cancan, or try and dance it yourself, which is not so easy as it seems; or, best of all, at the Théâtre de l'Odéon,* to see some piece of the classical *répertoire*.

Or, if it were not only fine,* but a Saturday afternoon into the bargain, the Laird would put on a necktie and a few other necessary things, and the three friends would walk arm-in-arm to Taffy's hotel in the Rue de Seine, and wait outside till he had made himself as presentable as the Laird, which did not take very long. And then (Little Billee was always presentable) they would, arm-in-arm, the huge Taffy in the middle, descend the Rue de Seine and cross a bridge to the Cité, and have a look in at the Morgue. Then back again to the quays on the *rive gauche** by the Pont Neuf,* to wend their way westward; now on one side to look at the print and picture shops and the *magasins** of bric-à-brac, and haply sometimes buy thereof, now on the other to finger and cheapen the secondhand books for sale on the parapet, and even pick up one or two utterly unwanted bargains, never to be read or opened again.

When they reached the Pont des Arts* they would cross it, stopping in the middle to look up the river towards the old Cité and Notre Dame, eastward, and dream unutterable things, and try to utter them. Then, turning westward, they would gaze at the glowing sky and all it glowed upon – the corner of the Tuileries* and the Louvre, the many bridges, the Chamber of Deputies,* the golden river narrowing its perspective and broadening its bed as it went flowing and winding on its way between Passy and Grenelle to St Cloud, to Rouen, to the Havre,* to England perhaps – where *they* didn't want to be just then; and they would try and express themselves to the effect that life was uncommonly well worth living in that particular city at that particular time of the day and year and century, at that particular epoch of their own mortal and uncertain lives.

Then, still arm-in-arm, and chatting gaily across the courtyard of the Louvre, through gilded gates well guarded by reckless imperial Zouaves,* up the arcaded Rue de Rivoli as far as the Rue Castiglione,* where they would stare with greedy eyes at the window of the great corner pastry-cook, and marvel at the beautiful assortment of bonbons, *pralines, dragées, marrons glacés** – saccharine, crystalline substances of all kinds and colours, as charming to look at as an illumination; precious stones, delicately-frosted sweets, pearls and diamonds so arranged as to melt in the mouth; especially, at this particular time of the year, the monstrous Easter-egg, of enchanting hue, enshrined like costly jewels in caskets of satin and gold; and the Laird, who was well read in his English classics and liked to show it, would opine that 'they managed these things better in France.'

Then across the street by a great gate into the Allée des Feuillants,* and up to the Place de la Concorde* – to gaze, but quite without base envy, at the smart people coming back from the Bois de Boulogne.* For even in Paris 'carriage people' have a way of looking bored, of taking their pleasure sadly, of having nothing to say to each other, as though the vibration of so many wheels all rolling home the same way every afternoon had hypnotised them into silence, idiocy, and melancholia.

And our three musketeers* of the brush would speculate on the vanity of wealth and rank and fashion; on the satiety that follows in the wake of self-indulgence and overtakes it; on the weariness of the pleasures that become a toil – as if they knew all about it, had found it all out for themselves, and nobody else had ever found it out before!

Then they found out something else – namely, that the sting of healthy appetite was becoming intolerable; so they would betake themselves to an English eating-house in the Rue de la Madeleine* (on the left-hand side near the top), where they would renovate their strength and their patriotism on British beef and beer, and household bread, and bracing, biting, stinging yellow mustard, and heroic horseradish, and noble apple-pie, and Cheshire cheese; and get through as much of these in an hour or so as they could for talking, talking, talking; such happy talk! as full of sanguine hope and enthusiasm, of cocksure commendation or condemnation of all painters, dead or alive, of modest but firm belief in themselves and each other, as a Paris Easter-egg is full of sweets and pleasantness (for the young).

And then a stroll on the crowded, well-lighted boulevards, and a bock at the café there, at a little three-legged marble table right out on the genial asphalt side pavement, still talking nineteen to the dozen.

Then home by dark, old, silent streets and some deserted bridge to their beloved Latin Quarter, the Morgue gleaming cold and still and fatal in the pale lamplight, and Notre Dame pricking up its watchful twin towers, which have looked down for so many centuries on so many happy, sanguine, expansive youths walking arm-in-arm by twos and threes, and for ever talking, talking talking . . .

The Laird and Little Billee would see Taffy safe to the door of his *hôtel garni** in the Rue de Seine, where they would find much to say to each other before they said good-night – so much that Taffy and Little Billee would see the Laird safe to *his* door, in the Place St Anatole des Arts. And then a discussion would arise between Taffy and the Laird on the immortality of the soul, let us say, or the exact meaning of the word 'gentle-

Three Musketeers of the Brush

man,' or the relative merits of Dickens and Thackeray, or some such recondite and quite unhackneyed theme, and Taffy and the Laird would escort Little Billee to *his* door, in the Place de l'Odéon, and he would re-escort them both back again, and so on till any hour you please.

Or again, if it rained, and Paris through the studio window loomed lead-coloured, with its shiny slate roofs under skies that were ashen and sober, and the wild west wind made woeful music among the chimney-pots, and little gray waves ran up the river the wrong way, and the Morgue looked chill and dark and wet, and almost uninviting (even to three healthy-minded young Britons), they would resolve to dine and spend a happy evening at home.

Little Billee, taking with him three francs (or even four), would dive into back streets and buy a yard or so of crusty new bread, well burned on the flat side, a fillet of beef, a litre of wine, potatoes and onions, butter, a little cylindrical cheese called 'bondon* de Neufchâtel,' tender curly lettuce, with chervil, parsley, spring onions, and other fine herbs, and a pod of garlic, which would be rubbed on a crust of bread to flavour things with.

Taffy would lay the cloth English-wise, and also make the salad, for which, like everybody else I ever met, he had a special receipt of his own (putting in the oil first and the vinegar after); and indeed his salads were quite as good as everybody else's.

The Laird, bending over the stove, would cook the onions and beef into a savoury Scotch mess so cunningly that you could not taste the beef for the onions — nor always the onions for the garlic.

And they would dine far better than at le Père Trin's, far better than at the English Restaurant in the Rue de la Madeleine — better than anywhere else on earth!

And after dinner, what coffee, roasted and ground on the spot, what pipes and cigarettes of *caporal*, by the light of the three shaded lamps, while the rain beat against the big north window, and the wind went howling round the quaint old mediæval tower at the corner of the Rue Vieille des Trois Mauvais Ladres* (the old street of the three bad lepers), and the damp logs hissed and crackled in the stove!

What jolly talk into the small hours! Thackeray and Dickens

Taffy makes the salad

'The glory that was Greece'

again, and Tennyson and Byron (who was 'not deed yet' in those days); and Titian and Velasquez, and young Millais and Holman Hunt* (just out); and Monsieur Ingres and Monsieur Delacroix,* and Balzac and Stendhal and George Sand; and the good Dumas! and Edgar Allan Poe; and the glory that was Greece and the grandeur that was Rome . . .

Good, honest, innocent, artless prattle – not of the wisest, perhaps, nor redolent of the very highest culture (which, by the way, can mar as well as make), nor leading to any very practical result; but quite pathetically sweet from the sincerity and fervour of its convictions, a profound belief in their importance, and a proud trust in their life-long immutability.

Oh, happy days and happy nights, sacred to art and friend-ship! oh, happy times of careless impecuniosity, and youth and hope and health and strength and freedom – with all Paris for a playground, and its dear old unregenerate Latin Quarter for a workshop, and a home!

And, up to then, no kill-joy complications of love!

No, decidedly no! Little Billee had never known such happi-ness as this – never dreamed of its possibility.

A day or two after this, our opening day, but in the afternoon, when the fencing and boxing had begun and the trapeze was in full swing, Trilby's 'Milk below!' was sounded at the door, and she appeared – clothed this time and in her right mind, as it seemed: a tall, straight, flat-backed, square-shouldered, deep-chested, full-bosomed young grisette, in a snowy frilled cap, a neat black gown and white apron, pretty faded, well-darned brown stockings, and well-worn, soft, gray, square-toed slippers of list, without heels and originally shapeless; but which her feet, uncompromising and inexorable as boot-trees, had en-nobled into everlasting classic shapeliness, and stamped with an unforgettable individuality, as does a beautiful hand its well-worn glove – a fact Little Billee was not slow to perceive, with a curious thrill that was only half æsthetic.

Then he looked into her freckled face, and met the kind and tender mirthfulness of her gaze and the plucky frankness of her fine wide smile with a thrill that was not æsthetic at all (nor the reverse), but all of the heart. And in one of his quick flashes of intuitive insight he divined far down beneath the shining surface of those eyes (which seemed for a moment to reflect only a little

image of himself against the sky beyond the big north window)
a well of sweetness; and floating somewhere in the midst of it
the very heart of compassion, generosity, and warm sisterly
love; and under that – alas! at the bottom of all – a thin slimy
layer of sorrow and shame. And just as long as it takes for a
tear to rise and gather and choke itself back again, this sudden
revelation shook his nervous little frame with a pang of pity and
the knightly wish to help. But he had no time to indulge in such
soft emotions. Trilby was met on her entrance by friendly
greetings on all sides.

'Tiens! c'est la grande Trilby!' exclaimed Jules Guinot through
his fencing mask. 'Comment! t'es déjà debout après hier soir?
Avons-nous assez rigolé chez Mathieu, hein? Crénom d'un nom,
quelle noce! V'là une crémaillère qui peut se vanter d'être
diantrement bien pendue, j'espère! Et la petite santé, c'matin?'

'Hé, hé! mon vieux,' answered Trilby. 'Ça boulotte, apparem-
ment! Et toi? et Victorine? Comment qu'a s' porte à c't'heure?
Elle avait un fier coup d'chasselas! c'est-y jobard, hein? de s' fich
'paf comme ça d'vant l' monde! Tiens, v'là, Gontran! ça marche-
t-y, Gontran, Zouzou* d' mon cœur?'

'Comme sur des roulettes, ma biche!' said Gontran, *alias*
l'Zouzou – a corporal in the Zouaves. 'Mais tu t'es donc mise
chiffonnière, à présent? T'as fait banque-route?'

(For Trilby had a chiffonnier's basket strapped on her back,
and carried a pick and lantern.)

'Mais-z-oui, mon bon!' she said. 'Dame! pas d' veine hier soir!
t'as bien vu! Dans la dêche jusqu'aux omoplates, mon pauv'
caporal-sous-off! nom d'un canon – faut bien vivre, s' pas?'*

Little Billee's heart-sluices had closed during this interchange
of courtesies. He felt it to be of a very slangy kind, because he
couldn't understand a word of it, and he hated slang. All he
could make out was the free use of the *tu* and the *toi*, and he
knew enough French to know that this implied a great familiar-
ity, which he misunderstood.

So that Jules Guinot's polite inquiries whether Trilby were
none the worse after Mathieu's house-warming (which was so
jolly), Trilby's kind solicitude about the health of Victorine,
who had very foolishly taken a drop too much on that occasion,
Trilby's mock regrets that her own bad luck at cards had made
it necessary that she should retrieve her fallen fortunes by rag-
picking – all these innocent, playful little amenities (which I

have tried to write down just as they were spoken) were couched
in a language that was as Greek to him – and he felt out of it,
jealous and indignant.

'Good-afternoon to you, Mr Taffy,' said Trilby, in English.
'I've brought you these objects of art and virtu* to make the
peace with you. They're the real thing, you know. I borrowed
'em from le père Martin, chiffonnier en gros et en détail, grand
officier de la Légion d'Honneur,* membre de l'Institut* et
cetera, treize bis Rue du Puits d'Amour,* rez-de-chaussée au
fond de la cour à gauche, vis-à-vis le mont-de-piété!* He's one
of my intimate friends, and—'

'You don't mean to say you're the intimate friend of a *rag-
picker!*' exclaimed the good Taffy.

'Oh yes! Pourquoi pas? I never brag; besides, there ain't any
beastly pride about le père Martin,' said Trilby, with a wink.
'You'd soon find that out if *you* were an intimate friend of his.
This is how it's put on. Do you see? If *you'll* put it on I'll fasten
it for you, and show you how to hold the lantern and handle
the pick. You may come to it yourself some day, you know. Il
ne faut jurer de rien!* Père Martin will pose for you in person if
you like. He's generally disengaged in the afternoon. He's poor
but honest, you know, and very nice and clean; quite the
gentleman. He likes artists, especially English – they pay. His
wife sells bric-à-brac and old masters: Rembrandts from two
francs fifty upwards. They've got a little grandson – a love of a
child. I'm his godmother. You know French, I suppose?'

'Oh yes,' said Taffy, much abashed. 'I'm very much obliged
to you – very much indeed – a – I – a—'

'Y a pas d' quoi!' said Trilby, divesting herself of her basket
and putting it, with the pick and lantern, in a corner. 'Et
maintenant, le temps d'absorber une fine de fin sec [a cigarette]
et je m' la brise [I'm off]. On m'attend à l'Ambassade d'Autriche.
Et puis zut! Allez toujours, mes enfants. En avant la boxe!'*

She sat herself down cross-legged on the model-throne, and
made herself a cigarette, and watched the fencing and boxing.
Little Billee brought her a chair, which she refused; so he sat
down on it himself by her side, and talked to her, just as he
would have talked to any young lady at home – about the
weather, about Verdi's new opera* (which she had never heard),
the impressiveness of Notre Dame, and Victor Hugo's beautiful
romance* (which she had never read), the mysterious charm of

Leonardo da Vinci's Lisa Gioconda's smile* (which she had never seen) – by all of which she was no doubt rather tickled and a little embarrassed, perhaps also a little touched.

Taffy brought her a cup of coffee, and conversed with her in polite formal French very well and carefully pronounced; and the Laird tried to do likewise. *His* French was of that honest English kind that breaks up the stiffness of even an English party; and his jolly manners were such as to put an end to all shyness and constraint, and make self-consciousness impossible.

Others dropped in from neighbouring studios – the usual cosmopolite crew. It was a perpetual come-and-go in this particular studio between four and six in the afternoon.

There were ladies too, *en cheveux*,* in caps and bonnets, some of whom knew Trilby, and thee'd and thou'd with familiar and friendly affection, while others mademoiselle'd her with distant politeness, and were mademoiselle'd and madame'd back again. 'Absolument comme à l'Ambassade d'Autriche,'* as Trilby observed to the Laird, with a British wink that was by no means ambassadorial.

Then Svengali came and made some of his grandest music, which was as completely thrown away on Trilby as fireworks on a blind beggar, for all she held her tongue so piously.

Fencing and boxing and trapezing seemed to be more in her line; and indeed, to a tone-deaf person, Taffy lunging his full spread with a foil, in all the splendour of his long, lithe, youthful strength, was a far gainlier sight than Svengali at the keyboard flashing his languid bold eyes with a sickly smile from one listener to another, as if to say: 'N'est-ce pas que che suis peau? N'est-ce pas que ch'ai tu chénie? Nest-ce pas que che suis suplime, enfin?'*

Then enter Durien the sculptor, who had been presented with a *baignoire** at the Porte St Martin* to see *La Dame aux Camélias*,* and he invited Trilby and another lady to dine with him *au cabaret** and share his box.

So Trilby didn't go to the Austrian embassy after all, as the Laird observed to Little Billee, with such a good imitation of her wink that Little Billee was bound to laugh.

But Little Billee was not inclined for fun; a dullness, a sense of disenchantment, had come over him; as he expressed it to himself, with pathetic self-pity:

A feeling of sadness and longing
That is not akin to pain,
And resembles sorrow only
As the mist resembles the rain.*

And the sadness, if he had known, was that all beautiful young women with kind sweet faces and noble figures and goddess-like extremities should not be good and pure as they were beautiful; and the longing was a longing that Trilby could be turned into a young lady – say the vicar's daughter in a little Devonshire village – his sister's friend and co-teacher at the Sunday-school, a simple, pure, and pious maiden of gentle birth.

For he adored piety in women, although he was not pious by any means. His inarticulate intuitive perceptions were not of form and colour secrets only, but strove to pierce the veil of deeper mysteries in impetuous and dogmatic boyish scorn of all received interpretations. For he flattered himself that he possessed the philosophical and scientific mind, and piqued himself on thinking clearly, and was intolerant of human inconsistency.

That small reserve portion of his ever-active brain which should have lain fallow while the rest of it was at work or play, perpetually plagued itself about the mysteries of life and death, and was for ever propounding unanswerable arguments against the Christian belief, through a kind of inverted sympathy with the believer. Fortunately for his friends, Little Billee was both shy and discreet, and very tender of other people's feelings; so he kept all his immature juvenile agnosticism to himself.

To atone for such ungainly strong-mindedness in one so young and tender, he was the slave of many little traditional observances which have no very solid foundation in either science or philosophy. For instance, he wouldn't walk under a ladder for worlds, nor sit down thirteen to dinner, nor have his hair cut on a Friday, and was quite upset if he happened to see the new moon through glass. And he believed in lucky and unlucky numbers, and dearly loved the sights and scents and sounds of high mass in some dim old French cathedral, and found them secretly comforting.

Let us hope that he sometimes laughed at himself, if only in his sleeve!

And with all his keenness of insight into life he had a well-brought-up, middle-class young Englishman's belief in the infallible efficacy of gentle birth – for gentle he considered his own and Taffy's and the Laird's, and that of most of the good people he had lived among in England – all people, in short, whose two parents and four grandparents had received a liberal education and belonged to the professional class. And with this belief he combined (or thought he did) a proper democratic scorn for bloated dukes and lords, and even poor inoffensive baronets, and all the landed gentry – everybody who was born an inch higher up than himself.

It is a fairly good middle-class social creed, if you can only stick to it through life in despite of life's experience. It fosters independence and self-respect, and not a few stodgy practical virtues as well. At all events, it keeps you out of bad company, which is to be found both above and below. *In medio tutissimus ibis!**

And all this melancholy preoccupation, on Little Billee's part, from the momentary gleam and dazzle of a pair of over-perfect feet in an over-æsthetic eye, too much enamoured of mere form!

Reversing the usual process, he had idealised from the base upward!

Many of us, older and wiser than Little Billee, have seen in lovely female shapes the outer garment of a lovely female soul. The instinct which guides us to do this is, perhaps, a right one, more often than not. But more often than not, also, lovely female shapes are terrible complicators of the difficulties and dangers of this earthly life, especially for their owner, and more especially if she be a humble daughter of the people, poor and ignorant, of a yielding nature, too quick to love and trust. This is all so true as to be trite – so trite as to be a common platitude!

A modern teller of tales,* most widely (and most justly) popular, tells us of Californian heroes and heroines who, like Lord Byron's Corsair,* were linked with one virtue and a thousand crimes. And so dexterously does he weave his story that the Young Person* may read it and learn nothing but good.

My poor heroine was the converse of these engaging criminals; she had all the virtues but one; but the virtue she lacked (the very one of all that plays the title-rôle, and gives its generic name to all the rest of that goodly company) was of such a kind that I have found it impossible so to tell her history as to make it quite fit and proper reading for the ubiquitous young person so dear to us all.

Most deeply to my regret. For I had fondly hoped it might one day be said of me that whatever my other literary shortcomings might be, I at least had never penned a line which a pure-minded young British mother might not read aloud to her little blue-eyed babe as it lies sucking its little bottle in its little bassinette.

Fate has willed it otherwise.

Would indeed that I could duly express poor Trilby's one shortcoming in some not too familiar medium – in Latin or Greek, let us say – lest the Young Person (in this ubiquitousness of hers, for which Heaven be praised) should happen to pry into these pages when her mother is looking another way.

Latin and Greek are languages the Young Person should not be taught to understand – seeing that they are highly improper languages, deservedly dead – in which pagan bards who should have known better have sung the filthy loves of their gods and goddesses.

But at least I am scholar enough to enter one little Latin plea on Trilby's behalf – the shortest, best, and most beautiful plea I can think of. It was once used in extenuation and condonation of the frailties of another poor weak woman, presumably beautiful, and a far worse offender than Trilby, but who, like Trilby, repented of her ways, and was most justly forgiven –

Quia multum amavit!*

Whether it be an aggravation of her misdeeds or an extenuating circumstance, no pressure of want, no temptations of greed or vanity, had ever been factors in urging Trilby on her downward career after her first false step in that direction – the result of ignorance, bad advice (from her mother, of all people in the world), and base betrayal. She might have lived in guilty splendour had she chosen, but her wants were few. She had no vanity, and her tastes were of the simplest, and she earned enough to gratify them all, and to spare.

So she followed love for love's sake only, now and then, as she would have followed art if she had been a man – capriciously, desultorily, more in a frolicsome spirit of *camaraderie** than anything else. Like an amateur, in short – a distinguished amateur who is too proud to sell his pictures, but willingly gives one away now and then to some highly-valued and much-admiring friend.

Sheer gaiety of heart and genial good-fellowship, the difficulty of saying nay to earnest pleading. She was *bonne camarade et bonne fille** before everything. Though her heart was not large enough to harbour more than one light love at a time (even in that Latin Quarter of genially capacious hearts), it had room for many warm friendships; and she was the warmest, most helpful, and most compassionate of friends, far more serious and faithful in friendship than in love.

Indeed, she might almost be said to possess a virginal heart, so little did she know of love's heartaches and raptures and torments and clingings and jealousies.

With her it was lightly come and lightly go, and never come back again; as one or two, or perhaps three, picturesque Bohemians* of the brush or chisel had found, at some cost to their vanity and self-esteem; perhaps even to a deeper feeling – who knows?

Trilby's father, as she had said, had been a gentleman, the son of a famous Dublin physician and friend of George the Fourth's.* He had been a Fellow of his college, and had entered holy orders. He also had all the virtues but one; he was a drunkard, and began to drink quite early in life. He soon left the Church and became a classical tutor, and failed through this besetting sin of his, and fell into disgrace.

Then he went to Paris, and picked up a few English pupils there, and lost them, and earned a precarious livelihood from hand to mouth, anyhow, and sank from bad to worse.

And when his worst was about reached, he married the famous tartaned and tam-o'-shantered barmaid at the Montagnards Écossais,* in the Rue du Paradis Poissonnière* (a very fishy paradise indeed); she was a most beautiful Highland lassie of low degree, and she managed to support him, or helped him to support himself, for ten or fifteen years. Trilby was born to them, and was dragged up in some way – *à la grâce de Dieu!**

Patrick O'Ferrall soon taught his wife to drown all care and responsibility in his own simple way, and opportunities for doing so were never lacking to her.

Then he died, and left a posthumous child – born ten months after his death, alas! and whose birth cost its mother her life.

Then Trilby became a *blanchisseuse de fin*,* and in two or three years came to grief through her trust in a friend of her mother's. Then she became a model besides, and was able to support her little brother, whom she dearly loved.

At the time this story begins, this small waif and stray was *en pension** with le père Martin, the rag-picker, and his wife, the dealer in bric-à-brac and inexpensive old masters. They were very good people, and had grown fond of the child, who was beautiful to look at, and full of pretty tricks and pluck and cleverness – a popular favourite in the Rue du Puits d'Amour and its humble neighbourhood.

Trilby, for some freak, always chose to speak of him as her godson, and as the grandchild of le père et la mère Martin, so that these good people had almost grown to believe he really belonged to them.

And almost every one else believed that he was the child of Trilby (in spite of her youth), and she was so fond of him that she didn't mind in the least.

He might have had a worse home.

La mère Martin was pious, or pretended to be; le père Martin was the reverse. But they were equally good for their kind, and though coarse and ignorant and unscrupulous in many ways (as was natural enough), they were gifted in a very full measure with the saving graces of love and charity, especially he. And if people are to be judged by their works, this worthy pair are no doubt both equally well compensated by now for the trials and struggle of their sordid earthly life.

So much for Trilby's parentage.

And as she sat and wept at Madame Doche's* impersonation of *La Dame aux Camélias* (with her hand in Durien's) she vaguely remembered, as in a waking dream, now the noble presence of Taffy as he towered cool and erect, foil in hand, gallantly waiting for his adversary to breathe, now the beautiful sensitive face of Little Billee and his deferential courtesy.

And during the *entr'actes** her heart went out in friendship to the jolly Scotch Laird of Cockpen, who came out now and then with such terrible French oaths and abominable expletives (and in the presence of ladies, too!), without the slightest notion of what they meant.

For the Laird had a quick ear, and a craving to be colloquial and idiomatic before everything else, and made many awkward and embarrassing mistakes.

It would be with him as though a polite Frenchman should

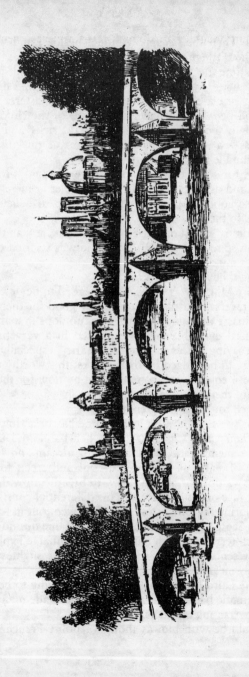

say to a fair daughter of Albion,* 'D— my eyes, mees, your tea
is getting — cold; let me tell that good old — of a Jules to bring
you another cup.'

And so forth, till time and experience taught him better. It is
perhaps well for him that his first experiments in conversational
French were made in the unconventional circle of the Place St
Anatole des Arts.

Part Second

Dieu! qu'il fait bon la regarder,
    La gracieuse, bonne et belle!
    Pour les grands biens qui sont en elle
Chacun est prêt de la louer.*

Nobody knew exactly how Svengali lived, and very few knew where (or why). He occupied a roomy dilapidated garret, *au sixième,* in the Rue Tire-Liard,* with a truckle-bed and a pianoforte for furniture, and very little else.

He was poor, for in spite of his talent he had not yet made his mark in Paris. His manners may have been accountable for this. He would either fawn or bully, and could be grossly impertinent. He had a kind of cynical humour, which was more offensive than amusing, and always laughed at the wrong thing, at the wrong time, in the wrong place. And his laughter was always derisive and full of malice. And his egotism and conceit were not to be borne; and then he was both tawdry and dirty in his person; more greasily, mattedly unkempt than even a really successful pianist has any right to be even in the best society.

He was not a nice man, and there was no pathos in his poverty – a poverty that was not honourable, and need not have existed at all; for he was constantly receiving supplies from his own people in Austria – his old father and mother, his sisters, his cousins, and his aunts, hard-working, frugal folk of whom he was the pride and the darling.

He had but one virtue – his love of his art; or, rather, his love of himself as a master of his art – *the* master; for he despised, or affected to despise, all other musicians, living or dead – even those whose work he interpreted so divinely, and pitied them for not hearing Svengali give utterance to their music, which of course they could not utter themselves.

'Ils safent tous un peu toucher du biâno, mais pas grand'chose!'*

He had been the best pianist of his time at the Conservatory in Leipsic;* and, indeed, there was perhaps some excuse for this overweening conceit, since he was able to lend a quite peculiar individual charm of his own to any music he played, except the highest and best of all, in which he conspicuously failed.

He had to draw the line just above Chopin, where he reached his highest level. It will not do to lend your own quite peculiar individual charm to Handel and Bach and Beethoven; and Chopin is not bad as a *pis-aller*.*

He had ardently wished to sing, and had studied hard to that end in Germany, in Italy, in France, with the forlorn hope of evolving from some inner recess a voice to sing with. But nature had been singularly harsh to him in this one respect – inexorable. He was absolutely without voice, beyond the harsh, hoarse, weak raven's croak he used to speak with, and no method availed to make one for him. But he grew to understand the human voice as perhaps no one has understood it – before or since.

So in his head he went for ever singing, singing, singing, as probably no human nightingale has ever yet been able to sing out loud for the glory and delight of his fellow-mortals; making unheard heavenly melody of the cheapest, trivialest tunes – tunes of the café concert, tunes of the nursery, the shop-parlour, the guard-room, the schoolroom, the pothouse, the slum. There was nothing so humble, so base even, but what his magic could transform it into the rarest beauty without altering a note. This seems impossible, I know. But if it didn't, where would the magic come in?

Whatever of heart or conscience – pity, love, tenderness, manliness, courage, reverence, charity – endowed him at his birth had been swallowed up by this one faculty, and nothing of them was left for the common uses of life. He poured them all into his little flexible flageolet.

Svengali playing Chopin on the pianoforte, even (or especially) Svengali playing 'Ben Bolt' on that penny whistle of his, was as one of the heavenly host.

Svengali walking up and down the earth seeking whom he might cheat, betray, exploit, borrow money from, make brutal fun of, bully if he dared, cringe to if he must – man, woman, child, or dog – was about as bad as they make 'em.

To earn a few pence when he couldn't borrow them he played accompaniments at café concerts, and even then he gave offence; for in his contempt for the singer he would play too loud, and embroider his accompaniments with brilliant improvisations of

As bad as they make 'em

his own, and lift his hands on high and bring them down with a
bang in the sentimental parts, and shake his dirty mane and
shrug his shoulders, and smile and leer at the audience, and do
all he could to attract their attention to himself. He also gave a
few music lessons (not at ladies' schools, let us hope), for which
he was not well paid, presumably, since he was always without
a sou, always borrowing money, that he never paid back, and
exhausting the pockets and the patience of one acquaintance
after another.

He had but two friends. There was Gecko, who lived in a
little garret close by in the Impasse des Ramoneurs,* and who
was second violin in the orchestra of the Gymnase,* and shared
his humble earnings with his master, to whom, indeed, he owed
his great talent, not yet revealed to the world.

Svengali's other friend and pupil was (or rather had been) the
mysterious Honorine, of whose conquest he was much given to
boast, hinting that she was *une jeune femme du monde.** This
was not the case. Mademoiselle Honorine Cahen (better known
in the Quartier Latin as Mimi la Salope*) was a dirty, drabby

little dolly-mop of a Jewess, a model for the figure – a very humble person indeed, socially.

She was, however, of a very lively disposition, and had a charming voice, and a natural gift of singing so sweetly that you forgot her accent, which was that of the *tout ce qu'il y a de plus canaille.**

She used to sit at Carrel's, and during the pose she would sing. When <u>Little Billee</u> first heard her he was so fascinated that 'it made him sick to think she sat for the figure' – an effect, by the way, that was always produced upon him by all specially attractive figure models of the gentler sex, for he had a reverence for woman. And before everything else, he had for the singing woman an absolute worship. He was especially thrall to the contralto – the deep low voice that breaks and changes in the middle and soars all at once into a magnified angelic boy treble. It pierced through his ears to his heart, and stirred his very vitals.

He had once heard Madame Alboni, and it had been an epoch in his life; he would have been an easy prey to the sirens! Even beauty paled before the lovely female voice singing in the middle of the note – the nightingale killed the bird of paradise.

I need hardly say that poor Mimi la Salope had not the voice of Madame Alboni, nor the art; but it was a beautiful voice of its little kind, always in the very middle of the note, and her artless art had its quick seduction.

She sang little songs of Béranger's* – 'Grand'mère, parlez-nous de lui!' or 'T'en souviens-tu? disait un capitaine—' or 'Enfants, c'est moi qui suis Lisette!' and such like pretty things, that almost brought the tears to Little Billee's easily-moistened eyes.

But soon she would sing little songs that were not by Béranger – little songs with slang words Little Billee hadn't French enough to understand; but from the kind of laughter with which the points were received by the 'rapins'* in Carrel's studio he guessed these little songs were vile, though the touching little voice was as that of the seraphim still; and he knew the pang of disenchantment and vicarious shame.

Svengali had heard her sing at the Brasserie des Porcherons in the Rue du Crapaud-volant,* and had volunteered to teach her; and she went to see him in his garret, and he played to her, and leered and ogled, and flashed his bold, black, beady Jew's eyes into hers, and she straightway mentally prostrated herself in reverence and adoration before this dazzling specimen of her race.

So that her sordid mercenary little gutter-draggled soul was filled with the sight and the sound of him, as of a lordly, godlike, shawm-playing,* cymbal-banging hero and prophet of the Lord God of Israel – David and Saul in one!*

And then he set himself to teach her – kindly and patiently at first, calling her sweet little pet names – his 'Rose of Sharon,'* his 'pearl of Pabylon,' his 'cazelle-eyed liddle Cherusalem skylark' – and promised her that she should be the queen of the nightingales.

But before he could teach her anything he had to unteach her all she knew; her breathing, the production of her voice, its emission – everything was wrong. She worked indefatigably to please him, and soon succeeded in forgetting all the pretty little sympathetic tricks of voice and phrasing Mother Nature had taught her.

But though she had an exquisite ear she had no real musical intelligence – no intelligence of any kind except about sous and centimes; she was as stupid as a little downy owl, and her voice was just a light native warble, a throstle's pipe, all in the head and nose and throat (a voice he *didn't* understand, for once), a thing of mere youth and health and bloom and high spirits – like her beauty, such as it was – *beauté du diable, beauté damnée.**

She did her very best, and practised all she could in this new way, and sang herself hoarse: she scarcely ate or slept for practising. He grew harsh and impatient and coldly severe, and of course she loved him all the more; and the more she loved him the more nervous she got and the worse she sang. Her voice cracked; her ear became demoralised; her attempts to vocalise grew almost as distressing as Trilby's. So that he lost his temper completely, and called her terrible names, and pinched and punched her with his big bony hands till she wept worse than Niobe,* and borrowed money of her – five-franc pieces, even francs and demifrancs – which he never paid her back; and browbeat and bullied and bully-ragged her till she went quite mad for love of him, and would have jumped out of his sixth-floor window to give him a moment's pleasure!

He did not ask her to do this – it never occurred to him, and

A voice he didn't understand

would have given him no pleasure to speak of. But one fine Sabbath morning (a Saturday, of course) he took her by the shoulders and chucked her, neck and crop, out of his garret, with the threat that if she ever dared to show her face there again he would denounce her to the police – an awful threat to the likes of poor Mimi la Salope!

'For where did all those five-franc pieces come from – *hein?* – with which she had tried to pay for all the singing lessons that had been thrown away upon her? Not from merely sitting to painters – *hein?*'

Thus the little gazelle-eyed Jerusalem skylark went back to her native streets again – a mere mud-lark of the Paris slums – her wings clipped, her spirit quenched and broken, and with no more singing left in her than a common or garden sparrow – not so much!

And so, no more of 'la betite Honorine!'

The morning after this adventure Svengali woke up in his garret with a tremendous longing to spend a happy day; for it was a Sunday, and a very fine one.

He made a long arm and reached his waistcoat and trousers off the floor, and emptied the contents of their pockets on to his tattered blanket; no silver, no gold, only a few sous and two-sou pieces, just enough to pay for a meagre *premier déjeuner!**

He had cleared out Gecko the day before, and spent the proceeds (ten francs, at least) in one night's riotous living – pleasures in which Gecko had had no share; and he could think of no one to borrow money from but Little Billee, Taffy, and the Laird, whom he had neglected and left untapped for days.

So he slipped into his clothes, and looked at himself in what remained of a little zinc mirror, and found that his forehead left little to be desired, but that his eyes and temples were decidedly grimy. Wherefore, he poured a little water out of a little jug into a little basin, and twisting the corner of his pocket-handkerchief round his dirty forefinger, he delicately dipped it, and removed the offending stains. His fingers, he thought, would do very well for another day or two as they were; he ran them through his matted black mane, pushed it behind his ears, and gave it the twist he liked (and that was so much disliked by his English friends). Then he put on his *béret* and his velveteen cloak, and went forth into the sunny street, with a sense of the fragrance

And so, no more

and freedom and pleasantness of Sunday morning in Paris in the month of May.

He found Little Billee sitting in a zinc hip-bath, busy with soap and sponge; and was so tickled and interested by the sight that he quite forgot for the moment what he had come for.

'Himmel! Why the devil are you doing that?' he asked, in his German-Hebrew-French.

'Doing *what?*' asked Little Billee, in his French of Stratford-atte-Bowe.*

'Sitting in water and playing with a cake of soap and a sponge!'

'Why, to try and get myself *clean*, I suppose!'

'Ach! And how the devil did you get yourself *dirty,* then?'

To this Little Billee found no immediate answer, and went on with his ablutions after the hissing, splashing, energetic fashion of Englishmen; and Svengali laughed loud and long at the spectacle of a little Englishman trying to get himself clean – *tâchant de se nettoyer!**

When such cleanliness had been attained as was possible under the circumstances, Svengali begged for the loan of two hundred francs, and Little Billee gave him a five-franc piece.

Content with this, *faute de mieux,** the German asked him when he would be trying to get himself clean again, as he would much like to come and see him do it.

'Demang mattang, à votre sairveece!'* said Little Billee, with a courteous bow.

'*What!! Monday too!!* Gott in Himmel!** you try to get yourself clean *every day?*'

And he laughed himself out of the room, out of the house, out of the Place de l'Odéon – all the way to the Rue de Seine, where dwelt the 'Man of Blood,' whom he meant to propitiate with the story of that original, Little Billee, trying to get himself clean – that he might borrow another five-franc piece, or perhaps two.

As the reader will no doubt anticipate, he found Taffy in his bath also, and fell to laughing with such convulsive laughter, such twistings, screwings, and doublings of himself up, such pointings of his dirty forefinger at the huge naked Briton, that Taffy was offended, and all but lost his temper.

'What the devil are you cackling at, sacred head of pig that you are? Do you want to be pitched out of that window into the

Rue de Seine? You filthy black Hebrew sweep!* Just you wait a bit; *I'll* wash your head for you!'

And Taffy jumped out of his bath, such a towering figure of righteous Herculean wrath that Svengali was appalled, and fled.

'Donnerwetter!'* he exclaimed as he tumbled down the narrow staircase of the Hôtel de Seine; 'What for a thick head! what for a pigdog! what for a rotten, brutal, *verfluchter kerl** of an Englander!'

Then he paused for thought.

'Now will I go to that Scottish Englander, in the Place St Anatole des Arts, for that other five-franc piece. But first will I wait a little while till he has perhaps finished trying to get himself clean.'

So he breakfasted at the crémerie Souchet, in the Rue Clopin-Clopant,* and, feeling quite safe again, he laughed and laughed till his very sides were sore.

Two Englanders in one day – as naked as your hand!* – a big one and a little one, trying to get themselves clean!

He rather flattered himself he had scored off those two Englanders.

After all, he was right perhaps, from his point of view; you can get as dirty in a week as in a lifetime, so what's the use of taking such a lot of trouble? Besides, so long as you are clean enough to suit your kind, to be any cleaner would be priggish and pedantic, and get you disliked.

Just as Svengali was about to knock at the Laird's door, Trilby came downstairs from Durien's, very unlike herself. Her eyes were red with weeping, and there were great black rings round them; she was pale under her freckles.

'Fous afez du chacrin, matemoiselle?'* asked he.

She told him that she had neuralgia in her eyes, a thing she was subject to; that the pain was maddening, and generally lasted twenty-four hours.

'Perhaps I can cure you; come in here with me.'

The Laird's ablutions (if he had indulged in any that morning) were evidently over for the day. He was breakfasting on a roll and butter, and coffee of his own brewing. He was deeply distressed at the sight of poor Trilby's sufferings, and offered whisky and coffee and gingernuts, which she would not touch.

Svengali told her to sit down on the divan, and sat opposite to her, and bade her look him well in the white of the eyes.

'Two Englanders in one day'

Klyponosis

'Recartez-moi pien tans le planc tes yeux.'*

Then he made little passes and counterpasses on her forehead and temples and down her cheek and neck. Soon her eyes closed and her face grew placid. After a while, a quarter of an hour perhaps, he asked her if she suffered still.

'Oh! presque plus du tout, monsieur – c'est le ciel.'*

In a few minutes more he asked the Laird if he knew German.

'Just enough to understand,' said the Laird (who had spent a year in Düsseldorf*), and Svengali said to him in German: 'See, she sleeps not, but she shall not open her eyes. Ask her.'

'Are you asleep, Miss Trilby?' asked the Laird.

'No.'

'Then open your eyes and look at me.'

She strained to open her eyes, but could not, and said so.

Then Svengali said, again in German, 'She shall not open her mouth. Ask her.'

'Why couldn't you open your eyes, Miss Trilby?'

She strained to open her mouth and speak, but in vain.

'She shall not rise from the divan. Ask her.'

But Trilby was spellbound, and could not move.

'I will now set her free,' said Svengali.

And, lo! she got up and waved her arms, and cried, 'Vive la Prusse! me v'là guérie!'* and in her gratitude she kissed Svengali's hand; and he leered, and showed his big brown teeth and the yellow whites at the top of his big black eyes, and drew his breath with a hiss.

'Now I'll go to Durien's and sit. How can I thank you, monsieur? You have taken all my pain away.'

'Yes, matemoiselle. I have got it myself; it is in my elbows. But I love it, because it comes from you. Every time you have pain you shall come to me, 12 Rue Tire-Liard, au sixième au-dessus de l'entresol,* and I will cure you and take your pain myself—'

'Oh, you are too good!' and in her high spirits she turned round on her heel and uttered her portentous war-cry, 'Milk below!' The very rafters rang with it, and the piano gave out a solemn response.

'What is that you say, matemoiselle?'

'Oh, it's what the milkmen say in England.'

'It is a wonderful cry, matemoiselle – *wunderschön!* It comes straight through the heart; it has its roots in the stomach, and blossoms into music on the lips like the voice of Madame Alboni – voce sulle labbre! It is good production – c'est un cri du cœur!'*

Trilby blushed with pride and pleasure.

'Yes, matemoiselle! I know only one person in the whole world who can produce the voice so well as you! I give you my word of honour.'

'Who is it, monsieur – yourself?'

'Ach, no, matemoiselle; I have not that privilege. I have unfortunately no voice to produce . . . It is a waiter at the Café de la Rotonde, in the Palais Royal;* when you call for coffee, he says "Boum!" in basso profondo. Tiefstimme – *F moll below the line – it is phenomenal! It is like a cannon – a cannon also has very good production, matemoiselle. They pay him for it a thousand francs a year, because he brings many customers to the Café de la Rotonde, where the coffee isn't very good, although it costs three sous a cup dearer than at the Café Larsouille in the Rue Flamberge-au-Vent.* When he dies they will search all Paris for another, and then all Germany, where the good big waiters come from – and the cannons – but they will not find him, and the Café de la Rotonde will be bankrupt – unless you will consent to take his place. Will you permit that I shall look into your mouth, matemoiselle?'

She opened her mouth wide, and he looked into it.

'Himmel! the roof in your mouth is like the dome of the Panthéon;* there is room in it for "toutes les gloires de la France," and a little to spare! The entrance to your throat is like the middle porch of St Sulpice* when the doors are open for the faithful on All Saints' Day;* and not one tooth is missing – thirty-two British teeth as white as milk and as big as knuckle-bones! and your little tongue is scooped out like the leaf of a pink peony, and the bridge of your nose is like the belly of a Stradivarius* – what a sounding-board! and inside your beautiful big chest the lungs are made of leather! and your breath, it embalms – like the breath of a beautiful white heifer fed on the buttercups and daisies of the Vaterland!* and you have a quick, soft, susceptible heart, a heart of gold, matemoiselle – all that sees itself in your face!

> Votre cœur est un luth suspendu!
> Aussitôt qu'on le touche, il résonne . . .*

'Himmel! The roof of your mouth'

What a pity you have not also the musical organisation!'

'Oh, but I *have*, monsieur; you heard me sing "Ben Bolt," didn't you? What makes you say that?'

Svengali was confused for a moment. Then he said: 'When I play the "Rosemonde" of Schubert, matemoiselle, you look another way and smoke a cigarette ... You look at the big Taffy, at the Little Billee, at the pictures on the walls, or out of window, at the sky, the chimney-pots of Notre Dame de Paris; you do not look at Svengali! – Svengali, who looks at you with all his eyes, and plays you the "Rosemonde" of Schubert!'

'Oh, maïe aïe!' exclaimed Trilby; 'you *do* use lovely language!'

'But never mind, matemoiselle; when your pain arrives, then shall you come once more to Svengali, and he shall take it away from you, and keep it himself for a soufenir of you when you are gone. And when you have it no more, he shall play you the "Rosemonde" of Schubert, all alone for you; and then "Messieurs les étutiants,* montez à la chaumière!" ... because it is gayer! *And you shall see nothing, hear nothing, think of nothing but Svengali, Svengali, Svengali!*'

Here he felt his peroration to be so happy and effective that he thought it well to go at once and make a good exit. So he bent over Trilby's shapely freckled hand and kissed it, and bowed himself out of the room, without even borrowing his five-franc piece.

'He's a rum 'un, ain't he?' said Trilby. 'He reminds me of a big hungry spider, and makes me feel like a fly! But he's cured my pain! he's cured my pain! Ah! you don't know what my pain is when it comes!'

'I wouldnt have much to do with him, all the same!' said the Laird. 'I'd sooner have any pain than have it cured in that unnatural way, and by such a man as that! He's a bad fellow, Svengali – I'm sure of it! He mesmerised you;* that's what it is – mesmerism! I've often heard of it, but never seen it done before. They get you into their power, and just make you do any blessed thing they please – lie, murder, steal – anything! and kill yourself into the bargain when they've done with you! It's just too terrible to think of!'

So spake the Laird, earnestly, solemnly, surprised out of his usual self, and most painfully impressed – and his own impressiveness grew upon him and impressed him still more. He loomed quite prophetic.

Tably easily influenced (handwritten)

Cold shivers went down Trilby's back as she listened. She had a singularly impressionable nature, as was shown by her quick and ready susceptibility to Svengali's hypnotic influence. And all that day, as she posed for Durien (to whom she did not mention her adventure), she was haunted by the memory of Svengali's big eyes and the touch of his soft, dirty finger-tips on her face; and her fear and her repulsion grew together.

obsession begins (handwritten)

And 'Svengali, Svengali, Svengali!' went ringing in her head and ears till it became an obsession, a dirge, a knell, an unendurable burden, almost as hard to bear as the pain in her eyes.

'*Svengali, Svengali, Svengali!*'

At last she asked Durian if he knew him.

'Parbleu! Si je connais Svengali!'

'Qu'est-ce que t'en penses?'

'Quand il sera mort, ça fera une fameuse crapule de moins!'*

Chez Carrel

Carrel's atelier (or painting-school) was in the Rue Notre Dame des Potirons St Michel,* at the end of a large courtyard, where there were many large dirty windows facing north, and each window let the light of heaven into a large dirty studio.

The largest of these studios, and the dirtiest, was Carrel's, where some thirty or forty art students drew and painted from the nude model every day but Sunday from eight till twelve, and for two hours in the afternoon, except on Saturdays when the afternoon was devoted to much-needed Augean sweepings* and cleanings.

One week the model was male, the next female, and so on, alternating through the year.

A stove, a model-throne, stools, boxes, some fifty strongly-built low chairs with backs, a couple of score easels and many drawing-boards, completed the *mobilier*.*

The bare walls were adorned with endless caricatures – *des charges** – in charcoal and white chalk; and also the scrapings of many palettes – a polychromous decoration not unpleasing.

For the freedom of the studio and the use of the model each student paid ten francs a month to the *massier*, or senior student, the responsible bell-wether* of the flock; besides this, it was expected of you, on your entrance or initiation, that you should pay for your footing – your *bienvenue** – some thirty, forty, or fifty francs, to be spent on cakes and rum punch all round.

Every Friday Monsieur Carrel, a great artist, and also a stately, well-dressed, and most courteous gentleman (duly decorated with the red rosette of the Legion of Honour), came for two or three hours and went the round, spending a few minutes at each drawing-board or easel – ten or even twelve when the pupil was an industrious and promising one.

He did this for love, not money, and deserved all the reverence with which he inspired this somewhat irreverent and most unruly company, which was made up of all sorts.

Graybeards who had been drawing and painting there for thirty years and more, and remembered other masters than Carrel, and who could draw and paint a torso almost as well as Titian or Velasquez – almost, but not quite – and who could never do anything else, and were fixtures at Carrel's for life.

Younger men who in a year or two, or three or five, or ten or twenty, were bound to make their mark, and perhaps follow in the footsteps of the master; others as conspicuously singled out for failure and future mischance – for the hospital, the garret, the river, the Morgue, or, worse, the traveller's bag, the road, or even the paternal counter.

Irresponsible boys, mere *rapins*, all laugh and chaff and mischief – *blague et bagout Parisien*;* little lords of misrule – wits, butts, bullies; the idle and industrious apprentice, the good and the bad, the clean and the dirty (especially the latter) – all more or less animated by a certain *esprit de corps*, and working very happily and genially together, on the whole, and always willing to help each other with sincere artistic counsel if it was asked for seriously, though it was not always couched in terms very flattering to one's self-love.

Before Little Billee became one of this band of brothers he had been working for three or four years in a London art school, drawing and painting from the life; he had also worked from the antique in the British Museum – so that he was no novice.

As he made his début at Carrel's one Monday morning he felt somewhat shy and ill at ease. He had studied French most earnestly at home in England, and could read it pretty well, and even write it and speak it after a fashion; but he spoke it with much difficulty, and found studio French a different language altogether from the formal and polite language he had been at

'Ça fera une fameuse crapule de moins'

such pains to acquire. Ollendorff* does not cater for the
Quartier Latin. Acting on Taffy's advice – for Taffy had worked
under Carrel – Little Billee handed sixty francs to the *massier*
for his *bienvenue* – a lordly sum – and this liberality made a
most favourable impression, and went far to destroy any little
prejudice that might have been caused by the daintiness of his
dress, the cleanliness of his person, and the politeness of his
manners. A place was assigned to him, and an easel and a
board; for he elected to stand at his work and begin with a
chalk drawing. The model (a male) was posed, and work began

in silence. Monday morning is always rather sulky everywhere (except perhaps in Judee*). During the ten minutes' rest three or four students came and looked at Little Billee's beginnings, and saw at a glance that he thoroughly well knew what he was about, and respected him for it.

Nature had given him a singularly light hand – or rather two, for he was ambidextrous, and could use both with equal skill; and a few months' practice at a London life school had quite cured him of that purposeless indecision of touch which often characterises the prentice hand for years of apprenticeship, and remains with the amateur for life. The lightest and most careless of his pencil strokes had a precision that was inimitable, and a charm that specially belonged to him, and was easy to recognise at a glance. His touch on either canvas or paper was like Svengali's on the keyboard – unique.

As the morning ripened little attempts at conversation were made – little breakings of the ice of silence. It was Lambert, a youth with a singularly facetious face, who first woke the stillness with the following uncalled-for remarks in English very badly pronounced:

'Av you seen my fahzere's ole shoes?'

'I av not seen your fahzere's ole shoes.'

Then, after a pause:

'Av you seen my fahzere's ole 'at?'

'I av not seen your fahzere's ole 'at!'

Presently another said, 'Je trouve qu'il a une jolie tête, l'Anglais.'

But I will put it all into English:

'I find that he has a pretty head – the Englishman! What say *you*, Barizel?'

'Yes; but why has he got eyes like brandy-balls, two a penny?'

'Because he's an Englishman!'

'Yes; but why has he got a mouth like a guinea-pig, with two big teeth in front like the double blank at dominoes?'

'Because he's an Englishman!'

'Yes; but why has he got a back without any bend in it, as if he'd swallowed the Colonne Vendôme* as far up as the battle of Austerlitz?'

'Because he's an Englishman!'

And so on, till all the supposed characteristics of Little Billee's outer man were exhausted. Then:

'Av you seen my fahzere's ole shoes?'

'Papelard!'

'What?'

'*I* should like to know if the Englishman says his prayers before going to bed.'

'Ask him.'

'Ask him yourself!'

'*I* should like to know if the Englishman has sisters; and if so, how old and how many and what sex.'

'Ask him.'

'Ask him yourself!'

'*I* should like to know the detailed and circumstantial history of the Englishman's first love, and how he lost his innocence!'

'Ask him,' etc. etc. etc.

Little Billee, conscious that he was the subject of conversation, grew somewhat nervous. Soon he was addressed directly.

Taffy a l'echelle!

'Dites donc, l'Anglais?'

'Kwaw?' said Little Billee.

'Avez-vous une sœur?'

'Wee.'

'Est-ce qu'elle vous ressemble?'

'Nong.'

'C'est bien dommage! Est-ce qu'elle dit ses prières, le soir, en se couchant?'

A fierce look came into Little Billee's eyes and a redness to his cheeks, and this particular form of overture to friendship was abandoned.

Presently Lambert said, 'Si nous mettions l'Anglais à l'échelle?'

Little Billee, who had been warned, knew what this ordeal meant.

They tied you to a ladder, and carried you in procession up and down the courtyard, and if you were nasty about it they put you under the pump.

During the next rest it was explained to him that he must submit to this indignity, and the ladder (which was used for reaching the high shelves round the studio) was got ready.

Little Billee smiled a singularly winning smile, and suffered himself to be bound with such good-humour that they voted it wasn't amusing, and unbound him, and he escaped the ordeal by ladder.

Taffy had also escaped, but in another way. When they tried to seize him he took up the first *rapin* that came to hand, and using him as a kind of club, he swung him about so freely and knocked down so many students and easels and drawing-boards with him, and made such a terrific rumpus, that the whole studio had to cry for 'pax!' Then he performed feats of strength of such a surprising kind that the memory of him remained in Carrel's studio for years, and he became a legend, a tradition, a myth! It is now said (in what still remains of the Quartier Latin) that he was seven feet high, and used to juggle with the *massier* and model as with a pair of billiard balls, using only his left hand!

To return to Little Billee. When it struck twelve, the cakes and rum punch arrived – a very goodly sight that put every one in a good temper.

The cakes were of three kinds – Babas, Madeleines, and

Savarins* – three sous* apiece, fourpence-halfpenny the set of three. No nicer cakes are made in France, and they are as good in the Quartier Latin as anywhere else; no nicer cakes are made in the whole world, that I know of. You must begin with the Madeleine, which is rich and rather heavy; then the Baba; and finish up with the Savarin, which is shaped like a ring, very light, and flavoured with rum. And then you must really leave off.

The rum punch was tepid, very sweet, and not a bit too strong.

They dragged the model-throne into the middle, and a chair was put on for Little Billee, who dispensed his hospitality in a very polite and attractive manner, helping the *massier* first, and then the other graybeards in the order of their grayness, and so on down to the model.

Presently, just as he was about to help himself, he was asked to sing them an English song. After a little pressing he sung them a song about a gay cavalier* who went to serenade his mistress (and a ladder of ropes, and a pair of masculine gloves that didn't belong to the gay cavalier, but which he found in his lady's bower) – a poor sort of song, but it was the nearest approach to a comic song he knew. There are four verses to it, and each verse is rather long. It does not sound at all funny to a French audience, and even with an English one Little Billee was not good at comic songs.

He was, however, much applauded at the end of each verse. When he had finished, he was asked if he were *quite* sure there wasn't any more of it, and they expressed a deep regret; and then each student, straddling on his little thick-set chair as on a horse, and clasping the back of it in both hands, galloped round Little Billee's throne quite seriously – the strangest procession he had ever seen. It made him laugh till he cried, so that he could not eat or drink.

Then he served more punch and cake all round; and just as he was going to begin himself, Papelard said:

'Say, you others, I find that the Englishman has something of truly distinguished in the voice, something of sympathetic, of touching – something of *je ne sais quoi!*'*

Bouchardy: 'Yes, yes – something of *je ne sais quoi!* That's the very phrase – n'est-ce pas, vous autres?* – that is a good phrase that Papelard has just invented to describe the voice of the Englishman. He is very intelligent – Papelard.'

Chorus: 'Perfect, perfect; he has the genius of characterisation – Papelard. Dites donc, l'Anglais! once more that beautiful song – *hein?* Nous vous en prions tous.'*

Little Billee willingly sang it again, with even greater applause, and again they galloped, but the other way round and faster, so that Little Billee became quite hysterical, and laughed till his sides ached.

Then Dubsoc: 'I find there is something of very capitous and exciting in English music – of very stimulating. And you, Bouchardy?'

Bouchardy: 'Oh me! It is above all the *words* that I admire; they have something of passionate, of romantic – "ze-ese glâ-âves, zese glâ-âves, zey do not belong to me." I don't know what that means, but I love that sort of – of – of – of *je ne sais quoi,* in short! Just *once* more, l'Anglais; only *once,* the *four* couplets.'

So he sang it a third time, all four verses, while they leisurely ate and drank and smoked and looked at each other, nodding solemn commendation of certain phrases in the song: 'Très bien!' 'Très bien!' 'Ah! voilà qui est bien réussi!' 'Épatant, ça!' 'Très fin!'* etc. etc. For, stimulated by success, and rising to the occasion, he did his very utmost to surpass himself in emphasis of gesture and accent and histrionic drollery – heedless of the fact that not one of his listeners had the slightest notion what his song was about.

It was a sorry performance.

And it was not till he had sung it four times that he discovered the whole thing was an elaborate impromptu farce, of which he was the butt, and that of all his royal spread not a crumb or a drop was left for himself.

It was the old fable of the fox and the crow!* And to do him justice, he laughed as heartily as any one, as if he thoroughly enjoyed the joke – and when you take jokes in that way people soon leave off poking fun at you. It is almost as good as being very big, like Taffy, and having a choleric blue eye!

Such was Little Billee's first experience of Carrel's studio, where he spent many happy mornings and made many good friends.

No more popular student had ever worked there within the memory of the grayest graybeards; none more amiable, more

The fox and the crow

genial, more cheerful, self-respecting, considerate, and polite, and certainly none with greater gifts for art.

Carrel would devote at least fifteen minutes to him, and invited him often to his own private studio. And often, on the fourth or fifth day of the week, a group of admiring students would be gathered by his easel watching him as he worked.

'C'est un rude lapin, l'Anglais! au moins il sait son orthographe en peinture, ce coco-là!'*

Such was the verdict on Little Billee at Carrel's studio; and I can conceive no much loftier praise.

Young as she was (seventeen or eighteen, or thereabouts), and also tender (like Little Billee), Trilby had singularly clear and quick perceptions in all matters that concerned her tastes, fancies, or affections, and thoroughly knew her own mind, and never lost much time in making it up.

On the occasion of her first visit to the studio in the Place St Anatole des Arts, it took her just five minutes to decide that it was quite the nicest, homeliest, genialest, jolliest studio in the whole Quartier Latin, or out of it, and its three inhabitants, individually and collectively, were more to her taste than any one else she had ever met.

In the first place, they were English, and she loved to hear her mother-tongue and speak it. It awoke all manner of tender recollections, sweet reminiscences of her childhood, her parents, her old home – such a home as it was – or, rather, such homes; for there had been many flittings from one poor nest to another. The O'Ferralls had been as birds on the bough.

She had loved her parents very dearly; and, indeed, with all their faults, they had many endearing qualities – the qualities that so often go with those particular faults – charm, geniality, kindness, warmth of heart, the constant wish to please, the generosity that comes before justice, and lends its last sixpence and forgets to pay its debts!

She knew other English and American artists, and had sat to them frequently for the head and hands; but none of these, for general agreeableness of aspect or manner, could compare in her mind with the stalwart and magnificent Taffy, the jolly fat Laird of Cockpen, the refined, sympathetic, and elegant Little Billee; and she resolved that she would see as much of them as she could, that she would make herself at home in that particular studio, and necessary to its *locataires*;* and without being the least bit vain or self-conscious, she had no doubts whatever of her power to please – to make herself both useful and ornamental if it suited her purpose to do so.

Her first step in this direction was to borrow Père Martin's basket and lantern and pick (he had more than one set of these trade properties) for the use of Taffy, whom she feared she might have offended by the freedom of her comments on his picture.

Then, as often as she felt it to be discreet, she sounded her war-cry at the studio door and went in and made kind inquiries, and, sitting cross-legged on the model-throne, ate her bread and cheese and smoked her cigarette and 'passed the time of day,' as she chose to call it; telling them all such news of the Quartier as had come within her own immediate ken. She was always full of little stories of other studios, which, to do her justice, were always good-natured, and probably true – quite so, as far as she was concerned; she was the most literal person alive; and she told all these *ragots, cancans, et potins d'atelier** in a quaint and amusing manner. The slightest look of gravity or boredom on one of those three faces, and she made herself scarce at once.

She soon found opportunities for usefulness also. If a costume were wanted, for instance, she knew where to borrow it, or hire it or buy it cheaper than any one anywhere else. She procured stuffs for them at cost price, as it seemed, and made them into draperies and female garments of any kind that was wanted, and sat in them for the toreador's sweetheart (she made the mantilla herself), for Taffy's starving dressmaker about to throw herself into the Seine, for Little Billee's studies of the beautiful French peasant girl in his picture, now so famous, called 'The Pitcher Goes to the Well.'

Then she darned their socks and mended their clothes, and got all their washing done properly and cheaply at her friend Madame Boisse's, in the Rue des Cloîtres Ste Pétronille.*

And then again, when they were hard up and wanted a good round sum of money for some little pleasure excursion, such as a trip to Fontainebleau or Barbizon* for two or three days, it was she who took their watches and scarf-pins and things to the Mount of Piety in the Street of the Well of Love (where dwelt *ma tante*,* which is French for 'my uncle' in this connection), in order to raise the necessary funds.

She was, of course, most liberally paid for all these little services, rendered with such pleasure and goodwill – far too liberally, she thought. She would have been really happier doing them for love.

Thus in a very short time she became a *persona gratissima** – a sunny and ever-welcome vision of health and grace and liveliness and unalterable good-humour, always ready to take any trouble to please her beloved 'Angliches,' as they were called by Madame Vinard, the handsome shrill-voiced *concierge*,* who was almost jealous; for she was devoted to the Angliches too – and so was Monsieur Vinard – and so were the little Vinards.

She knew when to talk and when to laugh and when to hold her tongue; and the sight of her sitting cross-legged on the model-throne darning the Laird's socks or sewing buttons on his shirts or repairing the smoke-holes in his trousers was so pleasant that it was painted by all three. One of these sketches (in water-colour by Little Billee) sold the other day at Christie's* for a sum so large that I hardly dare to mention it. It was done in an afternoon.

Sometimes on a rainy day, when it was decided they should dine at home, she would fetch the food and cook it, and lay the cloth, and even make the salad. She was a better saladist than Taffy, a better cook than the Laird, a better caterer than Little Billee. And she would be invited to take her share in the banquet. And on these occasions her tremulous happiness was so immense that it would be quite pathetic to see – almost painful; and their three British hearts were touched by thoughts of all the loneliness and homelessness, the expatriation, the half-conscious loss of caste, that all this eager childish clinging revealed.

And that is why (no doubt) that with all this familiar intimacy there was never any hint of gallantry or flirtation in any shape or form whatever – *bonne camaraderie voilà tout*.* Had she been Little Billee's sister she could not have been treated with more real respect. And her deep gratitude for this unwonted compliment transcended any passion she had ever felt. As the good Lafontaine so prettily says –

> Ces animaux vivaient entre eux comme cousins;
> Cette union si douce, et presque fraternelle,
> Edifiait tous les voisins!*

Cuisine Bourgeoise en Bohème

PART 2   75

And then their talk! It was to her as the talk of the gods in Olympus, save that it was easier to understand, and she could always understand it. For she was a very intelligent person, in spite of her woefully neglected education, and most ambitious to learn – a new ambition for her.

So they lent her books – English books: Dickens, Thackeray, Walter Scott – which she devoured in the silence of the night, the solitude of her little attic in the Rue des Pousse-Cailloux, and new worlds were revealed to her. She grew more English every day; and that was a good thing.

Trilby speaking English and Trilby speaking French were two different beings. Trilby's English was more or less that of her father, a highly-educated man; her mother, who was a Scotch-woman, although an uneducated one, had none of the ungainli-ness that mars the speech of so many Englishwomen in that humble rank – no droppings of the *h*, no broadening of the *o*'s and *a*'s.

Trilby's French was that of the Quartier Latin – droll, slangy, piquant, quaint, picturesque – quite the reverse of ungainly, but in which there was scarcely a turn of phrase that would not stamp the speaker as being hopelessly, emphatically 'no lady!' Though it was funny without being vulgar, it was perhaps a little *too* funny.

And she handled her knife and fork in the dainty English way, as no doubt her father had done – and his; 'like a lady' that it seemed quite odd (though very seductive) to see her in a grisette's cap and dress and apron. So much for her English training.

But enter a Frenchman or two, and a transformation effected itself immediately – a new incarnation of Trilbyness – so droll and amusing that it was difficult to decide which of her two incarnations was the more attractive.

It must be admitted that she had her faults – like Little Billee.

For instance, she would be miserably jealous of any other woman who came to the studio, to sit or scrub or sweep or do anything else, even of the dirty tipsy old hag who sat for Taffy's 'Found drowned'* – 'as if she couldn't have sat for it herself!'

And then she would be cross and sulky, but not for long – an injured martyr, soon ready to forgive and be forgiven.

She would give up any sitting to come and sit to her three English friends. Even Durien had serious cause for complaint.

Then her affection was exacting: she always wanted to be

The soft eyes

told one was fond of her, and she dearly loved her own way, even in the sewing on of buttons and the darning of socks, which was innocent enough. But when it came to the cutting and fashioning of garments for a toreador's bride, it was a nuisance not to be borne!

'What could *she* know of toreadors' brides and their wedding-dresses?' the Laird would indignantly ask – as if he were a toreador himself; and this was the aggravating side of her irrepressible Trilbyness.

In the caressing, demonstrative tenderness of her friendship she 'made the soft eyes' at all three indiscriminately. But sometimes Little Billee would look up from his work as she was sitting to Taffy or the Laird, and find her gray eyes fixed on him with an all-enfolding gaze, so piercingly, penetratingly, unutterably sweet and kind and tender, such a brooding, dovelike look of soft and warm solicitude, that he would feel a flutter at his heart, and his hand would shake so that he could not paint; and in a waking dream he would remember that his mother had often looked at him like that when he was a small boy, and she a beautiful young woman untouched by care or sorrow; and the tear that always lay in readiness so close to the corner of Little Billee's eye would find it very difficult to keep itself in its proper place – unshed.

And at such moments the thought that Trilby sat for the figure would go through him like a knife.

She did not sit promiscuously to anybody who asked, it is true. But she still sat to Durien; to the great Gérôme;* to M. Carrel, who scarcely used any other model.

It was poor Trilby's sad distinction that she surpassed all other models as Calypso* surpassed her nymphs; and whether by long habit, or through some obtuseness in her nature, or lack of imagination, she was equally unconscious of self with her clothes on or without! Truly, she could be naked and unashamed – in this respect an absolute savage.

She would have ridden through Coventry, like Lady Godiva* – but without giving it a thought beyond wondering why the streets were empty and the shops closed and the blinds pulled down – would even have looked up to Peeping Tom's shutter with a friendly nod, had she known he was behind it.

In fact, she was absolutely without that kind of shame, as she was without any kind of fear. But she was destined soon to know both fear and shame.

And here it would not be amiss for me to state a fact well known to all painters and sculptors who have used the nude model (except a few shady pretenders, whose purity, not being of the right sort, has gone rank from too much watching), namely, that nothing is so chaste as nudity. Venus herself, as she drops her garments and steps on to the model-throne, leaves behind her on the floor every weapon in her armoury by which she can pierce to the grosser passions of man. The more perfect her unveiled beauty, the more keenly it appeals to his higher instincts. And where her beauty fails (as it almost always does somewhere in the Venuses who sit for hire), the failure is so lamentably conspicuous in the studio light – the fierce light that beats on this particular throne – that Don Juan himself,* who has not got to paint, were fain to hide his eyes in sorrow and disenchantment, and fly to other climes.

All beauty is sexless in the eyes of the artist at his work – the beauty of man, the beauty of woman, the heavenly beauty of the child, which is the sweetest and best of all.

Indeed it is woman, lovely woman, whose beauty falls the shortest, for sheer lack of proper physical training.

As for Trilby,* G—, to whom she sat for his Phryne, once told me that the sight of her thus was a thing to melt Sir Galahad,* yet sober Silenus,* and chasten Jove* himself – a thing to Quixotise* a modern French master! I can well believe him. For myself, I only speak of Trilby as I have seen her – clothed and in her right mind. She never sat to me for any Phryne,* never bared herself to me, nor did I ever dream of asking her. I would as soon have asked the Queen of Spain to let me paint her legs!* But I have worked from many female models in many countries, some of them the best of their kind. I have also, like Svengali, seen Taffy 'trying to get himself clean,' either at home or in the swimming-baths of the Seine; and never a sitting woman among them all who could match for grace or finish or splendour of outward form that mighty Yorkshireman sitting in his tub, or sunning himself, like Ilyssus,* at the Bains Henri Quatre,* or taking his running header *à la hussarde*,* off the springboard at the Bains Deligny,* with a group of wondering Frenchmen gathered round.

Up he shot himself into mid-air with a sounding double downward kick, parabolically; then, turning a splendid semi-demi-somersault against the sky, down he came headlong, his body straight and stiff as an arrow, and made his clean hole in the water without splash or sound, to reappear a hundred yards farther on!

'Sac à papier! quel gaillard que cet Anglais, hein?'

'A-t-on jamais vu un torse pareil!'

'Et les bras, donc!'

'Et les jambes, nom d'un tonnerre!'

'Mâtin! J'aimerais mieux être en colère contre lui qu'il ne soit en colère contre moi!'* etc. etc. etc.

Omne ignotum pro magnifico!*

If our climate were such that we could go about without any clothes on, we probably should; in which case, although we should still murder and lie and steal and bear false witness against our neighbour, and break the Sabbath Day, and take the Lord's name in vain, much deplorable wickedness of another

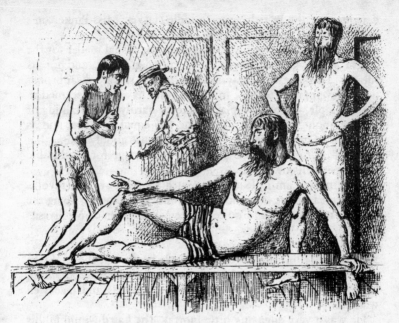

Illyssus

kind would cease to exist for sheer lack of mystery; and
Christianity would be relieved of its hardest task in this sinful
world, and Venus Aphrodite (*alias* Aselgeia)* would have to go
a-begging along with the tailors and dressmakers and bootmak-
ers, and perhaps our bodies and limbs would be as those of the
Theseus and Venus of Milo; who was no Venus, except in good
looks!

At all events, there would be no cunning, cruel deceptions, no
artful taking in of artless inexperience, no unduly hurried
waking-up from Love's young dream, no handing down to
posterity of hidden uglinesses and weaknesses, and worse!

And also many a flower, now born to blush unseen, would be
reclaimed from its desert, and suffered to hold its own, and
flaunt away with the best in the inner garden of roses! And poor
Miss Gale, the figure-model, would be permitted to eke out her
slender earnings by teaching calisthenics and deportment to the

daughters of the British upper middle-class at Miss Pinkerton's academy* for young ladies, The Mall, Chiswick.

And here let me humbly apologise to the casual reader for the length and possible irrelevancy of this digression, and for its subject. To those who may find matter for sincere disapprobation or even grave offence in a thing that has always seemed to me so simple, so commonplace, as to be hardly worth talking or writing about, I can only plead sincerity equal to theirs, and as deep a love and reverence for the gracious, goodly shape that God is said to have made after His own image for inscrutable purposes of His own.

Nor, indeed, am I pleading for such a subversive and revolutionary measure as the wholesale abolition of clothes, being the chilliest of mortals, and quite unlike Mr Theseus or Mr Ilyssus either.*

Sometimes Trilby would bring her little brother to the studio in the Place St Anatole des Arts, in his *beaux habits de Pâques*,* his hair well curled and pomatumed, his hands and face well washed.

He was a very engaging little mortal. The Laird would fill his pockets full of Scotch goodies, and paint him as a little Spaniard, in 'Le Fils du Toréador,' a sweet little Spaniard with blue eyes, and curly locks as light as tow, and a complexion of milk and roses, in singular and piquant constrast to his swarthy progenitors.

Taffy would use him as an Indian club or a dumb-bell, to the child's infinite delight, and swing him on the trapeze, and teach him *la boxe*.

And the sweetness and fun of his shrill, happy, infantile laughter (which was like an echo of Trilby's, only an octave higher) so moved and touched and tickled one that Taffy had to look quite fierce, so he might hide the strange delight of tenderness that somehow filled his manly bosom at the mere sound of it (lest Little Billee and the Laird should think him goody-goody); and the fiercer Taffy looked, the less this small mite was afraid of him.

Little Billee made a beautiful water-colour sketch of him, just as he was, and gave it to Trilby, who gave it to le père Martin, who gave it to his wife with strict instructions not to sell it as an old master. Alas! it *is* an old master now, and Heaven only knows who has got it!

Those were happy days for Trilby's little brother, happy days for Trilby, who was immensely fond of him, and very proud. And the happiest day of all was when the *trois* Angliches took Trilby and Jeannot (for so the mite was called) to spend the Sunday in the woods at Meudon,* and breakfast and dine at the *garde champêtre*'s.* Swings, peep-shows, donkey-rides; shooting at a mark with crossbows and little pellets of clay, and smashing little plaster figures and winning macaroons; losing one's self in the beautiful forest; catching newts and tadpoles and young frogs; making music on *mirlitons*.* Trilby singing 'Ben Bolt' into a *mirliton* was a thing to be remembered, whether one would or no!

Trilby on this occasion came out in a new character, *en demoiselle*, with a little black bonnet, and a gray jacket of her own making.

To look at (but for her loose, square-toed, heel-less silk boots laced up the inner side), she might have been the daughter of an English dean – until she undertook to teach the Laird some favourite cancan steps. And then the Laird himself, it must be admitted, no longer looked like the son of a worthy, god-fearing, Sabbath-keeping Scotch solicitor.

This was after dinner, in the garden, at *la loge* du garde champétre*. Taffy and Jeannot and Little Billee made the necessary music on their *mirlitons*, and the dancing soon became general, with plenty also to look on, for the *garde* had many customers who dined there on summer Sundays.

It is no exaggeration to say that Trilby was far and away the belle of that particular ball, and there have been worse balls in much finer company, and far plainer women!

Trilby lightly dancing the cancan (there are cancans and cancans) was a singularly gainly and seductive person – *et vera incessu patuit dea!** Here, again, she was funny without being vulgar. And for mere grace (even in the cancan), she was the forerunner of Miss Kate Vaughan;*. and for sheer fun, the precursor of Miss Nelly Farren!*

And the Laird, trying to dance after her ('dongsong le konkong,'* as he called it), was too funny for words; and if genuine popular success is a true test of humour, no greater humorist ever danced a *pas seul*.*

'Voila l'espayce de hom ker jer swee!'

What Englishmen could do in France during the fifties, and yet manage to preserve their self-respect, and even the respect of their respectable French friends!

'Voilà l'espayce de hom ker jer swee!'* said the Laird, every time he bowed in acknowledgment of the applause that greeted his performance of various solo steps of his own – Scotch reels and sword-dances that came in admirably . . .

Then, one fine day (as a judgment on him, no doubt), the Laird fell ill, and the doctor had to be sent for, and he ordered a nurse. But Trilby would hear of no nurses, not even a Sister of Charity! She did all the nursing herself, and never slept a wink for three successive days and nights.

On the third day the Laird was out of all danger, the delirium was past, and the doctor found poor Trilby fast asleep by the bedside.

Madame Vinard, at the bedroom door, put her finger to her lips, and whispered: 'Quel bonheur! il est sauvé, M. le Docteur; écoutez! il dit ses prières en Anglais, ce brave garçon!'*

The good old doctor, who didn't understand a word of English, listened, and heard the Laird's voice, weak and low, but quite clear, and full of heartfelt fervour, intoning, solemnly:

> Green herbs, red peppers, mussels, saffron,
>   Soles, onions, garlic, roach, and dace –
> All these you eat at Terré's Tavern
>   In that one dish of bouillabaisse!*

'Ah! mais c'est très bien de sa part, ce brave jeune homme! rendre grâces au ciel comme cela, quand le danger est passé! très bien, très bien!'*

Sceptic and Voltairian as he was, and not the friend of prayer, the good doctor was touched, for he was old, and therefore kind and tolerant, and made allowances.

And afterwards he said such sweet things to Trilby about it all, and about her admirable care of his patient, that she positively wept with delight – like sweet Alice with hair so brown, whenever Ben Bolt gave her a smile.

All this sounds very goody-goody, but it's true.

So it will be easily understood how the *trois* Angliches came in time to feel for Trilby quite a peculiar regard, and looked forward with sorrowful forebodings to the day when this singular and pleasant little quartet would have to be broken up, each of them to spread his wings and fly away on his own account, and poor Trilby to be left behind all by herself. They would even frame little plans whereby she might better herself in life, and avoid the many snares and pitfalls that would beset her lonely path in the Quartier Latin when they were gone.

Trilby never thought of such things as these; she took short views of life, and troubled herself about no morrows.

There was, however, one jarring figure in her little fool's paradise, a baleful and most ominous figure that constantly crossed her path, and came between her and the sun, and threw its shadow over her, and that was Svengali.

He also was a frequent visitor at the studio in the Place St Anatole, where much was forgiven him for the sake of his music, especially when he came with Gecko and they made music together. But it soon became apparent that they did not come there to play to the three Angliches; it was to see Trilby, whom they both had taken it into their heads to adore, each in a different fashion:

Gecko, with a humble, doglike worship that expressed itself in mute, pathetic deference and looks of lowly self-depreciation, of apology for his own unworthy existence, as though the only requital he would ever dare to dream of were a word of decent politeness, a glance of tolerance or good-will – a mere bone to a dog.

Svengali was a bolder wooer. When he cringed, it was with mock humility full of sardonic threats; when he was playful, it was with a terrible playfulness, like that of a cat with a mouse – a weird, ungainly cat, and most unclean; a sticky, haunting, long, lean, uncanny, black spider-cat, if there is such an animal outside a bad dream.

It was a great grievance to him that she had suffered from no more pains in her eyes. She had; but preferred to endure them rather than seek relief from *him*.

So he would playfully try to mesmerise her with his glance, and sidle up nearer and nearer to her, making passes and counter-passes, with stern command in his eyes, till she would shake and shiver and almost sicken with fear, and all but feel the spell come over her, as in a nightmare, and rouse herself with a great effort and escape.

If Taffy were there he would interfere with a friendly 'Now then, old fellow, none of that!' and a jolly slap on the back, which would make Svengali cough for an hour, and paralyse his mesmeric powers for a week.

Svengali had a stroke of good-fortune. He played at three grand concerts with Gecko, and had a well-deserved success. He even gave a concert of his own, which made a furore, and blossomed out into beautiful and costly clothes of quite original colour and shape and pattern, so that people would turn round and stare at him in the street – a thing he loved. He felt his fortune was secure, and ran into debt with tailors, hatters, shoemakers, jewellers, but paid none of his old debts to his friends. His pockets were always full of printed slips – things that had been written about him in the papers – and he would read them aloud to everybody he knew, especially to Trilby, as she sat darning socks on the model-throne while the fencing and boxing were in train. And he would lay his fame and his fortune at her feet, on condition that she should share her life with him.

'Ach, himmel, Drilpy!' he would say 'you don't know what it is to be a great pianist like me – *hein?** What is your Little Billee, with his stinking oil-bladders, sitting mum in his corner, his mahlstick* and his palette in one hand, and his twiddling little footle pig's-hair brush in the other! What noise does *he* make? When his little fool of a picture is finished he will send it to London, and they will hang it on a wall with a lot of others, all in a line, like recruits called out for inspection, and the yawning public will walk by in procession and inspect and say "damn!" Svengali will go to London *himself*. Ha! ha! He will be all alone on a platform, and play as nobody else can play; and hundreds of beautiful Engländerinnen will see and hear and go mad with love for him – Prinzessen, Comtessen, Serene English Altessen.* They will soon lose their Serenity and their Highness when they hear Svengali! They will invite him to their palaces, and pay him a thousand francs to play for them; and after, he will loll in the best armchair, and they will sit all round him on footstools, and bring him tea and gin and *küchen** and *marrons glacés*, and lean over him and fan him – for he is tired after playing them for a thousand francs of Chopin! Ha, ha! I know all about it – *hein?*

'And he will not look at them, even! He will look inward, at his own dream – and his dream will be about Drilpy – to lay his talent, his glory, his thousand francs at her beautiful white feet!

'Their stupid, big, fat, tow-headed, putty-nosed husbands will be mad with jealousy, and long to box him, but they will be afraid. Ach! those beautiful Anclaises! they will think it an honour to mend his shirts, to sew buttons on his pantaloons; to darn his socks, as you are doing now for that sacred imbecile of a Scotchman who is always trying to paint toréadors, or that sweating, pig-headed bullock of an Englander who is always trying to get himself dirty and then to get himself clean again! – *e da capo!**

'Himmel! what big socks are those! what potato-sacks!

'Look at your Taffy! what is he good for but to bang great musicians on the back with his big bear's paw! He finds that droll, the bullock! . . .

'Look at your Frenchmen there – your damned conceited *verfluchte* pig-dogs of Frenchmen – Durien, Barizel, Bouchardy!

What can a Frenchman talk of, *hein?* Only himself, and run down everybody else! His vanity makes me sick! He always thinks the world is talking about *him*, the fool! He forgets that there is a fellow called *Svengali* for the world to talk about! I tell you, Drilpy, it is about *me* the world is talking – me and nobody else – me, me, me!

'Listen what they say in the *Figaro** (reads it).

'What do you think of that, *hein?* What would your Durien say if people wrote of *him* like that?

'But you are not listening, sapperment! great big she-fool that you are – sheep's-head! Dummkopf!* Donner wetter! you are looking at the chimney-pots when Svengali talks! Look a little lower down between the houses, on the other side of the river! There is a little ugly gray building there, and inside are eight slanting slabs of brass, all of a row, like beds in a school dormitory, and one fine day you shall lie asleep on one of those slabs – you, Drilpy, who would not listen to Svengali, and therefore lost him! . . . And over the middle of you will be a little leather apron, and over your head a little brass tap, and all day long and all night the cold water shall trickle, trickle, trickle all the way down your beautiful white body to your beautiful white feet till they turn green, and your poor, damp, draggled, muddy rags will hang above you from the ceiling for your friends to know you by; drip, drip, drip! But you will have no friends . . .

'And people of all sorts, strangers, will stare at you through the big plate-glass window – Englanders, chiffonniers, painters and sculptors, workmen, piou-pious, old hags of washerwomen – and say, "Ah! what a beautiful woman was that! Look at her! She ought to be rolling in her carriage and pair!" And just then who should come by, rolling in his carriage and pair, smothered in furs, and smoking a big cigar of the Havana, but Svengali, who will jump out, and push the canaille* aside, and say, "Ha! ha! that is la grande Drilpy, who would not listen to Svengali, but looked at the chimney-pots when he told her of his manly love, and—"'

'Hi! damn it, Svengali, what the devil are you talking to Trilby about? You're making her sick; can't you see? Leave off, and go to the piano, man, or I'll come and slap you on the back again!'

Thus would that sweating, pig-headed bullock of an Eng-

Tit for tat

lander stop Svengali's love-making and release Trilby from bad quarters of an hour.

Then Svengali, who had a wholesome dread of the pig-headed bullock, would go to the piano and make impossible discords, and say: 'Dear Drilpy, come and sing "Pen Polt!" I am thirsting for those so beautiful chest notes! Come!'

Poor Trilby needed little pressing when she was asked to sing, and would go through her lamentable performance, to the great discomfort of Little Billee. It lost nothing of its grotesqueness from Svengali's accompaniment, which was a triumph of cacophony, and he would encourage her – *Très pien, très pien, ça y est!*

When it was over, Svengali would test her ear, as he called it, and strike the C in the middle and then the F just above, and ask which was the highest; and she would declare they were both exactly the same. It was only when he struck a note in the bass and another in the treble that she could perceive any difference, and said that the first sounded like Père Martin blowing up his wife, and the second like her little godson trying to make the peace between them.

She was quite tone-deaf, and didn't know it; and he would pay her extravagant compliments on her musical talent, till Taffy would say: 'Look here, Svengali, let's hear *you* sing a song!'

And he would tickle him so masterfully under the ribs that the creature howled and became quite hysterical.

Then Svengali would vent his love of teasing on Little Billee, and pin his arms behind his back and swing him round, saying: 'Himmel! what's this for an arm? It's like a girl's!'

'It's strong enough to paint!' said Little Billee.

'And what's this for a leg? It's like a mahlstick!'

'It's strong enough to kick, if you don't leave off!'

And Little Billee, the young and tender, would let out his little heel and kick the German's shins; and just as the German was going to retaliate, big Taffy would pin *his* arms and make him sing another song, more discordant than Trilby's – for he didn't dream of kicking Taffy: of that you may be sure!

Such was Svengali – only to be endured for the sake of his music – always ready to vex, frighten, bully, or torment anybody or anything smaller and weaker than himself – from a woman or a child to a mouse or a fly.

Part Third

Par deçà, ne dela la mer
  Ne sçay dame ni damoiselle
  Qui soit en tous biens parfaits telle –
C'est un songe que d'y penser:
Dieu! qu'il fait bon la regarder!*

One lovely Monday morning in late September, at about eleven or so, Taffy and the Laird sat in the studio – each opposite his picture, smoking, nursing his knee, and saying nothing. The heaviness of Monday weighed on their spirits more than usual, for the three friends had returned late on the previous night from a week spent at Barbizon and in the forest of Fontainebleau – a heavenly week among the painters; Rousseau, Millet, Corot, Daubigny,* let us suppose, and others less known to fame this day. Little Billee, especially, had been fascinated by all this artistic life in blouses and sabots and immense straw hats and panamas, and had sworn to himself and to his friends that he would some day live and die there – painting the forest as it is, and peopling it with beautiful people out of his own fancy – leading a healthy outdoor life of simple wants and lofty aspirations.

At length Taffy said: 'Bother work this morning! I feel much more like a stroll in the Luxembourg Gardens* and lunch at the Café de l'Odéon, where the omelets are good and the wine isn't blue.'

'The very thing I was thinking of myself,' said the Laird.

So Taffy sliped on his old shooting-jacket and his old Harrow cricket cap, with the peak turned the wrong way, and the Laird put on an old greatcoat of Taffy's that reached to his heels, and a battered straw hat they had found in the studio when they took it; and both sallied forth into the mellow sunshine on the way to Carrel's. For they meant to seduce Little Billee from his work, that he might share in their laziness, greediness, and general demoralisation.

And whom should they meet coming down the narrow turreted Rue Vieille des Trois Mauvais Ladres but Little Billee himself, with an air of general demoralisation so tragic that they were quite alarmed. He had his paint-box and field-easel in one hand and his little valise in the other. He was pale, his hat on the back of his head, his hair starting all at sixes and sevens, like a sick Scotch terrier's.

'Good Lord! what's the matter?' said Taffy.

'Oh! oh! oh! she's sitting at Carrel's!'

'Who's sitting at Carrel's?'

'Trilby! sitting to all those ruffians! There she was, just as I opened the door; I saw her, I tell you! The sight of her was like a blow between the eyes, and I bolted! I shall never go back to that beastly hole again! I'm off to Barbizon, to paint the forest; I was coming round to tell you. Good-bye! . . .'

'Stop a minute – are you mad?' said Taffy, collaring him.

'Let me go, Taffy – let me go, damn it! I'll come back in a week – but I'm going now! Let me go; do you hear?'

'But look here – I'll go with you.'

'No; I want to be alone – quite alone. Let me go, I tell you!'

'I shan't let you go unless you swear to me, on your honour, that you'll write directly you get there, and every day till you come back. Swear!'

'All right; I swear – honour bright! Now there! Good-bye – good-bye; back on Sunday – good-bye!' And he was off.

'Now, what the devil does all that mean?' asked Taffy, much perturbed.

'I suppose he's shocked at seeing Trilby in that guise, or disguise, or unguise, sitting at Carrel's – he's such an odd little chap. And I must say, I'm surprised at Trilby. It's a bad thing for her when we're away. What could have induced her? She never sat in a studio of that kind before. I thought she only sat to Durien and old Carrel.'

They walked for a while in silence.

'Do you know, I've got a horrid idea that the little fool's in love with her!'

'I've long had a horrid idea that *she's* in love with *him*.'

'That would be a very stupid business,' said Taffy.

They walked on, brooding over those two horrid ideas, and the more they brooded, considered, and remembered, the more convinced they became that both were right.

'Here's a pretty kettle of fish!' said the Laird – 'and talking of fish, let's go and lunch.'

And so demoralised were they that Taffy ate three omelets

'Let me go, Taffy . . .'

without thinking, and the Laird drank two half-bottles of wine, and Taffy three, and they walked about the whole of that afternoon for fear Trilby should come to the studio – and were very unhappy.

This is how Trilby came to sit at Carrel's studio:

Carrel had suddenly taken it into his head that he would spend a week there, and paint a figure among his pupils, that they might see and paint with – and if possible like – him. And he had asked Trilby as a great favour to be the model, and Trilby was so devoted to the great Carrel that she readily consented. So that Monday morning found her there, and Carrel posed her as Ingres's famous figure* in his picture called 'La Source,' holding an earthenware pitcher on her shoulder.

And the work began in religious silence. Then in five minutes or so Little Billee came bursting in, and as soon as he caught sight of her he stopped and stood as one petrified, his shoulders up, his eyes staring. Then lifting his arms, he turned and fled.

'Qu'est ce qu'il a donc, ce Litrebili?'* exclaimed one or two students (for they had turned his English nickname into French).

'Perhaps he's forgotten something,' said another.

'Perhaps he's forgotten to brush his teeth and part his hair!'

'Perhaps he's forgotten to say his prayers!' said Barizel.

'He'll come back, I hope!' exclaimed the master.

And the incident gave rise to no further comment.

But Trilby was much disquieted, and fell to wondering what on earth was the matter.

At first she wondered in French: French of the Quartier Latin. She had not seen Little Billee for a week, and wondered if he were ill. She had looked forward so much to his painting her – painting her beautifully – and hoped he would soon come back, and lose no time.

Then she began to wonder in English – nice clean English of the studio in the Place St Anatole des Arts – her father's English – and suddenly a quick thought pierced her through and through, and made the flesh tingle on her insteps and the backs of her hands, and bathed her brow and temples with sweat.

She had good eyes, and Little Billee had a singularly expressive face.

Could it possibly be that he was *shocked* at seeing her sitting there?

'Qu'est-ce qui'il a donc, ce Litrebili?'

Repentance

She knew that he was peculiar in many ways. She remembered that neither he nor Taffy nor the Laird had ever asked her to sit for the figure, though she would have been only too delighted to do so for them. She also remembered how Little Billee had always been silent whenever she alluded to her posing for the 'altogether,' as she called it, and had sometimes looked pained and always very grave.

She turned alternately pale and red, pale and red all over, again and again, as the thought grew up in her – and soon the growing thought became a torment.

This new-born feeling of shame was unendurable – its birth a travail that racked and rent every fibre of her moral being, and she suffered agonies beyond anything she had ever felt in her life.

'What is the matter with you, my child? Are you ill?' asked Carrel, who, like every one else, was very fond of her, and to whom she had sat as a child ('L'Enfance de Psyché,'* now in the Luxembourg Gallery, was painted from her).

She shook her head, and the work went on.

Presently she dropped her pitcher, that broke into bits; and putting her two hands to her face she burst into tears and sobs – and there, to the amazement of everybody, she stood crying like a big baby – *La source aux larmes?**

'What *is* the matter, my poor dear child?' said Carrel, jumping up and helping her off the throne.

'Oh, I don't know – I don't know – I'm ill – very ill – let me go home!'

And with kind solicitude and despatch they helped her on with her clothes, and Carrel sent for a cab and took her home.

And on the way she dropped her head on his shoulders, and wept, and told him all about it as well as she could, and Monsieur Carrel had tears in his eyes too, and wished to Heaven he had never induced her to sit for the figure, either then or at any other time. And pondering deeply and sorrowfully on such terrible responsibility (he had grown-up daughters on his own), he went back to the studio; and in an hour's time they got another model and another pitcher, and went to work again. So the pitcher went to the well once more.*

And Trilby, as she lay disconsolate on her bed all that day and all the next, and all the next again, thought of her past life with

agonies of shame and remorse that made the pain in her eyes
seem as a light and welcome relief. For it came, and tortured
worse and lasted longer than it had ever done before. But she
soon found, to her miserable bewilderment, that mind-aches are
the worst of all.

Then she decided that she must write to one of the *trois
Angliches*, and chose the Laird.

She was more familiar with him than with the other two: it
was impossible not to be familiar with the Laird if he liked one,
as he was so easy-going and demonstrative, for all that he was
such a canny Scot! Then she had nursed him through his illness;
she had often hugged and kissed him before the whole studio
full of people – and even when alone with him it had always
seemed quite natural for her to do so. It was like a child
caressing a favourite young uncle or elder brother. And though
the good Laird was the least susceptible of mortals, he would
often find these innocent blandishments a somewhat trying
ordeal! She had never taken such a liberty with Taffy; and as
for Little Billee, she would sooner have died!

So she wrote to the Laird. I give her letter without the spelling,
which was often faulty, although her nightly readings had much
improved it:

My dear Friend – I am very unhappy. I was sitting at Carrel's in
the Rue des Potirons, and Little Billee came in, and was so
shocked and disgusted that he ran away and never came back.

I saw it all in his face.

I sat there because M. Carrel asked me to. He has always
been very kind to me – M. Carrel – ever since I was a child; and
I would do anything to please him, but never *that* again.

He was there too.

I never thought anything about sitting before. I sat first as a
child to M. Carrel. Mamma made me, and made me promise
not to tell papa, and so I didn't. It soon seemed as natural to sit
for people as to run errands for them, or wash and mend their
clothes. Papa wouldn't have liked my doing that either, though
we wanted the money badly. And so he never knew.

I sat for the "altogether" to several other people besides* –
M. Gérôme, Durien, the two Hennequins, and Émile Baratier;
and for the head and hands to lots of people, and for the feet

only to Charles Faure, André Besson, Mathieu Dumoulin, and Collinet. Nobody else.

It seemed as natural for me to sit as for a man. Now I see the awful difference.

And I have done dreadful things besides, as you must know — as all the Quartier knows. Baratier and Besson; but not Durien, though people think so. Nobody else, I swear — except old Monsieur Penque at the beginning, who was mamma's friend.

It makes me almost die of shame and misery to think of it; for that's not like sitting. I knew how wrong it was all along — and there's no excuse for me, none. Though lots of people do as bad, and nobody in the Quartier seems to think any the worse of them.

If you and Taffy and Little Billee cut me, I really think I shall go mad and die. Without your friendship I shouldn't care to live a bit. Dear Sandy, I love your little finger better than any man or woman I ever met; and Taffy's and Little Billee's little fingers too.

What shall I do? I daren't go out for fear of meeting one of you. Will you come and see me?

I am never going to sit again, not even for the face and hands. I am going back to be a *blanchisseuse de fin* with my old friend Angèle Boisse, who is getting on very well indeed, in the Rue des Cloîtres Ste Pétronille.

You *will* come and see me, won't you? I shall be in all day till you do. Or else I will meet you some where, if you will tell me where and when; or else I will go and see you in the studio, if you are sure to be alone. Please don't keep me waiting long for an answer.

You don't know what I'm suffering.

Your ever loving, faithful friend,

                                        Trilby O'Ferrall.

She sent this letter by hand, and the Laird came in less than ten minutes after she had sent it; and she hugged and kissed and cried over him so that he was almost ready to cry himself; but he burst out laughing instead — which was better and more in his line, and very much more comforting — and talked to her so nicely and kindly and naturally that by the time he left her humble attic in the Rue des Pousse-Cailloux her very aspect,

Confession

which had quite shocked him when he first saw her, had almost
become what it usually was.

The little room under the leads, with its sloping roof and
mansard window, was as scrupulously neat and clean as if its
tenant had been a holy sister who taught the noble daughters of
France at some Convent of the Sacred Heart. There were
nasturtiums and mignonette on the outer window-sill, and
convolvulus was trained to climb round the window.

As she sat by his side on the narrow white bed, clasping and
stroking his painty, turpentiny hand, and kissing it every five
minutes, he talked to her like a father – as he told Taffy
afterwards – and scolded her for having been so silly as not to
send for him directly, or come to the studio. He said how glad
he was, how glad they would all be, that she was going to give
up sitting for the figure – not, of course, that there was any real
harm in it, but it was better not – and especially how happy it
would make them to feel she intended to live straight for the
future. Little Billee was to remain at Barbizon for a little while;
but she must promise to come and dine with Taffy and himself
that very day, and cook the dinner; and when he went back to
his picture, 'Les Noces du Toréador'* – saying to her as he left,
'à ce soir donc, mille sacreés tonnerres de nong de Dew!'* – he
left the happiest woman in the whole Latin Quarter behind him:
she had confessed and been forgiven.

And with shame and repentence and confession and forgiveness had come a strange new feeling – that of a dawning self-
respect.

Hitherto, for Trilby, self-respect had meant little more than
the mere cleanliness of her body, in which she had always
revelled; alas! it was one of the conditions of her humble calling.
It now meant another kind of cleanliness, and she would
luxuriate in it for evermore; and the dreadful past – never to be
forgotten by her – should be so lived down as in time, perhaps,
to be forgotten by others.

The dinner that evening was a memorable one for Trilby.
After she had washed up the knives and forks and plates and
dishes, and put them by, she sat and sewed. She wouldn't even
smoke her cigarette, it reminded her so of things and scenes she
now hated. No more cigarettes for Trilby O'Farrell.

They all talked of Little Billee. She heard about the way he
had been brought up, about his mother and sister, the people he

had always lived among. She also heard (and her heart alternately rose and sank as she listened) what his future was likely to be, and how rare his genius was, and how great – if his friends were to be trusted. Fame and Fortune would soon be his – such fame and fortune as fall to the lot of very few – unless anything should happen to spoil his promise and mar his prospects in life, and ruin a splendid career; and the rising of the heart was all for him, the sinking for herself. How could she ever hope to be even the friend of such a man? Might she ever hope to be his servant – his faithful, humble servant?

Little Billee spent a month at Barbizon, and when he came back it was with such a brown face that his friends hardly knew him; and he brought with him such studies as made his friends 'sit up.'

The crushing sense of their own hopeless inferiority was lost in wonder at his work, in love and enthusiasm for the workman.

Their Little Billee, so young and tender, so weak of body, so strong of purpose, so warm of heart, so light of hand, so keen and quick and piercing of brain and eye, was their master, to be stuck on a pedestal and looked up to and bowed down to, to be watched and warded and worshipped for evermore.

When Trilby came in for her work at six, and he shook hands with her and said 'Hullo, Trilby!' her face turned pale to the lips, her under lip quivered, and she gazed down at him (for she was among the tallest of her sex) with such a moist, hungry, wide-eyed look of humble craving adoration that the Laird felt his worst fear were realised: and the look Little Billee sent up in return filled the manly bosom of Taffy with an equal apprehension.

Then they all four went and dined together at le père Trin's, and Trilby went back to her *blanchisserie de fin.**

Next day Little Billee took his work to show Carrel, and Carrel invited him to come and finish his picture 'The Pitcher Goes to the Well' at his own private studio – an unheard-of favour, which the boy accepted with a thrill of proud gratitude and affectionate reverence.

So little was seen for some time of Little Billee at the studio in the Place St. Anatole des Arts, and little of Trilby; a *blanchisseuse de fin* has not many minutes to spare from her irons. But they often met at dinner. And on Sunday mornings Trilby came to repair the Laird's linen and darn his socks and look after his little comforts, as usual, and spend a happy day. And on Sunday afternoons the studio would be as lively as ever, with the fencing and boxing, the piano-playing and fiddling – all as it used to be.

And week by week the friends noticed a gradual and subtle change in Trilby. She was no long slangy in French, unless it were now and then by a slip of the tongue, no longer so facetious and droll, and yet she seemed even happier than she had ever seemed before.

Also, she grew thinner, especially in the face, where the bones of her cheeks and jaws began to show themselves, and these bones were constructed on such right principles (as were those of her brow and chin and the bridge of her nose) that the improvement was astonishing, almost inexplicable.

Also, she lost her freckles as the summer waned and she herself went less into the open air. And she let her hair grow, and made of it a small knot at the back of her head, and showed her little flat ears, which were charming, and just in the right place, very far back and rather high; Little Billee could not have placed them better himself. Also, her mouth, always too large, took on a firmer and sweeter outline, and her big British teeth were so white and regular that even Frenchmen forgave them their British bigness. And a new soft brightness came into her eyes that no one had ever seen there before. They were stars. just twin gray stars – or rather planets just thrown off by some new sun, for the steady mellow light they gave out was not entirely their own.

Favourite types of beauty change with each succeeding generation. These were the days of Buckner's* aristocractic Album beauties,* with lofty foreheads, oval faces, little aquiline noses, heart-shaped little mouths, soft dimpled chins, drooping shoulders, and long side ringlets that fell over them – the Lady Arabellas amd the Lady Clementinas, Musidoras and Medoras!* A type that will perhaps come back to us some day.

May the present scribe be dead!

Trilby's type would be infinitely more admired now than in the fifties. Her photograph would be in the shop-windows. Sir Edward Burne-Jones* – if I may make so bold as to say so – would perhaps have marked her for his own, in spite of her almost too exuberant joyousness and irrepressible vitality. Rossetti* might have evolved another new formula from her;

All as it used to be

Twin grey stars

Sir John Millais another old one of the kind that is always new and never sates nor palls – like Clytie, let us say – ever old and ever new as love itself!

Trilby's type was in singular contrast to the type Gavarni* had made so popular in the Latin Quarter at the period we are writing of, so that those who fell so readily under her charm were rather apt to wonder why. Moreover, she was thought much too tall for her sex, and her day, and her station in life, and especially for the country she lived in. She hardly looked up to a bold gendarme! and a bold gendarme* was nearly as tall as a *dragon de la garde**, who was nearly as tall as an average English policeman. Not that she was a giantess, by any means. She was about as tall as Miss Ellen Terry* – and that is a charming height, *I* think.

One day Taffy remarked to the Laird: 'Hang it! I'm blest if Trilby isn't the handsomest woman I know! She looks like a grande dame masquerading as a grisette – almost like a joyful saint at times. She's lovely! By Jove! I couldn't stand her hugging

me as she does you! There'd be a tragedy — say the slaughter of
Little Billee.'

'Ah! Taffy, my boy,' rejoined the Laird, 'when those long
sisterly arms are round my neck it isn't *me* she's hugging.'

'And then,' said Taffy, 'what a trump she is! Why, she's as
upright and straight and honourable as a man! And what she
says to one about one's self is always so pleasant to hear! That's
Irish, I suppose. And, what's more, it's always true.'

'Ah, that's Scotch!' said the Laird, and tried to wink at Little
Billee, but Little Billee wasn't there.

Even Svengali percieved the strange metamorphosis. 'Ach,
Drilpy,' he would say, on a Sunday-afternoon, 'how beautiful
you are! It drives me mad! I adore you. I like you thinner; you
have such beautiful bones! Why do you not answer my letters?
What! you do not *read* them? You *burn* them? And yet I—
Donnerrwetter! I forgot! The grisettes of the Quartier Latin
have not learned how to read or write; they have only learned
how to dance the cancan with the dirty little pig-dog monkeys
they call men. Sacrement!* *We* will teach the little pig-dog
monkeys to dance something else some day, we Germans. We
will make music for them to dance to! Boum! boum! Better than
the waiter at the Café de la Rotonde, *hein?* And the grisettes of
the Quartier Latin shall pour us out your little white wine —
*fotre betit fin planc,** as your pig-dog monkey of a poet says,
your rotten *verfluchter* De Musset, "who has got such a splendid
future behind him!" Bah! What do *you* know of Monsieur
Alfred de Musset? We have got a poet too, my Drilpy. His name
is Heinrich Heine.* If he's still alive, he lives in Paris, in a little
street off the Champs Élysées. He lies in bed all day long, and
only sees out of one eye, like the Countess Hahn-Hahn,* ha! ha!
He adores French grisettes. He married one. Her name is
Mathilde,* and she has got *süssen füssen,** like you. He would
adore you too, for your beautiful bones; he would like to count
them one by one, for he is very playful, like me. And, ach! what
a beautiful skeleton you will make! And very soon, too, because
you do not smile on your madly-loving Svengali. You burn his
letters without reading them! You shall have a nice little
mahogany glass case all to yourself in the museum of the École
de Médecine,* and Svengali shall come in his new fur-lined coat,
smoking his big cigar of the Havana, and push the dirty
carabins* out of the way, and look through the holes of your

eyes into your stupid empty skull, and up the nostrils of your high, bony sounding-board of a nose without either a tip or a lip to it, and into the roof of your big mouth, with your thirty-two big English teeth, and between your big ribs into your big chest, where the big leather lungs used to be, and say, "Ach! what a pity she had no more music in her than a big tom-cat!" And then he will look all down your bones to your poor crumbling feet, and say, "Ach! what a fool she was not to answer Svengali's letters!" and the dirty carabins shall—'

'Shut up, you sacred fool, or I'll precious soon spoil *your* skeleton for you.'

Thus the short-tempered Taffy, who had been listening.

Then Svengali, scowling, would play Chopin's funeral march* more divinely than ever; and where the pretty soft part comes in, he would whisper to Trilby, 'That is Svengali coming to look at you in your little mahogany glass case!'

And here let me say that these vicious imaginations of Svengali's, which look so tame in English print, sounded much more ghastly in French, pronounced with a Hebrew-German accent, and uttered in his hoarse, rasping, nasal, throaty rook's caw, his big yellow teeth baring themselves in a mongrel canine snarl, his heavy upper eyelids drooping over his insolent black eyes.

Besides which, as he played the lovely melody he would go through a ghoulish pantomime, as though he were taking stock of the different bones in her skeleton with greedy but discriminating approval. And when he came down to the feet, he was almost droll in the intensity of his terrible realism. But Trilby did not appreciate this exquisite fooling, and felt cold all over.

He seemed to her a dread powerful demon, who, but for Taffy (who alone could hold him in check), oppressed and weighed on her like an incubus – and she dreamed of him oftener than she dreamed of Taffy, the Laird, or even Little Billee!

Thus pleasantly and smoothly, and without much change or adventure, things went on till Christmas-time.

Little Billee seldom spoke of Trilby, or Trilby of him. Work went on every morning at the studio in the Place St. Anatole des Arts, and pictures were begun and finished – little pictures that didn't take long to paint – the Laird's Spanish bull-fighting

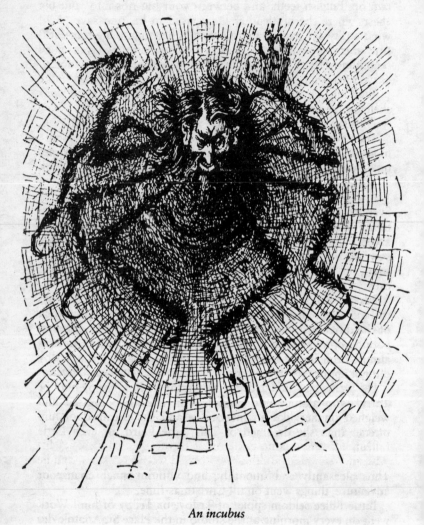

An incubus

scenes, in which the bull never appeared, and which he sent to his native Dundee and sold there; Taffy's tragic little dramas of life in the slums of Paris — starvings, drownings — suicides by charcoal and poison — which he sent everywhere, but did not sell.

Little Billee was painting all this time at Carrel's studio — his private one — and seemed preoccupied and happy when they all met at meal-time, and less talkative even than usual.

He had always been the least talkative of the three; more prone to listen, and no doubt to think the more.

In the afternoon people came and went as usual, and boxed and fenced and did gymnastic feats, and felt Taffy's biceps, which by this time equalled Mr Sandow's!*

Some of these people were very pleasant and remarkable, and have become famous since then in England, France, America — or have died, or married, and come to grief or glory in other ways. It is the Ballad of the Bouillabaisse all over again!

It might be worth while my trying to sketch some of the more noteworthy, now that my story is slowing for a while — like a French train when the engine-driver sees a long curved tunnel in front of him, as I do — and no light at the other end!

My humble attempts at characterisation might be useful as *mémoires pour servir** to future biographers. Besides, there are other reasons, as the reader will soon discover.

There was Durien, for instance — Trilby's especial French adorer, *pour le bon motif!** a son of the people, a splendid sculptor, a very fine character in every way — so perfect, indeed, that there is less to say about him than any of the others — modest, earnest, simple, frugal, chaste, and of untiring industry; living for his art, and perhaps also a little for Trilby, whom he would have been only too glad to marry. He was Pygmalion;* she was his Galatea — a Galatea whose marble heart would never beat for *him!*

Durien's house is now the finest in the Parc Monceau;* his wife and daughters are the best-dressed women in Paris, and he one of the happiest of men; but he will never quite forget poor Galatea:

'La belle aux pieds d'albâtre — aux deux talons de rose!'*

Then there was Vincent,* a Yankee medical student, who could both work and play.

He is now one of the greatest oculists in the world, and

Europeans cross the Atlantic to consult him. He can still play, and when he crosses the Atlantic himself for that purpose he has to travel incognito like a royalty, lest his play should be marred by work. And his daughters are so beautiful and accomplished that British dukes have sighed after them in vain. Indeed, these fair young ladies spend their autumn holiday in refusing the British aristocracy. We are told so in the society papers, and I can quite believe it. Love is not always blind; and if he is, Vincent is the man to cure him.

In those days he prescribed for us all round, and punched and stethoscoped us, and looked at our tongues for love, and told us what to eat, drink, and avoid, and even where to go for it.

For instance: late one night Little Billee woke up in a cold sweat, and thought himself a dying man – he had felt seedy all day and taken no food; so he dressed and dragged himself to Vincent's hotel, and woke him up, and said, 'Oh, Vincent, Vincent! I'm a dying man!' and all but fainted on his bed. Vincent felt him all over with the greatest care, and asked him many questions. Then, looking at his watch, he delivered himself thus: 'Humph! 3.30! rather late – but still – look here, Little Billee – do you know the Halle,* on the other side of the water, where they sell vegetables?'

'Oh yes! yes! What vegetable shall I—'

'Listen! On the north side are two restaurants – Bordier and Baratte. They remain open all night. Now go straight off to one of those tuck shops, and tuck in as big a supper as you possibly can. Some people prefer Baratte. I prefer Bordier myself. Perhaps you'd better try Bordier first and Baratte after. At all events, lose no time; so off you go!'

Thus he saved Little Billee from an early grave.

Then there was the Greek,* a boy of only sixteen, but six feet high, and looking ten years older than he was, and able to smoke even stronger tobacco than Taffy himself, and colour pipes divinely; he was a great favourite in the Place St. Anatole, for his *bonhomie*,* his niceness, his warm geniality. He was the capitalist of this select circle (and nobly lavish of his capital). He went by the name of Poluphloisboiospaleapologos Petrilopetrolicoconose – for so he was christened by the Laird – because his real name was thought much too long; and much too lovely for the Quartier Latin, and reminded one too much of the Isles of Greece – where burning Sappho loved and sang.

What was he learning in the Latin Quarter? French? He spoke French like a native! Nobody knows. But when his Paris friends transferred their Bohemia to London, where were they ever made happier and more at home than in his lordly parental abode – or fed with nicer things?

That abode is now his, and lordlier than ever, as becomes the dwelling of a millionaire and city magnate; and its gray-bearded owner is as genial, as jolly, and as hospitable as in the old Paris days, but he no longer colours pipes.

Then there was Carnegie,* fresh from Balliol,* redolent of the 'varsity. He intended himself then for the diplomatic service, and came to Paris to learn French as it is spoke; and spent most of his time with his fashionable English friends on the right side of the river, and the rest with Taffy, the Laird, and Little Billee on the left. Perhaps that is why he has not become an ambassador. he is now only a rural dean, and speaks the worst French I know, and speaks it wherever and whenever he can.

It serves him right, I think.

He was fond of lords, and knew some (at least, he gave one that impression), and often talked of them, and dressed so beautifully that even Little Billee was abashed in his presence. Only Taffy, in his threadbare, out-at-elbow shooting-jacket and cricket-cap, and the Laird, in his tattered straw hat and Taffy's old overcoat down to his heels, dared to walk arm-in-arm with him – nay, insisted on doing so – as they listened to the band in the Luxembourg Gardens.*

And his whiskers were even longer and thicker and more golden than Taffy's own. But the mere sight of a boxing-glove made him sick.

Then there was the yellow-haired Antony,* a Swiss – the idle apprentice, *le roi des truands*,* as we called him – to whom everything was forgiven, as to François Villon,* *à cause de ses gentillesses** – surely, for all his reprehensible pranks, the gentlest and most lovable creature that ever lived in Bohemia, or out of it.

Always in debt, like Svengali, for he had no more notion of the value of money than a humming-bird, and gave away in

The Capitalist and the Swell

reckless generosity to friends what in strictness belonged to his endless creditors; like Svengali, humorous, witty, and a most exquisite and original artist, and also somewhat eccentric in his attire (though scrupulously clean), so that people would stare at him as he walked along – a thing that always gave him dire offence! But, unlike Svengali, full of delicacy, refinement, and distinction of mind and manner, void of any self-conceit; and, in spite of the irregularities of his life, the very soul of truth and honour, as gentle as he was chivalrous and brave; the warmest, staunchest, sincerest, most unselfish friend in the world; and, as long as his purse was full, the best and drollest boon companion in the world – but that was not for ever!

When the money was gone, then would Antony hie him to some beggarly attic in some lost Parisian slum, and write his own epitaph in lovely French or German verse – or even English (for he was an astounding linguist); and telling himself that he was forsaken by family, friends, and mistress alike, look out of his casement over the Paris chimney-pots for the last time, and listen once more to 'the harmonies of nature,' as he called it, and 'aspire towards the infinite,' and bewail 'the cruel deceptions of his life,' and finally lay himself down to die of sheer starvation.

And as he lay and waited for his release, that was so long in coming, he would beguile the weary hours by mumbling a crust 'watered with his own salt tears,' and decorating his epitaph with fanciful designs of the most exquisite humour, pathos, and beauty; these early illustrated epitaphs of the young Antony, of which there still exist a goodly number, are now priceless, as all collectors know all over the world.

Fainter and fainter would he grow, and finally, on the third day or thereabouts, a remittance would reach him from some long-suffering sister or aunt in far Lausanne; or else the fickle mistress or faithless friend (who had been looking for him all over Paris) would discover his hiding-place, the beautiful epitaph would be walked off in triumph to le père Marcas in the Rue du Ghette* and sold for twenty, fifty, a hundred francs; and then *vogue la galère!** and back again to Bohemia, dear Bohemia and all its joys, as long as the money lasted . . . *e poi, da capo!**

And now that his name is a household word in two hemispheres, and he himself an honour and a glory to the land he had adopted as his own, he loves to remember all this, and look

back from the lofty pinnacle on which he sits perched up aloft
to the impecunious days of his idle apprenticeship – *le bon
temps où l'on était si malheureux!**

And with all that Quixotic dignity of his, so famous is he as a
wit that when he jokes (and he is always joking), people laugh
first, and then ask what he was joking about, and you can make
your own mild funniments raise a roar by merely prefacing them
'as Antony once said!'

The present scribe has often done so. And if by a happy fluke
you should some day hit upon a really good thing of your own
– good enough to be quoted – be sure it will come back to you
after many days prefaced 'as Antony once said!'

And these jokes are so good-natured that you almost resent
their being made at anybody's expense but your own! Never
from Antony:

> The aimless jest that striking has caused pain,
> The idle word that he'd wish back again!*

Indeed, in spite of his success, I don't suppose he ever made
an enemy in his life.

And here let me add (lest there be any doubt as to his identity)
that he is now tall and stout and strikingly handsome, though
rather bald; and such an aristocrat in bearing, aspect, and
manner, that you would take him for a blue-blooded descendant
of the Crusaders* instead of the son of a respectable burgher in
Lausanne.

Then there was Lorrimer,* the industrious apprentice, who is
now also well pinnacled on high; himself a pillar of the Royal
Academy – probably, if he lives long enough, its future president
– the duly knighted or baroneted Lord Mayor of 'all the plastic
arts' (except one or two perhaps, here and there, that are not
altogether without some importance).

May this not be for many, many years! Lorrimer himself
would be the first to say so!

Tall, thin, red-haired, and well-favoured, he was a most eager,
earnest, and painstaking young enthusiast, of precocious culture,
who read improving books, and did not share in the amusements
of the Quartier Latin, but spent his evenings at home with
Handel, Michael Angelo, and Dante, on the respectable side of

the river. Also, he went into good society sometimes, with dress-coat on, and a white tie, and his hair parted in the middle!

But in spite of these blemishes on his otherwise exemplary record as an art student, he was the most delightful companion – the most affectionate, helpful, and sympathetic of friends. May he live long and prosper!

Enthusiast as he was, he could only worship one god at a time. It was either Michael Angelo, Phidias,* Paul Veronese, Tintoret, Raphael, or Titian – never a modern – moderns didn't exist! And so thoroughgoing was he in his worship, and so pesistent in voicing it, that he made those immortals quite unpopular in the Place St Anatole des Arts. We grew to dread their very names. Each of them would last him a couple of months or so; then he would give us a month's holiday, and take up another.

Antony did not think much of Lorrimer in those days, nor Lorrimer of him, for all they were such good friends. And neither of them thought much of Little Billee, whose pinnacle (of pure unadulterated fame) is now the highest of all – the highest probably that can be for a mere painter of pictures!

And what is so nice about Lorrimer, now that he is a graybeard, an Academician,* an accomplished man of the world and society, is that he admires Antony's genius more than he can say – and reads Mr Rudyard Kipling's* delightful stories as well as Dante's *Inferno** – and can listen with delight to the lovely songs of Signor Tosti,* who has not precisely founded himself on Handel – can even scream with laughter at a comic song – even a nigger melody – so, at least, that it but be sung in well-bred and distinguished company – for Lorrimer is no Bohemian.

> Shoo, fly! don'tcher bother me!
> For I belong to the Comp'ny G!*

Both these famous men are happily (and most beautifully) married – grandfathers for all I know – and 'move in the very best society' (Lorrimer always, I'm told; Antony now and then); *la haute*, as it used to be called in French Bohemia – meaning dukes and lords and even royalties, I suppose, and those who love them, and whom they love!

That *is* the best society, isn't it? At all events, we are assured it used to be; but that must have been before the present scribe (a meek and somewhat innocent outsider) had been privileged to see it with his own little eye.

And when they happen to meet there (Antony and Lorrimer, I mean), I don't expect they rush very wildly into each other's arms, or talk very fluently about old times. Nor do I suppose their wives are very intimate. None of our wives are. Not even Taffy's and the Laird's.*

Oh, Orestes! Oh, Pylades!*

Oh, ye impecunious, unpinnacled young inseparables of eighteen, nineteen, twenty, even twenty-five, who share each other's thoughts and purses, and wear each other's clothes, and swear each other's oaths, and smoke each other's pipes, and respect each other's lights o' love, and keep each other's secrets, and tell each other's jokes, and pawn each other's watches and merrymake together on the proceeds, and sit all night by each other's bedsides in sickness, and comfort each other in sorrow and disappointment with silent, manly sympathy – 'wait till you get to forty year!'*

Wait even till each or either of you gets himself a little pinnacle of his own – be it ever so humble!

Nay, wait till either or each of you gets himself a wife!

History goes on repeating itself,* and so do novels, and this is a platitude, and there's nothing new under the sun.

May too cecee (as the idiomatic Laird would say in the language he adores) – may too cecee ay nee eecee nee lâh!*

Then there was Dodor,* the handsome young *dragon de la garde* – a full private, if you please, with a beardless face, and damask-rosy cheeks, and a small waist, and narrow feet like a lady's, and who, strange to say, spoke English just like an Englishman.

And his friend Gontran, *alias* l'Zouzou – a corporal in the Zouaves.

Both of these worthies had met Taffy in the Crimea, and frequented the studios in the Quartier Latin, where they adored (and were adored by) the grisettes and models, especially Trilby.

Both of them were distinguished for being the worst subjects (*les plus mauvais garnements*)* of their respective regiments; yet both were special favourites not only with their fellow-rankers, but with those in command, from their colonels downward.

Both were in the habit of being promoted to the rank of

corporal or brigadier, and degraded to the rank of private next day for general misconduct, the result of a too exuberant delight in their promotion.

Neither of them knew fear, envy, malice, temper, or low spirits; ever said or did an ill-natured thing; ever even thought one; ever had an enemy but himself. Both had the best or the worst manners going, according to their company, whose manners they reflected; they were true chameleons!

Both were always ready to share their last ten-sou piece (not that they ever seemed to have one) with each other or anybody else, or anybody else's last ten-sou piece with you; to offer you a friend's cigar; to invite you to dine with any friend they had; to fight with you, or for you, at a moment's notice. And they made up for all the anxiety, tribulation, and sorrow they caused at home by the endless fun and amusement they gave to all outside.

It was a pretty dance they led; but our three friends of the Place St. Anatole (who hadn't got to pay the pipers) loved them both, especially Dodor.

One fine Sunday afternoon Little Billee found himself studying life and character in that most delightful and festive scene la Fête de St Cloud, and met Dodor and l'Zouzou there, who hailed him with delight, saying:

'Nous allons joliment jubiler, nom d'une pipe!'* and insisted on his joining in their amusements and paying for them – round-abouts, swings, the giant, the dwarf, the strong man, the fat woman – to whom they made love and were taken too seriously, and turned out – the menagerie of wild beasts, whom they teased and aggravated till the police had to interfere. Also *al fresco* dances, where their cancan step was of the wildest and most unbridled character, till a *sous-officier** or a gendarme came in sight, and then they danced quite mincingly and demurely, *en maître d'école,** as they called it, to the huge delight of an immense and ever-increasing crowd, and the disgust of all truly respectable men.

They also insisted on Little Billee's walking between them, arm-in-arm, and talking to them in English whenever they saw coming towards them a respectable English family with daughters. It was the dragoon's delight to get himself stared at by fair daughters of Albion for speaking as good English as themselves – a rare accomplishment in a French trooper – and Zouzou's happiness to be thought English too, though the only English he knew was the phrase, 'I will not! I will not!' which he had picked up in the Crimea, and repeated over and over again when he came within ear-shot of a pretty English girl.

Little Billee was not happy in these circumstances. He was no snob. But he was a respectably-brought-up young Briton of the higher middle class, and it was not quite pleasant for him to be seen (by fair country-women of his own) walking arm-in-arm on a Sunday afternoon with a couple of French private soldiers, and uncommonly rowdy ones at that.

Later they came back to Paris together on the top of an omnibus, among a very proletarian crowd; and there the two facetious warriors immediately made themselves pleasant all round and became very popular, espcially with the women and children; but not, I regret to say, through the propriety, refinement, and discretion of their behaviour. Little Billee resolved that he would not go a-pleasuring with them any more.

However, they stuck to him through thick and thin, and insisted on escorting him all the way back to the Quartier Latin by the Pont de la Concorde* and the Rue de Lille* in the Faubourg St. Germain.

Little Billee loved the Faubourg St Germain, especially the Rue de Lille. He was fond of gazing at the magnificent old mansions, the *hôtels* of the old French noblesse, or rather the outside walls thereof, the grand sculptured portals with the armorial bearings and the splendid old historic names above them – Hôtel de This, Hôtel de That, Rohan-Chabot, Montmorency, La Rochefoucauld-Liancourt, La Tour d'Auvergne.*

He would not forget himself in romantic dreams of past and forgotten French chivalry which these glorious names called up; for he knew a little of French history, loving to read Froissart* and Saint Simon* and the genial Brantôme.*

Halting opposite one of the finest and oldest of all these gateways, his especial favourite, labelled 'Hôtel de la Rochemartel' in letters of faded gold over a ducal coronet and a huge escutcheon of stone, he began to descant upon its architectural beauties and noble proportions to l'Zouzou.

'*Parbleu!*' said l'Zouzou, '*connu, farceur!*'* why, I was *born* there, on the 6th of March 1834* at 5.30 in the morning. Lucky day for France – *hein?*'

'Born there? what do you mean – in the porter's lodge?'

'I will not! I will not!'

Dodor in his glory

At this juncture the two great gates rolled back, a liveried
*Suisse** appeared, and an open carriage and pair came out, and
in it were two elderly ladies and a younger one.

To Little Billee's indignation, the two incorrigible warriors
made the military salute, and the three ladies bowed stiffly and
gravely.

And then (to Little Billee horror this time) one of them
happened to look back, and Zouzou actually kissed his hand to
her.

Hôtel de la Rochemartel

'Do you *know* that lady?' asked Little Billee, very sternly.

'*Parbleu! si je la connais!** Why, it's my mother! Isn't she nice? She's rather cross with me just now.'

'Your *mother!* Why, what do you mean? What on earth would your mother be doing in that big carriage and at that big house?'

'*Parbleu, farceur!* She lives there!'

'*Lives* there? Why, who and what is she, your mother?'

'The Duchesse de le Rochemartel, *parbleu!* and that's my sister; and that's my aunt, Princesse de Chevagné-Bauffremont! She's the "*patronne*"* of that *chic* equipage. She's a millionaire, my aunt Chevagné!'

'Well, I never! What's *your* name, then?'

'Oh, *my* name! Hang it – let me see! Well – Gontran – Xavier – François – Marie – Joseph d'Amaury de Brissac de Ronces-vaulx* de la Rochemartel-Boisségur, at your service!'

'Quite correct!' said Dodor; '*l'enfant dit vrai!*'*

'Well – I – never! And what's *your* name, Dodor?'

'Oh! I'm only a humble individual, and answer to the one-horse name of Théodore Rigolot de Lafarce.* But Zouzou's an awful swell, you know – his brother's the Duke!'

Little Billee was no snob. But he was a respectably-brought-up young Briton of the higher middle class, and these revel-ations, which he could not but believe, astounded him so that he could hardly speak. Much as he flattered himself that he scorned the bloated aristocracy, titles are titles – even French titles! – and when it comes to dukes and princesses who live in houses like the Hôtel de la Rochemartel . . .!

It's enough to take a respectably-brought-up young Briton's breath away.

When he saw Taffy that evening, he exclaimed: 'I say, Zouzou's mother's a duchess!'

'Yes – the Duchesse de la Rochemartel-Boisségur.'

'You never told me!'

'You never asked me. It's one of the greatest names in France. They're very poor, I believe.'

'Poor! You should see the house they live in!'

'I've been there, to dinner; and the dinner wasn't very good. They let a great part of it, and live mostly in the country. The Duke is Zouzou's brother; very unlike Zouzou; he's consumptive and unmarried, and the most respectable man in Paris. Zouzou will be the Duke some day.'

'And Dodor – he's a swell, too, I suppose – he says he's *de* something or other!'

'Yes – Rigolot de Lafarce. I've no doubt he descends from the Crusaders too; the name seems to favour it, anyhow; and such lots of them do in this country. His mother was English, and bore the worthy name of Brown. He was at school in England; that's why he speaks English so well – and behaves so badly, perhaps! He's got a very beautiful sister, married to a man in the 60th Rifles – Jack Reeve, a son of Lord Reevely's; a selfish sort of chap. I don't suppose he gets on very well with his brother-in-law. Poor Dodor! His sister's about the only living thing he cares for – except Zouzou.'

I wonder if the bland and genial Monsieur Théodore – 'notre Sieur Théodore' – now junior partner in the great haberdashery firm of 'Passefil* et Rigolot,' on the Boulevard des Capucines,* and a pillar of the English chapel in the Rue Marbœuf,* is very hard on his employés and employées if they are a little late at their counters on a Monday morning?

I wonder if that stuck-up, stingy, stodgy, communard-shooting, church-going, time-serving, place-hunting, pious-eyed, pompous old prig, martinet, and philistine, Monsieur le Maréchal-Duc de la Rochemartel-Boisségur, ever tells Madame la Maréchale-Duchesse (*née* Hunks, of Chicago) how once upon a time Dodor and he –

We will tell no tales out of school.

The present scribe is no snob. He is a respectably-brought-up old Briton of the higher middle class – at least, he flatters himself so. And he writes for just such old philistines as himself, who date from a time when titles were not thought so cheap as to-day. Alas! all reverence for all that is high and time-honoured and beautiful seems at a discount.

So he has kept his blackguard ducal Zouave for the bouquet of this little show – the final *bonne bouche** in his Bohemian *menu* – that he may make it palatable to those who only look upon the good old Quartier Latin (now no more to speak of) as a very low, common, vulgar quarter indeed, deservedly swept away, where misters the students (shocking bounders and cads)

had nothing better to do, day and night, than mount up to a
horrid place called the thatched house – *la chaumière* –

> Pour y danser le cancan
> Ou le Robert Macaire –
> Toujours – toujours – toujours –
> La nuit comme le jour . . .
> Et youp! youp! youp!
> Tra la la la la . . . la la la!*

*

Christmas was drawing near.

There were days when the whole Quartier Latin would veil its
iniquities under fogs almost worthy of the Thames Valley
between London Bridge and Westminster, and out of the studio
window the prospect was a dreary blank. No Morgue! no
towers of Notre Dame! not even the chimney-pots over the way
– not even the little mediæval toy turret at the corner of the Rue
Vieille des Trois Mauvais Ladres, Little Billee's delight!

The stove had to be crammed till its sides grew a dull deep
red before one's fingers could hold a brush or squeeze a bladder;
one had to box or fence at nine in the morning, that one might
recover from the cold bath, and get warm for the rest of the
day!

Taffy and the Laird grew pensive and dreamy, child-like and
bland; and when they talked it was generally about Christmas
at home in Merry England and the distant Land of Cakes, and
how good it was to be there at such a time – hunting, shooting,
curling, and endless carouse!

It was Ho! for the jolly West Riding,* and Hey! for the
bonnets of Bonnie Dundee, till they grew quite homesick, and
wanted to start by the very next train.

They didn't do anything so foolish. They wrote over to friends
in London for the biggest turkey, the biggest plum-pudding, that
could be got for love or money, with mince-pies, and holly and
mistletoe, and sturdy, short, thick English sausages; half a
Stilton cheese, and a sirloin beef – two sirloins, in case one
should not be enough.

For they meant to have a Homeric feast* in the studio on
Christmas Day – Taffy, the Laird, and Little Billee – and invite
all the delightful chums I have been trying to describe; and that

is just why I tried to describe them – Durien, Vincent, Antony, Lorrimer, Carnegie, Petrolicoconose, l'Zouzou, and Dodor!

The cooking and waiting should be done by Trilby, her friend Angèle Boisse, M. et Mme. Vinard, and such little Vinards as could be trusted with glass and crockery and mince-pies; and if that was not enough, they would also cook themselves, and wait upon each other.

When dinner should be over, supper was to follow with scarcely any interval to speak of; and to partake of this other guests should be bidden – Svengali and Gecko, and perhaps one or two more. No ladies!

For, as the unsusceptible Laird expressed it, in the language of a gillie he had once met at a servant's dance in a Highland country-house, 'Them wimmen spiles the ball!'

Elaborate cards of invitation were sent out, in the designing and ornamentation of which the Laird and Taffy exhausted all their fancy (Little Billee had no time).

Wines and spirits and English beers were procured at great cost from M. E. Delevingne's, in the Rue St Honoré,* and liqueurs of every description – chartreuse, curaçoa, *ratafia de cassis*, and anisette;* no expense was spared.

Also, truffled galantines of turkey, tongues, hams, *rillettes de Tours,* pâtés de foie gras, fromage d'Italie** (which has nothing to do with cheese), *saucissons* d'Arles et de Lyon*, with and without garlic, cold jellies peppery and salt – everything that French *charcutiers** and their wives can make out of French pigs, or any other animal whatever, beast, bird, or fowl (even cats and rats), for the supper; and sweet jellies, and cakes, and sweetmeats, and confections of all kinds, from the famous pastry-cook at the corner of the Rue Castiglione.

Mouths went watering all day long in joyful anticipation. They water somewhat sadly now at the mere remembrance of these delicious things – the mere immediate sight or scent of which in these degenerate latter days would no longer avail to promote any such delectable secretion. *Hélas! ahimè! ach weh! ay de mi! eheu! οιμοι* – in point of fact, *alas!*

That is the very exclamation I wanted.

Christmas Eve came round. The pieces of resistance and plum-pudding and mince-pies had not yet arrived from London – but there was plenty of time.

Les trois Angliches dined at le père Trin's as usual, and played

Christmas Eve

billiards and dominoes at the Café du Luxembourg, and possessed their souls in patience till it was time to go and hear the midnight mass at the Madeleine, where Roucouly,* the great baritone of the Opéra Comique,* was retained to sing Adam's* famous Noël.

The whole Quartier seemed alive with the *réveillon.** It was a clear, frosty night, with a splendid moon just past the full, and most exhilarating was the walk along the quays on the Rive Gauche, over the Pont de la Concorde and across the Place thereof, and up the thronged Rue de la Madeleine to the massive Parthenaic* place of worship that always has such a pagan, worldly look of smug and prosperous modernity.

They struggled manfully, and found standing and kneeling room among that fervent crowd, and heard the impressive service with mixed feelings, as became true Britons of very advanced liberal and religious opinions; not with the unmixed contempt of the proper British Orthodox (who were there in full force, one may be sure).

But their susceptible hearts soon melted at the beautiful music, and in mere sensuous *attendrissement** they were quickly in unison with all the rest.

For as the clock struck twelve out pealed the organ, and up rose the finest voice in France:

> Minuit, Chrétiens! c'est l'heure solennelle
> Où l'Homme-Dieu descendit parmi nous!*

And a wave of religious emotion rolled over Little Billee and submerged him; swept him off his little legs, swept him out of his little self, drowned him in a great seething surge of love – love of his kind, love of love, love of life, love of death, love of all that is and ever was and ever will be – a very large order indeed, even for Little Billee.

And it seemed to him that he stretched out his arms for love to one figure especially beloved beyond all the rest – one finger erect on high with arms outstretched to him, in more than common fellowship of need; not the sorrowful figure crowned with thorns, for it was in the likeness of a woman; but never that of the Virgin Mother of Our Lord.

It was Trilby, Trilby, Trilby! a poor fallen sinner and waif all but lost amid the scum of the most corrupt city on earth. Trilby weak and mortal like himself, and in woeful want of pardon! and in her gray dove-like eyes he saw the shining of so great a love that he was abashed; for well he knew that all that love was his, and would be his for ever, come what would or could.

> Peuple, debout! Chante ta délivrance!
> Noël! Noël! Voici le Rédempteur!*

So sang and rang and pealed and echoed the big, deep, metallic baritone bass – above the organ, above the incense, above everything else in the world – till the very universe seemed to shake with the rolling thunder of that great message of love and forgiveness!

Thus at least felt Little Billee, whose way it was to magnify and exaggerate all things under the subtle stimulus of sound, and the singing human voice had especially strange power to penetrate into his inmost depths – even the voice of man!

And what voice but the deepest and gravest and grandest there is can give worthy utterance to such a message as that, the epitome, the abstract, the very essence of all collective humanity's wisdom at its best!

Little Billee reached the Hôtel Corneille that night in a very exalted frame of mind indeed; the loftiest, lowliest mood of all.

Now see what sport we are of trivial, base, ignoble earthly things!

Sitting on the doorstep, and smoking two cigars at once he found Ribot, one of his fellow-lodgers, whose room was just under his own. Ribot was so tipsy that he could not ring. But he could still sing, and did so at the top of his voice. It was not the Noël of Adam that he sang. He had not spent his réveillon in any church.

With the help of a sleepy waiter, Little Billee got the bacchanalian into his room and lit his candle for him, and, disengaging himself from his maudlin embraces, left him to wallow in solitude.

As he lay awake in his bed, trying to recall the deep and high emotions of the evening, he heard the tipsy hog below tumbling about his room and still trying to sing his senseless ditty:

> Allons, Gycère!
> Rougis mon verre
> Du jus divin dont mon cœur est toujours jaloux . . .
> Et puis à table,

'Allons, Gycère! Rougis mon verre . . .

Bacchante aimable!
Enivrons-nous (hic) Les g'glougloux sont des rendezvous! . . .*

Then the song ceased for a while, and soon there were other sounds, as on a Channel steamer. Gougloux indeed!

Then the fear arose in Little Billee's mind lest the drunken beast should set fire to his bedroom curtains. All heavenly visions were chased away for the night . . .

Our hero, half crazed with fear, disgust, and irritation, lay wide awake, his nostrils on the watch for the smell of burning chintz or muslin, and wondered how an educated man – for

Ribot was a law-student — could ever make such a filthy beast of himself as that! It was a scandal — a disgrace; it was not to be borne; there should be no forgiveness for such as Ribot — not even on Christmas Day! He would complain to Madame Paul, the *patronne*;* he would have Ribot turned out into the street; he would leave the hotel himself the very next morning! At last he fell asleep, thinking of all he would do; and thus, ridiculously and ignominiously for Little Billee, ended the *réveillon*.

Next morning he complained to Madame Paul; and though he did not give her warning, nor even insist on the expulsion of Ribot (who, as he heard with a hard heart, was *bien malade ce matin*),* he expressed himself very severely on the conduct of that gentleman, and on the dangers from fire that might arise from a tipsy man being trusted alone in a small bedroom with chintz curtains and a lighted candle. If it hadn't been for himself, he told her, Ribot would have slept on the door-step, and serve him right! He was really grand in his virtuous indignation, in spite of his imperfect French; and Madame Paul was deeply contrite for her peccant lodger, and profuse in her apologies; and Little Billee began his twenty-first Christmas Day like a Pharisee,* thanking his star that he was not as Ribot!

Part Fourth

Félicité passée
Qui ne peux revenir,
Tourment de ma pensée
Que n'ay-je, en te perdant, perdu le souvenir!*

Mid-day had struck.* The expected hamper had not turned up in the Place St Anatole des Arts.

All Madame Vinard's* kitchen battery was in readiness; Trilby and Madame Angèle Boisse were in the studio, their sleeves turned up, and ready to begin.

At twelve the *trois* Angliches and the two fair *blanchisseuses* sat down to lunch in a very anxious frame of mind, and finished a *pâté de foie gras* and two bottles of Burgundy between them, such was their disquietude.

The guests had been invited for six o'clock.

Most elaborately they laid the cloth on the table they had borrowed from the Hôtel de Seine, and settled who was to sit next to whom, and then unsettled it, and quarrelled over it – Trilby, as was her wont in such matters, assuming an authority that did not rightly belong to her, and of course getting her own way in the end.

And that, as the Laird remarked, was her confounded Trilbyness.

Two o'clock – three – four – but no hamper! Darkness had almost set in. It was simply maddening. They knelt on the divan, with their elbows on the window-sill, and watched the street-lamps popping into life along the quays – and looked out through the gathering dusk for the van from the Chemin de Fer du Nord* – and gloomily thought of the Morgue, which they could still make out across the river.

At length the Laird and Trilby went off in a cab to the station – a long drive – and, lo! before they came back the long-expected hamper arrived, at six o'clock.

And with it Durien, Vincent, Antony, Lorrimer, Carnegie, Petrolicoconose, Dodor, and l'Zouzou – the last two in uniform, as usual.

And suddenly the studio, which had been so silent, dark, and dull, with Taffy and Little Billee sitting hopeless and despondent round the stove, became a scene of the noisiest, busiest, and cheerfullest animation. The three big lamps were lit, and all the Chinese lanterns. The pieces of resistance and the pudding were whisked off by Trilby, Angèle, and Madame Vinard to other regions – the porter's lodge and Durien's studio (which had been lent for the purpose); and every one was pressed into the preparations for the banquet. There was planty for idle hands to do. Sausages to be fried for the turkey, stuffing made, and sauces, salads mixed, and punch – holly hung in festoons all round and about – a thousand things. Everybody was so clever and good-humoured that nobody got in anybody's way – not even Carnegie, who was in evening dress (to the Laird's delight). So they made him do the scullion's work – cleaning, rinsing, peeling, etc.

The cooking of the dinner was almost better fun than the eating of it. And though there were so many cooks, not even the broth was spoiled (cockaleekie, from a receipt of the Laird's).

It was ten o'clock before they sat down to that most memorable repast.

Zouzou and Dodor, who had been the most useful and energetic of all its cooks, apparently quite forgot they were due at their respective barracks at that very moment; they had only been able to obtain *la permission de dix heures.** If they remembered it, the certainty that next day Zouzou would be reduced to the ranks for the fifth time, and Dodor confined to his barracks for a month, did not trouble them in the least.

The waiting was as good as the cooking. The handsome, quick, authoritative Madame Vinard was in a dozen places at once, and openly prompted, rebuked, and bully-ragged her husband into a proper smartness. The pretty little Madame Angèle moved about as deftly and as quietly as a mouse; which of course did not prevent them both from genially joining in the general conversation whenever it wandered into French.

Trilby, tall, graceful, and stately, and also swift of action, though more like Juno or Diana than Hebe,* devoted herself more especially to her own particular favourites – Durien, Taffy, the Laird, Little Billee – and Dodor and Zouzou, whom she loved, and *tutoyé'd en bonne camarade** as she served them with all there was of the choicest.

The two little Vinards did their little best – they scrupulously respected the mince-pies, and only broke two bottles of oil and one of Harvey sauce,* which made their mother furious. To console them, the Laird took one of them on each knee and gave them of his share of plum-pudding and many other unaccustomed good things, so bad for their little French tumtums.

The genteel Carnegie had never been at such a queer scene in his life. It opened his mind – and Dodor and Zouzou, between whom he sat (the Laird thought it would do him good to sit between a private soldier and a humble corporal), taught him more French than he had learned during the three months he had spent in Paris. It was a specialty of theirs. It was more colloquial than what is generally used in diplomatic circles, and stuck longer in the memory; but it hasn't interfered with his preferment in the Church.

He quite unbent. He was the first to volunteer a song (without being asked) when the pipes and cigars were lit, and after the usual toasts had been drunk – Her Majesty's health, Tennyson, Thackeray, and Dickens; and John Leech.*

He sang, with a very cracked and rather hiccupy voice, his only song (it seems) – an English one, of which the burden, he explained, was French:

> Veeverler veeverler veeverler vee
> Veeverler companyee!*

And Zouzou and Dodor complimented him so profusely on his French accent that he was with difficulty prevented from singing it all over again.

Then everybody sang in rotation.

The Laird, with a capital baritone, sang

> Hie diddle dee for the Lowlands low,*

which was encored.

Little Billee sang 'Little Billee.'

Vincent sang

> Old Joe kicking up behind and afore,
> And the yaller gal a-kicking up behind old Joe.*

A capital song, with words of quite a masterly scansion.

Anthony sang 'Le Sire de Framboisy.'* Enthusiastic encore.

Lorrimer, inspired no doubt by the occasion, sang the 'Halle-

'My sister dear'

lujah Chorus,'* and accompanied himself on the piano, but failed to obtain an encore.

Durien sang

> Plaisir d'amour ne dure qu'un moment;
> Chagrin d'amour dure toute la vie . . .*

It was his favourite song, and is one of the beautiful songs of the world, and he sang it very well – and it became popular in the Quartier Latin ever after.

The Greek couldn't sing, and very wisely didn't.

Zouzou sang capitally a capital song in praise of *le vin à quat' sous!**

Taffy, in a voice like a high wind (and with a very good imitation of the Yorkshire brogue), sang a Somersetshire hunting ditty, ending:

> Of this 'ere song should I be axed the reason for to show,
> I don't exactly know, I don't exactly know!
> But all my fancy dwells upon Nancy,
>   And I sing Tally-ho!*

It is a quite super-excellent ditty, and haunts my memory to this day; and one felt sure that Nancy was a dear and a sweet, wherever she lived, and when. So Taffy was encored twice – once for her sake, once for his own.

And finally, to the surprise of all, the bold dragoon sang (in English) 'My Sister Dear,' out of *Masaniello*,* with such pathos, and in a voice so sweet and high and well in tune, that his audience felt almost weepy in the midst of their jollification; and grew quite sentimental, as Englishmen abroad are apt to do when they are rather tipsy and hear pretty music, and think of their dear sisters across the sea, or their friends' dear sisters.

Madame Vinard interrupted her Christmas dinner on the model-throne to listen, and wept and wiped her eyes quite openly, and remarked to Madame Boisse, who stood modestly close by: 'Il est gentil tout plein, ce dragon! Mon Dieu! comme il chante bien! Il est Angliche aussi, il paraît. Ils sont joliment bien élevés, tous ces Angliches – tous plus gentils les uns que les autres! e quant à Monsieur Litrebili, on lui donnerait le bon Dieu sans confession!'*

And Madame Boisse agreed.

Then Svengali and Gecko came, and the table had to be laid and decorated anew, for it was supper-time.

Supper was even jollier than dinner, which had taken off the keen edge of the appetites, so that every one talked at once – the true test of a successful supper – except when Antony told some of his experiences of Bohemia; for instance, how, after staying at home all day for a month to avoid his creditors, he became reckless one Sunday morning, and went to the Bains Deligny, and jumped into a deep part by mistake, and was saved from a watery grave by a bold swimmer, who turned out to be his bootmaker, Satory, to whom he owed sixty francs – of all his duns the one he dreaded the most, and who didn't let him go in a hurry.

Whereupon Svengali remarked that he also owed sixty francs to Satory – 'Mais comme che ne me baigne chamais, che n'ai rien à craindre!'*

Whereupon there was such a laugh that Svengali felt he had scored off Antony at last, and had a prettier wit. He flattered himself that he'd got the laugh of Antony *this* time.

After supper Svengali and Gecko made such lovely music that everybody was sobered and athirst again, and the punch-bowl, wreathed with holly and mistletoe, was placed in the middle of the table, and clean glasses set all round it.

The Dodor and l'Zouzou stood up to dance with Trilby and Madame Angèle, and executed a series of cancan steps, which, though they were so inimitably droll that they had each and all to be encored, were such that not one of them need have brought the blush of shame to the cheek of modesty.

Then the Laird danced a sword-dance* over two T-squares and broke them both. And Taffy, baring his mighty arms to the admiring gaze of all, did dumb-bell exercises, with Little Billee for a dumb-bell, and all but dropped him into the punch-bowl; and tried to cut a pewter ladle in two with Dodor's sabre, and sent it through the window; and this made him cross, so that he abused French sabres, and said they were made of worse pewter than even French ladles; and the Laird sententiously opined that they managed these things better in England, and winked at Little Billee.

Then they played at 'cock-fighting,' with their wrists tied across their shins, and a broomstick thrust in between; thus manacled, you are placed opposite your antagonist, and try to

A Ducal French fighting cock

upset him with your feet, and he you. It is a very good game. The cuirassier* and the Zouave playing at this got so angry, and were so irresistibly funny a sight, that the shouts of laughter could be heard on the other side of the river, so that a *sergent-de-ville** came in and civilly requested them not to make so much noise. They were disturbing the whole Quartier, he said, and there was quite a *rassemblement** outside. So they made him tipsy, and also another policeman, who came to look after his comrade, and yet another; and these guardians of the peace of Paris were trussed and made to play at cock-fighting, and were still funnier than the two soldiers, and laughed louder and made more noise than any one else, so that Madame Vinard had to remonstrate with them, till they got too tipsy to speak, and fell fast asleep, and were laid next to each other behind the stove.

The *fin-de-siècle** reader, disgusted at the thought of such an orgy as I have been trying to describe, must remember that it happened in the fifties, when men calling themselves gentlemen, and being called so, still wrenched off door-knockers and came back drunk from the Derby,* and even drank too much after dinner before joining the ladies, as is all duly chronicled and set down in John Leech's immortal pictures of life and character out of *Punch*.*

Then M. and Mme. Vinard and Trilby and Angèle Boisse bade the company good-night, Trilby being the last of them to leave.

Little Billee took her to the top of the staircase, and there he said to her:

'Trilby, I have asked you nineteen times, and you have refused. Trilby, once more, on Christmas night, for the twentieth time – *will* you marry me? If not, I leave Paris to-morrow morning, and never come back. I swear it on my word of honour!'

Trilby turned very pale, and leaned her back against the wall, and covered her face with her hands.

Little Billee pulled them away.

'Answer me, Trilby!'

'God forgive me, *yes!*' said Trilby, and she ran downstairs, weeping.

It was now very late.

It soon became evident that Little Billee was in extraordinarily high spirits – in an abnormal state of excitement.

He challenged Svengali to spar, and made his nose bleed, and frightened him out of his sardonic wits. He performed wonderful and quite unsuspected feats of strength. He swore eternal friendship to Dodor and Zouzou, and filled their glasses again and again, and also (in his innocence) his own, and *trinquéd** with them many times running. They were the last to leave (except the three helpless policemen); and at about five or six in the morning, to his surprise, he found himself walking between Dodor and Zouzou by a late windy moonlight in the Rue Vieille des Trois Mauvais Ladres, now on one side of the frozen gutter, now on the other, now in the middle of it, stopping them now and then to tell them how jolly they were and how dearly he loved them.

'Answer me, Trilby!'

Presently his hat flew away, and went rolling and skipping and bounding up the narrow street, and they discovered that as soon as they let each other go to run after it, they all three sat down.

So Dodor and Little Billee remained sitting, with their arms round each other's necks and their feet in the gutter, while Zouzou went after the hat on all fours, and caught it, and brought it back in his mouth like a tipsy retriever. Little Billee wept for sheer love and gratitude, and called him a cary*hat*tide* (in English), and laughed loudly at his own wit, which was quite thrown away on Zouzou! 'No man ever *had* such dear, dear frenge! no man ever *was* s'happy!'

After sitting for a while in love and amity, they managed to get up on their feet again, each helping the other; and in some never-to-be-remembered way they reached the Hôtel Corneille.

There they sat Little Billee on the door-step and rang the bell, and seeing some one coming up the Place de l'Odéon, and fearing he might be a *sergent-de-ville*, they bid Little Billee a most affectionate but hasty farewell, kissing him on both cheeks in French fashion, and contrived to get themselves round the corner and out of sight.

Little Billee tried to sing Zouzou's drinking-song:

> Quoi de plus doux
> Que les glougloux –
> Les glougloux du vin à quat' sous . . .*

The stranger came up. Fortunately, it was no *sergent-de-ville*, but Ribot, just back from a Christmas-tree and a little family dance at his aunt's, Madame Kolb (the Alsatian banker's wife, in the Rue de la Chaussée d'Antin*).

Next morning poor Little Billee was dreadfully ill.

He had passed a terrible night. His bed had heaved like the ocean, with oceanic results. He had forgotten to put out his candle, but fortunately Ribot had blown it out for him, after putting him to bed and tucking him up like a real good Samaritan.

And next morning, when Madame Paul brought him a cup of *tisane de chiendent** (which does not happen to mean a hair of the dog that bit him), she was kind, but very severe on the dangers and disgrace of intoxication, and talked to him like a mother.

'Les Glougloux du vin à quat' sous . . .

'If it had not been for kind Monsieur Ribot' (she told him),
'the door-step would have been his portion; and who could say
he didn't deserve it? And then think of the danger of fire from a
tipsy man all alone in a small bedroom with chintz curtains and
a lighted candle!'

'Ribot was kind enough to blow out my candle,' said Little
Billee, humbly.

'Ah, Dame!' said Madame Paul, with much meaning – 'au
moins il a *bon cœur,** Monsieur Ribot!'

And the cruellest sting of all was when the good-natured and incorrigibly festive Ribot came and sat by his bedside, and was kind and tenderly sympathetic, and got him a pick-me-up from the chemist's (unbeknown to Madame Paul).

'Credieu! vous vous êtes crânement bien amusé, hier soir! quelle bosse, hein! je parie que c'était plus drôle que chez ma tante Kolb!'*

All of which, of course, it is unnecessary to translate; except, perhaps, the word *bosse*, which stands for *noce*, which stands for a 'jolly good spree.'

In all his innocent little life Little Billee had never dreamed of such humiliation as this – such ignominious depths of shame and misery and remorse! He did not care to live. He had but one longing: that Trilby, dear Trilby, kind Trilby, would come and pillow his head on her beautiful white English bosom, and lay her soft, cool, tender hand on his aching brow, and there let him go to sleep, and sleeping, die!

He slept and slept, with no better rest for his aching brow than the pillow of his bed in the Hôtel Corneille, and failed to die this time. And when, after some forty-eight hours or so, he had quite slept off the fumes of that memorable Christmas debauch, he found that a sad thing had happened to him, and a strange!

It was as though a tarnishing breath had swept over the reminiscent mirror of his mind and left a little film behind it, so that no past thing he wished to see therein was reflected with quite the old pristine clearness. As though the keen, quick, razor-like edge of his power to reach and re-evoke the bygone charm and glamour and essence of things had been blunted and coarsened. As though the bloom of that special joy, the gift he unconsciously had of recalling past emotions and sensations and situations, and making them actual once more by a mere effort of the will, had been brushed away.

And he never recovered the full use of that most precious faculty, the boon of youth and happy childhood, and which he had once possessed, without knowing it, in such singular and exceptional completeness. He was to lose other previous faculties of his over-rich and complex nature – to be pruned and clipped and thinned – that his one supreme faculty of painting might have elbow-room to reach its fullest, or else you could never have seen the wood for the trees (or *vice versa* – which is it?).

On New Year's Day* Taffy and the Laird were at their work in the studio, when there was a knock at the door, and Monsieur Vinard, cap in hand, respectfully introduced a pair of visitors, an English lady and gentleman.

The gentleman was a clergyman, small, thin, round-shouldered, with a long neck; weak-eyed and dryly polite. The lady was middle-aged, though still young-looking; very pretty, with gray hair; very well dressed; very small, full of nervous energy, with tiny hands and feet. It was Little Billee's mother; and the clergyman, the Rev. Thomas Bagot, was her brother-in-law.

Their faces were full of trouble – so much so that the two painters did not even apologise for the carelessness of their attire, or for the odour of tobacco that filled the room. Little Billee's mother recognised the two painters at a glance, from the sketches and descriptions of which her son's letters were always full.

They all sat down.

After a moment's embarrassed silence, Mrs Bagot exclaimed, addressing Taffy: 'Mr Wynne, we are in terrible distress of mind. I don't know if my son has told you, but on Christmas day he engaged himself to be married!'

'To – be – *married!*' exclaimed Taffy and the Laird, for whom this was news indeed.

'Yes – to be married to a Miss Trilby O'Ferrall, who from what he implies, is in quite a different position in life from himself. Do you know the lady, Mr Wynne?'

'Oh yes! I know her very well indeed; we *all* know her.'

'Is she English?'

'She's an English subject, I believe.'

'Is she a Protestant or a Roman Catholic?' inquired the clergyman.

'A – a – upon my word. I really don't know!'

'You know her very well indeed, and you *don't – know – that*, Mr Wynne!' exclaimed Mr Bagot.

'Is she a *lady*, Mr Wynne?' asked Mrs Bagot, somewhat impatiently, as if that were a much more important matter.

By this time the Laird had managed to basely desert his friend;

'Is she a lady, My Wynne?'

had got himself into his bedroom, and from thence, by another
door, into the street and away.

'A lady?' said Taffy; 'a – it so much depends upon what that
word exactly means, you know; things are so – a – so different
here. Her father was a gentleman, I believe – a Fellow of Trinity,
Cambridge – and a clergyman, if *that* means anything! ... he
was unfortunate and all that – a – intemperate, I fear, and not
successful in life. He has been dead six or seven years.'

'And her mother?'

'I really know very little about her mother, except that she
was very handsome, I believe, and of inferior social rank to her
husband. She's also dead; she died soon after him.'

'What is the young lady, then? An English governess, or
something of that sort?'

'Oh no, no – a – nothing of *that* sort,' said Taffy (and inwardly, 'You coward – you cad of a Scotch thief of a sneak of a Laird – to leave all this to me!').

'What? Has she independent means of her own, then?'

'A – not that I know of; I should even say, decidedly not!'

'What *is* she, then? She's at least respectable, I hope?'

'At present she's a – a *blanchisseuse de fin* – that is considered respectable here.'

'Why, that's a washerwoman, isn't it?'

'Well – rather better than that, perhaps – *de fin*, you know! – things are so different in Paris! I don't think you'd say she was very much like a washerwoman – to look at!'

'Is she so good-looking, then?'

'Oh yes; extremely so. You may well say that – very beautiful, indeed – about that, at least, there is no doubt whatever!'

'And of unblemished character?'

Taffy, red and perspiring as if he were going through his Indian-club exercise, was silent – and his face expressed a miserable perplexity. But nothing could equal the anxious misery of those two maternal eyes, so wistfully fixed on his.

After some seconds of a most painful stillness, the lady said, 'Can't you – oh, *can't* you give me an answer, Mr Wynne?'

'Oh, Mrs Bagot, you have placed me in a terrible position! I – I love your son just as if he were my own brother! This engagement is a complete surprise to me – a most painful surprise! I'd thought of many possible things, but never of *that*! I cannot – I really *must* not conceal from you that it would be an unfortunate marriage for your son – from a – a worldly point of view, you know – although both I and M'Allister have a very deep and warm regard for poor Trilby O'Ferrall – indeed, a great admiration and affection and respect. She was once a model.'

'A *model*, Mr Wynne? What *sort* of a model – there are models and models, of course.'

'Well, a model of every sort, in every possible sense of the word – head, hands, feet, everything!'

'A model for the *figure?*'

'Well – yes!'

'Oh, my God! my God! my God!' cried Mrs Bagot – and she got up and walked up and down the studio in a most terrible state of agitation, her brother-in-law following her and begging her to control herself. Her exclamations seemed to shock him, and she didn't seem to care.

'Oh! Mr Wynne! Mr Wynne! If you only *knew* what my son is to me – to all of us – always has been! He has been with us all his life, till he came to this wicked, accursed city! My poor husband would never hear of his going to any school, for fear of all the harm he might learn there. My son was as innocent and pure-minded as any girl, Mr Wynne – I could have trusted him anywhere – and that's why I gave way and allowed him to come *here*, of all places in the world – all alone. Oh! I should have come with him! Fool – fool – fool that I was! . . .

'Oh, Mr Wynne, he won't see either his mother or his uncle! I found a letter from him at the hotel, saying he'd left Paris – and I don't even know where he's gone! . . . Can't *you*, can't Mr M'Allister do *anything* to avert this miserable disaster? You don't know how he loves you both – you should see his letters to me and to his sister! they are always full of you!'

'Indeed, Mrs Bagot – you can count on M'Allister and me for doing everything in our power! But it is of no use our trying to influence you son – I feel quite sure of *that!* It is to *her* we must make our appeal.'

'Oh, Mr Wynne! to a washerwoman – a figure model – and Heaven knows what besides! and with such a chance as this!'

'Mrs Bagot, you don't know her! She may have been all that. But strange as it may seem to you – and seems to me, for that matter – she's a – she's – upon my word of honour, I really think she's about the best woman I ever met – the most unselfish – the most—'

'Ah! She's a *beautiful* woman – I can well see *that!*'

'She has a beautiful nature, Mrs Bagot – you may believe me or not as you like – and it is to that I shall make my appeal, as your son's friend, who has his interests at heart. And let me tell you that deeply as I grieve for you in your present distress, my grief and concern for her are far greater!'

'What! grief for her if she marries my son!'

'No, indeed – but if she refuses to marry him. She may not do so, of course – but my instinct tells me she will!'

'Oh! Mr Wynne, is that likely?'

'I will do my best to make it so – with such an utter trust in her unselfish goodness of heart and her passionate affection for your son as—'

'How do you know she has all this passionate affection for him?'

'Oh, M'Allister and I have long guessed it – though we never thought this particular thing would come of it. I think, perhaps, that first of all you ought to see her yourself – you would get quite a new idea of what she really is – you would be surprised, I assure you!

Mrs Bagot shrugged her shoulders impatiently, and there was silence for a minute or two.

And then, just as in a play, Trilby's 'Milk below!' was sounded at the door, and Trilby came into the little antechamber, and seeing strangers, was about to turn back. She was dressed as a grisette, in her Sunday gown and pretty white cap (for it was New Year's Day), looking her very best.

Taffy called out, 'Come in, Trilby!'

And Trilby came into the studio.

As soon as she saw Mrs Bagot's face she stopped short – erect, her shoulders a little high, her mouth a little open, her eyes wide with fright – and pale to the lips – a pathetic, yet commanding, magnificent, and most distinguished apparition, in spite of her humble attire.

The little lady got up and walked straight to her, and looked up into her face, that seemed to tower so. Trilby breathed hard.

At length Mrs Bagot said, in her high accents, 'You are Miss Trilby O'Farrell?'

'Oh yes – yes – I am Trilby O'Ferrall, and you are Mrs Bagot; I can see that!'

A new tone had come into her large, deep, soft voice, so tragic, so touching, so strangely in accord with her whole aspect just then – so strangely in accord with the whole situation – that Taffy felt his cheeks and lips turn cold, and his big spine thrill and tickle all down his back.

'Oh yes; you are very, very beautiful – there's no doubt about *that!* You wish to marry my son?'

'I've refused to marry him nineteen times – for his own sake; he will tell you so himself. I am not the right person for him to marry. I know that. On Christmas night he asked me for the twentieth time; he swore he would leave Paris next day for ever if I refused him. I hadn't the courage. I was weak, you see! It was a dreadful mistake.'

'Are you so fond of him?'

'Fond of him? Aren't You?'

'*Fond* of him? Aren't *you*?'

'I'm his mother, my good girl!'

To this Trilby seemed to have nothing to say.

'You have just said yourself you are not a fit wife for him. If you are so *fond* of him, will you ruin him by marrying him; drag him down; prevent him from getting on in life; separate him from his sister, his family, his friends?'

Trilby turned her miserable eyes to Taffy's miserable face, and said, 'Will it really be all that, Taffy?'

'Oh, Trilby, things have got all wrong, and can't be righted! I'm afraid it might be so. Dear Trilby – I can't tell you what I feel – but I can't tell you lies, you know!'

'Oh no – Taffy – you don't tell lies!'

Then Trilby began to tremble very much, and Taffy tried to

make her sit down, but she wouldn't. Mrs Bagot looked up into her face, herself breathless with keen suspense and cruel anxiety – almost imploring.

Trilby looked down at Mrs Bagot very kindly, put out her shaking hand, and said: 'Good-bye, Mrs Bagot. I will not marry your son. I *promise* you. I will never see him again.'

Mrs Bagot caught and clasped her hand and tried to kiss it, and said: 'Don't go yet, my dear good girl. I want to talk to you. I want to tell you how deeply I—'

'Good-bye, Mrs Bagot,' said Trilby, once more; and disengaging her hand, she walked swiftly out of the room.

Mrs Bagot seemed stupefied, and only half content with her quick triumph.

'She will not marry your son, Mrs Bagot. I only wish to God she'd marry *me!*'

'Oh, Mr Wynne!' said Mrs Bagot, and burst into tears.

'Ah!' exclaimed the clergyman, with a feebly satirical smile and a little cough and sniff that were not sympathetic, 'now if *that* could be arranged – and I've no doubt there wouldn't be much opposition on the part of the lady' (here he made a little complimentary bow), 'it would be a very desirable thing all round!'

'It's tremendously good of you, I'm sure – to interest yourself in *my* humble affairs,' said Taffy. 'Look here, sir – I'm not a great genius like your nephew – and it doesn't much matter to any one but myself what I make of my life – but I can assure you that if Trilby's heart were set on me as it is on him, I would gladly cast in my lot with hers for life. She's one in a thousand. She's the one sinner that repenteth, you know?'

'Ah, yes – to be sure! – to be sure! I know all about that; still, facts are facts, and the world is the world, and we've got to live in it,' said Mr Bagot, whose satirical smile had died away under the gleam of Taffy's choleric blue eye.

Then said the good Taffy, frowning down on the parson (who looked mean and foolish, as people can sometimes do even with right on their side): 'And now, Mr Bagot – I can't tell you how very keenly I have suffered during this – a – this most painful interview – on account of my very deep regard for Trilby O'Ferrall. I congratulate you and your sister-in-law on its complete success. I also feel very deeply for your nephew. I'm not sure that he has not lost more than he will gain by – a – by the – a – the success of this – a – this interview, in short!'

Taffy's eloquence was exhausted, and his quick temper was getting the better of him.

Then Mrs Bagot, drying her eyes, came and took his hand in a very charming and simple manner, and said: 'Mr Wynne, I think I know what you are feeling just now. You must try and make some allowance for us. You will, I am sure, when we are gone, and you have had time to think a little. As for that noble and beautiful girl, I only wish that she were such that my son *could* marry her – in her past life, I mean. It is not her humble rank that would frighten me; *pray* believe that I am quite sincere in this – and don't think too hardly of your friend's mother. Think of all I shall have to go through with my poor son – who is deeply in love – and no wonder! and who has won the love of such a woman as that! and who cannot see at present how fatal to him such a marriage would be. I can see all the charm and believe in all the goodness, in spite of all. And, oh, how beautiful she is, and what a voice! All that counts for so much, doesn't it? I cannot tell you how I grieve for her. I can make no amends – who could, for such a thing? There are no amends, and I shall not even try. I will only write and tell her all I think and feel. You will forgive us, won't you?'

And in the quick, impulsive warmth and grace and sincerity of her manner as she said all this, Mrs Bagot was so absurdly like Little Billee that it touched big Taffy's heart, and he would have forgiven anything, and there was nothing to forgive.

'Oh, Mrs Bagot, there's no question of forgiveness. Good heavens! it is all so unfortunate, you know! Nobody's to blame, that I can see. Good-bye, Mrs Bagot; good-bye, sir,' and so saying, he saw them down to their *remise*,* in which sat a singularly pretty young lady of seventeen or so, pale and anxious, and so like Little Billee that it was quite funny, and touched big Taffy's heart again.

When Trilby went out into the courtyard in the Place St Anatole des Arts, she saw Miss Bagot looking out of the carriage window, and in the young lady's face, as she caught her eye, an expression of sweet surprise and sympathetic admiration, with lifted eyebrows and parted lips – just such a look as she had often got from Little Billee! She knew her for his sister at once. It was a sharp pang.

She turned away, saying to herself: 'Oh no; I will not separate him from his sister, his family, his friends! That would *never* do! *That's* settled, anyhow!'

Feeling a little dazed, and wishing to think, she turned up the Rue Vieille des Mauvais Ladres, which was always deserted at this hour. It was empty, but for a solitary figure sitting on a post, with its legs dangling, its hands in its trousers-pockets, an inverted pipe in its mouth, a tattered straw hat on the back of its head, and a long gray coat down to its heels. It was the Laird.

As soon as he saw her he jumped off his post and came to her, saying: 'Oh, Trilby – what's it all about? I couldn't stand it! I ran away! Little Billee's mother's there!'

'Yes, Sandy dear, I've just seen her.'

'Well, what's up?'

'I've promised her never to see Little Billee any more. I was foolish enough to promise to marry him. I refused many times these last three months, and then he said he'd leave Paris and never come back, and so, like a fool, I gave way. I've offered to live with him and take care of him and be his servant – to be everything he wished but his wife! But he wouldn't hear of it. Dear, dear Little Billee! he's an angel – and I'll take precious good care no harm shall ever come to him through me! I shall leave this hateful place and go and live in the country: I suppose I must manage to get through life somehow . . . Days are so long – *aren't* they! and there's *such* a lot of 'em! I know of some poor people who were once very fond of me, and I could live with them and help them and keep myself. The difficulty is about Jeannot. I thought it all out before it came to this. I was well prepared, you see.'

She smiled in a forlorn sort of way, with her upper lip drawn tight against her teeth, as if some one were pulling her back by the lobes of her ears.

'Oh! but Trilby – what shall we do without you? Taffy and I, you know! You've become one of us!'

'Now, how good and kind of you to say that!' exclaimed poor Trilby, her eyes filling. 'Why, that's just all I lived for, till all this happened. But it can't be any more now, can it? Everything is changed for me – the very sky seems different. Ah! Durien's little song – "*Plaisir d'amour – chagrin d'amour!*" it's all quite

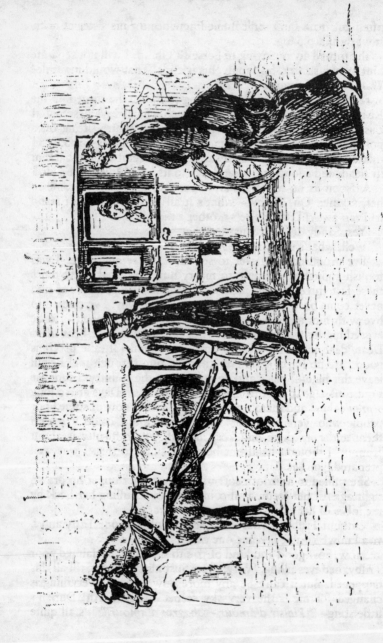

So like Little Billee

true, isn't it. I shall start immediately, and take Jeannot with me, I think.'

'But where do you think of going?'

'Ah! I mayn't tell you that, Sandy dear – not for a long time! Think of all the trouble there'd be. Well, there's no time to be lost. I must take the bull by the horns.'

She tried to laugh, and took him by his big side whiskers and kissed him on the eyes and mouth, and her tears fell on his face.

Then, feeling unable to speak, she nodded farewell, and walked quickly up the narrow winding street. When she came to the first bend she turned round and waved her hand, and kissed it two or three times, and then disappeared.

The Laird stared for several minutes up the empty thorough-fare – wretched, full of sorrow and compassion. Then he filled himself another pipe and lit it, and hitched himself on to another post, and sat there dangling his legs and kicking his heels, and waited for the Bagots' cab to depart, that he might go up and face the righteous wrath of Taffy like a man, and bear up against his bitter reproaches for cowardice and desertion before the foe.

Next morning Taffy received two letters: one, a very long one, was from Mrs Bagot. He read it twice over, and was forced to acknowledge that it was a very good letter – the letter of a clever, warm-hearted woman, but a woman also whose son was to her as the very apple of her eye. One felt she was ready to flay her dearest friend alive in order to make Little Billee a pair of gloves out of the skin, if he wanted a pair; but one also felt she would be genuinely sorry for the friend. Taffy's own mother had been a little like that, and he missed her every day of his life.

Full justice was done by Mrs Bagot to all Trilby's qualities of head and heart and person; but at the same time she pointed out, with all the cunning and ingeniously casuistic logic of her sex, when it takes to special pleading (even when it has right on its side), what the consequences of such a marriage must inevitably be in a few years – even sooner! The quick disenchant-ment, the lifelong regret,* on both sides!

He could not have found a word to controvert her arguments, save perhaps in his own private belief that Trilby and Little Billee were both exceptional people; and how could he hope to know Little Billee's nature better than the boy's own mother!

'I must take the Bull by the horns'

And if he had been the boy's elder brother in blood, as he already was in heart and affection, would he, should he, could he have given his fraternal sanction to such a match?

Both as his friend and his brother he felt it was out of the question.

The other letter was from Trilby, in her bold, careless handwriting, that sprawled all over the page, and her occasionally imperfect spelling. It ran thus: –

My dear, dear, Taffy – This is to say good-bye. I'm going away, to put an end to all this misery, for which nobody's to blame but myself.

The very moment after I'd said *yes* to Little Billee I knew perfectly well what a stupid fool I was, and I've been ashamed of myself ever since. I had a miserable week, I can tell you. I knew how it would all turn out.

I am dreadfully unhappy, but not half so unhappy as if I married him and he were ever to regret it and be ashamed of me; and of course he would, really, even if he didn't show it – good and kind as he is – an angel!

Besides – of course I could never be a lady – how could I? though I ought to have been one, I suppose. But everything seems to have gone wrong with me, though I never found it out before – and it can't be righted!

Poor papa!

I'm going away with Jeannot. I've been neglecting him shamefully. I mean to make up for it all now.

You mustn't try and find out where I am going; I know you won't if I beg you, nor any one else. It would make everything so much harder for me.

Angèle knows; she has promised me not to tell. I should like to have a line from you very much. If you send it to her she will send it on to me.

Dear Taffy, next to Little Billee, I love you and the Laird better than any one else in the whole world. I've never known real happiness till I met you. You have changed me into another person – you and Sandy and Little Billee.

Oh, it *has* been a jolly time, though it didn't last long. It will have to do for me for life. So good-bye. I shall never, never forget; and remain, with dearest love, your ever faithful and most affectionate friend,

Trilby O'Ferrall.

'P.S. – When it has all blown over and settled again, if it ever does, I shall come back to Paris, perhaps, and see you again some day.'

The good Taffy pondered deeply over this letter – read it half a dozen times at least; and then he kissed it, and put it back into its envelope and locked it up.

He knew what very deep anguish underlay this somewhat trivial expression of her sorrow.

He guessed how Trilby, so childishly impulsive and demonstrative in the ordinary intercourse of friendship, would be more reticent than most women in such a case as this.

He wrote to her warmly, affectionately, at great length, and sent the letter as she had told him.

The Laird also wrote a long letter full of tenderly-worded friendship and sincere regard. Both expressed their hope and belief that they would soon see her again, when the first bitterness of her grief would be over, and that the old pleasant relations would be renewed.

And then, feeling wretched, they went and silently lunched together at the Café de l'Odéon, where the omelets were good and the wine wasn't blue.

Late that evening they sat together in the studio, reading. They found they could not talk to each other very readily without Little Billee to listen – three's company sometimes and two's none!

Suddenly there was a tremendous getting up the dark stairs outside in a violent hurry, and Little Billee burst into the room like a small whirlwind – haggard, out of breath, almost speechless at first with excitement.

'Trilby! where is she? . . . what's become of her? . . . She's run away . . . oh! She's written me such a letter! . . . We were to have been married . . . at the Embassy . . . my mother . . . she's been meddling; and that cursed old ass . . . that beast . . . my uncle! . . . They've been here! I know all about it . . . Why didn't you stick up for her? . . .'

'I did . . . as well as I could. Sandy couldn't stand it, and cut.'

'*You* stuck up for her . . . *you* – why, you agreed with my mother that she oughtn't to marry me – you – you false friend –

'Trilby! Where is she?'

you! ... Why, she's an angel – far too good for the likes of *me*
... you know she is. As ... as for her social position and all
that, what degrading rot! Her father was as much a gentleman
as mine ... besides ... what the devil do I care for her father?
... it's *her* I want – *her* – *her* – *her*, I tell you ... I can't *live*
without her ... I must have her *back* – I must have her *back* ...
do you *hear*? We were to have lived together at Barbizon ... all
our lives – and I was to have painted stunning pictures ... like
those other fellows there. Who cares for their *social* position, I
should like to know ... or that of their wives? *Damn* social
position! ... we've often said so – over and over again. An
artist's life should be *away* from the world above all that
meanness and paltriness ... all in his work. Social position,

indeed! Over and over again we've said what fetid, bestial rot it all was – a thing to make one sick and shut one's self away from the world ... Why say one thing and act another? ... Love comes before all – love levels all – love and art ... and beauty – before such beauty as Trilby's rank doesn't exist. Such rank as mine, too! Good God! I'll never paint another stroke till I've got her back ... never, never, never, I tell you – I can't – I won't ...'

And so the poor boy went on, tearing and raving about in his rampage, knocking over chairs and easels, stammering and shrieking, mad with excitement.

They tried to reason with him, to make him listen, to point out that it was not her social position alone that unfitted her to be his wife and the mother of his children, etc.

It was no good. He grew more and more uncontrollable, became almost unintelligible, he stammered so – a pitiable sight and pitiable to hear.

'Oh! oh! good heavens! are you so precious immaculate, you two, that you should throw stones* at poor Trilby! What a shame, what a hideous shame it is that there should be one law for the woman and another for the man! ... poor weak women – poor, soft, affectionate things that beasts of men are always running after, and pestering, and ruining, and trampling under-foot ... Oh! oh! it makes me sick – it makes me sick!' And finally he gasped and screamed and fell down in a fit on the floor.

The doctor was sent for; Taffy went in a cab to the Hôtel de Lille et d'Albion to fetch his mother; and poor Little Billee, quite unconscious, was undressed by Sandy and Madame Vinard and put into the Laird's bed.

The doctor came, and not long after Mrs Bagot and her daughter. It was a serious case. Another doctor was called in. Beds were got and made up in the studio for the two grief-stricken ladies, and thus closed the eve of what was to have been poor Little Billee's wedding-day, it seems.

Little Billee's attack appears to have been a kind of epileptic seizure. It ended in brain fever and other complications – a long and tedious illness. It was many weeks before he was out of danger, and his convalescence was long and tedious too.

His nature seemed changed. He lay languid and listless – never even mentioned Trilby, except once to ask if she had come

La soeur de Litrebili

back, and if any one knew where she was, and if she had been
written to.

She had not, it appears. Mrs Bagot had thought it was better
not, and Taffy and the Laird agreed with her that no good could
come of writing.

Mrs Bagot felt bitterly against the woman who had been the
cause of all this trouble, and bitterly against herself for her
injustice. It was an unhappy time for everybody.

There was more unhappiness still to come.

One day in February Madame Angèle Boisse called on Taffy
and the Laird in the temporary studio where they worked. She
was in terrible tribulation.

Trilby's little brother had died of scarlet fever and was buried,
and Trilby had left her hiding-place the day after the funeral
and had never come back, and this was a week ago. She and

He fell a-weeping, quite desperately

Jeannot had been living at a village called Vibraye,* in La Sarthe,* lodging with some poor people she knew – she washing and working with her needle till her brother fell ill.

She had never left his bedside for a moment, night or day, and when he died her grief was so terrible that people thought she would go out of her mind; and the day after he was buried she was not to be found anywhere – she had disappeared, taking nothing with her, not even her clothes – simply vanished and left no sign, no message of any kind.

All the ponds had been searched – all the wells, and the small stream that flows through Vibraye – and the old forest.

Taffy went to Vibraye, cross-examined everybody he could, communicated with the Paris police, but with no result; and every afternoon, with a beating heart, he went to the Morgue . . .

The news was of course kept from Little Billee. There was no difficulty about this. He never asked a question, hardly ever spoke.

When he first got up and was carried into the studio he asked for his picture 'The Pitcher Goes to the Well,'* and looked at it for a while, and then shrugged his shoulders and laughed – a miserable sort of laugh, painful to hear and see – the laugh of a cold old man, who laughs so as not to cry! Then he looked at his mother and sister, and saw the sad havoc that grief and anxiety had wrought in them.

It seemed to him, as in a bad dream, that he had been mad for many years – a cause of endless sickening terror and distress; and that his poor weak wandering wits had come back at last, bringing in their train cruel remorse, and the remembrance of all the patient love and kindness that had been lavished on him; for many, many years! His sweet sister – his dear, long-suffering mother! what had really happened to make them look like this?

And taking them both in his feeble arms, he fell a-weeping, quite desperately and for a long time.

And when his weeping-fit was over, when he had quite wept himself out, he fell asleep.

And when he awoke he was conscious that another sad thing had happened to him, and that for some mysterious cause his power of loving had not come back with his wandering wits – had been left behind – and it seemed to him that it was gone for ever and ever – would never come back again – not even his

love for his mother and sister, not even his love for Trilby –
where all *that* had once been was a void, a gap, a blankness . . .

Truly, if Trilby had suffered much, she had also been the
innocent cause of terrible suffering. Poor Mrs Bagot, in her
heart, could not forgive her.

I feel this is getting to be quite a sad story, and that it is high
time to cut this part of it short.

As the warmer weather came, and Little Billee got stronger,
the studio became more lively. The ladies' beds were removed
to another studio on the next landing, which was vacant, and
the friends came to see Little Billee, and make life more easy for
him and his mother and sister.

As for Taffy and the Laird, they had already long been to Mrs
Bagot as a pair of crutches, without whose invaluable help she
could never have held herself upright to pick her way in all this
maze of trouble.

Then M. Carrel came every day to chat with his favourite
pupil and gladden Mrs Bagot's heart. And also Durien, Carnegie, Petrolicoconose, Vincent, Antony, Lorrimer, Dodor, and
l'Zouzou; Mrs Bagot thought the last two irresistible, when she
had once been satisfied that they were 'gentlemen,' in spite of
appearances. And, indeed, they showed themselves to great
advantage; and though they were so much the opposite to Little
Billee in everything, she felt almost maternal towards them, and
gave them innocent, good, motherly advice, which they swallowed *avec attendrissement,* not even stealing a look at each
other. And they held Mrs Bagot's wool, and listened to Miss
Bagot's sacred music with upturned pious eyes, and mealy
mouths that butter wouldn't melt in!

It is good to be a soldier and a detrimental; you touch the
hearts of women and charm them – old and young, high or low
(excepting, perhaps, a few wordly mothers of marriageable
daughters). They take the sticking of your tongue in the cheek
for the wearing of your heart on the sleeve.

Indeed, good women all over the world, and ever since it
began, have loved to be bamboozled by these genial, roistering
dare-devils, who haven't got a penny to bless themselves with
(which is so touching), and are supposed to carry their lives in
their hands, even in piping times of peace.* Nay, even a few
rare *bad* women sometimes; such women as the best and wisest
of us are often ready to sell our souls for!

> A lightsome eye, a soldier's mien,
>   A feather of the blue,
> A doublet of the Lincoln green –
>   No more of me you knew,
>   My love!
>   No more of me you knew . . .*

As if that wasn't enough, and to spare!

Little Billee could hardly realise that these two polite and gentle and sympathetic sons of Mars* were the lively grigs* who had made themselves so pleasant all round, and in such a singular manner, on the top of that St Cloud omnibus; and he admired how they added hypocrisy to their other crimes!

Svengali had gone back to Germany, it seemed, with his pockets full of napoleons* and big Havana cigars, and wrapped in an immense fur-lined coat, which he meant to wear all through the summer. But little Gecko often came with his violin and made lovely music, and that seemed to do Little Billee more good than anything else.

It made him realise in his brain all the love he could no longer feel in his heart. The sweet melodic phrase, rendered by a master, was as wholesome, refreshing balm to him while it lasted – as manna in the wilderness. It was the one good thing within his reach, never to be taken from him as long as his ear-drums remained and he could hear a master play.

Poor Gecko treated the two English ladies *de bas en haut** as if they had been goddesses, even when they accompanied him on the piano! He begged their pardon for every wrong note they struck, and adopted their 'tempi'* – that is the proper technical term, I believe – and turned scherzos and allegrettos into funeral dirges to please them; and agreed with them, poor little traitor, that it all sounded much better like that!

O Beethoven! O Mozart! did you turn in your graves?

Then, on fine afternoons, Little Billee was taken for drives to the Bois de Boulogne* with his mother and sister in an open fly, and generally Taffy as a fourth; to Passy, Auteuil, Boulogne, St Cloud, Meudon – there are many charming places within an easy drive of Paris.

And sometimes Taffy or the Laird would escort Mrs and Miss Bagot to the Luxembourg Gallery,* the Louvre, the Palais Royal; to the Comédie Française once or twice; and on Sundays, now and then, to the English chapel in the Rue Marbœuf. It was

The sweet, melodic phrase

all very pleasant; and Miss Bagot looks back on the days of her brother's convalescence as among the happiest in her life.

And they would all five dine together in the studio, with Madame Vinard to wait, and her mother (a cordon bleu)* for cook; and the whole aspect of the place was changed and made fragrant, sweet, and charming by all this new feminine invasion and occupation.

And what is sweeter to watch than the dawn and growth of love's young dream, when strength and beauty meet together by the couch of a beloved invalid?

Of course the sympathetic reader will foresee how readily the stalwart Taffy fell a victim to the charms of his friend's sweet sister, and how she grew to return his more than brotherly regard! and how, one lovely evening, just as March was going out like a lamb (to make room for the first of April), Little Billee joined their hands together, and gave them his brotherly blessing!

As a matter of fact, however, nothing of this kind happened. Nothing ever happens but the *un*foreseen. Pazienza!*

Then at length one day – it was a fine, sunny, showery day in April, by the bye, and the big studio window was open at the top and let in a pleasant breeze from the north-west, just as when our little story began – a railway omnibus drew up at the porte cochère* in the Place St Anatole des Arts, and carried away to the station of the Chemin de Fer du Nord Little Billee and his mother and sister, and all their belongings (the famous picture had gone before); and Taffy and the Laird rode with them, their faces very long, to see the last of the dear people, and of the train that was to bear them away from Paris; and Little Billee, with his quick, prehensile, æsthetic eye, took many a long and wistful parting gaze at many a French thing he loved, from the gray towers of Notre Dame downward – Heaven only knew when he might see them again! – so he tried to get their aspect well by heart, that he might have the better store of beloved shape and colour memories to chew the cud of when his lost powers of loving and remembering clearly should come back, and he lay awake at night and listened to the wash of the Atlantic along the beautiful red sandstone coast at home.

He had a faint hope that he should feel sorry at parting with Taffy and the Laird.

But when the time came for saying good-bye he couldn't feel sorry in the least, for all he tried and strained so hard!

So he thanked them so earnestly and profusely for all their kindness and patience and sympathy (as did also his mother and sister) that their hearts were too full to speak, and their manner was quite gruff – it was a way they had when they were deeply moved and didn't want to show it.

And as he gazed out of the carriage window at their two forlorn figures looking after him when the train steamed out of the station, his sorrow at not feeling sorry made him look so haggard and so woe-begone that they could scarcely bear the sight of him departing without them, and almost felt as if they must follow by the next train, and go and cheer him up in Devonshire, and themselves too.

They did not yield to this amiable weakness. Sorrowfully, arm-in-arm, with trailing umbrellas, they recrossed the river, and found their way to the Café de l'Odéon, where they ate many omelets in silence, and dejectedly drank of the best they could get, and were very sad indeed.

Nearly five years have elapsed since we bade farewell and *au revoir* to Taffy and the Laird at the Paris station of the Chemin de Fer du Nord, and wished Little Billee and his mother and sister Godspeed on their way to Devonshire, where the poor sufferer was to rest and lie fallow for a few months, and recruit his lost strength and energy, that he might follow up his first and well-deserved success, which perhaps contributed just a little to his recovery.

Many of my readers will remember his splendid *début* at the Royal Academy in Trafalgar Square* with that now so famous canvas 'The Pitcher Goes to the Well,' and how it was sold three times over on the morning of the private view, the third time for a thousand pounds – just five times what he got for it himself. And that was thought a large sum in those days for a beginner's picture two feet by four.

I am well aware that such a vulgar test is no criterion whatever of a picture's real merit. But this picture is well known to all the world by this time, and sold only last year at Christie's (more than thirty-six years after it was painted) for three thousand pounds.

Sorrowfully, arm-in-arm

Thirty-six years! That goes a long way to redeem even three thousand pounds of all their cumulative vulgarity.

'The Pitcher' is now in the National Gallery,* with that other canvas by the same hand, 'The Moon-Dial.' There they hang together for all who care to see them, his first and his last – the blossom and the fruit.

He had not long to live himself, and it was his good fortune, so rare among those whose work is probably destined to live for ever, that he succeeded at his first go off.

And his success was of the best and most flattering kind.

It began high up, where it should, among the masters of his own craft. But his fame filtered quickly down to those immediately beneath, and through these to wider circles. And there was quite enough of opposition and vilification and coarse abuse of him to clear it of any suspicion of cheapness or evanescence. What better antiseptic can there be than the philistine's deep hate? what sweeter, fresher, wholesomer music than the sound of his voice when he doth so furiously rage?

Yes! That is 'good production' – as Svengali would have said – 'C'est un cri du cœur.'

And then, when popular acclaim brings the great dealers and the big cheques, up rises the printed howl of the duffer, the disappointed one, the 'wounded thing with an angry cry'* – the prosperous and happy bagman that *should* have been, who has given up all for art, and finds he can't paint and make himself a name, after all, and never will, so falls to writing about those who can – and what writing!

To write in hissing dispraise of our more successful fellow-craftsman, and of those who admire him – that is not a clean or pretty trade. It seems, alas! an easy one, and it gives pleasure to so many. It does not even want good grammar. But it pays – well enough even to start and run a magazine with, instead of scholarship, and taste, and talent! humour, sense, wit, and wisdom! It is something like the purveying of pornographic pictures: some of us look at them and laugh, and even buy. To be a purchaser is bad enough; but to be the purveyor thereof – ugh!

A poor devil of a cracked soprano (are there such people still?) who has been turned out of the Pope's choir* because he can't sing in tune, *after all!* – think of him yelling and squeaking his treble rage at Santley – Sims Reeves – Lablache!*

Poor, lost, beardless nondescript! why not fly to other climes, where at least thou might'st hide from us thy woeful crack, and keep thy miserable secret to thyself! Are there no harems still left in Stamboul* for the likes of thee to sweep and clean, no women's beds to make and slops to empty, and doors and windows to bar – and tales to carry, and the pasha's* confidence and favour and protection to win? Even *that* is a better trade than pandering for hire to the basest instinct of all – the dirty pleasure we feel (some of us) in seeing mud and dead cats and rotten eggs flung at those we cannot but admire – and secretly envy!

All of which eloquence means that Little Billee was pitched into right and left, as well as overpraised. And it all rolled off him like water off a duck's back, both praise and blame.

It was a happy summer for Mrs Bagot, a sweet compensation for all the anguish of the winter that had gone before, with her two beloved children together under her wing, and all the world (for her) ringing with the praise of her boy, the apple of her eye, so providentially rescued from the very jaws of death, and from other dangers almost as terrible to her fiercely-jealous maternal heart.

And his affection for her *seemed* to grow with his returning health; but, alas! he was never again to be quite the same light-hearted, innocent, expansive lad he had been before that fatal year spent in Paris.

One chapter of his life was closed, never to be reopened, never to be spoken of again by him to her, by her to him. She could neither forgive nor forget. She could but be silent.

Otherwise he was pleasant and sweet to live with, and everything was done to make his life at home as sweet and pleasant as a loving mother could – as could a most charming sister – and others' sisters who were charming too, and much disposed to worship at the shrine of this young celebrity, who woke up one morning in their little village to find himself famous, and bore his blushing honours so meekly. And among them the vicar's daughter, his sister's friend and co-teacher at the Sunday-school, 'a simple, pure, and pious maiden of gentle birth,' everything he once thought a young lady should be; and her name it was Alice, and she was sweet,* and her hair was brown – as brown! . . .

And if he no longer found the simple country pleasures, the junketings and picnics, the garden-parties and innocent little musical evenings, quite so exciting as of old, he never showed it.

Indeed, there was much that he did not show, and that his mother and sister tried in vain to guess – many things.

And among them one thing that constantly preoccupied and distressed him – the numbness of his affections. He could be as easily demonstrative to his mother and sister as though nothing had ever happened to him – from the mere force of a sweet old habit – even more so, out of sheer gratitude and compunction.

But alas! he felt that in his heart he could no longer care for them in the least! – nor for Taffy, nor the Laird, nor for himself; not even for Trilby, of whom he constantly thought, but without emotion; and of whose strange disappearance he had been told, and the story had been confirmed in all its details by Angèle Boisse, to whom he had written.

It was as though some part of his brain where his affections were seated had been paralysed, while all the rest of it was as keen and as active as ever. He felt like some poor live bird or beast or reptile, a part of whose cerebrum (or cerebellum, or whatever it is) had been dug out by the vivisector for experimental purposes; and the strongest emotional feeling he seemed capable of was his anxiety and alarm about this curious symptom, and his concern as to whether he ought to mention it or not.

He did not do so, for fear of causing distress, hoping that it would pass away in time, and redoubled his caresses to his mother and sister, and clung to them more than ever; and became more considerate of others in thought and manner, word and deed, than he had ever been before, as though by constantly assuming the virtue he had no longer he would gradually coax it back again. There was no trouble he would not take to give pleasure to the humblest.

Also, his vanity about himself had become as nothing, and he missed it almost as much as his affection.

Yet he told himself over and over again that he was a great artist, and that he would spare no pains to make himself a greater. But that was no merit of his own.

$2 + 2 = 4$, also $2 \times 2 = 4$: that peculiarity was no reason why 4 should be conceited; for what was 4 but a result, either way?

Well, he was like 4 – just an inevitable result of circumstances over which he had no control – a mere product or sum; and though he meant to make himself as big a 4 as he could (to cultivate his peculiar *fourness*), he could no longer feel the old conceit and self-complacency; and they had been a joy, and it was hard to do without them.

At the bottom of it all was a vague, disquieting unhappiness, a constant fidget.

And it seemed to him, and much to his distress, that such mild unhappiness would be the greatest he could ever feel henceforward – but that, such as it was, it would never leave him, and that his moral existence would be for evermore one long gray gloomy blank – the glimmer of twilight – never glad, confident morning again!

So much for Little Billee's convalescence.

Then one day in the late autumn he spread his wings and flew away to London, which was very ready with open arms to welcome William Bagot, the already famous painter, *alias* Little Billee!

Part Fifth

Little Billee

An Interlude

Then the mortal coldness of the soul like death itself comes down;
It cannot feel for others' woes, it dare not dream its own;
That heavy chill has frozen o'er the fountain of our tears,
And, though the eye may sparkle yet, 'tis where the ice appears.

Though wit may flash from fluent lips, and mirth distract the breast,
Through midnight hours that yield no more their former hope of rest:
'Tis but as ivy leaves around a ruined turret wreathe,
All green and wildly fresh without, but worn and gray beneath.*

When Taffy and the Laird went back to the studio in the Place
St Anatole des Arts, and resumed their ordinary life there, it was
with a sense of desolation and dull bereavement beyond anything they could have imagined; and this did not seem to lessen
as the time wore on.

They realised for the first time how keen and penetrating and
unintermittent had been the charm of those two central figures
– Trilby and Little Billee – and how hard it was to live without
them, after such intimacy as had been theirs.

'Oh, it *has* been a jolly time, though it didn't last long!' So
Trilby had written in her farewell letter to Taffy; and these
words were true for Taffy and the Laird as well as for her.

And that is the worst of those dear people who have charm:
they are so terrible to do without, when once you have got
accustomed to them and all their ways.

And when, besides being charming, they are simple, clever,
affectionate, constant, and sincere, like Trilby and Little Billee!
Then the lamentable hole their disappearance makes is not to be
filled up! And when they are full of genius, like Little Billee –
and like Trilby, funny without being vulgar! For so she always
seemed to the Laird and Taffy, even in French (in spite of her
Gallic audacities of thought, speech, and gesture).

All seemed to have suffered change. The very boxing and
fencing were gone through perfunctorily, for mere health's sake;

and a thin layer of adipose deposit began to soften the outlines of the hills and dales on Taffy's mighty forearm.

Dodor and l'Zouzou no longer came so often, now that the charming Little Billee and his charming mother and still more charming sister had gone away – nor Carnegie, nor Antony, nor Lorrimer, nor Vincent, nor the Greek. Gecko never came at all. Even Svengali was missed, little as he had been liked. It is a dismal and sulky-looking piece of furniture, a grand piano that nobody ever plays – with all its sound and its souvenirs locked up inside – a kind of mausoleum! a lop-sided coffin, trestles and all! So it went back to London by the 'little quickness,' just as it had come!

Thus Taffy and the Laird grew quite sad and mopy, and lunched at the Café de l'Odéon every day – till the goodness of the omelets palled, and the redness of the wine there got on their nerves and into their heads and faces, and made them sleepy till dinner-time. And then, waking up, they dressed respectably, and dined expensively, 'like gentlemen,' in the Palais Royal, or the Passage Choiseul, or the Passage des Panoramas* – for three francs, three francs fifty, even five francs a head, and half a franc to the waiter! – and went to the theatre almost every night, on that side of the water – and more often than not they took a cab home, each smoking a Panatella,* which costs twenty-five centimes – five sous – 2½d.!

Then they feebly drifted into quite decent society – like Lorrimer and Carnegie – with dress-coats and white ties on, and their hair parted in the middle and down the back of the head, and brought over the ears in a bunch at each side, as was the English fashion in those days; and subscribed to *Galignani's Messenger;** and had themselves proposed and seconded for the Cercle Anglais* in the Rue Sainte-n'y Touche,* a circle of British philistines of the very deepest dye; and went to hear divine service on Sunday mornings in Rue Marbœuf!

Indeed, by the end of the summer they had sunk into such depths of demoralisation that they felt they must really have a change; and decided on giving up the studio in the Place St Anatole des Arts, and leaving Paris for good; and going to settle for the winter in Düsseldorf, which is a very pleasant place for English painters who do not wish to overwork themselves – as the Laird well knew, having spent a year there.

It ended in Taffy's going to Antwerp* for the Kermesse,* to

Demoralisation

paint the Flemish drunkard of our time just as he really is; and
the Laird's going to Spain, so that he might study toreadors
from the life.

I may as well state here that the Laird's toreador pictures,
which had had quite a vogue in Scotland as long as he had been
content to paint them in the Place St Anatole des Arts, quite
ceased to please (or sell) after he had been to Seville and Madrid;
so he took to painting Roman cardinals and Neapolitan pifferari* from the depths of his consciousness – and was so successful
that he made up his mind he would never spoil his market by
going to Italy!

So he went and painted his cardinals and his pifferari in
Algiers, and Taffy joined him there, and painted Algerian Jews
– just as they really are (and didn't sell them); and then they
spent a year in Munich,* and then a year in Düsseldorf, and a
winter in Cairo, and so on.

And all this time, Taffy, who took everything *au grand
sérieux** – especially the claims and obligations of friendship –
corresponded regularly with Little Billee, who wrote him long
and amusing letters back again, and had plenty to say about his
life in London – which was a series of triumphs, artistic and
social – and you would have thought from his letters, modest
though they were, that no happier young man, or more elate,
was to be found anywhere in the world.

It was a good time in England, just then, for young artists of
promise; a time of evolution, revolution, change, and development – of the founding of new schools and the crumbling away
of old ones – a keen struggle for existence – a surviving of the
fit – a preparation, let us hope, for the ultimate survival of the
fittest.

And among the many glories of this particular period two
names stand out very conspicuously – for the immediate and (so
far) lasting fame their bearers achieved, and the wide influence
they exerted, and continue to exert still.

The world will not easily forget Frederic Walker and William
Bagot, those two singularly gifted boys, whom it soon became
the fashion to bracket together, to compare and to contrast, as
one compares and contrasts Thackeray and Dickens, Carlyle
and Macaulay, Tennyson and Browning – a futile though
pleasant practice, of which the temptations seem irresistible!

Yet why compare the lily and the rose?

Fred Walker

These two young masters had the genius and the luck to be the progenitors of much of the best art work that has been done in England during the last thirty years, in oils, in water colour, in black and white.

They were both essentially English and of their own time; both absolutely original, receiving their impressions straight from nature itself; uninfluenced by any school, ancient or modern, they founded schools instead of following any, and each was a law unto himself, and a law-giver unto many others. Both were equally great in whatever they attempted – landscape, figures, birds, beasts, or fishes. Who does not remember the fishmonger's shop,* by F. Walker, or W. Bagot's little piebald piglings, and their venerable black mother, and their immense fat wallowing pink papa? An ineffable charm of poetry and refinement, of pathos and sympathy and delicate humour combined, an incomparable ease and grace and felicity of workmanship belong to each; and yet in their work are they not as wide apart as the poles; each complete in himself and yet a complement to the other?

And, oddly enough, they were both singularly alike in aspect – both small and slight, though beautifully made, with tiny hands and feet; always arrayed as the lilies of the field, for all they toiled and spun so arduously; both had regularly-featured faces of a noble cast and most winning character; both had the best and simplest manners in the world, and a way of getting themselves much and quickly and permanently liked . . .

*Que la terre leur soit légère!**

And who can say that the fame of one is greater than the other's!

Their pinnacles are twin, I venture to believe – of just an equal height and width and thickness, like their bodies in this life; but unlike their frail bodies in one respect: no taller pinnacles are to be seen, methinks, in all the garden of the deathless dead painters of our time, and none more built to last!

But it is not with the art of Little Billee, nor with his fame as a painter, that we are chiefly concerned in this unpretending little tale, except in so far as they have some bearing on his character and his fate.

'I should like to know the detailed history of the Englishman's first love, and how he lost his innocence!'

'Ask him!'

'Ask him yourself!'

Thus Papelard and Bouchardy, on the morning of Little Billee's first appearance at Carrel's studio, in the Rue des Potirons St Michel.

And that is the question the present scribe is doing his little best to answer.

A good-looking, famous, well-bred, and well-dressed youth finds that London society opens its doors very readily; he hasn't long to knock; and it would be difficult to find a youth more fortunately situated, handsomer, more famous, better dressed or better bred, more seemingly happy and successful, with more attractive qualities and more condonable faults, than Little Billee, as Taffy and the Laird found him when they came to London after their four or five years in foreign parts – their Wanderjahr.*

He had a fine studio and a handsome suite of rooms in Fitzroy Square.* Beautiful specimens of his unfinished work, endless studies, hung on his studio walls. Everything else was as nice as it could be – the furniture, the bibelots, and bric-à-brac, the artistic foreign and Eastern knick-knacks and draperies and hangings and curtains and rugs – the semi-grand piano by Collard and Collard.*

That immortal canvas, the 'Moon-Dial' (just begun, and already commissioned by Moses Lyon, the famous picture-dealer), lay on his easel.

No man worked harder and with teeth more clinched than Little Billee when he was at work – none rested or played more discreetly when it was time to rest or play.

The glass on his mantelpiece was full of cards of invitation, reminders, pretty mauve and pink and lilac scented notes; nor were coronets wanting on many of these hospitable little missives. He had quite overcome his fancied aversion for bloated dukes and lords and the rest (we all do sooner or later, if things go well with us); especially for their wives and sisters and daughters and female cousins; even their mothers and aunts. In point of fact, and in spite of his tender years, he was in some danger (for his art) of developing into that type so adored by sympathetic women who haven't got much to do: the friend, the tame cat, the platonic lover (with many loves) – the squire of dames, the trusty one, of whom husbands and brothers have no fear! – the delicate, harmless dilettante of Eros* – the dainty shepherd who dwells 'dans le pays du tendre!'* – and stops there!

The woman flatters and the man confides – and there is no danger whatever, I'm told – and I'm glad!

One man loves his fiddle (or, alas! his neighbour's sometimes) for all the melodies he can wake from it – it is but a selfish love!

Another, who is no fiddler, may love a fiddle too; for its symmetry, its neatness, its colour – its delicate grainings, the lovely lines and curves of its back and front – for its own sake, so to speak. He may have a whole galleryful of fiddles to love in this innocent way – a harem! – and yet not know a single note of music, or even care to hear one. He will dust them and stroke them, and take them down and try to put them in tune – *pizzicato!* – and put them back again, and call them ever such sweet little pet exotic names: viol, viola, viola d'amore, viol di gamba, violino mio!* and breathe his little troubles into them, and they will give back inaudible little murmurs in sympathetic response, like a damp Æolian harp;* but he will never draw a bow across the strings, nor wake a single chord – or discord!

And who shall say he is not wise in his generation? It is but an old-fashioned philistine notion that fiddles were only made to be played on – the fiddles themselves are beginning to resent it; and rightly, I wot!

In this harmless fashion Little Billee was friends with more than one fine lady *de par le monde.**

Indeed, he had been reproached by his more bohemian brothers of the brush for being something of a tuft-hunter – most unjustly. But nothing gives such keen offence to our unsuccessful brother, bohemian or bourgeois, as our sudden intimacy with the so-called great, the little lords and ladies of this little world! Not even our fame and success, and all the joy and pride they bring us, are so hard to condone – so embittering, so humiliating, to the jealous fraternal heart.

Alas! poor humanity – that the mere countenance of our betters (if they *are* our betters!) should be thought so priceless a boon, so consummate an achievement, so crowning a glory, as all that!

> A dirty bit of orange-peel,
>   The stump of a cigar –
> Once trod on by a princely heel,
>   How beautiful they are!*

Little Billee was no tuft-hunter – he was the tuft-hunted, or had been. No one of his kind was ever more persistently, resolutely, hospitably harried than this young 'hare with many friends' by people of rank and fashion.

And at first he thought them most charming; as they so often are, these graceful, gracious, gay, good-natured stoics and barbarians, whose manners are as easy and simple as their morals – but how much better! – and who, at least, have this charm, that they can wallow in untold gold (when they happen to possess it) without ever seeming to stink of the same: yes, they bear wealth gracefully – and the want of it more gracefully still! and these are pretty accomplishments that have yet to be learned by our new aristocracy of the shop and counting-house, Jew or Gentile, which is everywhere elbowing its irresistible way to the top and front of everything, both here and abroad.

Then he discovered that, much as you might be with them,

Darlings, old or young

you could never be *of* them, unless perchance you managed to hook on by marrying one of their ugly ducklings – their failures – their remnants! and even then life isn't all beer and skittles for a rank outsider, I'm told! Then he discovered that he didn't want to be *of* them in the least; especially at such a cost as that! and that to be very much *with* them was apt to pall, like everything else!

Also, he found that they were very mixed – good, bad, and indifferent; and not always very dainty or select in their predilections, since they took unto their bosoms such queer outsiders (just for the sake of being amused a little while) that their capricious favour ceased to be an honour and a glory – if it ever was! And then, their fickleness!

Indeed, he found, or thought he found, that they could be just as clever, as liberal, as polite or refined – as narrow, insolent, swaggering, coarse, and vulgar – as handsome, as ugly – as graceful, as ungainly – as modest or conceited, as any other upper class of the community – and indeed some lower ones!

Beautiful young women, who had been taught how to paint pretty little landscapes (with an ivy-mantled ruin in the middle distance), talked technically of painting to him, *de pair à pair,** as though they were quite on the same artistic level, and didn't mind admitting it, in spite of the social gulf between.

Hideous old frumps (osseous* or obese, yet with unduly bared necks and shoulders that made him sick) patronised him and gave him good advice, and told him to emulate Mr Buckner both in his genius and his manners – since Mr Buckner was the only 'gentleman' who ever painted for hire; and they promised him, in time, an equal success!

Here and there some sweet old darling specially enslaved him by her kindness, grace, knowledge of life, and tender womanly sympathy, like the dowager Lady Chiselhurst – or some sweet young one, like the lovely Duchess of Towers,* by her beauty, wit, good-humour, and sisterly interest in all he did, and who in some vague, distant manner constantly reminded him of Trilby, although she was such a great and fashionable lady!

But just such darlings, old or young, were to be found, with still higher ideals, in less exalted spheres; and were easier of access, with no impassable gulf between – spheres where there was no patronising, nothing but deference and warm appreciation and delicate flattery, from men and women alike – and where the aged Venuses, whose prime was of the days of Waterloo,* went with their historical remains duly shrouded, like ivy-mantled ruins (and in the middle distance!).

So he actually grew tired of the great before they had time to tire of him – incredible as it may seem, and against nature; and this saved him many a heart-burning; and he ceased to be seen at fashionable drums or gatherings of any kind, except in one or two houses where he was especially liked and made welcome for his own sake; such as Lord Chiselhurst's in Piccadilly,* where the 'Moon-Dial' found a home for a few years before going to its last home and final resting-place in the National Gallery (*R.I.P.*); or Baron Stoppenheim's in Cavendish Square,* where many lovely little water-colours signed W. B. occupied places of honour on gorgeously-gilded walls; or the gorgeously-gilded bachelor rooms of Mr Moses Lyon, the picture-dealer in Upper Conduit Street* – for Little Billee (I much grieve to say it of a hero of romance) was an excellent man of business. That infinitesimal dose of the good old Oriental blood kept him straight, and not only made him stick to his last through thick and thin, but also to those whose foot his last was found to match (for he couldn't or wouldn't alter his last).

He loved to make as much money as he could, that he might spend it royally in pretty gifts to his mother and sister, whom it was his pleasure to load in this way, and whose circumstances had been very much altered by his quick success. There was never a more generous son or brother than Little Billee of the clouded heart, that couldn't love any longer!

As a set-off to all these splendours, it was also his pleasure now and again to study London life at its lower den – the eastest end of all. Whitechapel, the Minories, the Docks, Ratcliffe Highway, Rotherhithe,* soon got to know him well, and he found much to interest him and much to like among their denizens, and made as many friends there among ship-carpenters, excisemen, long-shoremen, jack-tars, and what not, as in Bayswater and Belgravia (or Bloomsbury).

He was especially fond of frequenting sing-songs, or 'free-and-easies,' where good hard-working fellows met of an evening to relax and smoke and drink and sing, round a table well loaded with steaming tumblers and pewter pots, at one end of which sits Mr Chairman in all his glory, and at the other 'Mr

The moon-dial

Vice.' They are open to any one who can afford a pipe, a screw of tobacco, and a pint of beer, and who is willing to do his best and sing a song.

No introduction is needed; as soon as any one has seated himself and made himself comfortable, Mr Chairman taps the table with his long clay pipe, begs for silence, and says to his vis-à-vis: 'Mr Vice, it strikes me as the gen'l'man as is just come in 'as got a singing face. Per'aps, Mr Vice, you'll be so very kind as juster harsk the aforesaid gentl'man to oblige us with a 'armony.'

Mr Vice then puts it to the new-comer, who, thus appealed to simulates a modest surprise, and finally professes his willingness, like Mr Barkis;* then, clearing his throat a good many times, looks up to the ceiling, and after one or two unsuccessful starts in different keys, bravely sings 'Kathleen Mavourneen,' let us say – perhaps in a touchingly sweet tenor voice:

The Chairman

> Kathleen Mavourneen, the gry dawn is brykin,
> The 'orn of the 'unter is 'eard on the 'ill . . .*

And Little Billee didn't mind the dropping of all these aitches if the voice was sympathetic and well in tune, and the sentiment simple, tender, and sincere.

Or else, with a good rolling jingo bass, it was,

> 'Earts o' hoak are our ships; 'earts o' hoak are our men;
> And we'll fight and we'll conkwer agen and agen!*

And no imperfection of accent, in Little Billee's estimation, subtracted one jot from the manly British pluck that found expression in these noble sentiments, nor added one tittle to their swaggering, blatant, and idiotically aggressive vulgarity!

Well, the song finishes with general applause all round. Then the chairman says, 'Your 'ealth and song, sir!' And drinks, and all do the same.

Then Mr Vice asks, 'What shall we 'ave the pleasure of saying, sir, after that very nice 'armony?'

And the blushing vocalist, if he knows the ropes, replies, 'A roast leg o' mutton in Newgate, and nobody to eat it!' Or else, 'May 'im as is going up the 'ill o' prosperity never meet a friend coming down!' Or else, ''Ere's to 'er as shares our sorrers and doubles our joys!' Or else, ''Ere's to 'er as shares our joys and doubles our expenses!' and so forth.

More drink, more applause, and many 'ear 'ear's. And Mr Vice says to the singer: 'You call, sir. Will you be so good as to call on some other gen'l'man for a 'armony?' And so the evening goes on.

And nobody was more quickly popular at such gatherings, or sang better songs, or proposed more touching sentiments, or filled either chair or vice-chair with more grace and dignity than Little Billee. Not even Dodor or l'Zouzou could have beaten him at that.

And he was as happy, as genial, and polite, as much at his ease, in these humble gatherings as in the gilded saloons of the great, where grand-pianos are, and hired accompanists, and highly paid singers, and a good deal of talk while they sing.

So his powers of quick, wide, universal sympathy grew and grew, and made up to him a little for his lost power of being specially fond of special individuals. For he made no close friends among men, and ruthlessly snubbed all attempts at intimacy – all advances towards an affection which he felt he could not return; and more than one enthusiastic admirer of his talent and his charm was forced to acknowledge that, with all his gifts, he seemed heartless and capricious; as ready to drop you as he had been to take you up.

He loved to be wherever he could meet his kind, high or low; and felt as happy on a penny steamer as on the yacht of a millionaire – on the crowded knifeboard of an omnibus as on the box-seat of a nobleman's drag – happier; he liked to feel the warm contact of his fellow-man at either shoulder and at his back, and didn't object to a little honest grime! And I think all this genial caressing love of his kind, this depth and breadth of human sympathy, are patent in all his work.

One the whole, however, he came to prefer for society that of the best and cleverest of his own class – those who live and prevail by the professional exercise of their own specially-trained and highly-educated wits, the skilled workmen of the brain – from the Lord Chief-Justice of England downward – the salt of the earth, in his opinion; and stuck to them.

There is no class so genial and sympathetic as *our own*, in the long run – even if it be but the criminal class! none where the welcome is likely to be so genuine and sincere, so easy to win, so difficult to outstay, if we be but decently pleasant and successful; none where the memory of us will be kept so green (if we leave any memory at all!).

So Little Billee found it expedient, when he wanted rest and play, to seek them at the houses of those whose rest and play were like his own – little halts in a seeming happy life-journey, full of toil and strain and endeavour; oases of sweet water and cooling shade, where the food was good and plentiful, though the tents might not be of cloth of gold; where the talk was of something more to his taste than court or sport or narrow party politics; the new beauty; the coming match of the season; the coming ducal conversion to Rome; the last elopement in high life – the next! and where the music was that of the greatest music-makers that can be, who found rest and play in making better music for love than they ever made for hire – and were listened to as they should be, with understanding and religious silence, and all the fervent gratitude they deserved.

There were several such houses in London then – and are still – thank Heaven! And Little Billee had his little billet there – and there he was wont to drown himself in waves of lovely sound, or streams of clever talk, or rivers of sweet feminine adulation, seas! oceans! – a somewhat relaxing bath! – and forget a while his everlasting chronic plague of heart-insensibility, which no doctor could explain or cure, and to which he was becoming gradually resigned – as one does to deafness or blindness or locomotor ataxia* – for it had lasted nearly five years! But now and again, during sleep, and in a blissful dream, the lost power of loving – of loving mother, sister, friend – would be restored to him, just as with a blind man who sometimes dreams he has recovered his sight; and the joy of it would wake him to the sad reality: till he got to know, even in his dream, that he was only dreaming after all, whenever that priceless boon seemed to be his own once more – and did his utmost not to wake. And these were nights to be marked with a white stone, and remembered!

And nowhere was he happier than at the houses of the great surgeons and physicians who interested themselves in his strange disease. When the Little Billees of this world fall ill, the great surgeons and physicians (like the great singers and musicians) do better for them, out of mere love and kindness, than for the princes of the earth, who pay them thousand-guinea fees and load them with honours.

And of all these notable London houses none was pleasanter than that of Cornelys, the great sculptor, and Little Billee was such a favourite in that house that he was able to take his friends Taffy and the Laird there the very day they came to London.

First of all they dined together at a delightful little Franco-Italian pothouse near Leicester Square,* where they had *bouillabaisse* (imagine the Laird's delight), and *spaghetti,* and a *poulet rôti,* which is *such* a different affair from a roast fowl! and salad, which Taffy was allowed to make and mix himself; and they all smoked just where they sat, the moment they had swallowed their food – as had been their way in the good old Paris days.

That dinner was a happy one for Taffy and the Laird, with their Little Billee apparently unchanged – as demonstrative, as genial and caressing as ever, and with no swagger to speak of; and with so many things to talk about that were new to them, and of such delightful interest! They also had much to say – but

A happy dinner

they didn't say very much about Paris, for fear of waking up Heaven knows what sleeping dogs!

And every now and again, in the midst of all this pleasant forgathering and communion of long-parted friends, the pangs of Little Billee's miserable mind-malady would shoot through him like poisoned arrows.

He would catch himself thinking how fat and fussy and serious about trifles Taffy had become; and what a shiftless, feckless, futile duffer was the Laird; and how greedy they both were, and how red and coarse their ears and gills and cheeks grew as they fed, and how shiny their faces; and how little he would care, try as he might, if they both fell down dead under the table! And this would make him behave more caressingly to them, more genially and demonstratively than ever – for he knew it was all a gruesome physical ailment of his own, which he could no more help than a cataract in his eye!

Then, catching sight of his own face and form in a mirror, he would curse himself for a puny, misbegotten shrimp, an imp – an abortion – no bigger, by the side of the herculean Taffy or the burly Laird of Cockpen, than sixpennorth o' halfpence: a wretched little overrated follower of a poor trivial craft – a mere light amuser! For what did pictures matter, or whether they were good or bad, except to the triflers who painted them, the dealers who sold them, the idle, uneducated, purse-proud fools who bought them and stuck them up on their walls because they were told!

And he felt that if a dynamite shell were beneath the table where they sat, and its fuse were smoking under their very noses, he would neither wish to warn his friends nor move himself. He didn't care a d—!

And all this made him so lively and brilliant in his talk, so fascinating and droll and witty, that Taffy and the Laird wondered at the improvement success and the experience of life had wrought in him, and marvelled at the happiness of his lot, and almost found it in their warm affectionate hearts to feel a touch of envy!

Oddly enough, in a brief flash of silence, 'entre la poire et le fromage,' they heard a foreigner at an adjoining table (one of a very noisy group) exclaim: 'Mais quand je vous dis que j'l'ai entendue, moi, La Svengali! et même qu'elle a chanté l'Im-

A-smokin' their poipes and cigyars

promptu de Chopin absolument comme si c'était un piano qu'on jouait! voyons! . . .'

'Farceur! la bonne blague!' said another – and then the conversation became so noisily general it was no good listening any more.

'Svengali! how funny that name should turn up! I wonder what's become of *our* Svengali, by the way?' observed Taffy.

'I remember *his* playing Chopin's Impromptu,' said Little Billee; 'what a singular coincidence!'

There were to be more coincidences that night; it never rains them but it pours!

So our three friends finished their coffee and liqueured up, and went to Cornelys's three in a hansom –

> Like Mars,
> A-smokin' their poipes and cigyars.*

Sir Louis Cornelys,* as everybody knows, lives in a palace on Campden Hill, a house of many windows; and whichever window he looks out of, he sees his own garden and very little else. In spite of his eighty years, he works as hard as ever, and his hand has lost but little of its cunning. But he no longer gives those splendid parties that made him almost as famous a host as he was an artist.

When his beautiful wife died he shut himself up from the world; and now he never stirs out of his house and grounds except to fulfil his duties at the Royal Academy, and dine once a year with the Queen.

It was very different in the early sixties. There was no pleasanter or more festive house than his in London, winter or summer – no lordier host than he – no more irresistible hostesses than Lady Cornelys and her lovely daughters; and if ever music had a right to call itself divine, it was there you heard it – on late Saturday nights during the London season – when the foreign birds of song come over to reap their harvest in London Town.

It was on one of the most brilliant of these Saturday nights that Taffy and the Laird, chaperoned by Little Billee, made their *début* at Mechelen Lodge, and were received at the door of the immense music-room by a tall, powerful man with splendid eyes and a gray beard, and a small velvet cap on his head – and by a Greek matron* so beautiful and stately and magnificently attired that they felt inclined to sink them on their bended knees as in the presence of some overwhelming Eastern royalty – and were only prevented from doing so, perhaps, by the simple, sweet, and cordial graciousness of her welcome.

And whom should they be shaking hands with next but Antony, Lorrimer, and the Greek – each with a beard and moustache of nearly five years' growth!

But they had no time for much exuberant greeting, for there was a sudden piano crash – and then an immediate silence, as though for pins to drop – and Signor Giuglini* and the wondrous maiden Adelina Patti* sang the 'Miserere'* out of Signor Verdi's most famous opera – to the delight of all but a few very superior ones who had just read Mendelssohn's letters* (or misread them) and despised Italian music, and thought cheaply of 'mere virtuosity,' either vocal or instrumental.

When this was over, Little Billee pointed out all the lions to his friends – from the Prime Minister* down to the present scribe – who was right glad to meet them again and talk of auld lang syne, and present them to the daughters of the house and other charming ladies.

Then Roucouly, the great French baritone, sang Durien's favourite song –

> Plaisir d'amour ne dure qu'un moment;
> Chagrin d'amour dure toute la vie . . .

with quite a little drawing-room voice – but quite as divinely as he had sung 'Noël, noël' at the Madeleine in full blast one certain Christmas Eve our three friends remembered well.

Then there was a violin solo by young Joachim,* then as now the greatest violinist of his time; and a solo on the pianoforte by Madame Schumann,* his only peeress! and these came as a wholesome check to the levity of those for whom all music is but an agreeable pastime, a mere emotional delight, in which the intellect has no part; and also as a well-deserved humiliation to all virtuosi who play so charmingly that they make their listeners forget the master who invented the music in the lesser master who interprets it!

For these two – man and woman – the highest of their kind, never let you forget it was Sebastian Bach* they were playing – playing in absolute perfection, in absolute forgetfulness of themselves – so that if you weren't up to Bach, you didn't have a very good time!

But if you were (or wished it to be understood or thought you were), you seized your opportunity and you scored; and by the earnestness of your rapt and tranced immobility, and the stony, gorgon-like intensity of your gaze, you rebuked the frivolous – as you had rebuked them before by the listlessness and careless-ness of your bored resignation to the Signorina Patti's trills and fioritures, or M. Roucouly's pretty little French mannerisms.

And what added so much to the charm of this delightful concert was that the guests were not packed together sardine-wise, as they are at most concerts; they were comparatively few and well chosen, and could get up and walk about and talk to their friends between the pieces, and wander off into other rooms and look at endless beautiful things, and stroll in the lovely grounds, by moon or star or Chinese-lantern light.

And there the frivolous could sit and chat and laugh and flirt when Bach was being played inside; and the earnest wander up and down together in soul-communion, through darkened walks and groves and alleys where the sound of French or Italian warblings could not reach them, and talk in earnest tones of the great Zola,* or Guy de Maupassant* and Pierre Loti,* and exult in beautiful English over the inferiority of English literature, English art, English music, English everything else.

For these high-minded ones who can only bear the sight of classical pictures and the sound of classical music do not necessarily read classical books in any language – no Shake-speares or Dantes or Molières or Goethes for *them*. They know a trick worth two of that!

And the mere fact that these three immortal French writers of light books I have just named had never been heard of at this particular period doesn't very much matter; they had cognate predecessors whose names I happen to forget. Any stick will do to beat a dog with, and history is always repeating itself.

Feydeau,* or Flaubert, let us say – or for those who don't know French and cultivate an innocent mind, Miss Austen* (for to be dead and buried is almost as good as to be French and immoral!) – and Sebastian Bach, and Sandro Botticelli – that all the arts should be represented. These names are rather discrep-ant, but they make very good sticks for dog-beating; and with a thorough knowledge and appreciation of these (or the semblance

'Bonjour, Suzon!'

thereof), you were well equipped in those days to hold your own among the elect of intellectual London circles, and snub the philistine to rights.

Then, very late, a tall, good-looking, swarthy foreigner came in, with a roll of music in his hands, and his entrance made quite a stir; you heard all round, 'Here's Glorioli,' or 'Ecco Glorioli,' or 'Voici Glorioli,' till Glorioli got on your nerves. And beautiful ladies, ambassadresses, female celebrities of all kinds, fluttered up to him and cajoled and fawned; — as Svengali would have said, 'Prinzessen, Comtessen, Serene English Altessen!' — and they soon forgot their Highness and their Serenity!

For with very little pressing Glorioli stood up on the platform, with his accompanist by his side at the piano, and in his hands a sheet of music, at which he never looked. He looked at the beautiful ladies, and ogled and smiled; and from his scarcely-parted, moist, thick, bearded lips, which he always licked before singing, there issued the most ravishing sounds that had ever been heard from throat of man or woman or boy! He could sing both high and low and soft and loud, and the frivolous were bewitched, as was only to be expected; but even the earnestest of all, caught, surprised, rapt, astounded, shaken, tickled, teased, harrowed, tortured, tantalised, aggravated, seduced, demoral-ised, degraded, corrupted into mere naturalness, forgot to dissemble their delight.

And Sebastian Bach (the especially adored of all really great musicians, and also, alas! of many priggish outsiders who don't know a single note and can't remember a single tune) was well forgotten for the night; and who were more enthusiastic than the two great players who had been playing Bach that evening? For these, at all events, were broad and catholic and sincere, and knew what was beautiful, whatever its kind.

It was but a simple little song that Glorioli* sang, as light and pretty as it could well be, almost worthy of the words it was written to, and the words are De Musset's; and I love them so much I cannot resist the temptation of setting them down here, for the mere sensuous delight of writing them, as though I had just composed them myself:

> Bonjour, Suzon, ma fleur des bois!
>   Es-tu toujours la plus jolie?
> Je reviens, tel que tu me vois,

D'un grand voyage en Italie!
Du paradis j'ai fait le tour –
J'ai fait des vers – j'ai fait l'amour . . .
    Mais que t'importe!
Je passe devant ta maison:
    Ouvre ta porte!
    Bonjour, Suzon!

Je t'ai vue au temps des lilas.
    Ton cœur joyeux venait d'éclore,
Et tu disais: 'Je ne veux pas,
    Je ne veux pas qu'on m'aime encore.'
Qu'as-tu fait depuis mon départ?
Qui part trop tôt revient trop tard.
    Mais que m'importe?
Je passe devant ta maison:
    Ouvre ta porte!
    Bonjour, Suzon!*

And when it began, and while it lasted, and after it was over, one felt really sorry for all the other singers. And nobody sang any more that night; for Glorioli was tired, and wouldn't sing again, and none were bold enough or disinterested enough to sing after him.

Some of my readers may remember that meteoric bird of song, who, though a mere amateur, would condescend to sing for a hundred guineas in the saloons of the great (as Monsieur Jourdain* sold cloth); who would sing still better for love and glory in the studios of his friends.

For Glorioli – the biggest, handsomest, and most distinguished-looking Jew that ever was – one of the Sephardim* (one of the Seraphim!) – hailed from Spain, where he was junior partner in the great firm of Moralés, Peralés, Gonzalés, and Glorioli, wine merchants, Malaga. He travelled for his own firm; his wine was good, and he sold much of it in England. But his voice would bring him far more gold in the month he spent here; for his wines have been equalled – if it be not libellous to say so – but there was no voice like his anywhere in the world, and no more finished singer.

Anyhow his voice got into Little Billee's head more than any wine, and the boy could talk of nothing else for days and weeks; and was so exuberant in his expressions of delight and gratitude that the great singer took a real fancy to him (especially when he was told that this fervent boyish admirer was one of the greatest of English painters); and as a mark of his esteem, privately confided to him after supper that every century two human nightingales were born – only two! a male and a female; and that he, Glorioli, was the representative 'male rossignol of this soi-disant dix-neuvième siècle.'*

'I can well believe that! And the female, your mate that should be – *la rossignolle,** if there is such a word?' inquired Little Billee.

'Ah! mon ami ... it was Alboni, till la petite Adelina Patti came out a year or two ago; and now it is *La Svengali.*'

'La Svengali?'

'Oui, mon fy! You will hear her some day – et vous m'en direz des nouvelles!'*

'Why, you don't mean to say that she's got a better voice than Madame Alboni?'

'Mon ami, an apple is an excellent thing – until you have tried a peach! Her voice to that of Alboni is as a peach to an apple – I give you my word of honour! but bah! the voice is a detail. It's what she does with it – it's incredible! it gives one cold all down the back! it drives you mad! it makes you weep hot tears by the spoonful! Ah! the tear, mon fy! tenez! I can draw everything but *that!* Ça n'est pas dans mes cordes!* *I* can only madden with *love!* But La Svengali! ... And then, in the middle of it all, prrrout! ... she makes you laugh! Ah! le beau rire! faire rire avec des larmes plein les yeux – voilà qui me passe! ... Mon ami,* when I heard her it made me swear that even *I* would never try to sing any more – it seemed *too* absurd! and I kept my word for a month at least – and you know, je sais ce que je vaux, moi!'*

'You are talking of La Svengali, I bet,' said Signor Spartia.

'Oui, parbleu! You have heard her?'

'Yes – at Vienna last winter,' rejoined the greatest singing-master in the world. 'J'en suis fou! hélas!* I thought *I* could teach a woman how to sing, till I heard that blackguard Svengali's pupil. He had married her, they say?'

'That *blackguard* Svengali!' exclaimed Little Billee ... 'why, that must be a Svengali I knew in Paris – a famous pianist! a friend of mine!'

'That's the man! also une fameuse crapule (sauf vot' respect);* his real name is Adler; his mother was a Polish singer; and he

A human nightingale

was a pupil at the Leipsic Conservatorio. But he's an immense artist, and a great singing-master, to teach a woman like that! and such a woman! belle comme un ange – mais bête comme un pot.* I tried to talk to her – all she can say is 'ja wohl,' or 'doch,' or 'nein,' or 'soh!' not a word of English or French or Italian, though she sings them, oh! but *divinely!* It is *'il bel canto'* come back to the world after a hundred years . . .'

'But what voice is it?' asked Little Billee.

'Every voice a mortal woman can have – three octaves – four! and of such a quality that people who can't tell one tune from another cry with pleasure at the mere sound of it directly they hear her; just like anybody else. Everything that Paganini* could do with his violin, she does with her voice – only better – and what a voice! un vrai baume!'

'Now I don't mind petting zat you are schbeaking of La Sfencali,' said Herr Kreutzer,* the famous composer, joining in. 'Quelle merfeille, hein? I heard her in St Betersburg, at ze Vinter Balace.* Ze vomen all vent mat, and pulled off zeir bearls and tiamonts and kave zem to her – vent town on zeir knees and gried and gissed her hants. She tit not say vun vort! She tit not efen schmile! Ze men schnifelled in ze gorners, and looked at ze bictures, and tissempled – efen I, Johann Kreutzer! efen ze Emperor?'

'You're joking,' said Little Billee.

'My vrent, I neffer choke ven I talk apout zinging. You vill hear her zum tay yourzellof, and you vill acree viz me zat zere are two classes of beoble who zing. In ze vun class, La Sfencali; in ze ozzer, all ze ozzer zingers!'

'And does she sing good music?'

'I ton't know. *All* music is koot ven *she* sings it. I forket ze zong; I can only sink of ze zinger. Any koot zinger can zing a peautiful zong and kif bleasure, I zubboce! But I voot zooner hear La Sfencali zing a scale zan anypotty else zing ze most peautiful zong in ze vorldt – efen vun of my own! Zat is berhaps how zung ze crate Italian zingers of ze last century. It vas a lost art, and she has found it; and she must haf pecun to zing pefore she pecan to schpeak – or else she voot not haf hat ze time to learn all zat she knows, for she is not yet zirty! She zings in Paris in Ogdoper, Gott sei dank! and gums here after Christmas to zing at Trury Lane.* Chullien* kifs her ten sousand bounts!'

'I wonder, now? Why, that must be the woman I heard at

Warsaw two years ago – or three,' said young Lord Witlow. 'It was at Count Siloszech's. He'd heard her sing in the streets, with a tall black-bearded ruffian, who accompanied her on a guitar, and a little fiddling gypsy fellow. She was a handsome woman, with hair down to her knees, but stupid as an owl. She sang at Siloszech's, and all the fellows went mad and gave her their watches and diamond studs and gold scarf-pins. By gad! I never heard or saw anything like it. I don't know much about music myself – couldn't tell 'God save the Queen'* from 'Pop goes the Weasel,'* if the people didn't get up and stand and take their hats off; but I was as mad as the rest – why, I gave her a little German-silver vinaigrette I'd just bought for my wife; hanged if I didn't – and I was only just married, you know! It's the peculiar twang of her voice, I suppose!'

And hearing all this, Little Billee made up his mind that life had still something in store for him, since he would some day hear La Svengali. Anyhow, he wouldn't shoot himself till then!

Thus the night wore itself away. The Prinzessen, Comtessen, and Serene English Altessen (and other ladies of less exalted rank) departed home in cabs and carriages; and hostess and daughters went to bed. Late sitters of the ruder sex supped again, and smoked and chatted and listened to comic songs and recitations by celebrated actors. Noble dukes hobnobbed with low comedians; world-famous painters and sculptors sat at the feet of Hebrew capitalists and aitchless millionaires. Judges, cabinet ministers, eminent physicians and warriors and philosophers saw Sunday morning steal over Campden Hill and through the many windows of Mechelen Lodge, and listened to the pipe of half-awakened birds, and smelt the freshness of the dark summer dawn. And as Taffy and the Laird walked home to the Old Hummums* by daylight, they felt that last night was ages ago, and that since then they had forgathered with 'much there was of the best in London.' And then they reflected that 'much there was of the best in London' were still strangers to them – except by reputation – for there had not been time for many introductions: and this had made them feel a little out of it; and they found they hadn't had such a very good time after all. And there were no cabs. And they were tired, and their boots were tight.

And the last they had seen of Little Billee before leaving was a glimpse of their old friend in a corner of Lady Cornelys's boudoir, gravely playing cup and ball with Fred Walker for sixpences – both so rapt in the game that they were unconscious of anything else, and both playing so well (with either hand) that they might have been professional champions!

And that saturnine young sawbones, Jakes Talboys* (now Sir Jakes and one of the most genial of Her Majesty's physicians), who, sometimes after supper and champagne, was given to thoughtful, sympathetic, and acute observation of his fellow-men, remarked to the Laird in a whisper that was almost convivial:–

'Rather an enviable pair! Their united ages amount to forty-eight or so, their united weights to about fifteen stone, and they couldn't carry you or me between them. But if you were to roll all the other brains that have been under this roof to-night into one, you wouldn't reach the sum of their united genius ... I wonder which of the two is the most unhappy!'

The season over, the song-birds flown, summer on the wane, his picture, the 'Moon-Dial,' sent to Moses Lyon's (the picture-dealer in Conduit Street), Little Billee felt the time had come to go and see his mother and sister in Devonshire, and make the sun shine twice as brightly for them during a month or so, and the dew fall softer!

So one fine August morning found him at the Great Western Station* – the nicest station in all London, I think – except the stations that book you to France and far away.

It always seems so pleasant to be going west! Little Billee loved that station, and often went there for a mere stroll, to watch the people starting on their westward way, following the sun towards Heaven knows what joys or sorrows, and envy them their sorrows or their joys – any sorrows or joys that were not merely physical, like a chocolate drop or a pretty tune, a bad smell or a toothache.

And as he took a seat in a second-class carriage (it would be third in these democratic days), south corner, back to the engine, with *Silas Marner,** and Darwin's *Origin of Species** (which he was reading for the third time), and *Punch* and other literature of a lighter kind to beguile him on his journey, he felt rather bitterly how happy he could be if the little spot, or knot, or blot, or clot which paralysed that convolution of his brain where he kept his affections could but be conjured away!

Cup-and-ball

The dearest mother, the dearest sister in the world, in the dearest little seaside village (or town) that ever was! and other dear people – especially Alice, sweet Alice with hair so brown, his sister's friend, the simple, pure, and pious maiden of his boyish dreams: and himself, but for that wretched little kill-joy cerebral occlusion, as sound, as healthy, as full of life and energy, as he had ever been!

And when he wasn't reading *Silas Marner,* or looking out of window at the flying landscape, and watching it revolve round its middle distance (as it always seems to do), he was sympathetically taking stock of his fellow-passengers, and mildly envying them, one after another, indiscriminately!

A fat, old, wheezy philistine, with a bulbous nose and only one eye, who had a plain, sickly daughter, to whom he seemed devoted, body and soul; an old lady, who still wept furtively at recollections of the parting with her grandchildren, which had taken place at the station (they had borne up wonderfully, as grandchildren do); a consumptive curate, on the opposite corner seat by the window, whose tender, anxious wife (sitting by his side) seemed to have no thoughts in the whole world but for him; and her patient eyes were his stars of consolation, since he turned to look into them almost every minute, and always seemed a little the happier for doing so. There is no better star-gazing than that!

So Little Billee gave her up *his* corner seat, that the poor sufferer might have those stars where he could look into them comfortably without turning his head.

Indeed (as was his wont with everybody), Little Billee made himself useful and pleasant to his fellow-travellers in many ways – so many that long before they had reached their respective journeys' ends they had almost grown to love him as an old friend, and longed to know who this singularly attractive and brilliant youth, this genial, dainty, benevolent little princekin could possibly be, who was dressed so fashionably, and yet went second class, and took such kind thought of others; and they wondered at the happiness that must be his at merely being alive, and told him more of their troubles in six hours than they told many an old friend in a year.

But he told them nothing about himself – that self he was so sick of – and left them to wonder.

And at his own journey's end, the farthest end of all, he found his mother and sister waiting for him, in a beautiful little pony-carriage – his last gift – and with them sweet Alice, and in her eyes, for one brief moment, that unconscious look of love surprised which is not to be forgotten for years and years and years – which can only be seen by the eyes that meet it, and which, for the time it lasts (just a flash), makes all women's eyes look exactly the same (I'm told): and it seemed to Little Billee that, for the twentieth part of a second, Alice had looked at him with Trilby's eyes; or his mother's, when that he was a little tiny boy.

It all but gave him the thrill he thirsted for! Another twentieth part of a second, perhaps, and his brain-trouble would have melted away; and Little Billee would have come into his own again – the kingdom of love!

A beautiful human eye! *Any* beautiful eye – a dog's, a deer's, a donkey's, an owl's even! To think of all that it can look, and all that it can see! all that it can even *seem,* sometimes! What a prince among gems! what a star!

But a beautiful eye that lets the broad white light of infinite space (so bewildering and garish and diffused) into one pure virgin heart, to be filtered there! and lets it out again, duly warmed, softened, concentrated, sublimated, focused to a point as in a precious stone, that it may shed itself (a love-laden effulgence) into some stray fellow-heart close by – through pupil and iris, entre quatre-z-yeux – the very elixir of life!

Alas! that such a crown-jewel should ever lose its lustre and go blind!

Not so blind or dim, however, but it can still see well enough to look before and after, and inward and upward, and drown itself in tears, and yet not die! And that's the dreadful pity of it. And this is a quite uncalled-for digression; and I can't think why I should have gone out of my way (at considerable pains) to invent it! In fact –

> Of this 'ere song, should I be axed the reason for to show,
> I don't exactly know, I don't exactly know!
> *But all my family dwells upon Nancy.**

'How pretty Alice has grown, mother! quite lovely, I think! and so nice; but she was always as nice as she could be!'

So observed Little Billee to his mother that evening as they sat

Sweet Alice

in the garden and watched the crescent moon sink to the Atlantic.

'Ah! my darling Willie! If you *could* only guess how happy you would make your poor old mammy by growing fond of Alice . . . And Blanche, too! what a joy for *her!*'

'Good heavens! mother . . . Alice is not for the like of *me!* She's for some splendid young Devon squire, six foot high, and acred and whiskered within an inch of his life! . . .'

'Ah, my darling Willie! you are not of those who ask for love in vain . . . If you only *knew* how she believes in you! She almost beats your poor old mammy at *that!*'

And that night he dreamed of Alice – that he loved her as a sweet good woman should be loved; and knew, even in his dream, that it was but a dream; but, oh! it was good! and he managed not to wake; and it was a night to be marked with a white stone! And (still in his dream) she had kissed him, and healed him of his brain-trouble for ever. But when he woke next morning, alas! his brain-trouble was with him still, and he felt that no dream kiss would ever cure it – nothing but a real kiss from Alice's own pure lips!

And he rose thinking of Alice, and dressed and breakfasted thinking of her – and how fair she was, and how innocent, and how well and carefully trained up the way she should go – the beau ideal of a wife . . . Could she possibly care for a shrimp like himself?

For in his love of outward form he could not understand that any woman who had eyes to see should ever quite condone the signs of physical weakness in man, in favour of any mental gifts or graces whatsoever.

Little Greek that he was, he worshipped the athlete, and opined that all women without exception – all English women especially – must see with the same eyes as himself.

He had once been vain and weak enough to believe in Trilby's love (with a Taffy standing by – a careless, unsusceptible Taffy, who was like unto the gods of Olympus!) – and Trilby had given him up at a word, a hint – for all his frantic clinging.

She would not have given up Taffy *pour si peu*,* had Taffy but lifted a little finger! It is always 'just whistle, and I'll come to you, my lad!' with the likes of Taffy . . . but Taffy hadn't even whistled! Yet still he kept thinking of Alice – and he felt he couldn't think of her well enough till he went out for a stroll by himself on a sheep-trimmed down. So he took his pipe and his Darwin, and out he strolled into the early sunshine – up the green Red Lane, past the pretty church, Alice's father's church – and there, at the gate, patiently waiting for his mistress, sat Alice's dog – an old friend of his, whose welcome was a very warm one.

Little Billee thought of Thackeray's lovely poem in *Pendennis*:

> She comes – she's here – she's past!
> May heaven go with her! . . .*

Then he and the dog went on together to a little bench on the edge of the cliff – within sight of Alice's bedroom window. It was called 'the Honeymooners' Bench.'

'That look – that look – that look! Ah – but Trilby had looked like that, too! And there are many Taffys in Devon!'

He sat himself down and smoked and gazed at the sea below, which the sun (still in the east) had not yet filled with glare and robbed of the lovely sapphire-blue, shot with purple and dark green, that comes over it now and again of a morning on that most beautiful coast.

There was a fresh breeze from the west, and the long, slow billows broke into creamier foam than ever, which reflected itself as a tender white gleam in the blue concavities of their shining shoreward curves as they came rolling in. The sky was all of turquoise but for the smoke of a distant steamer – a long thin horizontal streak of dun – and there were little brown or white sails here and there, dotting; and the stately ships went on . . .

Little Billee tried hard to feel all this beauty with his heart as well as his brain – as he had so often done when a boy – and cursed his insensibility out loud for at least the thousand-and-first time.

Why couldn't these waves of air and water be turned into equivalent waves of sound, that he might feel them through the only channel that reached his emotions! That one joy was still left to him – but, alas! alas! he was only a painter of pictures – and not a maker of music!

He recited 'Break, break, break,'* to Alice's dog, who loved him and looked up into his face with sapient, affectionate eyes – and whose name, like that of so many dogs in fiction and so few in fact, was simply Tray. For Little Billee was much given to monologues out loud, and profuse quotations from his favourite bards.

Everybody quoted that particular poem either mentally or aloud when they sat on that particular bench – except a few old-fashioned people, who still said,

> Roll on, thou deep and dark blue ocean, roll!*

or people of the very highest culture, who only quoted the nascent (and crescent) Robert Browning; or people of no culture at all, who simply held their tongues – and only felt the more!

Tray listened silently.

'Ah, Tray, the best thing but one to do with the sea is to paint it. The next best thing to that is to bathe in it. The best of all is to lie asleep at the bottom. How would *you* like that?

> And on thy ribs the limpet sticks,
> And in thy heart the scrawl shall play . . .*

Tray's tail became as a wagging point of interrogation, and he turned his head first on one side and then on the other – his eyes fixed on Little Billee's, his face irresistible in its genial doggy wistfulness.

'Tray, what a singularly good listener you are – and therefore what singularly good manners you've got! I suppose all dogs have!' said Little Billee; and then, in a very tender voice, he exclaimed,

'Alice, Alice, Alice!'

And Tray uttered a soft, cooing, nasal croon in his head register, though he was a baritone dog by nature, with portentous, warlike chest-notes of the jingo order.

'Tray, your mistress is a parson's daughter, and therefore twice as much of a mystery as any other woman in this puzzling world!

'Tray, if my heart weren't stopped with wax, like the ears of the companions of Ulysses* when they rowed past the sirens – you've heard of Ulysses, Tray? he loved a dog – if my heart weren't stopped with wax, I should be deeply in love with your mistress; perhaps she would marry me if I asked her – there's no accounting for tastes! – and I know enough of myself to know that I should make her a good husband – that I should make her happy – and I should make two other women happy besides.

'As for myself personally, Tray, it doesn't very much matter. One good woman would do as well as another, if she's equally good-looking. You doubt it? Wait till you get a pimple inside your bump of – your bump of – wherever you keep your fondnesses, Tray.

'For that's what's the matter with me – a pimple – just a little clot of blood at the root of a nerve, and no bigger than a pin's point!

'That's a small thing to cause such a lot of wretchedness, and wreck a fellow's life, isn't it? Oh, curse it, curse it, curse it – every day and all day long.

'And just as small a thing will take it away, I'm told!

'Ah! grains of sand are small things – and so are diamonds! But diamond or grain of sand, only Alice has got that small thing! Alice alone, in all the world, has got the healing touch for me now; the hands, the lips, the eyes! I know it – I feel it! I dreamed it last night! She looked me well in the face, and took my hand – both hands – and kissed me, eyes and mouth, and told me how she loved me. Ah! what a dream it was! And my little clot melted away like a snowflake on the lips, and I was my old self again, after many years – and all through that kiss of a pure woman.

'I've never been kissed by a pure woman in my life – never! except by my dear mother and sister; and mothers and sisters don't count, when it comes to kissing.

'Ah! sweet physician that she is, and better than all! It will all come back again with a rush, just as I dreamed, and we will have a good time together, we three! . . .

'But your mistress is a parson's daughter, and believes everything she's been taught from a child, just as you do – at least, I hope so. And I like her for it – and you too.

'She has believed her father – will she ever believe me, who think so differently? And if she does, will it be good for her? – and then, where will her father come in?

'Oh! it's a bad thing to live and no longer believe and trust in your father, Tray! to doubt either his honesty or his intelligence. For he (with your mother to help) has taught you all the best he knows, if he has been a good father – till some one else comes and teaches you better – or worse!

'And then, what are you to believe of what good still remains of all that early teaching – and how are you to sift the wheat from the chaff? . . .

'Kneel undisturbed, fair saint! I, for one, will never seek to undermine thy faith in any father, on earth or above it!

'Yes, there she kneels in her father's church, her pretty head bowed over her clasped hands, her cloak and skirts falling in happy folds about her: I see it all!

'And underneath, that poor, sweet, soft, pathetic thing of flesh and blood, the eternal woman – great heart and slender brain – for ever enslaved or enslaving, never self-sufficing, never free . . . that dear, weak, delicate shape, so cherishable, so perishable, that I've had to paint so often, and know so well by heart! and love . . . ah, how I love it! Only painter-fellows and sculptor-fellows can ever quite know the fullness of that pure love.

'There she kneels and pours forth her praise or plaint, meekly and duly. Perhaps it's for me she's praying.

Leave thou thy sister when she prays.*

'She believes her poor little prayer will be heard and answered somewhere up aloft. The impossible will be done. She wants what she wants so badly, and prays for it so hard.

'She believes – she believes – what *doesn't* she believe, Tray?

'The world was made in six days. It is just six thousand years old. Once it all lay smothered under rain-water for many weeks, miles deep, because there were so many wicked people about somewhere down in Judea,* where they didn't know everything! A costly kind of clearance! And then there was Noah, who *wasn't* wicked, and his most respectable family, and his ark – and Jonah* and his whale – and Joshua* and the sun, and what not. I remember it all, you see, and oh! such wonderful things that have happened since! And there's everlasting agony for those who don't believe as she does; and yet she is happy; and good, and very kind; for the mere thought of any live creature in pain makes her wretched!

'After all, if she believes in me, she'll believe in anything; let her!

'Indeed, I'm not sure that it's not rather ungainly for a pretty woman *not* to believe in all these good old cosmic taradiddles, as it is for a pretty child not to believe in Little Red Riding-hood, and Jack and the Beanstalk, and Morgiana and the Forty Thieves;* we learn them at our mother's knee, and how nice they are! Let us go on believing them as long as we can, till the child grows up and the woman dies and it's all found out.

'Yes, Tray, I will be dishonest for her dear sake. I will kneel by her side if ever I have the happy chance, and ever after, night and morning, and all day long on Sundays if she wants me to! What will I *not* do for that one pretty woman who believes in *me*? I will respect even *that* belief, and do my little best to keep it alive for ever. It is much too precious an earthly boon for *me* to play ducks and drakes with . . .

'So much for Alice, Tray – your sweet mistress and mine.

'But then, there's Alice's papa – and that's another pair of sleeves,* as we say in France.

'Ought one ever to play at make-believe with a full-grown man for any consideration whatever – even though he be a parson, and a possible father-in-law? *There's* a case of conscience for you!

'When I ask him for his daughter, as I must, and he asks me

'So much for Alive, Tray'

for my profession of faith, as he will, what can I tell him? The truth?'

(And now, I regret to say, the reticent Little Billee is going to show his trusty four-footed friend the least attractive side of his many-sided nature, its modernity, its dreary scepticism – his own unhappy portion of *la maladie du siècle*)* . . .

'But then, what will *he* say? What allowances will *he* make for a poor little weak-kneed, well-meaning waif of a painter-fellow like me, whose only choice lay between Mr Darwin and the Pope of Rome, and who has chosen once and for ever – and that long ago – before he'd ever even heard of Mr Darwin's name.

'Besides, why should he make allowances for me? I don't for him. I think no more of a parson than he does of a painter-fellow – and that's precious little, I'm afraid.

'What will he think of a man who says:

' "Look here! the God of your belief isn't mine and never will be – but I love your daughter, and she loves me, and I'm the only man to make her happy!"

'He's no Jephthah;* he's made of flesh and blood, although he's a parson – and loves his daughter as much as Shylock* loved his.

'Tell me, Tray – thou that livest among parsons – what man, not being a parson himself, can guess how a parson would think, an average parson, confronted by such a poser as that?

'Does he, dare he, *can* he ever think straight or simply on any subject as any other man thinks, hedged in as he is by so many limitations?

'He is as shrewd, vain, wordly, self-seeking, ambitious, jealous, censorious, and all the rest, as you or I, Tray – for all his Christian profession – and just as fond of his kith and kin!

'He is considered a gentleman – which perhaps you and I are not – unless we happen to behave as such; it is a condition of his noble calling. Perhaps it's in order to become a gentleman that he's become a parson! It's about as short a royal road as any to that enviable distinction – as short almost as Her Majesty's commission,* and much safer, and much less expensive – within reach of the sons of most fairly successful butchers and bakers and candlestick-makers.*

'While still a boy he has bound himself irrevocably to certain beliefs, which he will be paid to preserve and preach and enforce through life, and act up to through thick and thin – at all events in the eyes of others – even his nearest and dearest – even the wife of his bosom.

'They are his bread and butter, these beliefs – and a man mustn't quarrel with his bread and butter. But a parson must quarrel with those who don't believe as he tells them!

'Yet a few years' thinking and reading and experience of life, one would suppose, might possibly just shake his faith a little (just as though, instead of being parson, he had been tinker, tailor, soldier, sailor, gentleman, apothecary, ploughboy, thief),* and teach him that many of these beliefs are simply childish – and some of them very wicked indeed – and most immoral.

'It is very wicked and most immoral to believe, or affect to believe, and tell others to believe, that the unseen, unspeakable, unthinkable Immensity we're all part and parcel of, source of eternal, infinite, indestructible life and light and might, is a kind of wrathful, glorified, and self-glorifying ogre in human shape, with human passions, and most inhuman hates – who suddenly made us out of nothing, one fine day – just for a freak – and made us so badly that we fell the next – and turned us adrift the day after – damned us from the very beginning – *ab ovo* – *ab ovo usque ad malum** – ha, ha! – and ever since! never gave us a chance!

'All-merciful Father, indeed! Why, the Prince of Darkness was an angel in comparison (and a gentleman into the bargain).

'Just think of it, Tray – a finger in every little paltry pie – an eye and an ear at every keyhole, even that of the larder, to catch us tripping, and find out if we're praising loud enough, or grovelling low enough, or fasting hard enough – poor God-forsaken worms!

'And if we're naughty and disobedient, everlasting torment for us; torture of so hideous a kind that *we* wouldn't inflict it on the basest criminal, not for one single moment!

'Or else, if we're good and do as we are bid, an eternity of bliss so futile, so idle, and so tame that we couldn't stand it for a week, but for thinking of its one horrible alternative, and of our poor brother for ever and ever roasting away, and howling for the drop of water he never gets.

'Everlasting flame, or everlasting dishonour – nothing between!

'Isn't it ludicrous as well as pitiful – a thing to make one snigger through one's tears? Isn't it a grievous sin to believe in such things as these, and go about teaching and preaching them, and being paid for it – a sin to be heavily chastised, and a shame? What a legacy!

'They were shocking bad artists, those conceited, narrow-minded Jews, those poor old doting monks and priests and bigots of the gruesome, dark age of faith! They couldn't draw a bit – no perspective, no anatomy, no chiaro-oscuro;* and it's a woeful image they managed to evolve for us out of the depths of their fathomless ignorance, in their zeal to keep us off all the forbidden fruit we're all so fond of, because we were built like that! And by whom? By our Maker, I suppose (who also made the forbidden fruit, and made it very nice – and put it so conveniently for you and me to see and smell and reach, Tray – and sometimes even pick, alas!).

'And even at that it's a failure, this precious image! Only the very foolish little birds are frightened into good behaviour. The naughty ones laugh and wink at each other, and pull out its hair and beard when nobody's looking, and build their nests out of the straw it's stuffed with (the naughty little birds in black, especially), and pick up what they want under its very nose, and thrive uncommonly well; and the good ones fly away out of sight; and some day, perhaps, find a home in some happy, useful fatherland far away where the Father isn't a bit like this. Who knows?

'And I'm one of the good little birds, Tray – at least, I hope so. And that unknown Father lives in me whether I will or no, and I love Him whether He be or not, just because I can't help it, and with the best and bravest love that can be – the perfect love that believeth no evil, and seeketh no reward, and casteth out fear. For I'm His father as much as He's mine, since I've conceived the thought of Him after my own fashion!

'And He lives in you too, Tray – you and all your kind. Yes, good dog, you king of beasts, I see it in your eyes . . .

'Ah, bon Dieu Père, le Dieu des bonnes gens!* Oh! if we only knew for *certain,* Tray! what martyrdom would we not endure, you and I, with a happy smile and a grateful heart – for sheer *love* of such a father! How little should *we* care for the things of this earth!

'But the poor parson?

'He must willy-nilly go on believing, or affecting to believe, just as he is told, *word for word,* or else good-bye to his wife and children's bread and butter, his own preferment, perhaps even his very gentility – that gentility of which his Master thought so little, and he and his are apt to think so much – with possibly the Archbishopric of Canterbury at the end of it, the *bâton de maréchal** that lies in every clerical knapsack.

'What a temptation! one is but human!

'So how can he be honest without believing certain things, to believe which (without shame) one must be as simple as a little child; as, by the way, he is so cleverly told to be in these matters, and so cleverly tells us – and so seldom is himself on any other matter whatever – his own interests, other people's affairs, the world, the flesh, and the devil! And that's clever of him too . . .

'And if he chooses to be as simple as a little child, why shouldn't I treat him as a little child, for his own good, and fool him to the top of his little bent for his dear daughter's sake, that I may make her happy, and thereby him too?

'And if he's *not* quite so simple as all that, and makes artful little compromises with his conscience – for a good purpose, of course – why shouldn't I make artful little compromises with mine, and for a better purpose still, and try to get what I want in the way *he* does? I want to marry his daughter far worse than he can ever want to live in a palace, and ride in a carriage and pair with a mitre on the panels.

'If he *cheats,* why shouldn't I cheat too?

'If *he* cheats, he cheats everybody all round – the wide, wide world, and something wider and higher still that can't be measured, something in himself. *I* only cheat *him!*

'*If* he cheats, he cheats for the sake of very worldly things indeed – tithes, honours, influence, power, authority, social consideration and respect – not to speak of bread and butter! *I* only cheat for the love of a lady fair – and cheating for cheating, I like my cheating best.

'So, whether he cheats or not, I'll—

'Confound it! what would old Taffy do in such a case, I wonder? . . .

'Oh, bother! it's no good wondering what old Taffy would do.

'Taffy never wants to marry *anybody's* daughter; he doesn't even want to paint her! He only wants to paint his beastly ragamuffins and thieves and drunkards, and be left alone.

'Besides, Taffy's as simple as a little child himself, and couldn't fool any one, and wouldn't if he could – not even a parson. But if any one tries to fool *him,* my eyes! don't he cut up rough, and call names, and kick up a shindy, and even knock people down! That's the worst of fellows like Taffy. They're too good for this world and too solemn. They're impossible, and lack all sense of humour. In point of fact Taffy's a *gentleman* – poor fellow! *et puis voilà!*

'I'm not simple – worse luck; and I can't knock people down

– I only wish I could! I can only paint them! and not even *that* 'as they really are!' . . . Good old Taffy! . . .

'Faint heart never won fair lady!

'Oh, happy, happy thought – I'll be brave and win!

'I can't knock people down, or do doughty deeds, but I'll be brave in my own little way – the only way I can . . .

'I'll simply lie through thick and thin – I must – I will – nobody need ever be a bit the wiser! I can do more good by lying than by telling the truth, and make more deserving people happy, including myself and the sweetest girl alive – the end shall justify the means: that's my excuse, my only excuse! and this lie of mine is on so stupendous a scale that it will have to last me for life. It's my only one, but its name is *Lion!* and I'll never tell another as long as I live.

'And now that I know what temptation really is, I'll never think any harm of any parson any more . . . never, never, never!'

So the little man went on, as if he knew all about it, had found it all out for himself, and nobody else had ever found it out before! and I am not responsible for his ways of thinking (which are not necessarily my own).

It must be remembered, in extenuation, that he was very young, and not very wise: no philosopher, no scholar – just a painter of lovely pictures; only that and nothing more. Also, that he was reading Mr Darwin's immortal book for the third time, and it was a little too strong for him; also, that all this happened in the early sixties, long ere Religion had made up her mind to meet Science half-way, and hobnob and kiss and be friends. Alas! before such a lying down of the lion and the lamb can ever come to pass, Religion will have to perform a larger share of the journey than half, I fear!

Then, still carried away by the flood of his own eloquence (for he had never had such an innings as this, nor such a listener), he again apostrophised the dog Tray, who had been growing somewhat inattentive (like the reader, perhaps), in language more beautiful than ever:

'Oh, to be like you, Tray – and secrete love and goodwill from morn till night, from night till morning – like saliva, without effort! with never a moment's cessation of flow, even in disgrace and humiliation! How much better to love than to be loved – to love as you do, my Tray – so warmly, so easily, so unremittingly – to forgive all wrongs and neglect and injustice

so quickly and so well – and forget a kindness never! Lucky dog
that you are!

> Oh! could I feel as I have felt, or be as I have been,
> Or weep as I could once have wept, o'er many a vanished scene,
> As springs in deserts found seem sweet, all brackish tho' they be,
> So 'midst this withered waste of life those tears would flow to me!*

'What do you think of those lines, Tray? I *love* them, because
my mother taught them to me when I was about your age – six
years old, or seven! and before the bard who wrote them had
fallen; like Lucifer, son of the morning!* Have you ever heard
of Lord Byron, Tray? He too, like Ulysses, loved a dog,* and
many people think that's about the best there is to be said of
him nowadays! Poor Humpty Dumpty!* Such a swell as he once
was! Not all the king's horses, nor all the—'

Here Tray jumped up suddenly and bolted – he saw some one
else he was fond of, and ran to meet him. It was the vicar,
coming out of his vicarage.

A very nice-looking vicar – fresh, clean, alert, well tanned by
sun and wind and weather – a youngish vicar still; tall, stout,
gentlemanlike, shrewd, kindly, worldly, a trifle pompous, and
authoritative more than a trifle; not much given to abstract
speculation, and thinking fifty times more of any sporting and
orthodox young country squire, well-inched and well-acred (and
well-whiskered), than of all the painters in Christendom.

'"When Greeks joined Greeks, then was the tug of war,"'*
thought Little Billee; and he felt a little uncomfortable. Alice's
father had never loomed so big and impressive before, or so
distressingly nice to look at.

'Welcome, my Apelles,* to your ain countree, which is
growing quite proud of you, I declare! Young Lord Archie
Waring was saying only last night that he wished he had half
your talent! He's *crazed* about painting, you know, and actually
wants to be a painter himself! The poor dear old marquis is
quite sore about it!'

With this happy exordium the parson stopped and shook
hands; and they both stood for a while, looking seaward. The
parson said the usual things about the sea – its blueness, its
grayness, its greenness, its beauty, its sadness, its treachery.

> Who shall put forth on thee,
> Unfathomable sea!*

'Who indeed!' answered Little Billee, quite agreeing. 'I vote *we* don't, at all events.' So they turned inland. The parson said the usual things about the land (from the country-gentleman's point of view), and the talk began to flow quite pleasantly, with quoting of the usual poets, and capping of quotations in the usual way – for they had known each other many years, both here and in London. Indeed, the vicar had once been Little Billee's tutor.

And thus, amicably, they entered a small wooded hollow. Then the vicar, turning of a sudden his full blue gaze on the painter, asked, sternly –

'What book's that you've got in your hand, Willie?'

'A – a – it's the *Origin of Species*, by Charles Darwin. I'm very f-f-fond of it. I'm reading it for the third time . . . It's very g-g-good. It *accounts* for things, you know.'

Then, after a pause, and still more sternly –

'What place of worship do you most attend in London – especially of an evening, William?'

Then stammered Little Billee, all self-control forsaking him –

'I d-d-don't attend any place of worship at all – morning, afternoon, or evening. I've long given up going to church altogether. I can only be frank with you; I'll tell you why . . .'

And as they walked along the talk drifted on to very momentous subjects indeed, and led, unfortunately, to a serious falling out – for which probably both were to blame – and closed in a distressful way at the other end of the little wooded hollow – a way most sudden and unexpected, and quite grievous to relate. When they emerged into the open, the parson was quite white, and the painter crimson.

'Sir,' said the parson, squaring himself up to more than his full height and breadth and dignity, his face big with righteous wrath, his voice full of strong menace – 'sir, you're – you're a – you're a *thief,* sir, a *thief*! You're trying to *rob me of my Saviour!* Never you dare to darken *my* door-step again!'

'Sir,' said Little Billee, with a bow, 'if it comes to calling names, you're – you're a – no; you're Alice's father; and whatever else you are besides, I'm another for trying to be honest with a parson; so good-morning to you.'

And each walked off in an opposite direction, stiff as pokers; and Tray stood between, looking first at one receding figure, then at the other, disconsolate.

'You're a thief, *sir!*'

And thus Little Billee found out that he could no more lie than he could fly. And so he did not marry sweet Alice after all, and no doubt it was ordered for her good and his. But there was tribulation for many days in the house of Bagot, and for many months in one tender, pure, and pious bosom.

And the best and the worst of it all is that, not very many years after, the good vicar – more fortunate than most clergymen who dabble in stocks and shares – grew suddenly very rich through a lucky speculation in Irish beer, and suddenly, also, took to thinking seriously about things (as a man of business should) – more seriously than he had ever thought before. So at least the story goes in North Devon, and it is not so new as to be incredible. Little doubts grew into big ones – big doubts resolved themselves into downright negations. He quarrelled with his bishop; he quarrelled with his dean; he even quarrelled with his 'poor dear old marquis,' who died before there was time to make it up again. And finally he felt it his duty, in conscience, to secede from a Church which had become too narrow to hold him, and took himself and his belongings to London, where at least he could breathe. But there he fell into a great disquiet, for the long habit of feeling himself always *en évidence** – of being looked up to and listened to without contradiction; of exercising influence and authority in spiritual matters (and even temporal); of impressing women, especially, with his commanding presence, his fine sonorous voice, his lofty brow, so serious and smooth, his soft, big, waving hands, which soon lost their country tan – all this had grown as a second nature to him, the breath of his nostrils, a necessity of his life. So he rose to be the most popular Positivist* preacher of his day, and pretty broad at that.

But his dear daughter Alice, she stuck to the old faith, and married a venerable High-Church archdeacon, who very cleverly clutched at and caught her and saved her for himself just as she stood shivering on the very brink of Rome; and they were neither happy nor unhappy together – *un ménage bourgeois, ni beau ni laid, ni bon ni mauvais.** And thus, alas! the bond of religious sympathy, that counts for so much in united families, no longer existed between father and daughter, and the heart's division divided them. *Ce que c'est que de nous!** ... The pity of it!

And so no more of sweet Alice with hair so brown.

Part Sixth

Vraiment, la reine auprès d'elle était laide
    Quand, vers le soir,
Elle passait sur le pont de Tolède
    En corset noir!
Un chapelet du temps de Charlemagne
    Ornait son cou ...
Le vent qui vient à travers la montagne
    Me rendra fou!

Dansez, chantez, villageois! la nuit tombe ...
    Sabine, un jour,
A tout donné – sa beauté de colombe,
    Et son amour –
Pour un anneau du Comte de Saldagne,
    Pour un bijou ...
Le vent qui vient à travers la montagne
    M'a rendu fou!*

Behold our three musketeers of the brush once more reunited in Paris, famous, after long years.

In emulation of the good Dumas, we will call it 'cinq ans après.'* It was a little more.

Taffy stands for Porthos and Athos* rolled into one, since he is big and good-natured, and strong enough to 'assommer un homme d'un coup de poing,'* and also stately and solemn, of aristocratic and romantic appearance, and not too fat – not too much ongbongpwang,* as the Laird called it – and also he does not dislike a bottle of wine, or even two, and looks as if he had a history.

The Laird, of course, is D'Artagnan,* since he sells his pictures well, and by the time we are writing of has already become an Associate of the Royal Academy; like Quentin Durward,* this D'Artagnan was a Scotsman:

Ah, wasna he a Roguey, this piper of Dundee!*

And Little Billee, the dainty friend of duchesses, must stand for Aramis, I fear! It will not do to push the simile too far; besides, unlike the good Dumas, one has a conscience. One does not play ducks and drakes with historical facts, or tamper with

An atmosphere of bank-notes and gold

historical personages. And if Athos, Porthos, and Co. are not historical by this time, I should like to know who are!

Well, so are Taffy, the Laird, and Little Billee – *tout ce qu'il y a de plus historique!**

Our three friends, well groomed, frock-coated, shirt-collared within an inch of their lives, duly scarfed and scarf-pinned, chimney-pot-hatted, and most beautifully trousered, and balmorally booted, or neatly spatted (or whatever was most correct at the time), are breakfasting together on coffee, rolls, and butter at a little round table in the huge courtyard of an immense caravansérai, paved with asphalt, and covered in at the top with a glazed roof that admits the sun and keeps out the rain – and the air.

A magnificent old man as big as Taffy, in black cloth coat and breeches and black silk stockings, and a large metal chain round his neck and chest, looks down like Jove from a broad flight of marble steps – as though to welcome the coming guests, who arrive in cabs and railway omnibuses through a huge archway on the boulevard; or to speed those who part through a lesser archway opening on to a side street.

'Bon voyage, messieurs et dames!'

At countless other little tables other voyagers are breakfasting or ordering breakfast; or, having breakfasted, are smoking and chatting and looking about. It is a babel of tongues – the cheerfullest, busiest, merriest scene in the world, apparently the costly place of rendezvous for all wealthy Europe and America; an atmosphere of banknotes and gold.

Already Taffy has recognised (and been recognised by) half a dozen old fellow-Crimeans, of unmistakable military aspect like himself; and three canny Scotsmen have discreetly greeted the Laird; and as for Little Billee, he is constantly jumping up from his breakfast and running to this table or that, drawn by some irresistible British smile of surprised and delighted female recognition: 'What, *you* here? How nice! Come over to hear La Svengali, I suppose?'

At the top of the marble steps in a long terrace, with seats and people sitting, from which tall glazed doors, elaborately carved and gilded, give access to luxurious drawing-rooms, diningrooms, reading-rooms, lavatories, postal and telegraph offices; and all round and about are huge square green boxes, out of which grow tropical and exotic evergreens all the year round –

with beautiful names that I have forgotten. And leaning against these boxes are placards announcing what theatrical or musical entertainments will take place in Paris that day or night; and the biggest of these placards (and the most fantastically decorated) informs the cosmopolite world that Madame Svengali intends to make her first appearance in Paris that very evening, at nine punctually, in the Cirque des Bashibazoucks,* Rue St Honoré!

Our friends had only arrived the previous night, but they had managed to secure stalls a week beforehand. No places were any longer to be got for love or money. Many people had come to Paris on purpose to hear La Svengali – many famous musicians from England and everywhere else – but they would have to wait many days.

The fame of her was like a rolling snow-ball that had been rolling all over Europe for the last two years – wherever there was snow to be picked up in the shape of golden ducats.

Their breakfast over, Taffy, the Laird, and Little Billee, cigar in mouth, arm-in-arm, the huge Taffy in the middle (*comme autrefois*),* crossed the sunshiny boulevard into the shade, and went down the Rue de la Paix,* through the Place Vendôme and the Rue Castiglione to the Rue de Rivoli – quite leisurely, and with a tender midriff-warming sensation of freedom and delight at almost every step.

Arrived at the corner pastrycook's, they finished the stumps of their cigars as they looked at the well-remembered show in the window; then they went in and had, Taffy a Madeleine, the Laird a Baba, and Little Billee a Savarin – and each, I regret to say, a liqueur-glass of *rhum de la Jamaïque*.*

After this they sauntered through the Tuileries Gardens, and by the quay to their favourite Pont des Arts, and looked up and down the river – *comme autrefois!*

It is an enchanting prospect at any time and under any circumstances; but on a beautiful morning in mid-October, when you haven't seen it for five years, and are still young! and almost every stock and stone that meets your eye, every sound, every scent, has some sweet and subtle reminder for you –

Let the reader have no fear. I will not attempt to describe it. I shouldn't know where to begin (nor when to leave off).

Not but what many changes had been wrought; many old landmarks were missing. And among them, as they found out a few minutes later, and much to their chagrin, the good old Morgue!

They inquired of a *gardien de la paix*,* who told them that a new Morgue – 'une bien jolie Morgue, ma foi!'* – and much more commodious and comfortable than the old one, had been built beyond Notre Dame, a little to the right.

'Messieurs devraient voir ça – on y est très bien!'*

But Notre Dame herself was still there, and La Sainte Chapelle* and Le Pont Neuf, and the equestrian statue of Henri IV.* *C'est toujours ça!*

And as they gazed and gazed, each framed unto himself, mentally, a little picture of the Thames they had just left – and thought of Waterloo Bridge, and St Paul's, and London – but felt no home-sickness whatever, no desire to go back in a hurry!

And looking down the river westward there was but little change.

On the left-hand side the terraces and garden of the Hôtel de la Rochemartel (the sculptured entrance of which was in the Rue de Lille) still overtopped the neighbouring houses and shaded the quay with tall trees, whose lightly-falling leaves yellowed the pavement for at least a hundred yards of frontage – or backage, rather; for this was but the rear of that stately palace.

'I wonder if l'Zouzou has come into his dukedom yet?' said Taffy.

And Taffy the realist, Taffy the modern of moderns, also said many beautiful things about old historical French dukedoms; which, in spite of their plentifulness, were so much more picturesque than English ones, and constituted a far more poetical and romantic link with the past; partly on account of their beautiful, high-sounding names.

'Amaury de Brissac de Roncesvaulx de la Rochemartel-Boisségur! what a generous mouthful! Why, the very sound of it is redolent of the twelfth century! Not even Howard of Norfolk can beat that!'

For Taffy was getting sick of 'this ghastly thin-faced time of ours,' as he sadly called it (quoting from a strange and very beautiful poem called 'Faustine,'* which had just appeared in the *Spectator* – and which our three enthusiasts already knew by heart), and beginning to love all things that were old and

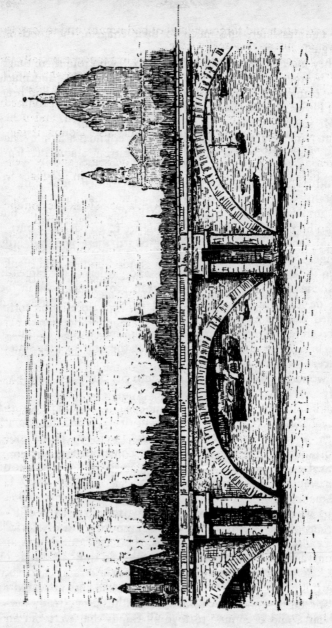

A little picture of the Thames

regal and rotten and forgotten and of bad repute, and to long to paint them just as they really were.

'Ah! they managed these things better in France, especially in the twelfth century, and even the thirteenth!' said the Laird. 'Still, Howard of Norfolk* isn't bad at a pinch – *fote de myoo!*'* he continued, winking at Little Billee. And they promised themselves that they would leave cards on Zouzou, and if he wasn't a duke, invite him to dinner; and also Dodor, if they could manage to find him.

Then along the quay and up the Rue de Seine, and by well-remembered little mystic ways to the old studio in the Place St Anatole des Arts.

Here they found many changes. A row of new houses on the north side, by Baron Haussmann* – the well-named – a boulevard was being constructed right through the place. But the old house had been respected; and looking up, they saw the big north window of their good old abode blindless and blank and black, but for a white placard in the middle of it with the words: 'À louer. Un atelier, et une chambre à coucher.'*

They entered the courtyard through the little door in the porte cochère, and beheld Madame Vinard standing on the step of her loge, her arms akimbo, giving orders to her husband – who was sawing logs for firewood, as usual at that time of the year – and telling him he was the most helpless log of the lot.

She gave them one look, threw up her arms, and rushed at them, saying, 'Ah, mon Dieu! les trois Angliches!'

And they could not have complained of any lack of warmth in her greeting, or in Monsieur Vinard's.

'Ah! mais quel bonheur de vous revoir! Et comme vous avez bonne mine, tous! Et Monsieur Litrebili, donc! il a grandi!' etc., etc.. 'Mais vous allez boire la gouette avant tout – vite, Vinard! Le ratafia de cassis que Monsieur Durien nous a envoyé la semaine dernière!'*

And they were taken into the loge* and made free of it – welcomed like prodigal sons; a fresh bottle of blackcurrant brandy was tapped, and did duty for the fatted calf. It was an ovation, and made quite a stir in the Quartier.

Le Retour des trois Angliches – cinq ans après!

She told them all the news: about Bouchardy; Papelard; Jules Guinot, who was now in the Ministère de la Guerre; Barizel, who had given up the arts and gone into his father's business

'Ah! The beautiful interment, messieurs!'

(umbrellas); Durien, who had married six months ago, and had a superb atelier in the Rue Taitbout,* and was coining money; about her own family – Aglaë, who was going to be married to the son of the charbonnier* at the corner of the Rue de la Canicule* – 'un bon mariage; bien solide!'* Niniche, who was studying the piano at the Conservatoire, and had won the silver medal; Isidore, who, alas! had gone to the bad – 'perdu par les femmes! un si joli garçon, vous concevez! ça ne lui a pas porté bonheur, par exemple!'* And yet she was proud! and said his father would never have had the pluck!

'A dix-huit ans, pensez donc!*

'And that good Monsieur Carrel; he is dead, you know! Ah, messieurs savaient ça?* Yes, he died at Dieppe, his natal town, during the winter, from the consequences of an indigestion – que voulez-vous!* He always had the stomach so feeble! . . . Ah, the beautiful interment, messieurs! Five thousand people, in spite of the rain! Car il pleuvait averse!* And M. le Maire and his adjunct walking behind the hearse, and the gendarmerie and the douaniers,* and a battalion of the douzième chasseurs-à-pied,* with their music, and all the sapper-pumpers, en grande tenue* with their beautiful brass helmets! All the town was there, following: so there was nobody left to see the procession go by! q'c'était beau! Mon Dieu, q'c'était beau! c'que j'ai pleuré, d'voir ça! n'est-ce-pas, Vinard?'

'Dame, oui, ma biche! j'crois bien!* It might have been Monsieur le Maire himself that one was interring in person!'

'Ah, ça! voyons, Vinard; thou'rt not going to compare the Maire of Dieppe to a painter like Monsieur Carrel?'

'Certainly not, ma biche! But still, M. Carrel was a great man all the same, in his way. Besides, I wasn't there – nor thou either, as to that!'

'Mon Dieu! comme il est idiot, ce Vinard* – of a stupidity to cut with a knife! Why, thou might'st almost be a Mayor thyself, sacred imbecile that thou art!'

And an animated discussion arose between husband and wife as to the respective merits of a country mayor on one side and a famous painter and a member of the Institute on the other, during which les trois Angliches were left out in the cold. When Madame Vinard had sufficiently routed her husband, which did not take very long, she turned to them again, and told them that she had started a magasin de bric-à-brac,* 'vous verrez ça!'*

Yes, the studio had been to let for three months. Would they like to see it? Here were the keys. They would, of course, prefer to see it by themselves, alone; 'je comprends ça! et vous verrez ce que vous verrez!' Then they must come and drink once more again the drop, and inspect her *magasin de bric-à-brac*.

So they went up, all three, and let themselves into the old place where they had been so happy – and one of them for a while so miserable!

It was changed indeed.

Bare of all furniture, for one thing; shabby and unswept, with a pathetic air of dilapidation, spoliation, desecration, and a musty, shut-up smell; the window so dirty you could hardly see the new houses opposite; the floor a disgrace!

All over the walls were caricatures in charcoal and white chalk, with more or less incomprehensible legends; very vulgar and trivial and coarse, some of them, and pointless for *trois Angliches*.

But among these (touching to relate) they found, under a square of plate-glass that had been fixed on the wall by means of an oak frame, Little Billee's old black-and-white-and-red chalk sketch of Trilby's left foot, as fresh as if it had been done only yesterday! Over it was written: 'Souvenir de la Grande Trilby, par W. B. (Litrebili).' And beneath, carefully engrossed on imperishable parchment, and pasted on the glass, the following stanzas: –

> Pauvre Trilby – la belle et bonne et chère!
> Je suis son pied. Devine qui voudra.
> Quel tendre ami, la chérissant naguère,
> Encadra d'elle (et d'un amour sincère)
> Ce souvenir charmant qu'un caprice inspira –
> Qu'un souffle emportera!
>
> J'étais jumeau: qu'est devenu mon frère?
> Hélas! Hélas: L'Amour nous égara.
> L'Éternité nous unira, j'espère;
> Et nous ferons comme autrefois la paire
> Au fond d'un lit bien chaste où nul ne troublera
> Trilby – qui dormira.
>
> Ô tendre ami, sans nous qu'allez-vous faire?
> La porte est close où Trilby demeura.
> Le Paradis est loin . . . et sur la terre
> (oui nous fut douce et lui sera légère)

'Pauvre Trilby'

Pour trouver nos pareils, si bien qu'on cherchera –
Beau chercher l'on aura!*

Taffy drew a long breath into his manly bosom, and kept it there as he read this characteristic French doggerel (for so he chose to call this touching little symphony in *ère* and *ra*). His huge frame thrilled with tenderness and pity and fond remembrance, and he said to himself (letting out his breath): 'Dear, dear Trilby! Ah! if you had only cared for *me*, *I* wouldn't have let you give me up – not for any one on earth. *You* were the mate for *me!*'

And that, as the reader has guessed long ago, was big Taffy's 'history.'

The Laird was also deeply touched, and could not speak. Had he been in love with Trilby, too? Had he ever been in love with any one?

He couldn't say. But he thought of Trilby's sweetness and unselfishness, her gaiety, her innocent kissings and caressings, her drollery and frolicsome grace, her way of filling whatever place she was in with her presence, the charming sight and the genial sound of her; and felt that no girl, no woman, no lady he had ever seen yet was a match for this poor waif and stray, this long-legged, cancan-dancing, Quartier Latin grisette, blanchisseuse de fin, 'and Heaven knows what besides!'

'Hang it all!' he mentally ejaculated, 'I wish to goodness I'd married her *myself!*'

Little Billee said nothing either. He felt unhappier than he had ever once felt for five long years – to think that he could gaze on such a memento as this, a thing so strongly personal to himself, with dry eyes and a quiet pulse! and he unemotionally, dispassionately, wished himself dead and buried for at least the thousand-and-first time!

All three possessed casts of Trilby's hands and feet, and photographs of herself. But nothing so charmingly suggestive of Trilby as this little masterpiece of a true artist, this happy fluke of a happy moment. It was Trilbyness itself, as the Laird thought, and should not be suffered to perish.

They took the keys back to Madame Vinard in silence.

She said: 'Vous avez vu – n'est-ce pas, messieurs? – le pied de Trilby! c'est bien gentil! C'est Monsieur Durien qui a fait mettre le verre, quand vous êtes partis; et Monsieur Guinot qui a composé *l'épitaphe*. Pauvre Trilby! qu'est-ce qu'elle est devenue! comme elle était bonne fille, hein? et si belle! et comme elle était vive elle était vive elle était vive! Et comme elle vous aimait tous bien – et surtout Monsieur Litrebili – n'est-ce pas?'*

Then she insisted on giving them each another liqueur-glass of Durien's ratafia de cassis, and took them to see her collection of *bric-à-brac* across the yard, a gorgeous show, and explained everything about it – how she had begun in quite a small way, but was making it a big business.

'Voyez cette pendule!* It is of the time of Louis Onze, who gave it with his own hands to Madame le Pompadour(!)*. I bought it at a sale in—'

'Combiang?' said the Laird.

'C'est cent-cinquante francs, monsieur – c'est bien bon marché – une véritable occasion,* et—'

'Je prong!' said the Laird, meaning 'I take it!'

Then she showed them a beautiful brocade gown 'which she had picked up a bargain at—'

'Combiang?' said the Laird.

'Ah, ça, c'est trois cents francs,* monsieur. Mais—'

'Je prong!' said the Laird.

'Et voici les souliers qui vont avec,* et que—'

'Je pr—'

But here Taffy took the Laird by the arm and dragged him by force out of this too seductive siren's cave.

The Laird told her where to send his purchases, and with many expressions of love and good-will on both sides, they tore themselves away from Monsieur and Madame Vinard.

The Laird, however, rushed back for a minute, and hurriedly whispered to Madame Vinard: 'Oh – er – le piay de Trilby – sur le mure, vous savvy – avec le verre et toot le reste – coopy le mure – comprenny? . . . Combiang?'

'Ah, Monsieur!' said Madame Vinard – 'c'est un peu difficile, vous savez – couper un mur comme ça! On parlera au proprié-taire si vous voulez, et ça pourrait peut-être s'arranger, si c'est en bois! seulement il fau—'

'Je prong!'* said the Laird, and waved his hand in farewell.

They went up the Rue Vieille des Trois Mauvais Ladres, and found that about twenty yards of a high wall had been pulled down – just at the bend where the Laird had seen the last of Trilby, as she turned round and kissed her hand to him – and

'Je Prong!'

they beheld, within, a quaint and ancient long-neglected garden;
a gray old garden, with tall, warty, black-boled trees, and damp,
green, mossy paths that lost themselves under the brown and
yellow leaves and mould and muck which had drifted into heaps
here and there, the accumulation of years – a queer old faded
pleasance, with wasted bowers and dilapidated carved stone
benches and weather-beaten discoloured marble statues – nose-
less, armless, earless fauns and hamadryads!* And at the end of
it, in a tumble-down state of utter ruin, a still inhabited little
house, with shabby blinds and window-curtains, and broken
window-panes mended with brown paper – a Pavillon de Flore,*
that must have been quite beautiful a hundred years ago – the
once mysterious love-resort of long-buried abbés with light

hearts, and well-forgotten lords and ladies gay – red-heeled, patched, powdered, frivolous, and shameless, but, oh! how charming to the imagination of the nineteenth century! And right through the ragged lawn (where lay, upset in the long dewy grass, a broken doll's perambulator by a tattered Polichinelle*) went a desecrating track made by cart-wheels and horses' hoofs; and this, no doubt, was to be a new street – perhaps, as Taffy suggested, 'La Rue *Neuve* des Trois Mauvais Ladres!' (The *new* street of the three bad lepers!)

'Ah, Taffy!' sententiously opined the Laird, with his usual wink at Little Billee – 'I've no doubt the *old* lepers were the best, bad as they were!'

'I'm quite *sure* of it!' said Taffy, with sad and sober conviction and a long-drawn sigh. 'I only wish I had a chance of painting one – just as he really was!'

How often they had speculated on what lay hidden behind that lofty old brick wall! and now this odd old poverty-stricken abode of Heaven knows what present grief and desolation, which a few strokes of the pickaxe had laid bare, seemed to chime in with their own gray mood that had been so bright and sunny an hour ago; and they went on their way quite dejectedly, for a stroll through the Luxembourg Gallery and Gardens.

The same people seemed to be still copying the same pictures in the long, quiet, genial room, so pleasantly smelling of oil-paint – Rosa Bonheur's 'Labourage Nivernais,' Hébert's 'Malaria,' Couture's 'Decadent Romans.'*

And in the formal dusty gardens were the same pioupious and zouzous still walking with the same nounous, or sitting by their sides on benches by formal ponds with gold and silver fish in them – and just the same old couples petting the same toutous and loulous![1]

Then they thought they would go and lunch at le père Trin's – the Restaurant de la Couronne, in the Rue du Luxembourg – for the sake of auld lang syne! But when they got there, the well-remembered fumes of that humble refectory, which had once seemed not unappetising, turned their stomachs. So they contented themselves with warmly greeting le père Trin, who was

[1] *Glossary.* – Pioupiou (*alias* pousse-caillou, *alias* tour-lourou) – a private soldier of the line. Zouzou – a Zouave. Nounou – a wet-nurse with a pretty ribboned cap and long streamers. Toutou – a nondescript French lapdog, of no breed known to Englishmen (a regular little beast!). Loulou – a Pomeranian dog – not much better.

'Oon pair de gong blong'

quite overjoyed to see them again, and anxious to turn the whole establishment topsy-turvy that he might entertain such guests as they deserved.

Then the Laird suggested an omelet at the Café de l'Odéon. but Taffy said, in his masterful way, 'Damn the Café de l'Odéon!'

And hailing a little open fly, they drove to Ledoyen's,* or some such place, in the Champs Élysées, where they feasted as became three prosperous Britons out for a holiday in Paris – three irresponsible musketeers, lords of themselves and Lutetia,* *beati possidentes!** – and afterwards had themselves driven in an open carriage and pair through the Bois de Boulogne to the fête de St Cloud (or what still remained of it, for it lasts six weeks), the scene of so many of Dodor's and Zouzou's exploits in past years, and found it more amusing than the Luxembourg Gardens; the lively and irrepressible spirit of Dodor seemed to pervade it still.

But it doesn't want the presence of a Dodor to make the blue-bloused sons of the Gallic people (and its neatly-shod, white-capped daughters) delightful to watch as they take their pleasure. And the Laird (thinking perhaps of Hampstead Heath* on an Easter Monday) must not be blamed for once more quoting his favourite phrase – the pretty little phrase with which the most humorous and least exemplary of British parsons began his famous journey to France.

When they came back to the hotel to dress and dine, the Laird found he wanted a pair of white gloves for the concert – 'Oon pair de gong blong,' as he called it – and they walked along the boulevards till they came to a haberdasher's shop of very good and prosperous appearance, and, going in, were received graciously by the 'patron,' a portly little bourgeois, who waved them to a tall and aristocratic and very well-dressed young commis behind the counter, saying, 'Une paire de gants blancs pour monsieur.'

And what was the surprise of our three friends in recognising Dodor!

The gay Dodor, Dodor *l'irrésistible*,* quite unembarrassed by his position, was exuberant in his delight at seeing them again, and introduced them to the patron and his wife and daughter, Monsieur, Madame, and Mademoiselle Passefil. And it soon became pretty evident that, in spite of his humble employment in that house, he was a great favourite in that family, and especially with mademoiselle.

Indeed, Monsieur Passefil invited our three heroes to stay and dine then and there; but they compromised matters by asking Dodor to come and dine with *them* at the hotel, and he accepted with alacrity.

Thanks to Dodor, the dinner was a very lively one, and they soon forgot the regretful impressions of the day.

They learned that he hadn't got a penny in the world, and had left the army, and had for two years kept the books at le père Passefil's and served his customers, and won his good opinion and his wife's, and especially his daughter's; and that soon he was to be not only his employer's partner, but his son-in-law; and that, in spite of his impecuniosity, he had managed to impress them with the fact that in marrying a Rigolot de Lafarce she was making a very splendid match indeed!

His brother-in-law, the Honourable Jack Reeve, had long cut him for a bad lot. But his sister, after a while, had made up her mind that to marry Mlle. Passefil wasn't the worst he could do; at all events, it would keep him out of England, and *that* was a comfort! And passing through Paris, she had actually called on the Passefil family, and they had fallen prostrate before such splendour; and no wonder, for Mrs Jack Reeve was one of the most beautiful, elegant, and fashionable women in London, the smartest of the smart.

'And how about l'Zouzou?' asked Little Billee.

'Ah, old Gontran! I don't see much of him. We no longer quite move in the same circles, you know; not that he's proud, or me either! but he's a sub-lieutenant in the Guides – an officer! Besides, his brother's dead, and he's the Duc de la Rochemartel, and a special pet of the Empress;* he makes her laugh more than anybody! He's looking out for the biggest heiress he can find, and he's pretty safe to catch her, with such a name as that! In fact, they say he's caught her already – Miss Lavinia Hunks, of Chicago. Twenty million dollars! – at least, so the *Figaro* says!'

Then he gave them news of other old friends; and they did not part till it was time for them to go to the Cirque des Bashibazoucks, and after they had arranged to dine with his future family on the following day.

In the Rue St Honoré was a long double file of cabs and carriages slowly moving along to the portals of that huge hall, Le Cirque des Bashibazoucks. Is it there still, I wonder? I don't mind betting not! Just at this period of the Second Empire* there was a mania for demolition and remolition (if there is such a word), and I have no doubt my Parisian readers would search the Rue St Honoré for the Salle des Bashibazoucks in vain!

Our friends were shown to their stalls, and looked round in surprise. This was before the days of the Albert Hall,* and they had never been in such a big place of the kind before, or one so regal in aspect, so gorgeously imperial with white and gold and crimson velvet, so dazzling with light, so crammed with people from floor to roof, and cramming itself still.

A platform carpeted with crimson cloth had been erected in front of the gates where the horses had once used to come in, and their fair riders, and the two jolly English clowns; and the beautiful nobleman with the long frock-coat and brass buttons, and soft high boots, and four-in-hand whip – *la chambrière*.

In front of this was a lower stand for the orchestra. The circus itself was filled with stalls – *stalles d'orchestre*. A pair of crimson curtains hid the entrance to the platform at the back, and by each of these stood a small page, ready to draw it aside and admit the diva.

The entrance to the orchestra was by a small door under the platform, and some thirty or forty chairs and music-stands, grouped around the conductor's *estrade*,* were waiting for the band.

Little Billee looked round, and recognised many countrymen and countrywomen of his own – many great musical celebrities especially, whom he had often met in London. Tiers upon tiers of people rose up all round in a widening circle, and lost themselves in a dazy mist of light at the top – it was like a picture by Martin!* In the imperial box were the English ambassador and his family, with an august British personage sitting in the middle, in front, his broad blue ribbon* across his breast and his opera-glass to his royal eyes.

Little Billee had never felt so excited, so exhilarated by such a show before, nor so full of eager anticipation. He looked at his programme, and saw that the Hungarian band (the first that had yet appeared in Western Europe, I believe) would play an overture of gypsy dances. Then Madame Svengali would sing 'un air connu, sans accompagnement' and afterwards other airs, including the 'Nussbaum' of Schumann* (for the first time in Paris, it seemed). Then a rest of ten minutes; then more *csárdás*; then the diva would sing 'Malbrouck s'en va-t'en guerre,'* of all things in the world! and finish up with 'un impromptu de Chopin, sans paroles.'*

Truly a somewhat incongruous bill of fare.

Close on the stroke of nine the musicians came in and took their seats. They were dressed in the foreign hussar uniform that has now become so familiar. The first violin had scarcely sat down before our friends recognised in him their old friend Gecko.

Just as the clock struck, Svengali, in irreproachable evening dress, tall and stout and quite splendid in appearance, notwithstanding his long black mane (which had been curled), took his place at his desk. Our friends would have known him at a glance, in spite of the wonderful alteration time and prosperity had wrought in his outward man.

He bowed right and left to the thunderous applause that greeted him, gave his three little bâton-taps, and the lovely music began at once. We have grown accustomed to strains of this kind during the last twenty years, but they were new then, and their strange seduction was a surprise as well as an enchantment.

Besides, no such band as Svengali's had ever been heard; and in listening to this overture the immense crowd almost forgot that it was a mere preparation for a great musical event, and tried to encore it. But Svengali merely turned round and bowed – there were to be no encores that night.

Then a moment of silence and breathless suspense – curiosity on tiptoe!

Then the two little page-boys each drew a silken rope, and the curtains parted and looped themselves up on each side symmetrically; and a tall female figure appeared, clad in what seemed like a classical dress of cloth of gold, embroidered with garnets and beetles' wings; her snowy arms and shoulders bare, a gold coronet of stars on her head, her thick light brown hair tied behind and flowing all down her back to nearly her knees, like those ladies in hair-dressers' shops who sit with their backs to the plate-glass window to advertise the merits of some particular hair-wash.

She walked slowly down to the front, her hands hanging at her sides in quite a simple fashion, and made a slight inclination

Gecko

of her head and body towards the imperial box, and then to right and left. Her lips and cheeks were rouged; her dark level eye-brows nearly met at the bridge of her short high nose. Through her parted lips you could see her large glistening white teeth; her gray eyes looked straight at Svengali.

Her face was thin, and had a rather haggard expression, in spite of its artificial freshness; but its contour was divine, and its character so tender, so humble, so touchingly simple and sweet, that one melted at the sight of her. No such magnificent or seductive apparition has ever been seen before or since on any stage or platform – not even Miss Ellen Terry as the priestess of Artemis* in the late laureate's play, *The Cup*.

The house rose at her as she came down to the front; and she bowed again to right and left, and put her hand to her heart quite simply and with a most winning natural gesture, an adorable *gaucherie** – like a graceful and unconscious school-girl, quite innocent of stage deportment.

It was Trilby!

Trilby the tone-deaf, who couldn't sing one single note in tune! Trilby, who couldn't tell a C from an F!!

What was going to happen?

Our three friends were almost turned to stone in the immensity of their surprise.

Yet the big Taffy was trembling all over; the Laird's jaw had all but fallen on to his chest; Little Billee was staring, staring his eyes almost out of his head. There was something, to them, so strange and uncanny about it all; so oppressive, so anxious, so momentous!

The applause had at last subsided. Trilby stood with her hands behind her, one foot (the left one) on a little stool that had been left there on purpose, her lips parted, her eyes on Svengali's, ready to begin.

He gave his three beats, and the band struck a chord. Then, at another beat from him, but in her direction, she began, without the slightest appearance of effort, without any accompaniment whatever, he still beating time – conducting her, in fact, just as if she had been an orchestra herself:

> Au clair de la lune,
> Mon ami Pierrot!

Au clair de la lune

Prête-moi ta plume
　　Pour écrire un mot.
Ma chandelle est morte . . .
　　Je n'ai plus de feu!
Ouvre-moi ta porte
　　Pour l'amour de Dieu!*

This was the absurd old nursery rhyme with which La Svengali chose to make her *début* before the most critical audience in the world! She sang it three times over – the same verse. There is but one.

The first time she sang it without any expression whatever – not the slightest. Just the words and the tune; in the middle of her voice, and not loud at all; just as a child sings who is thinking of something else; or just as a young French mother sings who is darning socks by a cradle, and rocking her baby to sleep with her foot.

But her voice was so immense in its softness, richness, freshness, that it seemed to be pouring itself out from all round; its intonation absolutely, mathematically pure; one felt it to be not only faultless, but infallible; and the seduction, the novelty of it, the strangely sympathetic quality! How can one describe the quality of a peach or a nectarine to those who have only known apples?

Until La Svengali appeared, the world had only known apples – Catalanis, Jenny Linds, Grisis,* Albonis, Pattis! The best apples that can be, for sure – but still only apples!

If she had spread a pair of large white wings and gracefully fluttered up to the roof and perched upon the chandelier, she could not have produced a greater sensation. The like of that voice has never been heard, nor ever will be again. A woman archangel might sing like that, or some enchanted princess out of a fairy tale.

Little Billee had already dropped his face into his hands and hid his eyes in his pocket-handkerchief; a big tear had fallen on to Taffy's left whisker; the Laird was trying hard to keep his tears back.

She sang the verse a second time, with but little added expression and no louder; but with a sort of breathy widening of her voice that made it like a broad heavenly smile of universal motherhood turned into sound. One felt all the genial gaiety and grace of impishness of Pierrot and Columbine* idealised into frolicsome beauty and holy innocence, as though they were performing for the saints in Paradise – a baby Columbine, with a cherub for clown! The dream of it all came over you for a second or two – a revelation of some impossible golden age – priceless – never to be forgotten! How on earth did she do it?

Little Billee had lost all control over himself, and was shaking with his suppressed sobs – Little Billee, who hadn't shed a single tear for five long years! Half the people in the house were in tears, but tears of sheer delight, of delicate inner laughter.

Then she came back to earth, and saddened and veiled and darkened her voice as she sang the verse for the third time; and it was a great and sombre tragedy, too deep for any more tears; and somehow or other poor Columbine, forlorn and betrayed and dying, out in the cold at midnight – sinking down to hell, perhaps – was making her last frantic appeal! It was no longer Pierrot and Columbine – it was Marguerite – it was Faust!* It was the most terrible and pathetic of all possible human tragedies, but expressed with no dramatic or histrionic exaggeration of any sort; by mere tone, slight, subtle changes in the quality of the sound – too quick and elusive to be taken count of, but to be felt with, oh, what poignant sympathy!

When the song was over, the applause did not come immediately, and she waited with her kind wide smile, as if she were well accustomed to wait like this; and then the storm began, and grew and spread and rattled and echoed – voice, hands, feet, sticks, umbrellas! – and down came the bouquets, which the little page-boys picked up; and Trilby bowed to front and right and left in her simple *débonnaire** fashion. It was her usual triumph. It had never failed, whatever the audience, whatever the country, whatever the song.

Little Billee didn't applaud. He sat with his head in his hands, his shoulders still heaving. He believed himself to be fast asleep and in a dream, and was trying his utmost not to wake; for a great happiness was his. It was one of those nights to be marked with a white stone!

As the first bars of the song came pouring out of her parted lips (whose shape he so well remembered), and her dove-like eyes looked straight over Svengali's head, straight in his own direction – nay, *at* him – something melted in his brain, and all his long-lost power of loving came back with a rush.

It was like the sudden curing of a deafness that has been

Ouvre-moi ta porte pour l'amour de dieu!'

lasting for years. The doctor blows through your nose into your Eustachian tube with a little india-rubber machine; some obstacle gives way, there is a snap in your head, and straightway you hear better than you had ever heard in all your life, almost too well; and all your life is once more changed for you!

At length he sat up again, in the middle of La Svengali's singing of the 'Nussbaum,' and saw her; and saw the Laird sitting by him, and Taffy, their eyes riveted on Trilby, and knew for certain that it was *no* dream this time, and his joy was almost a pain!

She sang the 'Nussbaum' (to its heavenly accompaniment) as simply as she had sung the previous song. Every separate note was a highly-finished gem of sound, linked to the next by a magic bond. You did not require to be a lover of music to fall beneath the spell of such a voice as that; the mere melodic phrase had all but ceased to matter. Her phrasing, consummate as it was, was as simple as a child's.

It was as if she said: 'See! what does the composer count for? Here is about as beautiful a song as was ever written, with beautiful words to match, and the words have been made French for you by one of your smartest poets! But what do the words signify, any more than the tune, or even the language? The "Nussbaum" is neither better nor worse than "Mon ami Pierrot" when I am the singer; for I am *Trilby*; and you shall hear nothing, see nothing, think of nothing, but *Svengali, Svengali, Svengali!*'

It was the apotheosis of voice and virtuosity! It was 'il bel canto' come back to earth after a hundred years – the bel canto of Vivarelli,* let us say, who sang the same song every night to the same King of Spain for a quarter of a century, and was rewarded with a dukedom, and wealth beyond the dreams of avarice.

And, indeed, here was this immense audience, made up of the most cynically critical people in the world, and the most anti-German, assisting with rapt ears and streaming eyes at the imagined spectacle of a simple German damsel, a Mädchen, a Fräulein,* just *verlobte** – a future Hausfrau – sitting under a walnut-tree in some suburban garden – à Berlin! – and around her, her family and her friends, probably drinking beer and smoking long porcelain pipes, and talking politics or business, and cracking innocent elaborate old German jokes; with bated breath, lest they should disturb her maiden dream of love! And all as though it were a scene in Elysium,* and the Fräulein a nymph of many-fountained Ida,* and her people Olympian gods and goddesses.

And such, indeed, they were when Trilby sang of them!

After this, when the long, frantic applause had subsided, she made a gracious bow to the royal British opera-glass (which had never left her face), and sang 'Ben Bolt' in English!

And then Little Billee remembered there was such a person as Svengali in the world, and recalled his little flexible flageolet!

'That is how I teach Gecko; that is how I teach la bedite Honorine; that is how I teach il bel canto . . . It was lost, il bel canto – and I found it in a dream – I, Svengali!'

And his old cosmic vision of the beauty and sadness of things, the very heart of them, and their pathetic evanescence, came back with a tenfold clearness – that heavenly glimpse beyond the veil! And with it a crushing sense of his own infinitesimal significance by the side of this glorious pair of artists, one of whom had been his friend and the other his love – a love who had offered to be his humble mistress and slave, not feeling herself good enough to be his wife!

It made him sick and faint to remember, and filled him with hot shame, and then and there his love for Trilby became as that of a dog for its master!

She sang once more – 'Chanson de Printemps,' by Gounod* (who was present, and seemed very hysterical), and the first part of the concert was over, and people had time to draw breath and talk over this new wonder, this revelation of what the human voice could achieve; and an immense hum filled the hall – astonishment, enthusiasm, ecstatic delight!

But our three friends found little to say – for what *they* felt there was as yet no words!

Taffy and the Laird looked at Little Billee, who seemed to be looking inward at some transcendent dream of his own; with red eyes, and his face all pale and drawn, and his nose very pink, and rather thicker than usual; and the dream appeared to be out of the common blissful, though his eyes were swimming still, for his smile was almost idiotic in its rapture!

The second part of the concert was still shorter than the first, and created, if possible, a wilder enthusiasm.

Trilby only sang twice.

Her first song was 'Malbrouck s'en va-t'en guerre.'

She began it quite lightly and merrily, like a jolly march; in the middle of her voice, which had not as yet revealed any exceptional compass or range. People laughed quite frankly at the first verse: –

> Malbrouck s'en va-t'en guerre –
> *Mironton, mironton, mirontaine!*
> Malbrouck s'en va-t'en guerre . . .
>> Ne sais quand reviendra!
>> Ne sais quand reviendra!
>> Ne sais quand reviendra!

The *mironton, mirontaine* was the very essence of high martial resolve and heroic self-confidence; one would have led a forlorn hope after hearing it once!

> Il reviendra-z à Pâques . . .
> *Mironton, mironton, mirontaine!*
> Il reviendra-z à Pâques. . . .
>> Ou . . . à la Trinité!*

People still laughed, though the *mironton, mirontaine,* betrayed an uncomfortable sense of the dawning of doubts and fears – vague forebodings!

> La Trinité se passe –
> *Mironton, mironton, mirontaine!*
> La Trinité se passe . . .
>> Malbrouck ne revient pas!*

And here, especially in the *mironton, mirontaine*, a note of anxiety revealed itself – so poignant, so acutely natural and human, that it became a personal anxiety of one's own, causing the heart to beat, and one's breath was short.

> Madame à sa tour monte –
> *Mironton, mironton, mirontaine!*
> Madame à sa tour monte,
>> Si haut qu'elle peut monter!

Oh! How one's heart went with her! Anne! Sister Anne! Do you see anything?

> Elle voit de loin son page –
> *Mironton, mironton, mirontaine!*

Malbrouck s'en va-t'en guerre

> Elle voit de loin son page,
>> Tout de noir habillé!

One is almost sick with the sense of impending calamity — it is all but unbearable!

> Mon page — mon beau page! —
>> *Mironton, mironton, mirontaine!*
> Mon page — mon beau page!
>> Quelle nouvelles apportez?*

And here Little Billee begins to weep again, and so does everybody else! The *mironton, mirontaine,* is an agonised wail of suspense — poor bereaved duchess! — poor Sarah Jennings!* Did it all announce itself to you just like that?

All this while the accompaniment had been quite simple — just a few obvious ordinary chords.

But now, quite suddenly, without a single modulation or note of warning, down goes the tune a full major third, from E to C — into the graver depths of Trilby's great contralto — so solemn and ominous that there is no more weeping, but the flesh creeps; the accompaniment slows and elaborates itself; the march becomes a funeral march, with muted strings, and quite slowly:

> Aux nouvelles que j'apporte —
>> *Mironton, mironton, mirontaine!*
> Aux nouvelles que j'apporte,
>> Vos beaux yeux vont pleurer!

Richer and richer grows the accompaniment. The *mironton, mirontaine,* becomes a dirge!

> Quittez vos habits roses —
>> *Mironton, mironton, mirontaine!*
> Quittez vos habits roses,
>> Et vos satins brochés!

Here the ding-donging of a big bell seems to mingle with the score; ... and very slowly, and so impressively that the news will ring for ever in the ears and hearts of those who hear it from La Svengali's lips:

> Le Sieur Malbrouck est mort —
>> *Mironton, mironton, mirontaine!*
> Le Sieur — Malbrouck — est — mort!
>> Est mort — et enterré!*

'*Aux nouvelles que j'apporte vos beaux yeux vont pleure*'

And thus it ends quite abruptly!

And this heartrending tragedy, this great historical epic in two dozen lines, at which some five or six thousand gay French people are sniffling and mopping their eyes like so many Niobes, is just a common old French comic song – a mere nursery ditty, like 'Little Bo-peep' – to the tune,

> We won't go home till morning,
> Till daylight doth appear.*

And after a second or two of silence (oppressive and impressive as that which occurs at a burial when the handful of earth is

being dropped on the coffin lid) the audience bursts once more
into madness; and La Svengali, who accepts no encores, has to
bow for nearly five minutes, standing amid a sea of flowers . . .

Then comes her great and final performance. The orchestra
swiftly plays the first four bars of the bass in Chopin's
Impromptu (A flat); and suddenly, without words, as a light
nymph catching the whirl of a double skipping-rope, La Svengali
breaks in, and vocalises that astounding piece of music that so
few pianists can even play; but no pianist has ever played it like
this; no piano has ever given out such notes as these!

Every single phrase is a string of perfect gems, of purest ray
serene, strung together on a loose golden thread! The higher and
shriller she sings, the sweeter it is; higher and shriller than any
woman had ever sung before.

Waves of sweet and tender laughter, the very heart and
essence of innocent, high-spirited girlhood, alive to all that is
simple and joyous and elementary in nature – the freshness of
the morning, the ripple of the stream, the click of the mill, the
lisp of the wind in the trees, the song of the lark in the cloudless
sky – the sun and the dew, the scent of early flowers and summer
woods and meadows – the sight of birds and bees and butterflies
and frolicsome young animals at play – all the sights and scents
and sounds that are the birthright of happy children, happy
savages in favoured climes – things within the remembrance and
the reach of most of us! All this, the memory and the feel of it
are in Trilby's voice as she warbles that long, smooth lilting,
dancing laugh, that shower of linked sweetness, that wondrous
song without words; and those who hear feel it all, and
remember it with her. It is irresistible; it forces itself on you; no
words, no pictures, could ever do the like! So that the tears that
are shed out of all these many French eyes are tears of pure,
unmixed delight in happy reminiscence! (Chopin, it is true, may
have meant something quite different – a hot-house, perhaps,
with orchids and arum lilies and tuberoses and hydrangeas –
but all this is neither here nor there, as the Laird would say in
French.)

Then comes the slow movement, the sudden adagio, with its
capricious ornaments – the waking of the virgin heart, the
stirring of the sap, the dawn of love; its doubts and fears and
questionings; and the mellow, powerful, deep chest notes are
like the pealing of great golden bells, with a light little pearl

Un Impromptu de Chopin

shower tinkling round – drops from the upper fringe of her grand voice as she shakes it . . .

Then back again the quick part, childhood once more, *da capo*, only quicker! hurry, hurry! but distinct as ever. Loud and shrill and sweet beyond compare – drowning the orchestra; of a piercing quality quite ineffable; a joy there is no telling; a clear, purling, crystal stream that gurgles and foams and bubbles along over sunlit stones; a wonder, a world's delight!

And there is not a sign of effort, of difficulty overcome. All through, Trilby smiles her broad, angelic smile; her lips well parted, her big white teeth glistening as she gently jerks her head from side to side in time to Svengali's bâton, as if to shake the willing notes out quicker and higher and shriller . . .

And in a minute or two it is all over, like the lovely bouquet of fireworks, at the end of the show, and she lets what remains of it die out and away like the afterglow of fading Bengal fires – her voice receding into the distance – coming back to you like an echo from all round, from anywhere you please – quite soft – hardly more than a breath; but *such* a breath! Then one last chromatically ascending rocket, *pianissimo*,* up to E in alt, and then darkness and silence!

And after a little pause the many-headed rises as one and waves its hats and sticks and handkerchiefs, and stamps and shouts . . . 'Vive La Svengali! Vive La Svengali!'

Svengali steps on to the platform by his wife's side and kisses her hand; and they both bow themselves backward through the curtains, which fall, to rise again and again and again on this astounding pair!

Such was La Svengali's *début* in Paris.

It had lasted little over an hour, one quarter of which, at least, had been spent in plaudits and courtesies!

The writer is no musician, alas! (as, no doubt, his musical readers have found out by this) save in his thraldom to music of not too severe a kind, and laments the clumsiness and inadequacy of this wild (though somewhat ambitious) attempt to recall an impression received more than thirty years ago; to revive the ever-blessed memory of that unforgettable first night at the Cirque des Bashibazoucks.

Would that I could transcribe here Berlioz's* famous series of twelve articles, entitled 'La Svengali,' which were republished from *La Lyre Éolienne*, and are now out of print!

Or Théophile Gautier's* elaborate rhapsody, 'Madame La Svengali – *Ange ou Femme?*' in which he proves that one need not have a musical ear (he hadn't) to be enslaved by such a voice as hers, any more than the eye for beauty (this he *had*) to fall the victim of 'her celestial form and face.' It is enough, he says, to be simply human! I forget in which journal this eloquent tribute appeared; it is not to be found in his collected works.

Or the intemperate diatribe by Herr Blagner* (as I will christen him) on the tyranny of the prima donna called 'Svengalismus'; in which he attempts to show that mere virtuosity carried to such a pitch is mere viciosity – base acrobatismus of the vocal chords, a hysteric appeal to morbid Gallic 'sentimentalismus'; and that this monstrous development of a phenomenal larynx, this degrading cultivation and practice of the abnormalismus of a mere physical peculiarity are death and destruction to all true music; since they place Mozart and Beethoven, and even *himself*, on a level with Bellini, Donizetti, Offenbach – any Italian tune-tinkler, any ballad-monger of the hated Paris pavement! and can make the highest music of all (even *his own*) go down with the common French herd at the very first hearing, just as if it were some idiotic refrain of the *café chantant!**

So much for Blagnerismus *v.* Svengalismus.

But I fear there is no space within the limits of this humble tale for these masterpieces of technical musical criticism.

Besides, there are other reasons.

Our three heroes walked back to the boulevards, the only silent ones amid the throng that poured through the Rue St Honoré, as the Cirque des Bashibazoucks emptied itself of its over-excited audience.

They went arm-in-arm, as usual; but this time Little Billee was in the middle. He wished to feel on each side of him the warm and genial contact of his two beloved old friends. It seemed as if they had suddenly been restored to him, after five long years of separation; his heart was overflowing with affection for them, too full to speak just yet! Overflowing, indeed, with the love of love, the love of life, the love of death – the love of all that is, and ever was, and ever will be! just as in his old way.

He could have hugged them both in the open street, before the whole world; and the delight of it was that this was no dream; about that there was no mistake. He was himself again at last, after five years, and wide awake; and he owed it all to Trilby!

And what did he feel for Trilby? He couldn't tell yet. It was too vast as yet to be measured; and, alas! it was weighted with such a burden of sorrow and regret that he might well put off the thought of it a little while longer, and gather in what bliss he might: like the man whose hearing has been restored after long years, he would revel in the mere physical delight of hearing for a space, and not go out of his way as yet to listen for the bad news that was already in the air, and would come to roost quite soon enough.

Taffy and the Laird were silent also; Trilby's voice was still in their ears and hearts, her image in their eyes, and utter bewilderment still oppressed them and kept them dumb.

It was a warm and balmy night, almost like mid-summer; and they stopped at the first café they met on the Boulevard de la Madeleine (*comme autrefois*), and ordered bocks of beer, and sat at a little table on the pavement, the only one unoccupied; for the café was already crowded, the hum of lively talk was great, and 'La Svengali' was in every mouth.

The Laird was the first to speak. He emptied his bock at a draught, and called for another, and lit a cigar, and said, 'I don't believe it was Trilby,, after all!' It was the first time her name had been mentioned between them that evening – and for five years!

'Good heavens!' said Taffy. 'Can you doubt it?'

'Oh yes! that was Trilby,' said Little Billee.

Then the Laird proceeded to explain that, putting aside the impossibility of Trilby's ever being taught to sing in tune, and her well-remembered loathing for Svengali, he had narrowly scanned her face through his opera-glass, and found that in spite of a likeness quite marvellous there were well-marked differences. Her face was narrower and longer, her eyes larger, and their expression not the same; then she seemed taller and stouter, and her shoulders broader and more drooping, and so forth.

But the others wouldn't hear of it, and voted him cracked, and declared they even recognised the peculiar twang of her old speaking voice in the voice she now sang with, especially when she sang low down. And they all three fell to discussing the wonders of her performance like everybody else all round; Little Billee leading with an eloquence and a seeming of technical musical knowledge that quite impressed them, and made them feel happy and at ease; for they were anxious for his sake about the effect this sudden and so unexpected sight of her would have upon him after all that had passed.

He seemed transcendently happy and elate – incomprehensibly so, in fact – and looked at them both with quite a new light in his eyes, as if all the music he had heard had trebled not only his joy in being alive, but his pleasure at being with them. Evidently he had quite outgrown his old passion for her, and that was a comfort indeed!

But Little Billee knew better.

He knew that his old passion for her had all come back, and was so overwhelming and immense that he could not feel it just yet, nor yet the hideous pangs of a jealousy so consuming that it would burn up his life. He gave himself another twenty-four hours.

But he had not to wait so long. He woke up after a short, uneasy sleep that very night, to find that the flood was over him; and he realised how hopelessly, desperately, wickedly, insanely he loved this woman, who might have been his, but was now the wife of another man; a greater than he, and one to whom she owed it that she was more glorious than any other woman on earth – a queen among queens – a goddess! for what was any earthly throne compared to that she established in the hearts and souls of all who came within the sight and hearing of her; beautiful as she was besides – beautiful, beautiful! And what must be her love for the man who had taught her and trained her, and revealed her towering genius to herself and to the world – a man resplendent also, handsome and tall and commanding – a great artist from the crown of his head to the sole of his foot!

And the remembrance of them – hand in hand, master and pupil, husband and wife – smiling and bowing in the face of all that splendid tumult they had called forth and could quell, stung and tortured and maddened him so that he could not lie still, but got up and raged and rampaged up and down his hot, narrow, stuffy bedroom, and longed for his old familiar brain-disease to come back and narcotise his trouble, and be his friend, and stay with him till he died!

Where was he to fly for relief from such new memories as these, which would never cease; and the old memories, and all

And the remembrance of them – hand in hand

the glamour and grace of them that had been so suddenly called out of the grave? And how could he escape, now that he felt the sight of her face and the sound of her voice would be a craving – a daily want – like that of some poor starving outcast for warmth and meat and drink?

And little innocent, pathetic, ineffable, well-remembered sweetness of her changing face kept painting themselves on his retina; and incomparable tones of this new thing, her voice, her infinite voice, went ringing in his head, till he all but shrieked aloud in his agony.

And then the poisoned and delirious sweetness of those mad kisses,

> by hopeless fancy feigned
> On lips that are for others!*

And then the gruesome physical jealousy, that miserable inheritance of all artistic sons of Adam, that plague and torment of the dramatic, plastic imagination, which can idealise so well, and yet realise, alas! so keenly. After three or four hours spent like this, he could stand it no longer; madness was lying his way. So he hurried on a garment, and went and knocked at Taffy's door.

'Good God! what's the matter with you?' exclaimed the good Taffy, as Little Billee tumbled into his room, calling out:

'Oh, Taffy, Taffy, I've g-g-gone mad, I think!' And then, shivering all over, and stammering incoherently, he tried to tell his friend what was the matter with him, with great simplicity.

Taffy, in much alarm, slipped on his trousers and made Little Billee get into his bed, and sat by his side holding his hand. He was greatly perplexed, fearing the recurrence of another attack like that of five years back. He didn't dare leave him for an instant to wake the Laird and send for a doctor.

Suddenly Little Billee buried his face in the pillow and began to sob, and some instinct told Taffy this was the best thing that could happen. The boy had always been a highly-strung, emotional, over-excitable, over-sensitive, and quite uncontrolled mammy's-darling, a cry-baby sort of chap, who had never been to school. It was all a part of his genius, and also a part of his charm. It would do him good once more to have a good blub after five years! After a while Little Billee grew quieter, and then suddenly he said: 'What a miserable ass you must think me, what an unmanly duffer!'

'Why, my friend?'

'Why, for going on in this idiotic way. I really couldn't help it. I went mad, I tell you. I've been walking up and down my room all night, till everything seemed to go round.'

'So have I.'

'You? What for?'

'The very same reason.'

'*What!*'

'I was just as fond of Trilby as you were. Only she happened to prefer *you.*'

'*What!*' cried Little Billee again. '*You* were fond of Trilby?'

'I believe you, my boy!'

'In *love* with her?'

"I believe you, my boy!"

'I believe you, my boy!'

'She never knew it, then!'

'Oh yes, she did.'

'She never told me, then!'

'Didn't she? That's like her. *I* told *her*, at all events. I asked her to marry me.'

'Well – I *am* damned! When?'

'That day we took her to Meudon, with Jeannot, and dined at the garde champêtre's, and she danced the cancan with Sandy.'

'Well – I *am*— And she *refused* you?'

'Apparently so.'

'Well, I— Why on earth did she refuse you?'

'Oh, I suppose she'd already begun to fancy *you*, my friend. *Il y en a toujours un autre!*'*

'Fancy *me* – prefer *me* – to *you*?'

'Well, yes. It *does* seem odd – eh, old fellow? But there's no accounting for tastes, you know. She's built on such an ample scale herself, I suppose, that she likes little 'uns – contrast, you see. She's very maternal, I think. Besides, you're a smart little chap; and you ain't half bad; and you've got brains and talent, and lots of cheek, and all that. I'm rather a *ponderous* kind of party.'

'Well – I *am* damned!'

'*C'est comme ça!* I took it lying down you see.'

'Does the Laird know?'

'No; and I don't want him to – nor anybody else.'

'Taffy, what a regular downright old trump you are!'

'Glad you think so; anyhow, we're both in the same boat, and we've got to make the best of it. She's another man's wife, and probably she's very fond of him. I'm sure she ought to be, cad as he is, after all he's done for her. So there's an end to it.'

'Ah! there'll never be an end of it for *me* – never – never – oh, never, my God! She would have married me but for my mother's meddling, and that stupid old ass, my uncle. What a wife! Think of all she must have in her heart and brain, only to *sing* like that! And, O Lord! how beautiful she is – a goddess! Oh, the brow and cheek and chin, and the way her head's put on! did you *ever* see anything like it? Oh, if only I hadn't written and told my mother I was going to marry her! why, we should have been man and wife for five years by this time – living at Barbizon – painting away like mad! Oh, what a heavenly life! Oh, curse all officious meddling with other people's affairs! Oh! oh! . . .'

'There you go again! What's the good? And where do *I* come in, my friend? *I* should have been no better off, old fellow – worse than ever, I think.'

Then there was a long silence.

At length Little Billee said:

'Taffy, I can't tell you what a trump you are. All I've ever thought of you – and God knows that's enough – will be nothing to what I shall always think of you after this.'

'All right, old chap!'

'And now I think *I'm* all right again, for a time – and I shall cut back to bed. Good night! Thanks more than I can ever express!' And Little Billee, restored to his balance, cut back to his own bed just as the day was breaking.

Part Seventh

The moon made thy lips pale, beloved,
   The wind made thy bosom chill;
      The night did shed
      On thy dear head
Its frozen dew, and thou didst lie
Where the bitter breath of the naked sky
      Might visit thee at will.*

Next morning our three friends lay late abed, and breakfasted in their rooms.

They had all three passed 'white nights' – even the Laird, who had tossed about and pressed a sleepless pillow till dawn, so excited had he been by the wonder of Trilby's reincarnation, so perplexed by his own doubts as to whether it was really Trilby or not.

And certain haunting tones of her voice, that voice so cruelly sweet (which clove the stillness with a clang so utterly new, so strangely heart-piercing and seductive, that the desire to hear it once more became nostalgic – almost an ache!), certain bits and bars and phrases of the music she had sung, unspeakable felicities and facilities of execution; sudden exotic warmths, fragrances, tendernesses, graces, depths, and breadths; quick changes from grave to gay, from rough to smooth, from great metallic brazen clangours to soft golden suavities; all the varied modes of sound we try so vainly to borrow from vocal nature by means of wind and reed and string – all this new 'Trilbyness' kept echoing in his brain all night (for he was of a nature deeply musical), and sleep had been impossible to him.

As when we dwell upon a word we know,
  Repeating, till the word we know so well
Becomes a wonder, and we know not why,*

so dwelt the Laird upon the poor old tune 'Ben Bolt,' which kept singing itself over and over again in his tired consciousness, and maddened him with novel, strange, unhackneyed, unsuspected beauties such as he had never dreamed of in any earthly music.

It had become a wonder, and he knew not why!

They spent what was left of the morning at the Louvre, and tried to interest themselves in the 'Marriage of Cana,' and the 'Woman at the Well,' and Vandyck's man with the glove, and the little Princess of Velasquez, and Lisa Gioconda's smile:* it was of no use trying. There was no sight worth looking at in all Paris but Trilby in her golden raiment; no other princess in the world; no smile but hers, when through her parted lips came bubbling Chopin's Impromptu. They had not long to stay in Paris, and they must drink of that bubbling fountain once more – *coûte que coûte!** They went to the Salle des Bashibazoucks, and found that all seats all over the house had been taken for days and weeks; and the 'queue' at the door had already begun! and they had to give up all hopes of slaking this particular thirst.

Then they went and lunched perfunctorily, and talked desultorily over lunch, and read criticisms of La Svengali's *début* in the morning papers – a chorus of journalistic acclamation gone mad, a frenzied eulogy in every key – but nothing was good enough for them! Brand-new words were wanted – another language!

Then they wanted a long walk, and could think of nowhere to go in all Paris – that immense Paris, where they had promised themselves to see so much that the week they were to spend there had seemed too short!

Looking in a paper, they saw it announced that the band of the Imperial Guides would play that afternoon in the Pré Catelan, Bois de Boulogne, and thought they might as well walk there as anywhere else, and walk back again in time to dine with the Passefils – a prandial function which did not promise to be very amusing; but still it was something to kill the evening with, since they couldn't go and hear Trilby again.

Outside the Pré Catelan* they found a crowd of cabs and carriages, saddle-horses and grooms. One might have thought one's self in the height of the Paris season. They went in, and strolled about here and there, and listened to the band, which was famous (it has performed in London at the Crystal Palace),* and they looked about and studied life, or tried to.

Suddenly they saw, sitting with three ladies (one of whom, the eldest, was in black), a very smart young officer, a Guide, all red and green and gold, and recognised their old friend Zouzou.

They bowed, and he knew them at once, and jumped up and came to them and greeted them warmly, especially his old friend Taffy, whom he took to his mother – the lady in black – and introduced to the other ladies, the younger of whom (strangely unlike the rest of her countrywomen) was so lamentably, so pathetically plain that it would be brutal to attempt the cheap and easy task of describing her. It was Miss Lavinia Hunks, the famous American millionairess, and her mother. Then the good Zouzou came back and talked to the Laird and Little Billee.

Zouzou, in some subtle and indescribable way, had become very ducal indeed.

He looked extremely distinguished, for one thing, in his beautiful Guides' uniform, and was most gracefully and winningly polite. He inquired warmly after Mrs and Miss Bagot, and begged Little Billee would recall him to their amiable remembrance when he saw them again. He expressed most sympathetically his delight to see Little Billee looking so strong and so well (Little Billee looked like a pallid little washed-out ghost, after his white night).

They talked of Dodor. He said how attached he was to Dodor, and always should be; but Dodor, it seemed, had made a great mistake in leaving the army and going into a retail business (*petit commerce*). He had done for himself – *dégringolé!** He should have stuck to the *dragons* – with a little patience and good conduct he would have 'won his epaulet' – and then one might have arranged for him a good little marriage – *un parti convenable* – for he was 'très joli garçon, Dodor! bonne tournure – et très gentiment né! C'est très ancien, les Rigolot – dans le Poitou, je crois – Lafarce, et tout ça; tout à fait bien!'*

It was difficult to realise that this polished and discreet and somewhat patronising young man of the world was the jolly dog who had gone after Little Billee's hat on all fours in the Rue Vieille des Trois Mauvais Ladres and brought it back in his mouth – the Caryhatide!

Little Billee little knew that Monsieur le Duc de la Rochemar-tel-Boisségur had quite recently delighted a very small and select and most august imperial supper-party at Compiègne* with this very story, not blinking a single detail of his own share in it – and had given a most touching and sympathetic description of 'le joli petit peintre anglais qui s'appelait Litrebili, et ne pouvait pas se tenir sur ses jambes – et qui pleurait d'amour fraternel dans les bras de mon copain Dodor!'*

'Ah! Monsieur Gontran, ce que je donnerais pour avoir vu ça!' had said the greatest lady in France; 'un de mes zouaves – à quatre pattes – dans la rue – un chapeau dans la bouche – oh – c'est impayable!'*

Zouzou kept these blackguard bohemian reminiscences for the imperial circle alone – to which it was suspected that he was secretly rallying himself. Among all outsiders – especially within the narrow precincts of the cream of the noble Faubourg (which remained aloof from the Tuileries) – he was a very proper and gentlemanlike person indeed, as his brother had been – and, in his mother's fond belief, 'très bien pensant, très bien vu, à Frohsdorf et à Rome.'*

On lui aurait donné le bon Dieu sans confession – as Madame Vinard had said of Little Billee – they would have shriven him at sight, and admitted him to the holy communion on trust!

He did not present Little Billee and the Laird to his mother, nor to Mrs and Miss Hunks; that honour was reserved for 'the Man of Blood' alone; nor did he ask where they were staying, nor invite them to call on him. But in parting he expressed the immense pleasure it had given him to meet them again, and the hope he had of some day shaking their hands in London.

As the friends walked back to Paris together, it transpired that 'the Man of Blood' had been invited by Madame Duchesse Mère (Mamam Duchesse, as Zouzou called her) to dine with her next day, and meet the Hunkses at a furnished apartment she had taken in the Place Vendôme; for they had let (to the Hunkses) the Hôtel de la Rochemartel in the Rue de Lille; they had also been obliged to let their place in the country, le château de Boisségur (to Monsieur Despoires, or 'des Poires,' as he chose to spell himself on his visiting cards – the famous soap manufacturer – 'Un très brave homme, à ce qu'on dit!'* and whose only son, by the way, soon after married Mademoiselle Jeanne-Adélaïde d'Amaury-Brissac de Roncesvaulx de Boisségur de la Rochemartel).

'Il ne fait pas gras chez nous à présent – je vous assure!'*

Maman Duchese

Madame Duchesse Mère had pathetically said to Taffy – but had given him to understand that things would be very much better for her son in the event of his marriage with Miss Hunks.

'Good heavens!' said Little Billee, on hearing this; 'that grotesque little bogy in blue? Why, she's deformed – she squints – she's a dwarf, and looks like an idiot! Millions or no millions, the man who marries her is a felon! As long as there are stones to break and a road to break them on, the able-bodied man who marries a woman like that for anything but pity and kindness – and even then – dishonours himself, insults his ancestry, and inflicts on his descendants a wrong that nothing will ever redeem – he nips them in the bud – he blasts them for ever! He ought to be cut by his fellow-men – sent to Coventry – to jail – to penal servitude for life! He ought to have a separate hell to himself when he dies – he ought to—'

'Shut up, you little blaspheming ruffian!' said the Laird. 'Where do *you* expect to go to, yourself, with such frightful sentiments? And what would become of your beautiful old twelfth-century dukedoms, with a hundred yards of back front-age opposite the Louvre, on a beautiful historic river, and a dozen beautiful historic names, and no money – if *you* had your way?' and the Laird wunk his historic wink.

'Twelfth-century dukedoms be damned!' said Taffy, *au grand sérieux*, as usual. 'Little Billee's quite right, and Zouzou makes me sick! Besides, what does she marry *him* for – not for his beauty either, I guess! She's his fellow-criminal, his deliberate accomplice, *particeps delicti*,* accessory before the act and after! She has no right to marry at all! tar and feathers and a rail for both of them – and for Maman Duchesse too – and I suppose that's why I refused her invitation to dinner! and now let's go and dine with Dodor – ... anyhow Dodor's young woman doesn't marry him for a dukedom – or even his 'de' – *mais bien pour ses beaux yeux!** and if the Rigolots of the future turn out less nice to look at than their sire, and not quite so amusing, they will probably be a great improvement on him in many other ways. There's room enough – and to spare!'

''Ear! 'ear!' said Little Billee (who always grew flippant when Taffy got on his high horse). 'Your 'ealth and song, sir – them's my sentiments to a T! What shall we 'ave the pleasure of drinkin', after that wery nice 'armony?'

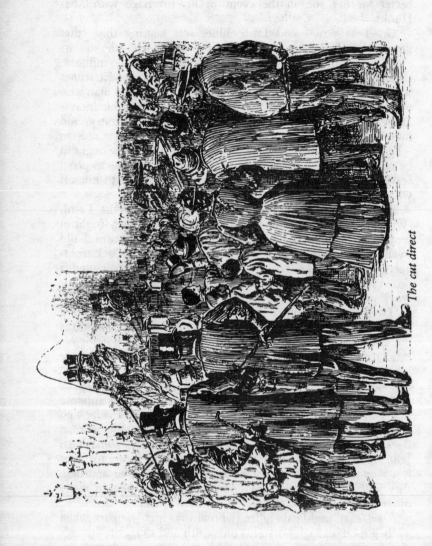

The cut direct

After which they walked on in silence, each, no doubt, musing on the general contrariness of things, and imagining what splendid little Wynnes, or Bagots, or M'Allisters might have been ushered into a decadent world for its regeneration if fate had so willed it that a certain magnificent and singularly gifted grisette, etc. etc. etc. . . .

Mrs and Miss Hunks passed them as they walked along, in a beautiful blue barouche with C-springs – *un 'huit-ressorts'*;* Maman Duchesse passed them in a hired fly; Zouzou passed them on horseback; 'tout Paris' passed them; but they were none the wiser, and agreed that the show was not a patch on that in Hyde Park during the London season.

When they reached the Place de la Concorde it was that lovely hour of a fine autumn day in beautiful bright cities when all the lamps are lit in the shops and streets and under the trees, and it is still daylight – a quickly fleeting joy; and as a special treat on this particular occasion the sun set, and up rose the yellow moon over eastern Paris, and floated above the chimney-pots of the Tuileries.

They stopped to gaze at the homeward procession of cabs and carriages, as they used to do in the old times. Tout Paris was still passing; tout Paris is very long.

They stood among a little crowd of sightseers like themselves. Little Billee right in front – in the road.

Presently a magnificent open carriage came by – more magnificent than even the Hunkses', with liveries and harness quite vulgarly resplendent – almost Napoleonic.

Lolling back in it lay Monsieur et Madame Svengali – he with his broad-brimmed felt sombrero over his long black curls, wrapped in costly furs, smoking his big cigar of the Havana.

By his side La Svengali – also in sables – with a large black velvet hat on, her light brown hair done up in a huge knot on the nape of her neck. She was rouged and pearl-powdered, and her eyes were blackened beneath, and thus made to look twice their size; but in spite of all such disfigurements she was a most splendid vision, and caused quite a little sensation in the crowd as she came slowly by.

Little Billee's heart was in his mouth. He caught Svengali's eye, and saw him speak to her. She turned her head and looked at him standing there – they both did. Little Billee bowed. She stared at him with a cold stare of disdain, and cut him dead –

so did Svengali. And as they passed he heard them both snigger – she with a little high-pitched flippant snigger worthy of a London barmaid.

Little Billee was utterly crushed, and everything seemed turning round.

The Laird and Taffy had seen it all without losing a detail. The Svengalis had not even looked their way. The Laird said:

'It's not Trilby – I swear! She could *never* have done that – it's not *in* her! and it's another face altogether – I'm sure of it!'

Taffy was also staggered and in doubt. They caught hold of Little Billee, each by an arm, and walked him off to the boulevards. He was quite demoralised, and wanted not to dine at Passefil's. He wanted to go straight home at once. He longed for his mother as he used to long for her when he was in trouble as a small boy and she was away from home – longed for her desperately – to hug her and hold her and fondle her, and be fondled, for his own sake and hers; all his old love for her had come back in full – with what arrears! all his old love for his sister, for his old home.

When they went back to the hotel to dress (for Dodor had begged them to put on their best evening war-paint, so as to impress his future mother-in-law), Little Billee became fractious and intractable. And it was only on Taffy's promising that he would go all the way to Devonshire with him on the morrow, and stay with him there, that he could be got to dress and dine.

The huge Taffy lived entirely by his affections, and he hadn't many to live by – the Laird, Trilby, and Little Billee.

Trilby was unattainable, the Laird was quite strong and independent enough to get on by himself, and Taffy had concentrated all his faculties of protection and affection on Little Billee, and was equal to any burden or responsibility all this instinctive young fathering might involve.

In the first place, Little Billee had always been able to do quite easily, and better than any one else in the world, the very things Taffy most longed to do himself and couldn't, and this inspired the good Taffy with a chronic reverence and wonder he could not have expressed in words.

Then Little Billee was physically small and weak, and incapable of self-control. Then he was generous, amiable, affectionate, transparent as crystal, without an atom of either egotism or conceit: and had a gift of amusing you and interesting you by his talk (and its complete sincerity) that never palled; and even his silence was charming – one felt so sure of him – so there was hardly any sacrifice, little or big, that big Taffy was not ready and glad to make for Little Billee. On the other hand, there lay deep down under Taffy's surface irascibility and earnestness about trifles (and beneath his harmless vanity of the strong man), a long-suffering patience, a real humility, a robustness of judgment, a sincerity and all-roundness, a completeness of sympathy, that made him very good to trust and safe to lean upon. Then his powerful, impressive aspect, his great stature, the gladiator-like poise of his small round head on his big neck and shoulders, his huge deltoids and deep chest and slender loins, his clean-cut ankles and wrists, all the long and bold and highly-finished athletic shapes of him, that easy grace of strength that made all his movements a pleasure to watch, and any garment look well when he wore it – all this was a perpetual feast to the quick, prehensile, aesthetic eye. And then he had such a solemn, earnest, lovable way of bending pokers round his neck, and breaking them on his arm, and jumping his own height (or near it), and lifting up armchairs by one leg with one hand, and what not else!

So that there was hardly any sacrifice, little or big, that Little Billee would not accept from big Taffy as a mere matter of course – a fitting and proper tribute rendered by bodily strength to genius.

Par nobile fratrum* – well met and well mated for fast and long-enduring friendship.

The family banquet at Monsieur Passefil's would have been dull but for the irrepressible Dodor, and still more for the Laird of Cockpen, who rose to the occasion, and surpassed himself in geniality, drollery, and eccentricity of French grammar and accent. Monsieur Passefil was also a droll in his way, and had the quickly familiar, jocose facetiousness that seems to belong to the successful middle-aged bourgeois all over the world, when he's not pompous instead (he can even be both sometimes).

Madame Passefil was not jocose. She was much impressed by the aristocratic splendour of Taffy, the romantic melancholy and refinement of Little Billee, and their quiet and dignified politeness. She always spoke of Dodor as Monsieur de Lafarce, though the rest of the family (and one or two friends who had

Petit enfant, j'amais d'un amour tendre
ma mère et Dieu – saintes affections!
Puis mon amour aux fleurs se fit entendre,
puis aux oiseaux, et puis aux papillons!

been invited) always called him Monsieur Théodore, and he was officially known as Monsieur Rigolot.

Whenever Madame Passefil addressed him or spoke of him in this aristocratic manner (which happened very often), Dodor would wink at his friends, with his tongue in his cheek. It seemed to amuse him beyond measure.

Mademoiselle Ernestine was evidently too much in love to say anything, and seldom took her eyes off Monsieur Théodore, whom she had never seen in evening dress before. It must be owned that he looked very nice – more ducal than even Zouzou – and to be Madame de Lafarce *en perspective*,* and the future owner of such a brilliant husband as Dodor, was enough to turn a stronger little bourgeois head than Mademoiselle Ernestine's.

She was not beautiful, but healthy, well grown, well brought up, and presumably of a sweet, kind, and amiable disposition – an *ingénue** fresh from her convent – innocent as a child, no doubt; and it was felt that Dodor had done better for himself (and for his race) than Monsieur le Duc. Little Dodors need have no fear.

After dinner the ladies and gentlemen left the dining-room together, and sat in a pretty salon overlooking the boulevard, where cigarettes were allowed, and there was music. Mademoiselle Ernestine laboriously played 'Les Cloches du Monastère'* (by Monsieur Lefébure-Wély, if I'm not mistaken). It's the most bourgeois piece of music I know.

Then Dodor, with his sweet high voice, so strangely pathetic and true, sang goody-goody little French songs of innocence (of which he seemed to have an endless *répertoire*) to his future wife's conscientious accompaniment – to the immense delight, also, of all his future family, who were almost in tears – and to the great amusement of the Laird, at whom he winked in the most pathetic parts, putting his forefinger to the side of his nose, like Noah Claypole in *Oliver Twist*.*

The wonder of the hour, La Svengali, was discussed, of course; it was unavoidable. But our friends did not think it necessary to reveal that she was 'la grande Trilby.' That would soon transpire by itself.

And, indeed, before the month was a week older the papers were full of nothing else.

Madame La Svengali – 'la grande Trilby' – was the only daughter of the honourable and reverend Sir Lord O'Ferrall.

She had run away from the primeval forests and lonely marshes of le Dublin, to lead a free-and-easy life among the artists of the Quartier Latin of Paris – *une vie de bohème!*

She was the Venus Anadyomene* from top to toe.

She was *blanche comme neige, avec un volcan dans le cœur.**

Casts of her alabaster feet could be had at Brucciani's, in the Rue de la Souricière St Denis.* (He made a fortune.)

Monsieur Ingres had painted her left foot on the wall of a studio in the Place St Anatole des Arts; and an eccentric Scotch milord (le Comte de Pencock) had bought the house containing the flat containing the studio containing the wall on which it was painted, had had the house pulled down and the wall framed and glazed and sent to his castle of Édimbourg.

(This, unfortunately, was in excess of the truth. It was found impossible to execute the Laird's wish, on account of the material the wall was made of. So the Lord Count of Pencock – such was Madame Vinard's version of Sandy's nickname – had to forgo his purchase.)

Next morning our friends were in readiness to leave Paris; even the Laird had had enough of it, and longed to get back to his work again – a 'Hari-Kari in Yokohama.'* (He had never been to Japan; but no more had any one else in those early days.)

They had just finished breakfast, and were sitting in the courtyard of the hotel, which was crowded, as usual.

Little Billee went into the hotel post-office to despatch a note to his mother. Sitting sideways there at a small table and reading letters was Svengali – of all people in the world. But for these two and a couple of clerks the room was empty.

Svengali looked up; they were quite close together.

Little Billee, in his nervousness, began to shake, and half put out his hand, and drew it back again, seeing the look of hate on Svengali's face.

Svengali jumped up, put his letters together, and passing by Little Billee on his way to the door, called him 'verfluchter Schweinhund,'* and deliberately spat in his face.

Little Billee was paralysed for a second or two; then he ran after Svengali, and caught him just at the top of the marble stairs, and kicked him, and knocked off his hat, and made him drop all his letters. Svengali turned round and struck him over the mouth and made it bleed, and Little Billee hit out like a fury, but with no effect: he couldn't reach high enough, for Svengali was well over six feet.

There was a crowd round them in a minute, including the beautiful old man in the court suit and gold chain, who called out:

'Vite! vite! un commissaire de police!' – a cry that was echoed all over the place.

Taffy saw the row, and shouted, 'Bravo, little 'un!' and jumping up from his table, jostled his way through the crowd; and Little Billee, bleeding and gasping and perspiring and stammering said:

'He spat in my face, Taffy – damn him! I'd never even spoken to him – not a word, I swear!'

Svengali had not reckoned on Taffy's being there; he recognised him at once, and turned white.

Taffy, who had dogskin gloves on, put out his right hand, and deftly seized Svengali's nose between his fore and middle fingers and nearly pulled it off, and swung his head two or three times backward and forward by it, and then from side to side, Svengali holding on to his wrist; and then, letting him go, gave him a sounding open-handed smack on his right cheek – and a smack on the face from Taffy (even in play) was no joke, I'm told; it made one smell brimstone, and see and hear things that didn't exist.

Svengali gasped worse than Little Billee, and couldn't speak for a while. Then he said:

'Lâche – grand lâche! che fous enferrai mes témoins!'*

'At your orders!' said Taffy, in beautiful French, and drew out his card-case, and gave him his card in quite the orthodox French manner, adding: 'I shall be here till tomorrow at twelve – but that is my London address, in case I don't hear from you before I leave. I'm sorry, but you really mustn't spit, you know – it's not done. I will come to you whenever you send for me – even if I have to come from the end of the world.'

'Très bien! très bien!' said a military-looking old gentleman close by, who gave Taffy *his* card, in case he might be of any service – and who seemed quite delighted at the row – and indeed it was really pleasant to note with what a smooth, flowing, rhythmical spontaneity the good Taffy could always improvise these swift little acts of summary retributive justice: no hurry or scurry or flurry whatever – not an inharmonious

'Vite! Vite! un commissaire de police!'

gesture, not an infelicitous line – the very poetry of violence, and almost its only excuse!

Whatever it was worth, this was Taffy's special gift, and it never failed him at a pinch.

When the commissaire de police arrived, all was over. Svengali had gone away in a cab, and Taffy put himself at the disposition of the commissaire.

They went into the post-office and discussed it all with the old military gentleman, and the majordome in velvet, and the two clerks who had seen the original insult. And all that was required of Taffy and his friends for the present was 'their names, prenames, titles, qualities, age, address, nationality, occupation,' etc.

'C'est une affaire qui s'arrangera autrement, et autre part!'* had said the military gentleman – monsieur le général Comte de la Tour-aux-Loups.

So it blew over quite simply, and all that day a fierce unholy joy burned in Taffy's choleric blue eye.

Not, indeed, that he had any wish to injure Trilby's husband, or meant to do him any grievous bodily harm, whatever happened. But he was glad to have given Svengali a lesson in manners.

That Svengali should injure *him* never entered into his calculations for a moment. Besides, he didn't believe Svengali would show fight; and in this he was not mistaken.

But he had, for hours, the feel of that long, thick, shapely Hebrew nose being kneaded between his gloved knuckles, and a pleasing sense of the effectiveness of the tweak he had given it. So he went about chewing the cud of that heavenly remembrance all day, till reflection brought remorse, and he felt sorry; for he was really the mildest-mannered man that ever broke a head!

Only the sight of Little Billee's blood (which had been made to flow by such an unequal antagonist) had roused the old Adam.

No message came from Svengali to ask for the names and addresses of Taffy's seconds; so Dodor and Zouzou (not to mention Mister the general Count of the Tooraloorals, as the Laird called him) were left undisturbed; and our three muska-teers went back to London clean of blood, whole of limb, and heartily sick of Paris.

Little Billee stayed with his mother and sister in Devonshire till Christmas, Taffy staying at the village inn.

It was Taffy who told Mrs Bagot about La Svengali's all but certain identity with Trilby, after Little Billee had gone to bed, tired and worn out, the night of their arrival.

'Good heavens!' said poor Mrs Bagot. 'Why, that's the new singing woman who's coming over here! There's an article about her in today's *Times*. It says she's a wonder, and that there's no one like her! Surely, that can't be the Miss O'Ferrall I saw in Paris!'

'It seems impossible – but I'm almost certain it is – and Willy has no doubts in the matter. On the other hand, M'Allister declares it isn't.'

'Oh, what trouble! So *that's* why poor Willy looks so ill and miserable! It's all come back again. Could she sing at all then, when you knew her in Paris?'

'Not a note – her attempts at singing were quite grotesque.'

'Is she still very beautiful?'

'Oh yes; there's no doubt about that; more than ever!'

'And her singing – is that so very wonderful? I remember that she had a beautiful voice in speaking.'

'Wonderful? Ah, yes; I never heard or dreamed the like of it. Grisi, Alboni, Patti – not one of them to be mentioned in the same breath!'

'Good heavens! Why, she must be simply irresistible! I wonder you're not in love with her yourself. How dreadful these sirens are, wrecking the peace of families!'

'You mustn't forget that she gave way at once at a word from you, Mrs Bagot; and she was very fond of Willy. She wasn't a siren then.'

'Oh yes – oh yes! that's true – she behaved very well – she did her duty – I can't deny that! You must try and forgive me, Mr Wynne – although I can't forgive *her!* – that dreadful illness of poor Willy's – that bitter time in Paris—'

And Mrs Bagot began to cry, and Taffy forgave. 'Oh, Mr Wynne, let us still hope that there's some mistake – that it's only somebody like her! Why, she's coming to sing in London after Christmas! My poor boy's infatuation will only increase. What *shall* I do?'

'Well – she's another man's wife, you see. So Willy's infatuation is bound to turn itself out as soon as he fully recognises

that important fact. Besides, she cut him dead in the Champs
Élysées – and her husband and Willy had a row next day at the
hotel, and cuffed and kicked each other – that's rather a bar to
any future intimacy, I think.'

'Oh, Mr Wynne! my son cuffing and kicking a man whose
wife he's in love with! Good heavens!'

'Oh, it was all right – the man had grossly insulted him; and
Willy behaved like a brick, and got the best of it in the end, and
nothing came of it. I saw it all.'

'Oh, Mr Wynne – and you didn't interfere?'

'Oh yes, I interfered – everybody interfered! It was all right, I
assure you. No bones were broken on either side, and there was
no nonsense about calling out, or swords or pistols, and all
that.'

'Thank Heaven!'

In a week or two Little Billee grew more like himself again,
and painted endless studies of rocks and cliffs and sea – and
Taffy painted with him, and was very content. The vicar and
Little Billee patched up their feud. The vicar also took an
immense fancy to Taffy, whose cousin, Sir Oscar Wynne, he had
known at college, and lost no opportunity of being hospitable
and civil to him. And his daughter was away in Algiers.

And all 'the nobility and gentry' of the neighbourhood,
including 'the poor dear marquis' (one of whose sons was in
Taffy's old regiment), were civil and hospitable also to the two
painters – and Taffy got as much sport as he wanted, and
became immensely popular. And they had, on the whole, a very
good time till Christmas, and a very pleasant Christmas, if not
an exuberantly merry one.

After Christmas Little Billee insisted on going back to London
– to paint a picture for the Royal Academy; and Taffy went
with him; and there was dullness in the house of Bagot – and
many misgivings in the maternal heart of its mistress.

And people of all kinds, high and low, from the family at the
Court to the fishermen on the little pier and their wives and
children, missed the two genial painters, who were the friends
of everybody, and made such beautiful sketches of their beautiful coast.

La Svengali has arrived in London. Her name is in every mouth.
Her photograph is in the shop-windows. She is to sing at J—'s

'I suppose you do all this kind of thing for mere amusement,
My Wynne?'

monster concerts next week. She was to have sung sooner, but it seems some hitch has occurred – a quarrel between Monsieur Svengali and his first violin, who is a very important person.

A crowd of people as usual, only bigger, is assembled in front of the windows of the Stereoscopic Company in Regent Street,* gazing at presentments of Madame Svengali in all sizes and costumes. She is very beautiful – there is no doubt of that; and the expression of her face is sweet and kind and sad, and of such a distinction that one feels an imperial crown would become her even better than her modest little coronet of golden stars. One of the photographs represents her in classical dress, with her left foot on a stool, in something of the attitude of the Venus of Milo, except that her hands are clasped behind her back; and the foot is bare but for a Greek sandal, and so smooth and delicate and charming, and with so rhythmical a set and curl of the five slender toes (the big one slightly tip-tilted and well apart from its longer and slighter and more aquiline neighbour), that this presentment of her sells quicker than all the rest.

And a little man who, with two bigger men, has just forced his way in front says to one of his friends: 'Look, Sandy, look – *the foot! Now* have you got any doubts?'

'Oh yes – those are Trilby's toes, sure enough!' says Sandy. And they all go in and purchase largely.

As far as I have been able to discover, the row between Svengali and his first violin had occurred at a rehearsal in Drury Lane Theatre.

Svengali, it seems, had never been quite the same since the 15th of October previous, and that was the day he had got his face slapped and his nose tweaked by Taffy in Paris. He had become short-tempered and irritable, especially with his wife (if she *was* his wife). Svengali, it seems, had reasons for passionately hating Little Billee.

He had not seen him for five years – not since the Christmas mass festivity in the Place St Anatole, when they had sparred together after supper, and Svengali's nose had got in the way on this occasion, and had been made to bleed; but that was not why he hated Little Billee.

When he caught sight of him standing on the kerb in the Place de la Concorde and watching the procession of 'tout Paris,' he knew him directly, and all his hate flared up; he cut him dead, and made his wife do the same.

Next morning he saw him again in the hotel post-office, looking small and weak and flurried, and apparently alone; and being an Oriental Israelite Hebrew Jew,* he had not been able to resist the temptation of spitting in his face, since he must not throttle him to death.

The minute he had done this he had regretted the folly of it. Little Billee had run after him, and kicked and struck him, and he had returned the blow and drawn blood; and then, suddenly and quite unexpected, had come upon the scene that apparition so loathed and dreaded of old – the pig-headed Yorkshireman – the huge British philistine, the irresponsible bull, the junker, the ex-Crimean, Front-de-Bœuf,* who had always reminded him of the brutal and contemptuous sword-clanking, spur-jingling aristocrats of his own country – ruffians that treated Jews like dogs.* Callous as he was to the woes of others, the self-indulgent and highly-strung musician was extra sensitive about himself – a very bundle of nerves – and especially sensitive to pain and rough usage, and by no means physically brave. The stern, choleric, invincible blue eye of the hated northern Gentile had cowed him at once. And that violent tweaking of his nose, that heavy open-handed blow on his face, had so shaken and demoralised him that he had never recovered from it.

He was thinking about it always – night and day – and constantly dreaming at night that he was being tweaked and slapped over again by a colossal nightmare Taffy, and waking up in agonies of terror, rage, and shame. All healthy sleep had forsaken him.

Moreover, he was much older than he looked – nearly fifty – and far from sound. His life had been a long, hard struggle.

He had for his wife, slave, and pupil a fierce, jealous kind of affection that was a source of endless torment to him; for indelibly graven in her heart, which he wished to occupy alone, was the never-fading image of the little English painter, and of this she made no secret.

Gecko no longer cared for the master. All Gecko's doglike devotion was concentrated on the slave and pupil, whom he worshipped with a fierce but pure and unselfish passion. The only living soul that Svengali could trust was the old Jewess who lived with them – his relative – but even she had come to love the pupil as much as the master.

On the occasion of this rehearsal at Drury Lane he (Svengali) was conducting and Madame Svengali was singing. He inter-rupted her several times, angrily and most unjustly, and told her she was singing out of tune, 'like a verfluchter tomcat,' which was quite untrue. She was singing beautifully, 'Home, Sweet Home.'*

Finally he struck her two or three smart blows on her knuckles with his little bâton, and she fell on her knees, weeping and crying out:

'Oh! oh! Svengali! ne me battez pas, mon ami – je fais tout ce que je peux!'*

On which little Gecko had suddenly jumped up and struck Svengali on the neck near the collar-bone, and then it was seen that he had a little bloody knife in his hand, and blood flowed from Svengali's neck, and at the sight of it Svengali had fainted; and Madame Svengali had taken his head on her lap, looking dazed and stupefied, as in a waking dream.

Gecko had been disarmed, but as Svengali recovered from his faint and was taken home, the police had not been sent for, and the affair was hushed up, and a public scandal avoided. But La Svengali's first appearance, to Monsieur J—'s despair, had to be put off for a week. For Svengali would not allow her to sing without him; nor, indeed, would he be parted from her for a minute, or trust her out of his sight.

The wound was a slight one. The doctor who attended Svengali described the wife as being quite imbecile, no doubt from grief and anxiety. But she never left her husband's bedside for a moment, and had the obedience and devotion of a dog.

When the night came round for the postponed *début*, Svengali was allowed by the doctor to go to the theatre, but he was absolutely forbidden to conduct. His grief and anxiety at this were uncontrollable; he raved like a madman; and Monsieur J— was almost as bad.

Monsieur J— had been conducting the Svengali band at rehearsals during the week, in the absence of its master – an easy task. It had been so thoroughly drilled and knew its business so well that it could almost conduct itself, and it had played all the music it had to play (much of which consisted of accompaniments to La Svengali's songs) many times before. Her *répertoire* was immense, and Svengali had written these orches-tral scores with great care and felicity.

On the famous night it was arranged that Svengali should sit

The first violin loses his temper

in a box alone, exactly opposite his wife's place on the platform, where she could see him well; and a code of simple signals was arranged between him and Monsieur J— and the band, so that virtually he might conduct, himself, from his box, should any hesitation or hitch occur. This arrangement was rehearsed the day before (a Sunday) and had turned out quite successfully, and La Svengali had sung in perfection in the empty theatre.

When Monday evening arrived everything seemed to be going smoothly; the house was soon crammed to suffocation, all but the middle box on the grand tier. It was not a promenade concert, and the pit was turned into guinea stalls (the promenade concerts were to begin a week later).

Right in the middle of these stalls sat the Laird and Taffy and Little Billee.

The band came in by degrees and tuned their instruments.

Eyes were constantly being turned to the empty box, and people wondered what royal personages would appear.

Monsieur J— took his place amid immense applause, and bowed in his inimitable way, looking often at the empty box.

Then he tapped and waved his bâton, and the band played its Hungarian dance music with immense success; when this was over there was a pause, and soon some signs of impatience from the gallery. Monsieur J— had disappeared.

Taffy stood up, his back to the orchestra, looking round.

Some one came into the empty box, and stood for a moment in front, gazing at the house. A tall man, deathly pale, with long black hair and a beard.

It was Svengali.

He caught sight of Taffy and met his eyes, and Taffy said: 'Good God! Look! Look!'

Then Little Billee and the Laird got up and looked.

And Svengali for a moment glared at them. And the expression of his face was so terrible with wonder, rage, and fear that they were quite appalled – and then he sat down, still glaring at Taffy, the whites of his eyes showing at the top, and his teeth bared in a spasmodic grin of hate.

Then thunders of applause filled the house, and turning round and seating themselves, Taffy and Little Billee and the Laird saw Trilby being led by J— down the platform, between the players, to the front, her face smiling rather vacantly, her eyes anxiously intent on Svengali in his box.

'Hast thou found me, o mine enemy?'

She made her bows to right and left just as she had done in Paris.

The band struck up the opening bars of 'Ben Bolt,' with which she was announced to make her *début*.

She still stared – but she didn't sing – and they played the little symphony three times.

One could hear Monsieur J— in a hoarse, anxious whisper saying,

'Mais chantez donc, madame – pour l'amour de Dieu, commencez donc – commencez!'

She turned round with an extraordinary expression of face,
and said,

'Chanter? pourquoi donc voulez-vous que je chante, moi?
chanter quoi, alors?'

'Mais "Ben Bolt," parbleu – chantez!'

'Ah – "Ben Bolt!" oui – je connais ça!'*

Then the band began again.

And she tried, but failed to begin herself. She turned round
and said,

'Comment diable voulez-vous que je chante avec tout ce train
qu'ils font, ces diables de musiciens!'

'Mais, mon Dieu, madame – qu'est-ce que vous avez donc?'
cried Monsieur J—.

'J'ai que j'aime mieux chanter sans toute cette satanée
musique, parbleu! J'aime mieux chanter toute seule!'

'Sans musique, alors – mais chantez – chantez!'*

The band was stopped – the house was in a state of indescribable wonder and suspense.

She looked all round, and down at herself, and fingered her
dress. Then she looked up to the chandelier with a tender,
sentimental smile and began –

> Oh, don't you remember sweet Alice, Ben Bolt?
>   Sweet Alice with hair so brown,
> Who wept with delight when you gave her a smile—

She had not got further than this when the whole house was
in an uproar – shouts from the gallery – shout of laughter,
hoots, hisses, cat-calls, cock-crows.

She stopped and glared like a brave lioness, and called out –

'Qu'est-ce que vous avez donc, tous! tas de vieilles pommes
cuites que vous êtes! Est-ce qu'on a peur de vous?'* and then,
suddenly –

'Why, you're all English, aren't you? – what's all the row
about? – what have you brought me here for? – what have I
done, I should like to know?'

And in asking these questions the depth and splendour of her
voice were so extraordinary – its tone so pathetically feminine,
yet so full of hurt and indignant command, that the tumult was
stilled for a moment.

'Oh, don't you remember Alice, Ben Bolt?'

It was the voice of some being from another world – some insulted daughter of a race more puissant and nobler than ours; a voice that seemed as if it could never utter a false note.

Then came a voice from the gods in answer –

'Oh, ye're Henglish, har yer? Why don't yer sing as yer *hought* to sing – yer've got *voice* enough, any'ow! why don't yer sing in *tune*?'

'Sing in *tune*!' cried Trilby. 'I didn't want to sing at all – I only sang because I was asked to sing – that gentleman asked me – that French gentleman with the white waistcoat! I won't sing another note!'

'Oh, yer won't, won't yer! then let us 'ave our money back, or we'll know what for!'

And again the din broke out, and the uproar was frightful.

Monsieur J— screamed out across the theatre: 'Svengali! Svengali! qu'est-ce qu'elle a donc, votre femme? ... elle est devenue folle!'*

Indeed she had tried to sing 'Ben Bolt,' but had sung it in her old way – as she used to sing it in the Quartier Latin – the most lamentably grotesque performance ever heard out of a human throat!

'Svengali! Svengali!' shrieked poor Monsieur J—, gesticulating towards the box where Svengali was sitting, quite impassible, gazing at Monsieur J—, and smiling a ghastly, sardonic smile, a *rictus* of hate and triumphant revenge – as if he were saying –

'I've got the laugh of you *all*, this time!'

Taffy, the Laird, Little Billee, the whole house were now staring at Svengali, and his wife was forgotten.

She stood vacantly looking at everybody and everything – the chandelier, Monsieur J—, Svengali in his box, the people in the stalls, in the gallery – and smiling as if the noisy scene amused and excited her.

'Svengali!' Svengali! Svengali!'

The whole house took up the cry, derisively. Monsieur J— led Madame Svengali away; she seemed quite passive. That terrible figure of Svengali still sat, immovable, watching his wife's retreat – still smiling his ghastly smile. All eyes were now turned on him once more.

Monsieur J— was then seen to enter his box with a policeman and two or three other men, one of them in evening dress. He quickly drew the curtains to; then, a minute or two after, he

The last they saw of Svengali

reappeared on the platform bowing and scraping to the audience, as pale as death, and called for silence, the gentleman in evening dress by his side; and this person explained that a very dreadful thing had happened – that Monsieur Svengali had suddenly died in that box – of apoplexy or heart disease; that his wife had seen it from her place on the stage, and had apparently gone out of her senses, which accounted for her extraordinary behaviour.

He added that the money would be returned at the doors, and begged the audience to disperse quietly.

Taffy, with his two friends behind him, forced his way to a stage door he knew. The Laird had no longer any doubts on the score of Trilby's identity – *this* Trilby, at all events.

Taffy knocked and thumped till the door was opened, and gave his card to the man who opened it, stating that he and his friends were old friends of Madame Svengali, and must see her at once.

The man tried to slam the door in his face, but Taffy pushed through, and shut it on the crowd outside, and insisted on being taken to Monsieur J— immediately; and was so authoritative and big, and looked such a swell, that the man was cowed, and led him.

They passed an open door, through which they had a glimpse of a prostrate form on a table – a man partially undressed, and some men bending over him, doctors probably.

That was the last they saw of Svengali.

Then they were taken to another door, and Monsieur J— came out, and Taffy explained who they were, and they were admitted.

La Svengali was there, sitting in an armchair by the fire, while several of the band stood round gesticulating, and talking German or Polish or Yiddish. Gecko, on his knees, was alternately chafing her hands and feet. She seemd quite dazed.

But at the sight of Taffy she jumped up and rushed to him, saying: 'Oh, Taffy dear – oh, Taffy! what's it all about? Where on earth am I? What an age since we met!'

Then she caught sight of the Laird, and kissed him; and then she recognised Little Billee.

She looked at him for a long while in great surprise, and then shook hands with him.

'How pale you are! and so changed – you've got a moustache!

What's the matter? Why are you all dressed in black, with white
cravats, as if you were going to a funeral? Where's Svengali? I
should like to go home!'

'Where – what do you call – home, I mean – where is it?'
asked Taffy.

'C'est à l'Hôtel de Normandie, dans le Haymarket.* On va
vous y conduire, madame!' said Monsieur J—.

'Oui – c'est ça!' said Trilby – 'Hôtel de Normandie – mais
Svengali – où est-ce qu'il est?'

'Hélas! Madame – il est très malade!'

'Malade? Qu'est-ce qu'il a?* How funny you look, with your
moustache, Little Billee! dear, *dear* Little Billee! so pale, so very
pale! Are you ill too? Oh, I hope not! How *glad* I am to see you
again – you can't tell! though I promised your mother I wouldn't
– never, never! Where are we now, dear Little Billée?'

Monsieur J— seemed to have lost his head. He was constantly
running in and out of the room, distracted. The bandsmen began
to talk and try to explain, in incomprehensible French, to Taffy.
Gecko seemed to have disappeared. It was a bewildering business – noises from outside, the tramp and bustle and shouts of
the departing crowd, people running in and out and asking for
Monsieur J—, policemen, firemen, and what not!

Then Little Billee, who had been exerting the most heroic self-
control, suggested that Trilby should come to his house in
Fitzroy Square, first of all, and be taken out of all this – and the
idea struck Taffy as a happy one – and it was proposed to
Monsieur J—, who saw that our three friends were old friends
of Madame Svengali's, and people to be trusted; and he was
only too glad to be relieved of her, and gave his consent.

Little Billee and Taffy drove to Fitzroy Square to prepare
Little Billee's landlady, who was much put out at first at having
such a novel and unexpected charge imposed on her. It was all
explained to her that it must be so. That Madame Svengali, the
greatest singer in Europe and an old friend of her tenant's, had
suddenly gone out of her mind from grief at the tragic death of
her husband, and that for this night at least the unhappy lady
must sleep under that roof – indeed, in Little Billee's own bed,
and that he would sleep at a hotel; and that a nurse would be
provided at once – it might be only for that one night; and that
the lady was as quiet as a lamb, and would probably recover her
faculties after a night's rest. A doctor was sent for from close

by, and soon Trilby appeared, with the Laird, and her appearance and her magnificent sables impressed Mrs Godwin, the landlady — brought her figuratively on her knees. Then Taffy, the Laird and Little Billee departed again and dispersed — to procure a nurse for the night, to find Gecko, to fetch some of Trilby's belongings from the Hôtel de Normandie, and her maid.

The maid (the old German Jewess and Svengali's relative), distracted by the news of her master's death, had gone to the theatre. Gecko was in the hands of the police. Things had got to a terrible pass. But our three friends did their best, and were up most of the nght.

So much for La Svengali's *début* in London.

The present scribe was not present on that memorable occasion, and has written this inadequate and most incomplete description partly from hearsay and private information, partly from the reports in the contemporary newspapers.

Should any surviving eye-witness of that lamentable fiasco read these pages, and see any gross inaccuracy in this bald account of it, the P. S. will feel deeply obliged to the same for any corrections or additions, and these will be duly acted upon and gratefully acknowledged in all subsequent editions; which will be numerous, no doubt, on account of the great interest still felt in 'La Svengali,' even by those who never saw or heard her (and they are many), and also because the present scribe is better qualified (by his opportunities) for the compiling of this brief biographical sketch than any person now living, with the exception, of course, of 'Taffy' and 'the Laird,' to whose kindness, even more than to his own personal recollections, he owes whatever it may contain of serious historical value.

Next morning they all three went to Fitzroy Square. Little Billee had slept at Taffy's rooms in Jermyn Street.*

Trilby seemed quite pathetically glad to see them again. She was dressed simply and plainly — in black; her trunks had been sent from the hotel.

The hospital nurse was with her; the doctor had just left. He had said that she was suffering from some great nervous shock — a pretty safe diagnosis!

Her wits had apparently not come back, and she seemed in no way to realise her position.

'Ah! what it is to see you again, all three! It makes one feel

Three nice clean Englishmen

glad to be alive! I've thought of many things, but never of this –
never! Three nice clean Englishmen, all speaking English – and
such dear old friends! Ah! J'aime tant ça – c'est le ciel!* I
wonder I've got a word of English left!'

Her voice was so soft and sweet and low that these ingenuous
remarks sounded like a beautiful song. And she 'made the soft
eyes' at them all three, one after another, in her old way; and
the soft eyes quickly filled with tears.

She seemed ill and weak and worn out, and insisted on
keeping the Laird's hand in hers.

'What's the matter with Svengali? He must be dead!'

They all three looked at each other, perplexed.

'Ah! he's dead! I can see it in your faces. He'd got heart

disease. I'm sorry! oh, very sorry indeed! He was always very kind, poor Svengali!'

'Yes. He's dead,' said Taffy.

'And Gecko – dear little Gecko – is he dead too? I saw him last night – he warmed my hands and feet: where were we?'

'No. Gecko's not dead. But he's had to be locked up for a little while. He struck Svengali, you know. You saw it all.'

'I? No! I never saw it. But I *dreamt* something like it! Gecko with a knife, and people holding him, and Svengali bleeding on the ground. That was just before Svengali's illness. He'd cut himself in the neck, you know – with a rusty nail, he told me. I wonder how? ... But it was wrong of Gecko to strike him. They were such friends. Why did he?'

'Well – it was because Svengali struck you with his conductor's wand when you were rehearsing. Struck you on the fingers and made you cry! don't you remember?'

'Struck *me! rehearsing?* – made me *cry!* what *are* you talking about, dear Taffy? Svengali never *struck* me! He was kindness itself – always! and what should *I* rehearse?'

'Well, the song you were to sing at the theatre in the evening.'

'Sing at the theatre! I never sang at any theatre – except last night, if that big place was a theatre! and they didn't seem to like it! I'll take precious good care never to sing in a theatre again! How they howled! and there was Svengali in the box opposite, laughing at me. Why was I taken there? and why did that funny little Frenchman in the white waistcoat ask me to sing? I know very well I can't sing well enough to sing in a place like that! What a fool I was! It all seems like a bad dream! What was it all about? *Was* it a dream, I wonder!'

'Well – but don't you remember singing at Paris, in the Salle des Bashibazoucks – and at Vienna – St Petersburg – lots of places?'

'What nonsense, dear – you're thinking of some one else! *I* never sang anywhere! I've been to Vienna and St Petersburg – but I never sang there – good heavens!'

Then there was a pause, and our three friends looked at her helplessly.

Little Billee said: 'Tell me, Trilby – what made you cut me dead when I bowed to you in the Place de la Concorde, and you were riding with Svengali in that swell cariage?'

'*I* never rode in a swell carriage with Svengali! Omnibuses

were more in *our* line! You're dreaming, dear Little Billee –
you're taking me for somebody else; and as for my cutting *you*
– why, I'd sooner cut myself – into little pieces!'

'*Where* were you staying with Svengali in Paris?'

'I really forget. *Were* we in Paris? Oh yes of course. Hôtel
Bertrand, Place Notre Dame des Victoires.'*

'How long have you been going about with Svengali?'

'Oh, months, years – I forget. I was very ill. He cured me.'

'Ill! What was the matter?'

'Oh! I was mad with grief, and pain in my eyes, and wanted
to kill myself, when I lost my dear little Jeannot, at Vibraye. I
fancied I hadn't been careful enough with him. I was crazed!
Don't you remember writing to me there, Taffy – through
Angèle Boisse? Such a sweet letter you wrote! I know it by
heart! And you too, Sandy;' and she kissed him. 'I wonder
where they are, your letters? I've got nothing of my own in the
world – not even your dear letters – nor Little Billee's – such
lots of them!

'Well, Svengali used to write to me too – and then he got my
address from Angèle . . .

'When Jeannot died, I felt I must kill myself or get away from
Vibraye – get away from the people there; so when he was
buried I cut my hair short and got a workman's cap and blouse
and trousers and walked all the way to Paris without saying
anything to anybody. I didn't want anybody to know; I wanted
to escape from Svengali, who wrote that he was coming there to
fetch me. I wanted to hide in Paris. When I got there at last it
was two o'clock in the morning, and I was in dreadful pain –
and I'd lost all my money – thirty francs – through a hole in my
trousers' pocket. Besides, I had a row with a carter in the Halle.
He thought I was a man, and hit me and gave me a black eye,
just because I patted his horse and fed it with a carrot I'd been
trying to eat myself. He was tipsy, I think. Well, I looked over
the bridge to the river – just by the Morgue – and wanted to
jump in. But the Morgue sickened me, so I hadn't the pluck.
Svengali used to be always talking about the Morgue, and my
going there some day. He used to say he'd come and look at me
there, and the idea made me so sick I couldn't. I got bewildered
and quite stupid.

'Then I went to Angèle's, in the Rue des Cloîtres Ste Pétronille,
and waited about; but I hadn't the courage to ring, so I went to

Pœna Pede Claudo

the Place St Anatole des Arts, and looked up at the old studio
window, and thought how comfortable it was in there, with the
big settee near the stove, and all that, and felt inclined to ring
up Madame Vinard; and then I remembered Little Billee was ill
there, and his mother and sister were with him. Angèle had
written me, you know. Poor Little Billee! There he was, very ill!

'So I walked about the place, and up and down the Rue des
Trois Mauvais Ladres. Then I went down the Rue de Seine to
the river again, and again I hadn't the pluck to jump in. Besides,
there was a *sergent-de-ville* who followed and watched me. And
the fun of it was that I knew him quite well, and he didn't know
me a bit. It was Célestin Beaumollet, who got so tipsy on
Christmas night. Don't you remember? The tall one, who was
pitted with the small-pox.

'Then I walked about till near daylight. Then I could stand it
no longer, and went to Svengali's, in the rue Tireliard, but he'd
moved to the Rue des Saints Pères;* and I went there and found
him. I didn't want to a bit, but I couldn't help myself. It was
fate, I suppose! He was very kind, and cured me almost directly,
and got me coffee and bread and butter – the best I ever tasted
– and a warm bath from Bidet Frères, in the Rue Savonarole. It
was heavenly! And I slept for two days and two nights! And
then he told me how fond he was of me, and how he would
always cure me, and take care of me, and marry me, if I would
go away with him. He said he would devote his whole life to
me, and took a small room for me, next to his.

'I stayed with him there a week, never going out or seeing any
one, mostly asleep. I'd caught a chill.

'He played in two concerts and made a lot of money; and
then we went away to Germany together; and no one was a bit
the wiser.'

'And *did* he marry you?'

'Well – no. He couldn't poor fellow! He'd already got a wife
living, and three children, which he declared were not his. They
live in Elberfeld in Prussia;* she keeps a small sweet-stuff shop
there. He behaved very badly to them. But it was not through
me! He'd deserted them long before; but he used to send them
plenty of money when he'd got any; I made him, for I was very
sorry for her. He was always talking about her, and what she
said and what she did, and imitating her saying her prayers and
eating pickled cucumber with one hand and drinking schnapps

The old Studio

with the other, so as not to lose any time; till he made me die of laughing. He could be very funny, Svengali, though he *was* German, poor dear! And then Gecko joined us, and Marta.'

'Who's Marta?'

'His aunt. She cooked for us, and all that. She's coming here presently; she sent word from the hotel; she's very fond of him. Poor Marta! Poor Gecko! What *will* they ever do without Svengali?'

'Then what did he do to live?'

'Oh! he played at concerts, I suppose – and all that.'

'Did you ever hear him?'

'Yes. Sometimes Marta took me; at the beginning, you know. He was always very much applauded. He plays beautifully. Everybody said so.'

'Did he never try and teach you to sing?'

'Oh, maïe aïe! not he! Why, he always laughed when I tried to sing; and so did Marta; and so did Gecko! It made them roar! I used to sing "Ben Bolt." They used to make me, just for fun – and go into fits. *I* didn't mind a scrap. I'd had no training, you know!'

'Was there anybody else he knew – any other woman?'

'Not that *I* know of! He always made out he was so fond of me that he couldn't even *look* at another woman. Poor Svengali!' (Here her eyes filled with tears again.) 'He was always very kind! But I never could be fond of him in the way he wished – never! It made me sick even to think of! Once I used to hate him – in Paris – in the studio; don't you remember?

'He hardly ever left me; and then Marta looked after me – for I've always been weak and ill, and often so languid that I could hardly walk across the room. It was that three days' walk from Vibraye to Paris. I never got over it.

'I used to try and do all I could – be a daughter to him, as I couldn't be anything else – mend his things, and all that, and cook him little French dishes. I fancy he was very poor at one time; we were always moving from place to place. But I always had the best of everything. He insisted on that – even if he had to go without himself. It made him quite unhappy when I wouldn't eat, so I used to force myself.

'Then, as soon as I felt uneasy about things, or had any pain, he would say, "Dors, ma mignonne!"* and I would sleep at once – for hours, I think – and wake up oh, so tired! and find him kneeling by me, always so anxious and kind – and Marta and Gecko! and sometimes we had the doctor, and I was ill in bed.

'Gecko used to dine and breakfast with us – you've no idea what an angel he is, poor little Gecko! But what a dreadful thing to strike Svengali! *Why* did he? Svengali taught him all he knows!'

'And you knew no one else – no other woman?'

'No one that I can remember – except Marta – not a soul!'

'And that beautiful dress you had on last night?'

'It isn't mine. It's on the bed upstairs, and so's the fur cloak. They belong to Marta. She's got lots of them, lovely things – silk, satin, velvet – and lots of beautiful jewels. Marta deals in them, and makes lots of money.

'I've often tried them on; I'm very easy to fit,' she said, 'being so tall and thin. And poor Svengali would kneel down and cry, and kiss my hands and feet, and tell me I was his goddess and empress, and all that, which I hate. And Marta used to cry, too. And then he would say –

' "Et maintenant dors, ma mignonne!"

'And when I woke up I was so tired that I went to sleep again on my own account.

'But he was very patient. Oh dear me! I've always been a poor, helpless, useless log and burden to him!

'Once I actually walked in my sleep – and woke up in the market-place at Prague – and found an immense crowd, and poor Svengali bleeding from the forehead, in a faint on the ground. He'd been knocked down by a horse and cart, he told me. He'd got his guitar with him. I suppose he and Gecko had been playing somewhere, for Gecko had his fiddle. If Gecko hadn't been there, I don't know what we should have done. You never saw such queer people as they were – such crowds – you'd think they'd never seen an Englishwoman before. The noise they made, and the things they gave me . . . some of them went down on their knees, and kissed my hands and the skirts of my gown.

'He was ill in bed for a week after that, and I nursed him, and he was very grateful. Poor Svengali! God knows *I* felt grateful to *him* for many things! Tell me how he died! I hope he hadn't much pain.'

They told her it was quite sudden, from heart disease.

'Et maintenant dors, ma mignonne!'

'Ah! I knew he had that; he wasn't a healthy man; he used to smoke too much. Marta used always to be very anxious.'

Just then Marta came in.

Marta was a fat elderly Jewess of rather a grotesque and ignoble type. She seemed overcome with grief – all but prostrate.

Trilby hugged and kissed her, and took off her bonnet and shawl, and made her sit down in a big arm-chair, and got her a foot-stool.

She couldn't speak a word of anything but Polish and a little German. Trilby had also picked up a little German, and with this and by means of signs, and no doubt through a long intimacy with each other's ways, they understood each other very well. She seemed a very good old creature, and very fond of Trilby, but in mortal terror of the three Englishmen.

Lunch was brought up for the two women and the nurse, and our friends left them, promising to come again that day.

They were utterly bewildered; and the Laird would have it that there was another Madame Svengali somewhere, the real one, and that Trilby was a fraud – self-deceived and self-deceiving – quite unconsciously so, of course.

Truth looked out of her eyes, as it always had done – truth was in every line of her face.

The truth only – nothing but the truth could ever be told in that 'voice of velvet,' which rang as true when she spoke as that of any thrush or nightingale, however rebellious it might be now (and for ever perhaps) to artificial melodic laws and limitations and restraints. The long training it had been subjected to had made it 'a wonder, a world's delight,' and though she might never sing another note, her mere speech would always be more golden than any silence, whatever she might say.

Except on the one particular point of her singing, she had seemed absolutely sane – so, at least, thought Taffy, the Laird, and Little Billee. And each thought to himself, besides, that this last incarnation of Trilbyness was quite the sweetest, most touching, most endearing of all.

They had not failed to note how rapidly she had aged, now that they had seen her without her rouge and pearl-powder; she looked thirty at least – she was only twenty-three.

Her hands were almost transparent in their waxen whiteness; delicate little frosty wrinkles had gathered round her eyes; there were gray streaks in her hair; all strength and straightness and elasticity seemed to have gone out of her with the memory of her endless triumphs (if she really *was* La Svengali), and of her many wanderings from city to city all over Europe.

It was evident enough that the sudden stroke which had destroyed her power of singing had left her physically a wreck.

But she was one of those rarely-gifted beings who cannot look or speak or even stir without waking up (and satisfying) some vague longing that lies dormant in the hearts of most of us, men and women alike; grace, charm, magnetism – whatever the nameless seduction should be called that she possessed to such an unusual degree – she had lost none of it when she lost her high spirits, her buoyant health and energy, her wits!

Tuneless and insane, she was more of a siren than ever – a quite unconscious siren – without any guile, who appealed to the heart all the more directly and irresistibly that she could no longer stir the passions.

All this was keenly felt by all three – each in his different way – by Taffy and Little Billee especially.

All her past life was forgiven – her sins of omission and commission! And whatever might be her fate – recovery, madness, disease, or death – the care of her till she died or recovered should be the principal business of their lives.

Both had loved her. All three, perhaps.* One had been loved by her as passionately, as purely, as unselfishly, as any man could wish to be loved, and in some extraordinary manner had recovered, afer many years, at the mere sudden sight and sound over her, his lost share in our common inheritance – the power to love, and all its joy and sorrow; without which he had found life not worth living, though he had possessed every other gift and blessing in such abundance.

'Oh, Circe,* poor Circe, dear Circe, divine enchantress that you were!' he said to himself, in his excitable way. 'A mere look from your eyes, a mere note of your heavenly voice, has turned a poor, miserable, callous brute back into a man again! and I will never forget it – never! And now that a still worse trouble than mine has befallen you, you shall always be first in my thoughts till the end!'

And Taffy felt pretty much the same, though he was not by way of talking to himself so eloquently about things as Little Billee.

As they lunched, they read the account of the previous evening's events in different papers, three or four of which (including the *Times*) had already got leaders about the famous but unhappy singer who had been so suddenly widowed and struck down in the midst of her glory. All these accounts were more or less correct. In one paper it was mentioned that Madame Svengali was under the roof and care of Mr William Bagot, the painter, in Fitzroy Square.

The inquest on Svengali was to take place that afternoon, and also Gecko's examination at the Bow Street Police Court, for his assault.

Taffy was allowed to see Gecko, who was remanded till the result of the *post-mortem* should be made public. But beyond inquiring most anxiously and minutely after Trilby, and betraying the most passionate concern for her, he would say nothing, and seemed indifferent as to his own fate.

When they went to Fitzroy Square, late in the afternoon, they found that many people, musical, literary, fashionable, and otherwise (and many foreigners), had called to inquire after Madame Svengali, but no one had been admitted to see her. Mrs Godwin was much elated by the importance of her new lodger.

Trilby had been writing to Angèle Boisse, at her old address in the Rue des Cloîtres Ste Pétronille, in the hope that this letter would find her still there. She was anxious to go back and be a *blanchisseuse de fin* with her friend. It was a kind of nostalgia for Paris, the Quartier Latin, her clean old trade.

This project our three heroes did not think it necessary to discuss with her just yet; she seemed quite unfit for work of any kind.

The doctor who had seen her again, had been puzzled by her strange physical weakness, and wished for a consultation with some special authority; Little Billee, who was intimate with most of the great physicians, wrote about her to Sir Oliver Calthorpe.

She seemed to find a deep happiness in being with her three old friends, and talked and listened with all her old eagerness and geniality, and much of her old gaiety, in spite of her strange and sorrowful position. But for this it was impossible to realise that her brain was affected in the slightest degree, except when some reference was made to her singing, and this seemed to annoy and irritate her, as though she were being made fun of.

Taffy was allowed to see Gecko

The whole of her marvellous musical career, and everything connected with it, had been clean wiped out of her recollection.

She was very anxious to get into other quarters, that Little Billee should suffer no inconvenience, and they promised to take rooms for her and Marta on the morrow.

They told her cautiously all about Svengali and Gecko; she was deeply concerned, but betrayed no such poignant anguish as might have been expected. The thought of Gecko troubled her most, and she showed much anxiety as to what might befall him.

Next day she moved with Marta to some lodgings in Charlotte Street, where everything was made as comfortable for them as possible.

Sir Oliver saw her with Dr Thorne (the doctor who was attending her) and Dr Jakes Talboys.*

Sir Oliver took the greatest interest in her case, both for her sake and his friend Little Billee's. Also his own, for he was charmed with her. He saw her three times in the course of the week, but could not say for certain what was the matter with her, beyond taking the very gravest view of her condition. For all he could advise or prescribe, her weakness and physical prostration increased rapidly, through no cause he could discover. Her insanity was not enough to account for it. She lost weight daily; she seemed to be wasting and fading away from sheer general atrophy.

Two or three times he took her and Marta for a drive.

On one of these occasions, as they went down Charlotte Street, she saw a shop with transparent French blinds in the window, and through them some Frenchwomen, with neat white caps, ironing. It was a French *blanchisserie de fin*, and the sight of it interested and excited her so much that she must needs insist on being put down and on going into it.

'Je voudrais bien parler à la patronne, si ça ne la dérange pas,'* she said.

The *patronne*, a genial Parisian, was much astonished to hear a great French lady, in costly garments, evidently a person of fashion and importance, applying to her rather humbly for employment in the business, and showing a thorough knowledge of the work (and of the Parisian work-woman's colloquial dialect). Marta managed to catch the *patronne*'s eye, and tapped her own forehead significantly, and Sir Oliver nodded. So the

A fair blanchisseuse de fin

good woman humoured the great lady's fancy, and promised her abundance of employment whenever she should want it.

Employment! Poor Trilby was hardly strong enough to walk back to the carriage; and this was her last outing.

But this little adventure had filled her with hope and good spirits – for she had as yet received no answer from Angèle Boisse (who was in Marseilles), and had begun to realise how dreary the Quartier Latin would be without Jeannot, without Angèle, without the *trois Angliches* in the Place St Anatole des Arts.

She was not allowed to see any of the strangers who came and made kind inquiries. This her doctors had strictly forbidden. Any reference to music or singing irritated her beyond measure. She would say to Marta in bad German –

'Tell them, Marta – what nonsense it is! They are taking me for another – they are mad. They are trying to make a fool of me!'

And Marta would betray great uneasiness – almost terror – when she was appealed to in this way.

Part Eighth

La vie est vaine:
 un peu d'amour,
Un peu de haine . . .
 Et puis – bonjour!

La vie est brève:
 Un peu d'espoir,
Un peu de rève . . .
 Et puis – bonsoir.*

Svengali had died from heart disease. The cut he had received from Gecko had not apparently (as far as the verdict of a coroner's inquest could be trusted) had any effect in aggravating his malady or hastening his death.

But Gecko was sent for trial at the Old Bailey, and sentenced to hard labour for six months (a sentence which, if I remember aright, gave rise to much comment at the time). Taffy saw him again, but with no better result than before. He chose to preserve an obstinate silence on his relations with the Svengalis and their relations with each other.

When he was told how hopelessly ill and insane Madame Svengali was, he shed a few tears, and said: 'Ah, pauvrette, pauvrette – ah! monsieur – je l'aimais tant, je l'aimais tant! il n'y en a pas beaucoup comme elle, Dieu de misère! C'est un ange du Paradis!'*

And not another word was to be got out of him.

It took some time to settle Svengali's affairs after his death. No will was found. His old mother came over from Germany, and two of his sisters, but no wife. The comic wife and the three children, and the sweet-stuff shop in Elberfeld, had been humorous inventions of his own – a kind of Mrs Harris!

He left three thousand pounds, every penny of which (and of far larger sums that he had spent) had been earned by 'La Svengali,' but nothing came to Trilby of this; nothing but the clothes and jewels he had given her, and in this respect he had been lavish enough; and there were countless costly gifts from emperors, kings, great people of all kinds. Trilby was under the impression that all these belonged to Marta. Marta behaved

admirably; she seemed bound hand and foot to Trilby by a kind
of slavish adoration, as that of a plain old mother for a brilliant
and beautiful but dying child.

It soon became evident that, whatever her disease might be,
Trilby had but a very short time to live.

She was soon too weak even to be taken out in a Bath chair,
and remained all day in her large sitting-room with Marta; and
there, to her great and only joy, she received her three old
friends every afternoon and gave them coffee, and made them
smoke cigarettes of caporal as of old; and their hearts were daily
harrowed as they watched her rapid decline.

Day by day she grew more beautiful in their eyes, in spite of
her increasing pallor and emaciation – her skin was so pure and
white and delicate, and the bones of her face so admirable!

Her eyes recovered all their old humorous brightness when *les
trois Angliches* were with her, and the expression of her face
was so wistful and tender for all her playfulness, so full of eager
clinging to existence and to them that they felt the memory of it
would haunt them for ever, and be the sweetest and saddest
memory of their lives.

Her quick, though feeble gestures, full of reminiscences of the
vigorous and lively girl they had known a few years back, sent
waves of pity through them and pure brotherly love; and the
incomparable tones and changes and modulations of her voice,
as she chatted and laughed, bewitched them almost as much as
when she had sung the 'Nuss-baum' of Schumann in the Salle
des Bashibazoucks.

Sometimes Lorrimer came, and Antony, and the Greek. It was
like a genial little court of bohemia. And Lorrimer, Antony, the
Laird, and Little Billee made those beautiful chalk and pencil
studies of her head which are now so well known – all so
singularly like her, and so singularly unlike each other! *Trilby
vue à travers quatre tempéraments!**

These afternoons were probably the happiest poor Trilby had
ever spent in her life – with these dear people round her,
speaking the language she loved; talking of old times and jolly
Paris days, she never thought of the morrow.

But later – at night, in the small hours – she would wake up
with a start from some dream full of tender and blissful
recollections, and suddenly realise her own mischance, and
feel the icy hand of that which was to come before many

A throne in Bohemia

morrows were over; and taste the bitterness of earth so keenly
that she longed to scream out loud, and get up, and walk up
and down, and wring her hands at the dreaful thought of parting
for ever!

But she lay motionless and mum as a poor little frightened
mouse in a trap, for fear of waking up the good old tired Marta,
who was snoring at her side.

And in an hour or two the bitterness would pass away, the
creeps and the horrors; and the stoical spirit of resignation
would steal over her – the balm, the blessed calm! and all her
old bravery would come back.

And then she would sink into sleep again, and dream more
blissfully than ever, till the good Marta woke her with a
motherly kiss and a fragrant cup of coffee; and she would find,
feeble as she was, and doomed as she felt herself to be, that joy
cometh of a morning; and life was still sweet for her, with yet a
whole day to look forward to.

One day she was deeply moved at receiving a visit from Mrs
Bagot, who, at Little Billee's earnest desire, had come all the
way from Devonshire to see her.

As the graceful little lady came in, pale and trembling all over,
Trilby rose from her chair to receive her, and rather timidly put
out her hand, and smiled in a frightened manner. Neither could
speak for a second. Mrs Bagot stood stock-still by the door
gazing (with all her heart in her eyes) at the so terribly altered
Trilby – the girl she had once so dreaded.

Trilby, who seemed also bereft of motion, and whose face
and lips were ashen, exclaimed, 'I'm afraid I haven't quite kept
my promise to you, after all! but things have turned out so
differently! anyhow, you needn't have any fear of me *now*.'

At the mere sound of that voice, Mrs Bagot, who was as
impulsive, emotional, and unregulated as her son, rushed forward, crying, 'Oh, my poor girl, my poor girl!' and caught her
in her arms, and kissed and caressed her, and burst into a flood
of tears, and forced her back into her chair, hugging her as if
she were a long-lost child.

'I love you now as much as I always admired you – pray
believe it!'

'Oh, how kind of you to say that!' said Trilby, her own eyes
filling. 'I'm not at all the dangerous or designing person you

'Oh, my poor girl, my poor girl!'

thought. I knew quite well I wasn't a proper person to marry your son all the time; and told him so again and again. It was very stupid of me to say yes at last. I was miserable directly after, I assure you. Somehow I couldn't help myself – I was driven.'

'Oh, don't talk of that! don't talk of that! You've never been to blame in any way – I've long known it – I've been full of remorse! You've been in my thoughts always, night and day. Forive a poor jealous mother. As if *any* man could help loving you – or any woman either. Forgive me!'

'Oh, Mrs Bagot – forgive *you!* What a funny idea! But, anyhow, you have forgiven *me*, and that's all I care for now. I was very fond of your son – as fond as could be. I am now, but in quite a different sort of way, you know – the sort of way *you* must be, I fancy! There was never another like him that I ever met – anywhere! You *must* be so proud of him; who wouldn't? *Nobody's* good enough for him. I would have been only too glad to be his servant, his humble servant! I used to tell him so – but he wouldn't hear of it – he was much too kind! He always thought of others before himself. And, oh! how rich and famous he's become! I've heard all about it, and it did me good. It does me more good to think of than anything else; far more than if I were to be ever so rich and famous myself, I can tell you!'

This from La Svengali, whose overpowering fame, so utterly forgotten by herself, was still ringing all over Europe; whose lamentable illness and approaching death were being mourned and discussed and commented upon in every capital of the civilised world, as one distressing bulletin appeared after another. She might have been a royal personage!

Mrs Bagot knew, of course, the strange form her insanity had taken, and made no allusion to the flood of thoughts that rushed through her own brain as she listened to this towering goddess of song, this poor mad queen of the nightingales, humbly gloating over her son's success ...

Poor Mrs Bagot had just come from Little Billee's, in Fitzroy Square, close by. There she had seen Taffy, in a corner of Little Billee's studio, laboriously answering endless letters and telegrams from all parts of Europe – for the good Taffy had constituted himself Trilby's secretary and *homme d'affaires** – unknown to her, of course. And this was no sinecure (though he liked it): putting aside the numerous people he had to see and be interviewed by, there were kind inquiries and messages of condolence and sympathy from nearly all the crowned heads of Europe, through their chamberlains; applications for help from unsuccessful musical strugglers all over the world to the pre-eminently successful one; beautiful letters from great and famous people, musical or otherwise; disinterested offers of service; interested proposals for engagements when the present trouble should be over; beggings for an interview from famous *impresarios*, to obtain which no distance would be thought too great, etc. etc. etc. It was endless, in English, French, German, Italian – in languages quite incomprehensible (many letters had to remain unanswered) – Taffy took an almost malicious pleasure in explaining all this to Mrs Bagot.

Then there was a constant rolling of carriages up to the door, and a thundering of Little Billee's knocker: Lord and Lady Palmerston wish to know – the Lord Chief Justice wishes to know – the Dean of Westminster wishes to know – the Marchioness of Westminster wishes to know – everybody wishes to know if there is any better news of Madame Svengali!

These were small things, truly; but Mrs Bagot was a small person from a small village in Devonshire, and one whose heart and eye had hitherto been filled by no larger image than that of Little Billee; and Little Billee's fame, as she now discovered for the first time, did not quite fill the entire universe.

And she mustn't be too much blamed if all these obvious signs of a world-wide colossal celebrity impressed and even awed her a little.

Madame Svengali! Why, this was the beautiful girl whom she remembered so well, whom she had so grandly discarded with a word, and who had accepted her *congé** so meekly in a minute; whom, indeed, she had been cursing in her heart for years, because – because what?

Poor Mrs Bagot felt herself turn hot and red all over, and humbled herself to the very dust, and almost forgot that she had been in the right, after all, and that 'la grande Trilby' was certainly no fit match for her son!

So she went quite humbly to see Trilby, and found a poor pathetic mad creature still more humble than herself, who still apologised for – for what?

A poor, pathetic, mad creature who had clean forgotten that she was the greatest singer in all the world – one of the greatest

artists that had ever lived; but who remembered with shame and
contrition that she had once taken the liberty of yielding (after
endless pressure and repeated disinterested refusals of her own,
and out of sheer irresistible affection) to the passionate pleadings
of a little obscure art student, a mere boy – no better off than
herself – just as penniless and insignificant a nobody; but – the
son of Mrs Bagot!

All due sense of proportion died out of the poor lady as she
remembered and realised all this!

And then Trilby's pathetic beauty, so touching, so winning, in
its rapid decay; the nameless charm of look and voice and
manner that was her special appanage, and which her malady
and singular madness had only increased; her childlike simplicity, her transparent forgetfulness of self – all these so
fascinated and entranced Mrs Bagot, whose quick susceptibility
to such impressions was just as keen as her son's, that she very
soon found herself all but worshipping this fast-fading lily – for
so she called her in her own mind – quite forgetting (or affecting
to forget) on what very questionable soil the lily had been
reared, and through what strange vicissitudes of evil and corruption it had managed to grow so tall and white and fragrant!

Oh, strange compelling power of weakness and grace and
prettiness combined, and sweet, sincere unconscious natural
manners! not to speak of world-wide fame!

For Mrs Bagot was just a shrewd little conventional British
country matron of the good upper middle-class type, bristling
all over with provincial proprieties and respectabilities, a philistine of the philistines, in spite of her artistic instincts; one who
for years had (rather unjustly) thought of Trilby as a wanton
and perilous siren, an unchaste and unprincipled and most
dangerous daughter of Heth, and the special enemy of her
house.

And here she was – like all the rest of us monads and nomads
and bohemians – just sitting at Trilby's feet . . .

'A washerwoman! a figure model! and Heaven knows what
besides!' and she had never even heard her sing!

It was truly comical to see and hear!

Mrs Bagot did not go back to Devonshire. She remained in
Fitzroy Square, at her son's, and spent most of her time with
Trilby, doing and devising all kinds of things to distract and

amuse her, and lead her thoughts gently to heaven, and soften for her the coming end of all.

Trilby had a way of saying, and especially of looking, 'Thank you' that made one wish to do as many things for her as one could, if only to make her say and look it again.

And she had retained much of her old, quaint, and amusing manner of telling things, and had much to tell still left of her wandering life, although there were so many strange lapses in her powers of memory – gaps – which, if they could only have been filled up, would have been full of such surpassing interest!

Then she was never tired of talking and hearing of Little Billee; and that was a subject of which Mrs Bagot could never tire either!

Then there were the recollections of her childhood. One day, in a drawer, Mrs Bagot came upon a faded daguerreotype of a woman in a Tam o' Shanter,* with a face so sweet and beautiful and saint-like that it almost took her breath away. It was Trilby's mother.

'Who and what was your mother, Trilby?'

'Ah, poor mamma!' said Trilby, and she looked at the portrait a long time. 'Ah, she was ever so much prettier than that! Mamma was once a *demoiselle de comptoir** – that's a barmaid, you know – at the Montagnards Écossais, in the Rue du Paradis Poissonnière – a place where men used to drink and smoke without sitting down. That was unfortunate, wasn't it?

'Papa loved her with all his heart, although, of course, she wasn't his equal. They were married at the Embassy, in the Rue du Faubourg St-Honoré.

'*Her* parents weren't married at all. Her mother was the daughter of a boatman on Loch Ness, near a place called Drumnadrochit; but her father was the Honourable Colonel Desmond. He was related to all sorts of great people in England and Ireland. He behaved very badly to my grandmother and to poor mamma – his own daughter! deserted them both! Not very *honourable* of him, *was* it? And that's all I know about him.'

And then she went on to tell of the home in Paris that might have been so happy but for her father's passion for drink; of her parents' deaths, and little Jeannot, and so forth. And Mrs Bagot was much moved and interested by these naïve revelations, which accounted in a measure for so much that seemed unaccountable in this extraordinary woman; who thus turned out to

'Ah, poor mamma! She was ever so much prettier than that!'

be a kind of cousin (though on the wrong side of the blanket) to no less a person than the famous Duchess of Towers.

With what joy would that ever kind and gracious lady have taken poor Trilby to her bosom had she only known! She had once been all the way from Paris to Vienna merely to hear her sing. But, unfortunately, the Svengalis had just left for St Petersburg, and she had had her long journey for nothing!

Mrs Bagot brought her many good books, and read them to her – Dr Cummings* on the approaching end of the world, and

other works of a like comforting tendency for those who are
just about to leave it; the *Pilgrim's Progress*,* sweet little tracts,
and what not.

Trilby was so grateful that she listened with much patient
attention. Only now and then a faint gleam of amusement
would steal over her face, and her lips would almost form
themselves to ejaculate, 'Oh, maïe, aïe!'

Then Mrs Bagot, as a reward for such winning docility, would
read her *David Copperfield*, and that was heavenly indeed!

But the best of all was for Trilby to look over John Leech's
Pictures of Life and Character,* just out. She had never seen
any drawings of Leech before, except now and then in an
occasional *Punch* that turned up in the studio in Paris. And they
never palled upon her, and taught her more of the aspect of
English life (the life she loved) than any book she had ever read.
She laughed and laughed; and it was almost as sweet to listen to
as if she were vocalising the quick part in Chopin's Impromptu.

One day she said, her lips trembling: 'I can't make out why
you're so wonderfully kind to me, Mrs Bagot. I hope you have
not forgotten who and what I am, and what my story is. I hope
you haven't forgotten that I'm not a respectable woman?'

'Oh, my dear child – don't ask me ... I only know that you
are you! ... and I am I! and that is enough for me ... you're
my poor, gentle, patient, suffering daughter, whatever else you
are – more sinned against than sinning, I feel sure! But there ...
I've misjudged you so, and been so unjust, that I would give
worlds to make you some amends ... besides, I should be just
as fond of you if you'd committed a murder, I really believe –
you're so strange! you're irresistible! Did you ever, in all your
life, meet anybody that *wasn't* fond of you?'

Trilby's eyes moistened with tender pleasure at such a pretty
compliment. Then, after a few minutes' thought, she said, with
engaging candour and quite simply: 'No, I can't say I ever did,
that I can think of just now. But I've forgotten such lots of
people!'

One day Mrs Bagot told Trilby that her brother-in-law, Mr
Thomas Bagot, would much like to come and talk to her.

'Was that the gentleman who came with you to the studio in
Paris?'

'Yes.'

'Why, he's a clergyman, isn't he? What does he want to come and talk to *me* about?'

'Ah! my dear child . . .' said Mrs Bagot, her eyes filling.

Trilby was thoughtful for a while, and then said: 'I'm going to die, I suppose. Oh yes! oh yes! There's no mistake about that!'

'Dear Trilby, we are all in the hands of an Almighty Merciful God!' And the tears rolled down Mrs Bagot's cheeks.

After a long pause, during which she gazed out of the window, Trilby said, in an abstracted kind of way, as though she were talking to herself: 'Après tout, c'est pas déjà si raide, de claquer! J'en ai tant vus, qui ont passé par la! Au bout du fossé la culbute, ma foi!'*

'What are you saying to yourself in French, Trilby? Your French is so difficult to understand!'

'Oh, I beg your pardon! I was thinking it's not so difficult to die, after all! I've seen such lots of people do it. I've nursed them, you know – papa and mamma and Jeannot, and Angèle Boisse's mother-in-law, and a poor *casseur de pierres*,* Colin Maigret, who lived in the Impasse des Taupes St Germain.* He'd been run over by an omnibus in the Rue Vaugirard, and had to have both his legs cut off just about the knee. They none of them seemed to mind dying a bit. They weren't a bit afraid! *I'm* not!

'Poor people don't think much of death. Rich people shouldn't either. They should be taught when they're quite young to laugh at it and despise it, like the Chinese. The Chinese die of laughing just as their heads are being cut off, and cheat the executioner! It's all in the day's work, and we're all in the same boat – so who's afraid!'

'Dying is not all, my poor child! Are you prepared to meet your Maker face to face! Have you thought about God, and the possible wrath to come if you should die unrepentant?'

'Oh, but I sha'n't! I've been repenting all my life! Besides, there'll be no wrath for any of us – not even the worst! *Il y aura amnistie générale!** Papa told me so, and he'd been a clergyman, like Mr Thomas Bagot. I often think about God. I'm very fond of Him. One *must* have something perfect to look up to and be fond of – even if it's only an idea! even if it's too good to be true!

'Though some people don't even believe He exists! Le père

'To sing like that is to pray!'

Martin didn't — but, of course, *he* was only a *chiffonnier*, and doesn't count.

'One day, though, Durien, the sculptor, who's very clever, and a very good fellow indeed, said:

'"Vois-tu, Trilby — I'm very much afraid He doesn't really exist, le bon Dieu! most unfortunately for *me*, for I *adore* Him! I never do a piece of work without thinking how nice it would be if I could only please *Him* with it!"

'And I've often thought, myself, how heavenly it must be to be able to paint, or sculpt, or make music, or write beautiful poetry, for that very reason!

'Why, once on a very hot afternoon we were sitting, a lot of us, in the court-yard outside la mère Martin's shop, drinking coffee with an old Invalide* called Bastide Lendormi, one of the Vieille Garde,* who'd only got one leg and one arm and one eye, and everybody was very fond of him. Well, a model called Mimi la Salope came out of the Mont-de-piété opposite, and Père Martin called out to her to come and sit down, and gave her a cup of coffee, and asked her to sing.

'She sang a song of Béranger's, about Napoleon the Great, in which it says —

> Parlez-nous de lui grandmère!
> Grandmère, parlez-nous de lui!*

I suppose she sang it very well, for it made old Bastide Lendormi cry; and when Père Martin *blagué*'d* him about it, he said —

'"C'est égal, voyez-vous!* to sing like that is *to pray!*"

'And then I thought how lovely it would be if *I* could only sing like Mimi la Salope, and I've thought so ever since — just to *pray!*'

'*What!* Trilby? if *you* could only sing like— Oh, but never mind, I forgot! Tell me, Trilby — do you ever pray to Him, as other people pray?'

'Pray to Him? Well, no — not often — not in words and on my knees and with my hands together, you know! *Thinking's* praying, very often — don't you think so? And so's being sorry and ashamed when one's done a mean thing, and glad when one's resisted a temptation, and grateful when it's a fine day and one's enjoying one's self without hurting any one else! What is it but praying when you try and bear up after losing all you cared to live for? And very good praying too! There can be prayers without words just as well as songs, I suppose; and Svengali used to say that songs without words are the best!

'And then it seems mean to be always asking for things. Besides, you don't get them any the faster that way, and that shows!

'La mère Martin used to be always praying. And Père Martin used always to laugh at her; yet he always seemed to get the thing *he* wanted oftenest!

'I prayed once, very hard indeed! I prayed for Jeannot not to die!'

'Well – but how do you *repent*, Trilby, if you do not humble yourself, and pray for forgiveness on your knees?'

'Oh, well – I don't exactly know! Look here, Mrs Bagot, I'll tell you the lowest and meanest thing I ever did . . .'

(Mrs Bagot felt a little nervous.)

'I'd promised to take Jeannot on Palm-Sunday* to St Philippe du Roule,* to hear l'abbé Bergamot. But Durien (that's the sculptor, you know) asked me to go with him to St Germain, where there was a fair, or something; and with Mathieu, who was a student in law; and a certain Victorine Letellier, who – who was Mathieu's mistress, in fact – a lace-mender in the Rue Ste Maritorne la Pocharde.* And so I went on Sunday morning to tell Jeannot that I couldn't take him.

'He cried so dreadfully that I thought I'd give up the others and take him to St Philippe, as I'd promised. But then Durien and Mathieu and Victorine drove up and waited outside, and so I *didn't* take him, and went with them, and I didn't enjoy anything all day, and was miserable.

'They were in an open carriage with two horses; it was Mathieu's treat, and Jeannot might have ridden on the box by the coachman without being in anybody's way. But I was afraid they didn't want him, as they didn't say anything, and so I didn't dare ask – and Jeannot saw us drive away, and I *couldn't* look back! And the worst of it is that when we were half-way to St Germain, Durien said, "What a pity you didn't bring Jeannot!" and they were all sorry I hadn't.

'It was six or seven years ago, and I really believe I've thought of it every day, and sometimes in the middle of the night!

'Ah! and when Jeannot was dying! and when he was dead – the remembrance of that Palm-Sunday!

'And if *that's* not repenting, I don't know what is!'

The remembrance of that Palm-Sunday!

'Oh, Trilby, what nonsense! *that's* nothing; good heavens! – putting off a small child! I'm thinking of far worse things – when you were in the Quartier Latin, you know – sitting to painters and sculptors . . . Surely, so attractive as you are . . .'

'Oh yes. . . . I know what you mean – it was horrid, and I was frightfully ashamed of myself; and it wasn't amusing a bit; *nothing* was, till I met your son and Taffy and dear Sandy M'Allister! But then it wasn't deceiving or disappointing anybody, or hurting their feelings – it was only hurting myself!

'Besides, all that sort of thing, in women, is punished severely enough down here, God knows! unless one's a Russian empress like Catherine the Great, or a grande dame like lots of them, or a great genius like Madame Rachael or George Sand!*

'Why, if it hadn't been for that, and sitting for the figure, I should have felt myself good enough to marry your son, *although* I was only a *blanchisseuse de fin* – you've said so yourself!

'And I should have made him a good wife – of that I feel sure. He wanted to live all his life at Barbizon, and paint, you know; and didn't care for society in the least. Anyhow, I should have been equal to such a life as that! Lots of their wives are *blanchisseuses* over there, or people of that sort; and they get on very well indeed, and nobody troubles about it!

'So I think I've been pretty well punished – richly as I've deserved to!'

'Trilby, have you ever been confirmed?'

'I forget. I fancy not!'

'Oh dear, oh dear! And do you know about our blessed Saviour, and the Atonement and the Incarnation* and the Resurrection . . .'

'Oh yes – I *used* to, at least. I used to have to learn the catechism on Sundays – mamma made me. Whatever her faults and mistakes were, poor mamma was always very particular about *that!* It all seemed very complicated. But papa told me not to bother too much about it, but to be good. He said that God would make it all right for us somehow, in the end – all of us. And that seems sensible, *doesn't* it?

'He told me to be good, and not to mind what priests and clergymen tell us. He'd been a clergyman himself, and knew all about it, he said.

'I haven't been very good – there's not much doubt about

that, I'm afraid! But God knows I've repented often enough and sore enough; I do now! But I'm rather glad to die, I think; and not a bit afraid – not a scrap! I believe in poor papa, though he *was* so unfortunate! He was the cleverest man I ever knew, and the best – except Taffy and the Laird and your dear son!

'There'll be no hell for any of us – he told me so – except what we make for ourselves and each other down here; and that's bad enough for anything. He told me that *he* was responsible for me – he often said so – and that mamma was too, and his parents for *him*, and his grandfathers and grandmothers for *them*, and so on up to Noah and ever so far beyond, and God for us all!

'He told me always to think of other people before myself; as Taffy does, and your son; and never to tell lies or be afraid, and keep away from drink, and I should be all right. But I've sometimes been all wrong, all the same; and it wasn't papa's fault, but poor mamma's and mine; and I've known it, and been miserable at the time, and after! and I'm sure to be forgiven – perfectly certain – and so will everybody else, even the wickedest that ever lived! Why, just give them sense enough in the next world to understand all their wickedness in this, and that'll punish them enough for anything, I think! That's simple enough, *isn't* it? Besides, there may be *no* next world – that's on the cards too, you know! – and that will be simpler still!

'Not all the clergymen in all the world, not even the Pope of Rome, will ever make me doubt papa, or believe in any punishment after what we've all got to go through here. *Ce serait trop bête!*[*]

'So that if you don't want me to very much, and he won't think it unkind, I'd rather not talk to Mr Thomas Bagot about it. I'd rather talk to Taffy if I *must*. He's very clever, Taffy, though he doesn't often say such clever things as your son does, or paint nearly so well; and I'm sure he'll think papa was right.'

And as a matter of fact the good Taffy, in his opinion on this solemn subject, was found to be at one with the late Reverend Patrick Michael O'Ferrall – and so was the Laird – and so (to his mother's shocked and pained surprise) was Little Billee.

And so were Sir Oliver Calthorpe and Sir Jakes (then Mr) Talboys and Doctor Thorne and Antony and Lorrimer and the Greek!

And so – in after-years, when grief had well pierced and torn and riddled her through and through, and time and age had healed the wounds, and nothing remained but the consciousness of great inward scars of recollection to remind her how deep and jagged and wide the wounds had once been – did Mrs Bagot herself!

Late on one memorable Saturday afternoon, just as it was getting dusk in Charlotte Street, Trilby, in her pretty blue dressing-gown, lay on the sofa by the fire – her head well propped, her knees drawn up – looking very placid and content.

She had spent the early part of the day dictating her will to the conscientious Taffy.

It was a simple document, although she was not without many valuable trinkets to leave; quite a fortune! Souvenirs from many men and women she had charmed by her singing, from royalties downward.

She had been looking them over with the faithful Marta, to whom she had always thought they belonged. It was explained to her that they were gifts of Svengali's; since she did not remember when and where and by whom they were presented to her, except a few that Svengali had given her himself, with many passionate expressions of his love, which seems to have been deep and constant and sincere; none the less so, perhaps, that she could never return it!

She had left the bulk of these to the faithful Marta.

But to each of the *trois Angliches* she had bequeathed a beautiful ring, which was to be worn by their brides if they ever married, and the brides didn't object.

To Mrs Bagot she left a pearl necklace, to Miss Bagot her gold coronet of stars; and pretty (and most costly) gifts to each of the three doctors who had attended her and been so assiduous in their care; and who, as she was told, would make no charge for attending on Madame Svengali. And studs and scarf-pins to Antony, Lorrimer, the Greek, Dodor, and Zouzou; and to Carnegie a little German-silver vinaigrette which had once belonged to Lord Witlow; and pretty souvenirs to the Vinards, Angèle Boisse, Durien, and others.

And she left a magnificent gold watch and chain to Gecko, with a most affectionate letter and a hundred pounds – which was all she had in money of her own.

She had taken great interest in discussing with Taffy the

For Grecko

particular kind of trinket which would best suit the idiosyncrasy of each particular legatee, and derived great comfort from the business-like and sympathetic conscientiousness with which the good Taffy entered upon all these minutiæ – he was so solemn and serious about it, and took such pains. She little guessed how his dumb but deeply feeling heart was harrowed!

This document had been duly signed and witnessed and entrusted to his care; and Trilby lay tranquil and happy, and with a sense that nothing remained for her but to enjoy the fleeting hour, and make the most of each precious moment as it went by.

She was quite without pain of either mind or body, and surrounded by the people she adored – Taffy, the Laird, and Little Billee, and Mrs Bagot, and Marta, who sat knitting in the corner with her black mittens on, and her brass spectacles.

She listened to the chat and joined in it, laughing as usual; 'love in her eyes sat playing' as she looked from one to another, for she loved them all beyond expression. 'Love on her lips was straying, and warbling in her breath,' whenever she spoke; and her weakened voice was still larger, fuller, softer than any other voice in the room, in the world – of another kind, from another sphere.

A cart drove up, there was a ring at the door, and presently a wooden packing-case was brought into the room.

At Trilby's request it was opened, and found to contain a large photograph, framed and glazed, of Svengali, in the military uniform of his own Hungarian band (which he had always worn until he came to Paris and London, where he conducted in ordinary evening dress), and looking straight out of the picture, straight at you. He was standing by his desk with his left hand turning over a leaf of music, and waving his bâton with his right. It was a splendid photograph, by a Viennese photographer, and a most speaking likeness; and Svengali looked truly fine – all made up of importance and authority, and his big black eyes were full of stern command.

Marta trembled as she looked. It was handed to Trilby, who exclaimed in surprise. She had never seen it. She had no photograph of him, and had never possessed one.

No message of any kind, no letter of explanation, accompanied this unexpected present, which, from the postmarks on the case, seemed to have travelled all over Europe to London, out of some remote province in eastern Russia – out of the mysterious East! The poisonous East – birthplace and home of an ill wind that blows nobody good.

Trilby laid it against her legs as on a lectern, and lay gazing at it with close attention for a long time, making a casual remark now and then, as, 'He was very handsome, I think'; or, 'That uniform becomes him very well. Why has he got it on, I wonder?'

The others went on talking, and Mrs Bagot made coffee.

Presently Mrs Bagot took a cup of coffee to Trilby, and found her still staring intently at the portrait, but with her eyes dilated, and quite a strange light in them.

'Trilby, Trilby, your coffee! What is the matter, Trilby?'

Trilby was smiling, with fixed eyes, and made no answer.

The others got up and gathered round her in some alarm.

Out of the mysterious East!

Marta seemed terror-stricken, and wished to snatch the photograph away, but was prevented from doing so; one didn't know what the consequences might be.

Taffy rang the bell, and sent a servant for Dr Thorne, who lived close by, in Fitzroy Square.

Presently Trilby began to speak, quite softly, in French: 'Encore une fois? bon! je veux bien! avec la voix blanche alors, n'est-ce pas? et puis foncer au milieu. Et pas trop vite en commençant! Battez bien la mesure, Svengali – que je puisse bien voir – car il fait déjà nuit! c'est ça! Allons, Gecko – donne-moi le ton!'*

Then she smiled, and seemed to beat time softly by moving her head a little from side to side, her eyes intent on Svengali's in the portrait, and suddenly she began to sing Chopin's Impromptu in A flat.

She hardly seemed to breathe as the notes came pouring out, without words – mere vocalising. It was as if breath were unnecessary for so little voice as she was using, though there was enough of it to fill the room – to fill the house – to drown her small audience in holy, heavenly sweetness.

She was a consummate mistres of her art. How that could be seen! And also how splendid had been her training. It all seemed as easy to her as opening and shutting her eyes, and yet how utterly impossible to anybody else!

Between wonder, enchantment, and alarm they were frozen to statues – all except Marta, who ran out of the room crying, 'Gott im Himmel! wieder zurück! wieder zurück!'*

She sang it just as she had sung it at the Salle des Bashibazoucks, only it sounded still more ineffably seductive, as she was using less voice – using the essence of her voice in fact – the pure spirit, the very cream of it.

There can be little doubt that these four watchers by that enchanted couch were listening to not only the most divinely beautiful, but also the most astounding feat of musical utterance ever heard out of a human throat.

The usual effect was produced. Tears were streaming down the cheeks of Mrs Bagot and Little Billee. Tears were in the Laird's eyes, a tear on one of Taffy's whiskers – tears of sheer delight.

When she came back to the quick movement again, after the adagio, her voice grew louder and shriller, and sweet with a sweetness not of this earth; and went on increasing in volume as she quickened the time, nearing the end; and then came the dying away into all but nothing – a mere melodic breath; and then the little soft chromtic ascending rocket, up to E in alt, the last parting caress (which Svengali had introduced as a finale, for it does not exist in the piano score).

When it was over, she said: 'Ça y est-il, cette fois, Svengali? Ah! tant mieux, à la fin! c'est pas malheureux! Et maintenant, mon ami, *je suis fatiguée – bon soir!*'*

Her head fell back on the pillow, and she lay fast asleep.

Mrs Bagot took the portrait away gently. Little Billee knelt down and held Trilby's hand in his and felt for her pulse, and could not find it.

He said, 'Trilby! Trilby!' and put his ear to her mouth to hear her breathe. Her breath was inaudible.

But soon she folded her hands across her breast, and uttered a little short sigh, and in a weak voice said: '*Svengali ...*
Svengali ... Svengali ...'

They remained in silence round her for several minutes, terror-stricken.

The doctor came; he put his hand to her heart, his ear to her lips. He turned up one of her eyelids and looked at her eye. And then, his voice quivering with strong emotion, he stood up and said, 'Madame Svengali's trials and sufferings are all over!'

'Oh, good God! is she *dead*?' cried Mrs Bagot.

'Yes, Mrs Bagot. She has been dead several minutes – perhaps a quarter of an hour.'

Vingt ans après

Porthos-Athos, *alias* Taffy Wynne, is sitting to breakfast (opposite his wife) at a little table in the courtyard of that huge caravansérai* on the Boulevard des Capucines, Paris, where he had sat more than twenty years ago with the Laird and Little Billee; where, in fact, he had pulled Svengali's nose.

Little is changed in the aspect of the place: the same cosmopolite company, with more of the American element perhaps; the same arrivals and departures in railway omnibuses, cabs, hired carriages; and airing his calves on the marble steps, stood just such another colossal and beautiful old man in black cloth coat and knee-breeches and silk stockings as of yore, with probably the very same pinchbeck chain. Where do they breed

'Svengali . . . Svengali . . . Svengali . . .'

these magnificent old Frenchmen? In Germany, perhaps, 'where all the good big waiters come from!'

And also the same fine weather. It is always fine weather in the courtyard of the Grand Hôtel. As the Laird would say, they manage these things better there!

Taffy wears a short beard, which is turning gray. His kind blue eye is no longer choleric, but mild and friendly – as frank as ever; and full of humorous patience. He has grown stouter; he is very big indeed, in all three dimensions, but the symmetry and the gainliness of the athlete belong to him still in movement and repose; and his clothes fit him beautifully, though they are not new, and show careful beating and brushing and ironing, and even a faint suspicion of all but imperceptible fine-drawing here and there.

What a magnificent old man *he* will make some day, should the Grand Hôtel ever run short of them! He looks as if he could be trusted down to the ground – in all things, little or big; as if his word were as good as his bond, and even better; his wink as good as his word, his nod as good as his wink; and, in truth, as he looks, so he is.

The most cynical disbeliever in 'the grand old name of gentleman,' and its virtues as a noun of definition, would almost be justified in quite dogmatically asserting at sight, and without even being introduced, that, at all events, Taffy is a 'gentleman,' inside and out, up and down – from the crown of his head (which is getting rather bald) to the sole of his foot (by no means a small one, or a lightly shod – *ex pede Herculem*)!*

Indeed, this is always the first thing people say of Taffy – and the last. It means, perhaps, that he may be a trifle dull. Well, one can't be everything!

Porthos was a trifle dull – and so was Athos, I think; and likewise his son, the faithful Viscount of Bragelonne – *bon chien chasse de race!** And so was Wilfred of Ivanhoe, the disinherited; and Edgar, the Lord of Ravenswood!* and so, for that matter, was Colonel Newcome,* of immortal memory!

Yet who does not love them – who would not wish to be like them, for better, for worse!

Taffy's wife is unlike Taffy in many ways; but fortunately for both) very like him in some. She is a little woman, very well shaped, very dark, with black, wavy hair, and very small hands and feet; a very graceful, handsome, and vivacious person; by

Tout vient à point, à qui sait attendre

no means dull; full, indeed, of quick perceptions and intuitions; deeply interested in all that is going on about and around her, and with always lots to say about it, but not too much.

She distinctly belongs to the rare, and ever-blessed, and most precious race of charmers.

She had fallen in love with the stalwart Taffy more than a quarter of a century ago in the Place St Anatole des Arts, where he and she and her mother had tended the sick couch of Little Billee — but she had never told her love. *Tout vient à point, à qui sait attendre!**

That is a capital proverb, and sometimes even a true one. Blanche Bagot had found it to be both!

One terrible night, never to be forgotten, Taffy lay fast asleep in bed, at his rooms in Jermyn Street, for he was very tired; grief tires more than anything, and brings a deeper slumber.

That day he had followed Trilby to her last home in Kensal Green, with Little Billee, Mrs Bagot, the Laird, Antony, the Greek, and Durien (who had come over from Paris on purpose) as chief mourners; and very many other people, noble, famous, or otherwise, English and foreign; a splendid and most representative gathering, as was duly chronicled in all the newspapers here and abroad; a fitting ceremony to close the brief but splendid career of the greatest pleasure-giver of our time.

He was awakened by a tremendous ringing at the street-door bell, as if the house were on fire; and then there was a hurried scrambling up in the dark, a tumbling over stairs and kicking against banisters, and Little Billee had burst into his room, calling out: 'Oh! Taffy, Taffy! I'm g-going mad – I'm g-going m-mad! I'm d-d-done for . . .'

'All right, old fellow – just wait till I strike a light!'

'Oh, Taffy! I haven't slept for four nights – not a wink! She d-d-died with Sv – Sv – Sv . . . damn it, I can't get it out! that ruffian's name on her lips! . . . it was just as if he were calling her from the t-t-tomb! She recovered her senses the very minute she saw his photograph – she was so f-fond of him she f-forgot everybody else! She's gone straight to him, after all – in some other life! . . . to slave for him, and sing for him, and help him to make better music than ever! Oh, T – T – oh – oh! Taffy – oh! oh! oh! catch hold! c-c-catch . . .' And Little Billie had all but fallen on the floor in a fit.

And all the old miserable business of five years before had begun over again!

There had been too much sickness in this story, so I will tell as little as possible of poor Little Billee's long illness, his slow and only partial recovery, the paralysis of his powers as a painter, his quick decline, his early death, his manly, calm, and most beautiful surrender – the wedding of the moth with the star, of the night with the morrow!

For all but blameless as his short life had been, and so full of splended promise and performance, nothing ever became him

'I, Pete Coelestes . . .

better than the way he left it. It was as if he were starting on some distant holy quest, like some gallant knight of old – 'A Bagot to the rescue!' in another life. It shook the infallibility of a certain vicar down to its very foundations, and made him think more deeply about things than he had ever thought yet. It gave him pause! . . . and so wrung his heart that when, at the last, he stooped to kiss his poor young dead friend's pure white forehead, he dropped a bigger tear on it than Little Billee (once so given to the dropping of big tears) had ever dropped in his life.

But it is all too sad to write about.

It was by Little Billee's bedside, in Devonshire, that Taffy had grown to love Blanche Bagot, and not very many weeks after it was all over that Taffy had asked her to be his wife; and in a year they were married, and a very happy marriage it turned out – the one thing that poor Mrs Bagot still looks upon as a compensation for all the griefs and troubles of her life.

During the first year or two Blanche had perhaps been the most ardently loving of this well-assorted pair. That beautiful look of love surprised (which makes all women's eyes look the same) came into hers whenever she looked at Taffy, and filled his heart with tender compunction, and a queer sense of his own unworthiness.

Then a boy was born to them, and that look fell on the boy, and the good Taffy caught it as it passed him by, and he felt a helpless, absurd jealousy, that was none the less painful for being so ridiculous! and then that look fell on another boy, and yet another, so that it was through these boys that she looked at their father. Then *his* eyes caught the look, and kept it for their own use; and he grew never to look at his wife without it; and as no daughter came, she retained for life the monopoly of that most sweet and expressive regard.

They are not very rich. He is a far better sportsman than he will ever be a painter; and he doesn't sell his pictures, it is not because they are too good for the public taste: indeed, he has no illusions on that score himself, even if his wife has! He is quite the least conceited art-duffer I ever met – and I have met many far worse duffers than Taffy.

Would only that I might kill off his cousin Sir Oscar, and Sir Oscar's five sons (the Wynnes are good at sons), and his seventeen grandsons, and the fourteen cousins (and their numerous male progeny), that stand between Taffy and the baronetcy, and whatever property goes with it; so that he might be Sir Taffy, and dear Blanche Bagot (that was) might be called 'my lady'! This Shakespearian holocaust would scarcely cost me a pang!

It is a great temptation, when you have duly slain your first hero, to enrich hero number two beyond the dreams of avarice, and provide him with a title and castle and park, as well as a handsome wife and a nice family! But truth is inexorable – and, besides, they are just as happy as they are.

They are well off enough, anyhow, to spend a week in Paris at last, and even to stop at the Grand Hôtel! now that two of their sons are at Harrow (where their father was before them), and the third is safe at a preparatory school at Elstree, Herts.

It is their first outing since the honeymoon, and the Laird should have come with them.

But the good Laird of Cockpen (who is now a famous Royal Academician) is preparing for a honeymoon of his own. He has gone to Scotland to be married himself – to wed a fair and clever countrywoman of just a suitable age, for he has known her ever since she was a bright little lassie in short frocks, and he a promising A.R.A.* (the pride of his native Dundee) – a marriage of reason, and well-seasoned affection, and mutual esteem – and therefore sure to turn out a happy one! and in another fortnight or so the pair of them will very possibly be sitting to breakfast opposite each other at that very corner table in the courtyard of the Grand Hôtel! and she will laugh at everything he says – and they will live happily ever after.

So much for hero number three – D'Artagnan? Here's to you, Sandy M'Allister, canniest, genialest, and most humorous of Scots? most delicate, and dainty, and fanciful of British painters? 'I trink your health, mit your family's – may you lif long – and brosper?'

So Taffy and his wife have come for their second honeymoon, their Indian-summer honeymoon, alone; and are well content that it should be so. Two's always company for such a pair – the amusing one and the amusable! – and they are making the most of it!

They have been all over the Quartier Latin, and revisited the well-remembered spots; and even been allowed to enter the old studio, through the kindness of the *concierge* (who is no longer Madame Vinard). It is tenanted by two American painters, who are coldly civil on being thus disturbed in the middle of their work.

The studio is very spick and span, and most respectable. Trilby's foot, and the poem, and the sheet of plateglass have been improved away, and a bookshelf put in their place. The new *concierge* (who has only been there a year) knows nothing of Trilby; and of the Vinards, only that they are rich and prosperous, and live somewhere in the south of France, and that Monsieur Vinard is mayor of its commune. *Que le bon Dieu les bénisse! c'étaient de bien braves gens.**

Then Mr and Mrs Taffy have also been driven (in an open *calèche* with two horses) through the Bois de Boulogne to St Cloud; and to Versailles, where they lunched at the Hôtel de Réservoirs – *parlez-moi de ça!** and to St Germain, and to Meudon (where they lunched at *la loge du garde champêtre* – a new one); they have visited the Salon, the Louvre, the porcelain manufactory at Sèvres, the Gobelins, the Hôtel Cluny, the Invalides,* with Napoleon's tomb; and seen half a dozen churches, including Notre Dame and the Sainte Chapelle; and dined with the Dodors at their charming villa near Asnières, and with the Zouzous at the splendid Hôtel de la Rochemartel, and with the Duriens in the Parc Monceau (Dodor's food was best and Zouzou's worst; and at Durien's the company and talk were so good that one forgot to notice the food – and that was a pity). And the young Dodors are all right – and so are the young Duriens. As for the young Zouzous, there aren't any – and *that's* a weight off one's mind!

And they've been to the Variétés* and seen Madame Chaumont,* and to the Français* and seen Sarah Bernhardt and Coquelin and Delaunay,* and to the Opéra and heard Monsieur Lassalle.*

And to-day being their last day, they are going to laze and flâne about the boulevards, and buy things, and lunch anywhere, *sur le pouce,** and do the Bois once more and see *tout* Paris, and dine early at Durand's,* or Bignon's (or else the Café des Ambassadeurs)*, and finish up the well-spent day at the 'Mouches d'Espagne' – the new theatre in the Boulevard Poissonnière – to see Madame Cantharidi* in 'Petits Bonheurs de Contrebande,'* which they are told is immensely droll and quite

Petits Bonheurs de Contrebande

proper – funny without being vulgar! Dodor was their informant
– he had taken Madame Dodor to see it three or four times.

Madame Cantharidi, as everybody knows, is a very clever but
extremely plain old woman with a cracked voice – of spotless
reputation, and the irreproachable mother of a grown-up family
whom she has brought up in perfection. They have never been
allowed to see their mother (and grandmother) act – not even
the sons. Their excellent father (who adores both them and her)
has drawn the line at that!

In private life she is 'quite the lady,' but on the stage – well,
go and see her, and you will understand how she comes to be
the idol of the Parisian public. For she is the true and liberal
dispenser to them of that modern *esprit gaulois* which would
make the good Rabelais turn uneasily in his grave and blush
there like a Benedictine Sister.

And truly she deserves the reverential love and gratitude of
her *chers Parisiens!* She amused them all through the Empire;
during the *année terrible* she was their only stay and comfort,
and has been their chief delight ever since, and is now.

When they come back from *La Revanche*,* may Madame
Cantharidi be still at her post, 'Les Mouches d'Espagne,' to
welcome the returning heroes, and exult and crow with them in
her funny cracked old voice; or, haply, even console them once
more, as the case may be.

Victors or vanquished, they will laugh the same!*

Mrs Taffy is a poor French scholar. One must know French
very well indeed (and many other things besides) to seize the
subtle points of Madame Cantharidi's play (and by-play)!

But Madame Cantharidi has so droll a face and voice, and
such very droll, odd movements, that Mrs Taffy goes into fits of
laughter as soon as the quaint little old lady comes on the stage.
So heartily does she laugh that a good Parisian bourgeois turns
round and remarks to his wife: 'V'là une jolie p'tite Anglaise qui
n'est pas bégueule, au moins! Et l' gros bœuf avec les yeux bleus
en boules de loto – c'est son mari, sans doute! il n'a pas l'air
trop content par exemple, celui-là!'*

The fact is that the good Taffy (who knows French very well
indeed) is quite scandalised, and very angry with Dodor for
sending them there; and as soon as the first act is finished he
means, without any fuss, to take his wife away.

As he sits patiently, too indignant to laugh at what is really funny in the piece (much of it is vulgar *without* being funny), he finds himself watching a little white-haired man in the orchestra, a fiddler, the shape of whose back seems somehow familiar, as he plays an *obbligato** accompaniment to a very broadly comic song of Madame Cantharidi's. He plays beautifully – like a master – and the loud applause is as much for him as for the vocalist.

Presently this fiddler turns his head so that his profile can be seen, and Taffy recognises him.

After five minutes' thought, Taffy takes a leaf out of his pocket-book and writes (in perfectly grammatical French): –

Dear Gecko – You have not forgotten Taffy Wynne, I hope; and Litrebili, and Litrebili's sister, who is now Mrs Taffy Wynne. We leave Paris to-morrow, and would like very much to see you once more. Will you, after the play, come and sup with us at the Café Anglais?* If so, look up and make 'yes' with the head, and enchant – Your well-devoted

Taffy Wynne.

He gives this, folded, to an attendant – for 'le premier violon – celui qui a des cheveux blancs.'*

Presently he sees Gecko receive the note and read it and ponder for a while.

Then Gecko looks round the theatre, and Taffy waves his handkerchief and catches the eye of the premier violon, who 'makes "yes" with the head.'

And then, the first act over, Mr and Mrs Wynne leave the theatre; Mr explaining why, and Mrs very ready to go, as she was beginning to feel strangely uncomfortable without quite realising as yet what was amiss with the lively Madame Cantharidi.

They went to the Café Anglais and bespoke a nice little room on the *entresol* overlooking the boulevard, and ordered a nice little supper; salmi of something very good, mayonnaise of lobster, and one or two other dishes better still – and chambertin* of the best. Taffy was particular about these things on a holiday, and regardless of expense. Porthos was very hospitable, and liked good food and plenty of it; and Athos dearly loved good wine!

And then they went and sat at a little round table outside the Café de la Paix on the boulevard, near the Grand Opéra, where it is always very gay, and studied Paris life, and nursed their appetites till supper-time.

At half-past eleven Gecko made his appearance – very meek and humble. He looked old – ten years older than he really was – much bowed down, and as if he had roughed it all his life, and had found living a desperate long, hard grind.

He kissed Mrs Taffy's hand, and seemed half inclined to kiss Taffy's too, and was almost tearful in his pleasure at meeting them again, and his gratitude at being asked to sup with them. He had soft, clinging, caressing manners, like a nice dog's, that made you his friend at once. He was obviously genuine and sincere, and quite pathetically simple, as he always had been.

At first he could scarcely eat for nervous excitement; but Taffy's fine example and Mrs Taffy's genial, easy-going cordiality (and a couple of glasses of chambertin) soon put him at his ease and woke up his dormant appetite, which was a very large one, poor fellow!

He was told all about Little Billee's death, and deeply moved to hear the cause which had brought it about, and then they talked of Trilby.

He pulled her watch out of his waistcoat-pocket and reverently kissed it, exclaiming: 'Ah! c'était un ange! un ange du Paradis!* when I tell you I lived with them for five years! Oh! her kindness, Dio, Dio Maria! It was "Gecko this!" and "Gecko that!" and "poor Gecko, your toothache, how it worries me!" and "Gecko, how tired and pale you look – you distress me so, looking like that! Shall I mix you a maitrank?" And "Gecko, you love artichokes à la Barigoule;* they remind you of Paris – I have heard you say so. Well, I have found out where to get artichokes, and I know how to do them à la Barigoule, and you shall have them for dinner to-day and to-morrow and all the week after!" and we did!

'Ach! dear kind one – what did I really care for artichokes à la Barigoule? . . .

'And it was always like that – always – and to Svengali and old Marta just the same! and she was never well – never! *toujours souffrante!**

'And it was she who supported us all – in luxury and splendour sometimes!'

Enter Grecko

'And *what* an artist!' said Taffy.

'Ah, yes! but all that was Svengali, you know. Svengali was the greatest artist I ever met! Monsieur, Svengali was a demon, a magician! I used to think him a god! He found me playing in the streets for copper coins, and took me by the hand, and was my only friend, and taught me all I ever knew – and yet he could not play my instrument!

'And now he is dead. I have forgotten how to play it myself! That English jail! it demoralised me, ruined me for ever! ach! quel enfer, nom de Dieu (pardon, madame)! I am just good enough to play the *obbligato* at the Mouches d'Espagne, when the old Cantharidi sings,

> V'là mon mari qui r'garde!
> Prends garde – ne m'chatouille plus!*

'It does not want much of an *obbligato, hein*, a song so noble and so beautiful as that!

'And that song, monsieur, all Paris is singing it now. And that is the Paris that went mad when Trilby sang the "Nussbaum" of Schumann at the Salle des Bashibazoucks. You heard her? Well!'

And here poor Gecko tried to laugh a little sardonic laugh in falsetto, like Svengali's, full of scorn and bitterness – and very nearly succeeded.

'But what made you strike him with – with that knife, you know?'

'Ah, monsieur, it had been coming on for a long time. He used to work Trilby too hard; it was killing her – it killed her at last! And then at the end he was unkind to her and scolded her and called her names – horrid names – and then one day in London he struck her. He struck her on the fingers with his bâton, and she fell down on her knees and cried . . .

'Monsieur, I would have defended Trilby against a locomotive going *grande vitesse!* against my own father – against the Emperor of Austria – against the Pope! and I am a good Catholic, monsieur! I would have gone to the scaffold for her, and to the devil after!'

And he piously crossed himself.

'But Svengali – wasn't *he* very fond of her?'

'Oh yes, monsieur! *quant à ça,** passionately! But she did not love him as he wished to be loved. She loved Litrebili, monsieur!

Litrebili, the brother of madame. And I suppose that Svengali grew angry and jealous at last. He changed as soon as he came to Paris. Perhaps Paris reminded him of Litrebili – and reminded Trilby too!'

'But how on earth did Svengali ever manage to teach her how to sing like that? She had no ear for music whatever when *we* knew her!'

Gecko was silent for a while, and Taffy filled his glass, and gave him a cigar, and lit one himself.

'Monsieur, no – that is true. She had not much ear. But she had such a voice as had never been heard. Svengali knew that. He had found it out long ago. Litolff had found it out, too. One day Svengali heard Litolff tell Meyerbeer that the most beautiful female voice in Europe belonged to an English grisette who sat as a model to sculptors in the Quartier Latin, but that unfortunately she was quite tone-deaf, and couldn't sing one single note in tune. Imagine how Svengali chuckled! I see it from here!

'Well, we both taught her together – for three years – morning, noon, and night – six – eight hours a day. It used to split me the heart to see her worked like that! We took her voice note by note – there was no end to her notes, each more beautiful than the other – velvet and gold, beautiful flowers, pearls, diamonds, rubies – drops of dew and honey; peaches, oranges, and lemons! *en veux-tu en voilà!** – all the perfumes and spices of the Garden of Eden! Svengali with his little flexible flageolet, I with my violin – that is how we taught her to make the sounds – and then how to use them. She was a *phénomène*, monsieur! She could keep on one note and make it go through all the colours in the rainbow – according to the way Svengali looked at her. It would make you laugh – it would make you cry – but, cry or laugh, it was the sweetest, the most touching, the most beautiful note you ever heard – except all her others! and each had as many overtones as the bells in the Carillon de Notre Dame. She could run up and down the scales, chromatic scales, quicker and better and smoother than Svengali on the piano, and more in tune than any piano! and her shake – *ach!* twin stars, monsieur! She was the greatest contralto, the greatest soprano the world has ever known! the like of her has never been! the like of her will never be again! and yet she only sang in public for two years!

'*Ach!* those breaks and runs and sudden leaps from darkness

'We took her voice note by note'

into light and back again – from earth to heaven! . . . those slurs and swoops and slides à la Paganini from one note to another, like a swallow flying! . . . or a gull? Do you remember them? how they drove you mad? Let any other singer in the world try to imitate them – they would make you sick! That was Svengali . . . he was a magician!

'And how she looked, singing! do you remember? her hands behind her – her dear, sweet, slender foot on a little stool – her thick hair lying down all along her back! and that good smile like the Madonna's, so soft and bright and kind! *Ach! Bel ucel di Dio!* it was to make you weep for love, merely to see her (*c'était à vous faire pleurer d'amour, rien que de la voir*)!* That was Trilby! Nightingale and bird of paradise in one!

'*Enfin* she could do anything – utter any sound she liked, when once Svengali had shown her how – and he was the greatest master that ever lived! and when once he knew a thing, she knew it. *Et voilà!*'

'How strange,' said Taffy, 'that she should have suddenly gone out of her senses that night at Drury Lane, and so completely forgotten it all! I suppose she saw Svengali die in the box opposite, and that drove her mad!'

And then Taffy told the little fiddler about Trilby's death-song, like a swan's, and Svengali's photograph. But Gecko had heard it all from Marta, who was now dead.

Gecko sat and smoked and pondered for a while, and looked from one to the other. Then he pulled himself together with an effort, so to speak, and said, 'Monsieur, she never went mad – not for one moment!'

'What? Do you mean to say she *deceived* us all?'

'Non, monsieur! She could never deceive anybody, and never would. *She had forgotten – voilà tout!*'

'But hang it all, my friend, one doesn't *forget* such a—'

'Monsieur, listen! She is dead. And Svengali is dead – and Marta also. And I have a good little malady that will kill me soon, *Gott sei dank* – and without much pain.

'I will tell you a secret.

'*There were two Trilbys.* There was the Trilby you knew, who could not sing one single note in tune. She was an angel of paradise. She is now! But she had no more idea of singing than I have of winning a steeplechase at the croix de Berny. She could no more sing than a fiddle can play itself! She could never tell

The nightingale's first song

one tune from another – one note from the next. Do you remember how she tried to sing 'Ben Bolt' that day when she first came to the studio in the Place St Anatole des Arts? It was droll, *hein? à se boucher les oreilles!** Well, that was Trilby, your Trilby! that was my Trilby too – and I loved her as one loves an only love, an only sister, an only child – a gentle martyr on earth, a blessed saint in heaven! And that Trilby was enough for *me!*

'And that was the Trilby that loved your brother, madame – oh! but with all the love that was in her! He did not know what he had lost, your brother! her love, it was immense, like her voice and just as full of celestial sweetness and sympathy! She told me everything! *ce pauvre Litrebili, ce qu'il a perdu!**

'But all at once – pr-r-r-out! presto! *augenblick!* . . . with one wave of his hand over her – with one look of his eye – with a word – Svengali could turn her into the other Trilby, *his* Trilby – and make her do whatever he liked . . . you might have run a red-hot needle into her and she would not have felt it . . .

'He had but to say *'Dors!'* and she suddenly became an unconscious Trilby of marble, who could produce wonderful sounds – just the sounds he wanted, and nothing else – and think his thoughts and wish his wishes – and love him at his bidding with a strange, unreal, factitious love . . . just his own love for himself turned inside out – à l'envers – and reflected back on him, as from a mirror . . . *un écho, un simulacre, quoi! pas autre chose!** . . . It was not worth having! I was not even jealous!

'Well, that was the Trilby he taught how to sing – and – and I helped him, God of heaven forgive me! That Trilby was just a singing-machine – an organ to play upon – an instrument of music – a Stradivarius – a flexible flageolet of flesh and blood – a voice, and nothing more – just the unconscious voice that Svengali sang with – for it takes two to sing like La Svengali, monsieur – the one who has got the voice, and the one who knows what to do with it . . . So that when you heard her sing the "Nussbaum," the "Impromptu," you heard Svengali singing with her voice, just as you heard Joachim play a *chaconne** of Bach with his fiddle! . . . Herr Joachim's fiddle . . . what does it know of Sebastian Bach? and as for *chaconnes . . . il s'en moque pas mal, ce fameux violon! . . .**

'And *our* Trilby . . . what did she know of Schumann,

Chopin? – nothing at all! She mocked herself not badly of
Nussbaums and Impromptus . . . they would make her yawn to
demantibulate* her jaws! . . . When Svengali's Trilby was being
taught to sing . . . when Svengali's Trilby was singing – or
seemed to *you* as if she were singing – *our* Trilby had ceased to
exist . . . *our* Trilby was fast asleep . . . in fact, *our* Trilby was
dead . . .

'Ah, monsieur . . . that Trilby of Svengali's! I have heard her
sing to kings and queens in royal palaces! . . . as no woman has
ever sung before or since . . . I have seen emperors and grand-
dukes kiss her hand, monsieur – and their wives and daughters
kiss her lips, and weep . . .

'I have seen the horses taken out of her sledge and the pick of
the nobility drag her home to the hotel . . . with torchlights and
choruses and shoutings of glory and long life to her! . . . and
serenades all night, under the window! . . . *she* never knew! she
heard nothing – felt nothing – saw nothing! and she bowed to
them, right and left, like a queen!

'I have played the fiddle for her while she sang in the street, at
fairs and festas and Kermessen . . . and seen the people go mad
to hear her . . . and once, at Prague, Svengali fell down in a fit
from sheer excitement! and then, suddenly, *our* Trilby woke up
and wondered what it was all about . . . and we took her home
and put her to bed and left him with Marta – and Trilby and I
went together arm-in-arm all over the town to fetch a doctor
and buy things for supper – and that was the happiest hour in
all my life!

'*Ach!* what an existence! What travels! what triumphs! what
adventures! Things to fill a book – a dozen books – Those five
happy years – with those two Trilbys! what recollections! . . . I
think of nothing else, night or day . . . even as I play the fiddle
for old Cantharidi. *Ach!* . . . To think how often I have played
the fiddle for La Svengali . . . to have done that is to have lived
. . . and then to come home to Trilby . . . *our* Trilby . . . the *real*
Trilby! . . . Gott sei dank! Ich habe *geliebt und gelebet!* geliebt
un gelebet! geliebt und gelebet!* Cristo di dio . . . Sweet sister in
heaven . . . Ô Dieu de Misère, ayez pitié de nous . . .'*

His eyes were red, and his voice was high and shrill and
tremulous and full of tears; these remembrances were too much
for him; and perhaps also the chambertin! He put his elbows on

'Ich habe Geliebt und Gelebet!'

the table and hid his face in his hands and wept, muttering to himself in his own language (whatever that might have been — Polish, probably) as if he were praying.

Taffy and his wife got up and leaned on the window-bar and looked out on the deserted boulevards, where an army of scavengers, noiseless and taciturn, was cleansing the asphalt roadway. The night above was dark, but 'star-dials hinted of morn,' and a fresh breeze had sprung up, making the leaves dance and rustle on the sycamore trees along the boulevard – a nice little breeze; just the sort of little breeze to do Paris good. A four-wheel came by at a foot pace, the driver humming a tune; Taffy hailed him; he said, 'V'là, m'sieur!' and drew up.

Taffy rang the bell, and asked for the bill, and paid it. Gecko had apparently fallen asleep. Taffy gently woke him up and told him how late it was. The poor little man seemed dazed and rather tipsy, and looked older than ever; sixty, seventy – any age you like. Taffy helped him on with his great-coat, and taking him by the arm, led him downstairs, giving him his card, and telling him how glad he was to have seen him, and that he would write to him from England – a promise that was kept, one may be sure.

Gecko uncovered his fuzzy white head, and took Mrs Taffy's hand and kissed it, and thanked her warmly for her 'si bon et sympathique accueil.'*

Then Taffy all but lifted him into the cab, the jolly cabman saying –

'Ah, bon – connais bien, celui là; vous savez – c'est lui qui joue du violon aux Mouches d'Espagne! Il a soupé, l'bourgeois; n'est-ce pas, m'sieur? "petits bonheurs de contrebande," hein? ... ayez pas peur! on vous aura soin de lui! il joue joliment bien, m'sieur; n'est-ce pas?'*

Taffy shook Gecko's hand and asked,

'Où restez-vous, Gecko?'

'Quarante-huit Rue des Pousse-cailloux, au cinquième.'*

'How strange!' said Taffy to his wife – 'how touching! why, that's where Trilby used to live – the very number! the very floor!'

'Oui, oui,' said Gecko, waking up; 'c'et l'ancienne mansarde à Trilby – j'y suis depuis douze ans – *j'y suis, j'y reste . . .*'*

And he laughed feebly at his mild little joke.

Taffy told the address to the cabman, and gave him five francs.

'Merci, m'sieur! C'est de l'aut'côté de l'eau – près de la Sorbonne, s'pas? On vous aura soin du bourgeois; soyez tranquille – ayez pas peur! quarante-huit; on y va. Bonsoir, monsieur et dame!'* And he cracked his whip and rattled away, singing: –

> V'là mon mari qui r'garde –
>   Prends garde!
> Ne m'chatouill' plus!'

Mr and Mrs Wynne walked back to the hotel, which was not far. She hung on to his big arm and crept close to him, and shivered a little. It was quite chilly. Their footsteps were very audible in the stillness; 'pit-pat, floppety-clop,' otherwise they were both silent. They were tired, yawny, sleepy, and very sad; and each was thinking (and knew the other was thinking) that a week in Paris was just enough – and how nice it would be, in just a few hours more, to hear the rooks cawing round their own quiet little English country home – where three jolly boys would soon be coming for the holidays.

And there we will leave them to their useful, humdrum, happy domestic existence – than which there is no better that I know of, at their time of life – and no better time of life than theirs!

> *Où peut-on être mieux qu'au sein de sa famille?**

That blessed harbour of refuge well within our reach, and having really cut our wisdom teeth at last, and learned the ropes, and left off hankering after the moon – we can do with so little down here . . .

> A little work, a little play
> To keep us going – and so, good-day!
>
> A little warmth, a little light
> Of love's bestowing – and so, good-night!
>
> A little fun, to match the sorrow
> Of each day's growing – and so, good-morrow!
>
> A little trust that when we die
> We reap our sowing! And so – good-bye!*

APPENDIX

Passages from *Trilby* originally published in *Harper's Magazine* but excised from the book editions

1 'Joe Sibley'

Then there was Joe Sibley, the idle apprentice, the king of bohemia, *le roi des truands*, to whom everything was forgiven, as to François Villon, 'à cause de ses gentillesses.'

Always in debt, like Svengali; like Svengali, vain, witty, and a most exquisite and original artist; and also eccentric in his attire (though clean), so that people would stare at him as he walked along – which he adored! But (unlike Svengali) he was genial, caressing, sympathetic, charming; the most irresistible friend in the world as long as his friendship lasted – but that was not forever!

The moment his friendship left off, his enmity began at once. Sometimes this enmity would take the simple and straightforward form of trying to punch his ex-friend's head; and when the ex-friend was too big, he would get some new friend to help him. And much bad blood would be caused in this way – though very little was spilt. And all this bad blood was not made better by the funny things he went on saying through life about the unlucky one who had managed to offend him – things that stuck forever! His bark was worse than his bite – he was better with his tongue than with his fists – a dangerous joker! But when he met another joker face to face, even an inferior joker – with a rougher wit, a coarser thrust, a louder laugh, a tougher hide – he would just collapse, like a pricked bladder!

He is now perched on such a topping pinnacle (of fame and notoriety combined) that people can stare at him from two hemispheres at once; and so famous as a wit that when he jokes (and he is always joking) people laugh first, and then ask what it was he was joking about. And you can even make your own mild funniments raise a roar by merely prefacing them, 'As Joe Sibley once said.'

The present scribe has often done so.

And if by any chance you should one day, by a happy fluke, hit upon a really good thing of your own – good enough to be quoted – be sure it will come back to you after many days prefaced, 'As Joe Sibley once said.'

Then there was Lorrimer, the industrious apprentice, who is now also well pinnacled on high; himself a pillar of the Royal Academy – probably, if he lives long enough, its future president – the duly knighted or baroneted Lord Mayor of 'all the plastic arts' (except one or two perhaps, here and there, that are not altogether without some importance).

May this not be for many, many years! Lorrimer himself would be the first to say so!

Tall, thin, red-haired, and well-favored, he was a most eager, earnest, and painstaking young enthusiast, of precocious culture, who read improving books, and did not share in the amusements of the quartier latin, but spent his evenings at home with Handel, Michael Angelo and Dante, on the respectable side of the river. Also, he went into good society sometimes, with a dress-coat on, and a white tie, and his hair parted in the middle!

But in spite of these blemishes on his otherwise exemplary record as an art student, he was the most delightful companion – the most affectionate, helpful, and sympathetic of friends. May he live long and prosper!

Enthusiast as he was, he could only worship one god at a time. It was either Michael Angelo, Phidias, Paul Veronese, Tintoret, Raphael, or Titian – never a modern – moderns didn't exist! And so thoroughgoing was he in his worship, and so persistent in voicing it, that he made those immortals quite unpopular in the Place St-Anatole des Arts. We grew to dread their very names. Each of them would last him a couple of months or so; then he would give us a month's holiday, and take up another.

Joe Sibley, equally enthusiastic, was more faithful. He was a monotheist, and had but one god, and was less tiresome in the expression of his worship. He is so still – and his god is still the same – no stodgy old master this divinity, but a modern of the moderns! For forty years the cosmopolite Joe has been singing his one god's praise in every tongue he knows and every country

– and also his contempt for all rivals to this godhead – whether quite sincerely or not, who can say? Men's motives are so mixed! But so eloquently, so wittily, so prettily, that he almost persuades you to be a fellow-worshipper – *almost*, only! – for if he did *quite*, you (being a capitalist) would buy nothing but 'Sibleys' (which you don't). For Sibley was the god of Joe's worship, and none other! and he would hear of no other genius in the world!

Let us hope that he sometimes laughed at himself in his sleeve – or winked at himself in his looking-glass, with his tongue in his cheek!

And here, lest there should be any doubt as to his identity, let me add that although quite young he had beautiful white hair like an Albino's, as soft and bright as floss silk – and also that he was tall and slim and graceful; and, like most of the other personages concerned in this light story, very nice to look at – with pretty manners (and an unimpeachable moral tone).

Joe Sibley did not think much of Lorrimer in those days, nor Lorrimer of him, for all they were such good friends. And neither of them thought much of Little Billee, whose pinnacle (of pure unadulterated fame) is now the highest of all – the highest probably that can be for a mere painter of pictures!

And what is so nice about Lorrimer, now that he is a graybeard, an academician, an accomplished man of the world and society, is that he admires Sibley's genius more than he can say – and reads Mr Rudyard Kipling's delightful stories as well as Dante's 'Inferno' – and can listen with delight to the lovely songs of Signor Tosti, who has not precisely founded himself on Handel – can even scream with laughter at a comic song – even a nigger melody – so, at least, that it but be sung in well-bred and distinguished company – for Lorrimer is no bohemian.

> 'Shoo, fly! don'tcher bother me!
> For I belong to the Comp'ny G!'

Both these famous men are happily (and most beautifully) married – grandfathers, for all I know – and 'move in the very best society' (Lorrimer always, I'm told; Sibley now and then); 'la haute,' as it used to be called in French bohemia – meaning dukes and lords and even royalties, I suppose, and those who love them, and whom they love!

That *is* the best society, isn't it? At all events, we are assured it used to be; but that must have been before the present scribe (a meek and somewhat innocent outsider) had been privileged to see it with his own little eye.

And when they happen to meet there (Sibley and Lorrimer, I mean), I don't expect they rush very wildly into each other's arms, or talk very fluently about old times. Nor do I suppose their wives are very intimate. None of our wives are. Not even Taffy's and the Laird's.

2 'Macey Sparks'

And the Rabelaisian Macey Sparks (now most respectable of Royal Academicians), who sometimes, in his lucid intervals after supper and champagne, was given to thoughtful, acute, and sympathetic observation of his fellow-men, had remarked, in a hoarse, smoky, hiccuppy whisper to the Laird: 'Rather an enviable pair! Their united ages amount to forty-eight or so, their united weights to about fifteen stone, and they couldn't carry you or me between them. But if you were to roll all the other brains that have been under this roof to-night into one, you wouldn't reach the sum of their united genius. . . . I wonder which of the two is the most unhappy!'

And for once the Rabelaisian Macey Sparks wasn't joking. . . .

NOTES

Paris locations have been identified by the number of the arrondissement, e.g., 1er, 2ème.

Title page The original title page had a quotation from the French song *'Malbrouck s'en va-t'en guerre'* (see p. 237). On the title verso were two lines from a Breton chanson:

> Hélas! Je sais un chant d'amour,
> Triste et gai, tour-à-tour!

These lines inspired *Chant d'Amour* by Edward Burne-Jones (1833–98), of which there are four versions (c1864, 1865, 1866 and 1878). Du Maurier lists the painting as a 'special favourite' in *Peter Ibbetson* of 1891.

Part First

p.3   Mimi Pinson: Alfred de Musset (1810–57), 'Mimi Pinson, Chanson', 1844.

> Mimi Pinson is a blonde,
>   A blonde we know;
> She has only one dress in all the world,
> Landerirette [Landerinette in the original poem]! and only one bonnet!

p.3   Broadwood: an instrument from a London piano manufacturer established in the eighteenth century. Beethoven was among their clients. Du Maurier's friends recalled that the hired piano was one of the few prized items in their studio and that Du Maurier spent his time playing and singing when he should have been at work.

p.3   Dante's mask: a copy of a plaster cast of Dante's face.

p.3   Michael Angelo's alto-rilievo of Leda and the swan: the relief sculpture by Michelangelo Buonarroti (1475–1564) in the Bargello Museum in Florence. Leda was the nymph wooed by Zeus in the form of a swan.

p.3   a centaur and Lapith from the Elgin Marbles: there are a number of metopes (square marble slabs) showing battles between lapiths (a race descended from the sun god, Apollo) and centaurs (mythical creatures, half human and half horse) among the sculptures from the Athenian Parthenon in the British Museum. They were brought to Britain by the Earl of Elgin (1766–1841).

p.3   Tintoret: Jacopo Robusti, known as Tintoretto, Venetian painter (1512–94).

p.3   Botticelli: Alessandro di Mariano Filpepi, known as Sandro Botticelli, Florentine painter (c1445–1510). The works of Botticelli were virtually unknown in the 1850s. Du Maurier is writing from the perspective of the 1890s after the artist had been 'discovered' and taken up by the aesthetic movement of the 1870s and 1880s.

p.3   Mantegna: Andrea Mantegna, Mantuan painter (1430/1–1506).

p.3   Theseus: a male figure from the pediment of the Parthenon, now in the British Museum, identified in the early nineteenth century as the Greek hero Theseus, but now thought to represent either Dionysus (the god of wine) or Heracles (or Hercules, the personification of strength in Greek mythology).

p.3   Venus of Milo: the famous statue of the Greek goddess of love and beauty (probably of 2 BC), excavated on the Island of Melos in 1820 and now in the Louvre, Paris. Du Maurier had a copy prominently displayed in his Hampstead house, and from time to time introduced the statue into his *Punch* cartoons.

p.3   discobolus: there are several surviving copies of the ancient Greek statue of an athlete stooping to throw a discus, but the cast referred to here was probably made from that in the collection left by Charles Townley (1737–1805) to the British Museum.

p.3   a little flayed man: presumably a copy of a statue of Marsyas, the faun who was flayed after losing to Apollo in a musical competition.

p.3   Barye: Antoine Louis Barye, French sculptor (1795–1875), particularly known for his animal pieces.

p.3   horse's head: the head of one of the horses from the chariot of Selene, the moon.

p.3   Clytie: a famous bust of a woman emerging from leaves, in the Townley Collection, British Museum. The name given to it here refers to the nymph who pined for Apollo, the sun god, and was turned into a sunflower. The bust is now thought to be a portrait of a Roman lady.

p.4   Taffy: several originals have been suggested for Taffy, among them a fellow student of Du Maurier, Joseph Rowley (d. 1908), who later became a colliery owner, and Valentine Cameron Prinsep (1838–1904), who trained at Gleyre's atelier at a later period. Both were men of powerful physique who took a good deal of exercise. Taffy's dependability seems to owe much to Du Maurier's closest friend, Thomas Armstrong (1835–1911), a painter and later Director of Art at the South Kensington Museum. Armstrong's *Memoir* (1912) is a valuable source for the biographical background to *Trilby*.

p.4   Balaklava: Black Sea port in the Crimea. Scene of a famous battle during the Crimean War on 25 October 1854 when the Light Brigade under Lord Cardigan charged the Russian guns, following an apparent error in the interpretation of a signal.

p.5   Piccadilly weepers: long flowing side-whiskers.

p.5   Mr Sothern in Lord Dundreary: Edward Askew Sothern (1826–81) played the part of Lord Dundreary in *Our American Cousin* (1858) by Tom Taylor (1817–80); the long side-whiskers which Sothern wore were known as Dundrearies.

p.5   What's become of all the gold . . .: Robert Browning (1812–89), 'A Toccata of Galuppi's', 1855.

p.5   Sandy, the Laird of Cockpen: drawn from Thomas Reynolds Lamont, Scottish genre painter (1826–98). 'The Laird of Cockpen' is the title of a poem by Lady Nairne (1766–1845).

p.6   Boulevard du Temple: runs south from the Place de la République in the 3ème. It was then the scene of a second-hand clothes market, set up on the site of the old church of the Templars.

p.6   A street there is in Paris . . .: 'The Ballad of the Bouillabaisse' by William Makepeace Thackeray (1811–63); 'Roo Nerve day Petty Shong' is the rue des Petits Champs in the 1er, where Du Maurier and his friends had a studio at no. 53.

p.7   'Little Billee': a poem by W. M. Thackeray in which two older sailors decide to eat Billee, the youngest, when food runs out. He is saved when land is sighted. Several writers believe that Du Maurier's Little Billee was drawn from the painter and illustrator Frederick Walker (1840–75). Du Maurier usually denied it, but, on at least one occasion, agreed that the character *was* in part derived from Walker. The American painter James McNeill Whistler (1834–1903) believed, with some justification, that the real original for Little Billee was Du Maurier himself.

p.7   Carrel: drawn from the Swiss painter Charles-Gabriel Gleyre (1806–74), in whose atelier or studio Du Maurier and several of his friends trained.

p.7   Quartier Latin: Latin Quarter, an area of Paris south of the Seine in the 5ème traditionally associated with students. Latin was once the language of the university.

p.8 *Tant pis pour les autres!*: too bad for the others!

p.8 **Place St Anatole des Arts**: presumably the Place St André des Arts in the 6ème, between the Boulevard St Michel and the Odéon. There is no apparent reason for this change of name.

p.8 **the river, the 'Cité', and the ominous old Morgue**: the Seine, the Ile de la Cité, on which stands the Cathedral of Notre Dame de Paris, and, in Du Maurier's day, the mortuary where unidentified bodies (often of those drowned in the river) were displayed for identification.

p.8 *ipsissimus*: very much himself.

p.10 **Hôtel de Seine**: at one point Thomas Armstrong lived in the Hôtel de Mont Blanc in the rue de Seine, which runs between the Institut Français and the rue St Sulpice in the 6ème.

p.10 **Hôtel Corneille**: in the adjoining rue Corneille beside the Théâtre de l'Odéon. Armstrong lived in the Hôtel Corneille in 1856 and first met Du Maurier and Lamont there.

p.10 **Place de l'Odéon**: the seventeenth-century crescent in front of the Théâtre de l'Odéon, near the Palais du Luxembourg in the 6ème.

p.11 **realist**: realism, painting from direct observation of the world. The leader of the school in France was Gustave Courbet (1819–77).

p.11 **Louvre**: site of a palace of the kings of France since the thirteenth century, the present structure having been built largely from the sixteenth to the nineteenth centuries. After the revolution of 1789 the royal picture galleries were opened to the public, and the Louvre is one of the richest museums in the world.

p.11 **Sairey Gamp and Betsey Prig**: characters from *Martin Chuzzlewit* (1844) by Charles Dickens (1812–70).

p.13 **Svengali**: Du Maurier and his friends knew a Greek musician and pianist, Sotiri, but Armstrong is adamant that Sotiri was not the original of Svengali. The characterisation of Svengali as a musician seems to owe something to the performance styles of Nicolo Paganini (see note for p. 197). Another possible contender is Henri Litolff (see note for p. 21).

p.13 **'Ponchour, mes enfants ... anche!'**: 'Hallo children', said Svengali. 'I've brought my friend Gecko to meet you. He plays the violin like an angel!'

p.13 'Ha! le biâno! . . . t'accord!': 'Ha! The piano!' exclaimed Svengali . . . 'I hope it's a good one, and well tuned!'

p.13 **Chopin's impromptu in A flat**: Frederic Chopin, Polish composer and pianist (1810–49). The Impromptu in A flat dates from 1837.

p.13 **'Annie Laurie,' 'The Last Rose of Summer,' 'The Blue Bells of Scotland'**: the words of 'Annie Laurie' are said to be by William Douglas (1672–1748) and the music is by Lady John Scott (1835); 'Tis the Last Rose of Summer' (to a traditional Irish tune) comes from the *Irish Melodies* of Thomas Moore (1779–1852); 'The Blue Bells of Scotland' ('O where tell me where is your Highland laddie gone?') was sung by Dorothea Jordan (1762–1816) in 1800. She claimed to have composed the music, but it was probably an adaptation of an original air which may have been a marching song and may even have been English.

p.14 **czardas**: Hungarian dance, mixing slow and fast passages.

p.16 **Trilby**: many attempts have been made to identify an original for Trilby. Two girls apparently contributed something to her. Thomas Armstrong and Luke Ionides (1837–1925) both thought that she might have been drawn from a model known as Héloise or 'Fumette' who worked for James Whistler. She was, incidentally, an admirer of Alfred de Musset's poems. Du Maurier's later friend Felix Moscheles (1833–1917) claimed that the original of Trilby was a girl called Octavie or 'Carry', whom they met in Malines in 1857–8. Trilby's name comes from the story of 'Trilby, le Lutain d'Argail' (the fairy of Argyll) by Charles Nodier (1780–1844). Alfred de Musset referred to Nodier's 'Trilby' in a poem of 1843, 'Réponse à M. Charles Nodier'. An operetta, *Trilby*, drawn from Nodier, with words by Mahiet de la Chesneraye and music by M. Laurent de Rillé was performed at the *Folies-Nouvelles* in 1857, when Du Maurier was in Paris.

p.16 *tenore robusto*: a robust tenor, a tenor able to sing with full dramatic and passionate expression. Du Maurier himself was a lyrical tenor.

p.16 **Durien**: Armstrong mentions a sculptor whose studio was in 53 rue Notre Dame des Champs, and who used to visit the Englishman.

p.16 **Olympian**: Mount Olympus was traditionally the home of the Greek gods.

p.17 **lovely slender feet**: the sister of the sculptor living near the English studio had beautiful feet. Du Maurier, an admirer, was too shy to enter into conversation with her.

p.18 *En voilà de l'éloquence . . . bottes!*: There's eloquence for you, on the subject of boots!

p.18   *fromage à la crème*: cream cheese.

p.18   Schubert's 'Rosemonde': Franz Schubert, Austrian composer (1797–1828). His incidental music to *Rosamunde* was first performed in 1823 but not published until 1867. Svengali's reference to a princess of Cyprus is probably anachronistic, as the score for *Rosamunde* was only discovered after the period of the novel. The famous theme, however, would have been known from the Impromptu in B Flat, D 935.

p.18   'Maïe, aïe! . . . s'appelle?': 'My eye, it's terribly well played that music! Only it isn't very cheerful, you know! What's it called?'

p.20   'Messieurs les étudiants . . .': 'Les Étudiants' of 1845 by Frédéric Soulié (1800–47).

> The young gentlemen, the students,
> Go to La Chaumière
> To dance the can-can.

La Chaumière was a popular dance hall at 112–36 Blvd Montparnasse in the 6ème, founded in 1783 by an Englishman called Tickson. In the 1830s it was run by Père Lahire. The first dance craze was the polka, then came the Robert Macaire (see note for p. 122), the 'danse osée' (a daring dance), and finally the can-can. This was a vigorous dance, usually for four women. The high kicks rendered it notorious. La Chaumière was popular with performers, politicians, writers and artists. It closed in 1855 when the can-can craze passed and was replaced by the Closerie des Lilas (see note for p. 28).

p.20   Oh, don't you remember sweet Alice, Ben Bolt? . . .: song of 1843 by the American writer Thomas Dunn English (1819–1902), with music of 1848 by the Philadelphia composer Nelson Kneass. Kneass adapted a German air and sang the song in *The Battle of Buena Vista*. Alice was the name of English's daughter.

p.21   Litolff: Henri Litolff, Anglo-Alsatian pianist, composer and music publisher (1818–91). Litolff was a child prodigy and pupil of Ignaz Moscheles (1794–1870), the father of Du Maurier's friend Felix. Litolff married at 17, against his parents' wishes, and moved to France. In 1851 he acquired a music publishing business in Brunswick, marrying as his second wife the widow of the former owner. On his third marriage, to the Comtesse de Rochefoucauld, he moved back to Paris. He produced several operas and much orchestral and piano music. The much married Litolff, resident in Paris, and with his sinister beard, may be a strong contender for the role of Svengali.

p.21   Madame Alboni: Marietta Alboni, Italian contralto (1826–94). Du Maurier greatly admired her.

p.21 'Qu'est-ce qu'elle dit?: 'What is she saying?'

p.21 Comédie Française: theatre in the rue de Richelieu within the Palais Royal in the 1er (see note for p. 58). Originally founded by Louis XIV in 1680, the theatre is associated with French classic drama.

p.21 Faubourg St Germain: an area south of the Seine in the 7ème. It was highly fashionable in the eighteenth century, when great mansions were built there.

p.21 'Barpleu!': parbleu, 'Yes indeed!'

p.22 Life ain't all beer and skittles: common expression meaning that life is not an unmixed pleasure.

p.22 chiffonnier: rag picker.

p.22 King Arthurs and Guineveres and Lancelots and Elaines, and floating Ladies of Shalott: characters from the Arthurian legends made popular by Alfred Tennyson (1809–92) in 'The Lady of Shalott' (1832) and *The Idylls of the King* (1859–85). In the second half and particularly in the last quarter of the nineteenth century, paintings of these subjects were a commonplace in the Royal Academy.

p.22 sabots: boots.

p.22 Rue des Pousse-Cailloux: there was apparently no such street in Paris. However, Du Maurier's footnote explains that in Parisian slang a Pompiou is short for a pousse-caillou, a private soldier of the line.

p.22 pose pour l'ensemble . . . orichinale: 'she poses in the altogether [the nude], when it amuses her! now I'm off to town to do everything I need to do!' . . . 'There's an eccentric', said Svengali.

p.22 'Qu'est-ce que c'est, Ben Bolt?': 'What is it, Ben Bolt?'

p.24 'Mais c'est tout-à-fait chentil! . . . chouez-nous ça!': 'But that's utterly charming! Come on Gecko, play it for us!'

p.24 in minor, in pizzicato, and in sordino – adagio, andante, allegretto, scherzo: in a minor key, plucking the strings with the hand, playing with a muted sound, slow, flowing and not fast, briskly, lively.

p.24 And the dear little nook . . .: 'Ben Bolt'.

p.25 'Sacrepleu! . . . du monte!': 'Damn it, Gecko plays well, doesn't he?' . . . 'He's my pupil! I make him sing on the violin, it's as if it were I who was singing. Ah! If I only had a bit of a voice, I would be the greatest singer in the world!'

p.25 la betite Honorine: little Honorine, otherwise known as Mimi la

Salope; drawn from an artists' model, La Petite Sara, who used to sing colloquial songs while she posed.

p.25   **flageolet**: tin whistle.

p.25   *pour se donner une contenance!*: to give an impression of composure!

p.27   *il bel canto!*: literally, beautiful singing; singing in the formal style of the seventeenth and eighteenth centuries.

p.27   **hussar**: a member of a light cavalry regiment; originally a Hungarian expression, but by Du Maurier's day generally current in Europe.

p.27   *maître d'armes*: fencing master.

p.27   '**Tiens!** ... **touchez plus!**': 'Ah! Trilby's foot! You did it from life?' 'No!' 'From memory, then?' 'Yes!' 'I give you my compliments! You were having a good day. I wish I had done it myself! It's a minor masterpiece you've drawn there – very good, my dear boy! But don't embellish it too much. Please don't touch it any more!'

p.28   **Restaurant de la Couronne, kept by the Père Trin (in the Rue de Monsieur)**: Trin's restaurant was behind the Théâtre de l'Odéon; the rue Monsier-le-Prince runs between the Carrefour de l'Odéon and the Boulevard St Michel in the 6ème.

p.28   **Trois Frères Provençaux**: The Three Brothers from Provence, a café at 88 Galerie de Beaujolais in the Palais Royal. It was founded in 1786 in rue Helvétius Ste Anne. Apparently the three founders were neither brothers nor from Provence, but they had married three sisters. Napoleon Bonaparte (1769–1821) was among those who dined at the café. It closed in 1877.

p.28   *brocs*: jugs.

p.28   *blanchisseuses*: washerwomen.

p.28   **grisettes**: strictly speaking, milliners, but also a general term for working-class girls in the Latin Quarter.

p.28   **Théâtre du Luxembourg, in the Rue de Madame**: the theatre no longer exists; the rue Madame runs south from the rue de Rennes to the rue de Assac in the 6ème.

p.28   **Jardin Bullier (la Closerie des Lilas)**: 171 Boulevard du Montparnasse, famed as a favourite café for artists and writers.

p.28   **Théâtre de l'Odéon**: now the Théâtre Royal de l'Odéon, this is the second classical theatre of Paris.

p.28   Or, if it were not only fine . . .: the passage describing the three students' walk through Paris apparently shows the influence of Chapter 4 of *L'Oeuvre* (1886) by Emile Zola (1840–1902). Henry James sent Du Maurier a copy in the year of its publication.

p.29   *rive gauche*: left (south) bank of the Seine, the intellectual quarter of Paris.

p.29   Pont Neuf: begun in 1578, the oldest surviving Paris bridge, it connects the Ile de la Cité with both banks of the Seine.

p.29   *magasins*: shops.

p.29   Pont des Arts: built in 1803, this iron bridge crosses the Seine to the Institut de France on the left bank.

p.29   Tuileries: a royal palace was built near the Louvre in the sixteenth century. It was still standing when Du Maurier was an art student, but was burnt down during the Commune of 1871.

p.29   Chamber of Deputies: elected French legislature. This was the Palais Bourbon, built in 1722.

p.29   Passy and Grenelle to St Cloud, to Rouen, to the Havre: Passy was the village near the Bois de Boulogne where Du Maurier spent the happiest part of his childhood, described in his first novel, *Peter Ibbetson*; by the 1890s it was entirely absorbed into the Paris suburbs. Grenelle (literally gravel pits) was an independent town on the Seine during Du Maurier's boyhood; it was annexed into Paris in 1860. St Cloud, near Versailles, was the site of a royal palace the grounds of which were loved by Du Maurier in childhood; it was burnt down in 1871 during the Franco-Prussian War. Rouen and Le Havre are both cities on the Seine; Le Havre is the port on the Normandy coast.

p.29   Zouaves: light cavalrymen, originally Algerian soldiers in the French army, but, in Du Maurier's day, French soldiers wearing North African uniform.

p.29   Rue de Rivoli as far as the Rue Castiglione: fashionable streets north of the Louvre in the Ier. Haussmann had begun his redevelopment of this part of Paris in 1854 (see note for p. 225).

p.29   *pralines, dragées, marrons glacés*: chocolate almonds, sugared almonds and crystallised chestnuts.

p.29   Allée des Feuillants: the Terrasse des Feuillants is the footpath on the north side of the Tuileries Gardens.

p.29   Place de la Concorde: the square at the western end of the Tuileries Gardens, marked by an Egyptian obelisk.

p.29   Bois de Boulogne: the largest park in Paris. Du Maurier remembered it before it was 'improved' in the 1850s.

p.30   three musketeers: a reference to the novel by Alexandre Dumas the elder (1802–70).

p.30   Rue de la Madeleine: Du Maurier probably means the Place de la Madeleine, where stands the fashionable church of Ste Marie-Madeleine built in the early nineteenth century. He may, however, be referring to the Boulevard de la Madeleine in the 8ème.

p.30   *hôtel garni*: a residential hotel, with lodging but no board.

p.32   bondon: a plug or bung.

p.32   Rue Vieille des Trois Mauvais Ladres: 'old street of the three bad lepers', apparently an invention of Du Maurier.

p.34   Millais and Holman Hunt: both Pre-Raphaelite painters; John Everett Millais (1827–1896) was a close friend of Du Maurier; William Holman Hunt (1827–1910).

p.34   Monsieur Ingres and Monsieur Delacroix: Jean-Auguste-Dominique Ingres, French neo-classical painter (1780–1867); Gleyre was one of his disciples. Eugène Delacroix, French romantic painter (1798–1863).

p.36   Zouzou: l'Zouzou (Zouave) may be partly drawn from the Prince de Ligne, the aristocratic friend of Du Maurier's younger brother Eugène, who was the original of Dodor (see note for p. 114).

p.36   'Tiens! ... s'pas?': 'Hello, it's the great Trilby!' ... 'What! You're already up, after last night? We had lots of fun at Mathieu's, didn't we? That was a damn good party! That was a house warming party which went off really well! But not too brilliant this morning, eh?'
     'Hey, old boy!' ... 'That was a great meal! And you and Victorine? How is she feeling now? She had a drop too much! That was a bit stupid of her, to go off like that in front of everyone! Hello, Gontran! How's things, Gontran, my darling Zouzou?'
     'Like clockwork, darling! ... But why are you dressed like a ragamuffin now? Have you gone broke?' ...
     'That's right, my man! ... I didn't have any luck last night! You saw perfectly well! I'm on my uppers, right up to my uppers [literally, shoulder blades] my poor corporal! Heck! We need to live, you know.'

p.37   objects of art and virtu: curios.

p.37   'le père Martin ... mont-de-piété!': 'Father Martin, wholesale and retail rag merchant, Legion of Honour, member of the Institut

Français etc., 13A rue du Puits d'Amour, on the ground floor at the back of the courtyard on the left opposite the pawnbroker's!'

p.37   Légion d'Honneur: an order set up by Napoleon in 1802 to reward outstanding civilian and military services.

p.37   membre de l'Institut: elected member of one of the five French academies.

p.37   Rue du Puits d'Amour: 'street of the wells of love', the old name for the rue de la Petite Truanderie in the 1er.

p.37   mont-de-piété: this was a state-run pawnbroker, founded by Louis XVI in 1777 in the rue des Francs Bourgeois, 3ème.

p.37   'Il ne faut jurer de rien!': 'You never can tell!'

p.37   'Y a pas d' quoi! ... la boxe!': 'Pray don't mention it! ... And now there's just time for me to smoke a cigarette and I'm off. They're waiting for me at the Austrian Embassy. And then, who knows? Keep going boys, and on with the boxing!' The Austrian Embassy, to which Trilby is not going, is part of the Hôtel de Bauffremont, 87 rue de Grenelle, in the 7ème.

p.37   Verdi's new opera: either La Traviata or Il Trovatore, both of 1853; Giuseppe Verdi (1813–1901). Du Maurier's friend Edward John Poynter (1836–1919) sang airs from Il Trovatore while he painted.

p.37   Victor Hugo's beautiful romance: Notre Dame de Paris of 1831; Victor Hugo, French poet and novelist (1802–85).

p.38   Lisa Gioconda's smile: Leonardo Da Vinci's Mona Lisa in the Louvre. In fact the painting was unlikely to have been a talking point in the 1850s; it achieved its fame later in the century. Du Maurier also apostrophises this portrait in Part the Fourth of Peter Ibbetson.

p.38   en cheveux: bare headed.

p.38   'Absolument comme à l'Ambassade d'Autriche': 'Just like the Austrian Embassy'.

p.38   'N'est-ce pas ... enfin?': 'Aren't I handsome? Aren't I a genius? Aren't I sublime, all in all?'

p.38   baignoire: a box in the pit.

p.38   Porte St Martin: 16 Boulevard St Martin in the 10ème, one of the most popular of Paris theatres. It was named as the Odéon in Harper's.

p.38   La Dame aux Camélias: a dramatisation by the novelist Alexandre Dumas the Younger (1824–95) of his own novel, it was first performed in 1852 at the Vaudeville. Verdi adapted it for *La Traviata*. It had a significant impact on Du Maurier's *Trilby*.

p.38   *au cabaret*: in a restaurant.

p.39   A feeling of sadness and longing . . .: Henry Wadsworth Longfellow (1807–82), 'The Day is Done', 1845.

p.40   *In medio tutissimus ibis!*: It is safest to go in the middle; Ovid, *Metamorphosis*, II, 137.

p.40   A modern teller of tales: this seems to be the American writer (Francis) Bret Harte (1836–1902), well known for his stories of the Californian mining camps, including 'The Luck of Roaring Camp' (1868) and 'The Outcasts of Poker Flat' (1870). Du Maurier met him at the house of George Eliot in 1880.

p.40   Lord Byron's Corsair: George Gordon, Lord Byron (1788–1824). His romantic poem about a pirate chief of 1814. It was a particular favourite with the young Du Maurier.

p.40   Young Person: a reference to Dickens's novel *Our Mutual Friend* (1865), where the insular Mr Podsnap cannot condone anything which might 'bring a blush to the cheek of the young person'.

p.41   Quia multum amavit!: Because she loved so much; Luke 7: 47. These words are part of Christ's defence of Mary Magdalen.

p.41   *camaraderie*: companionship.

p.42   *bonne camarade et bonne fille*: a good companion and a fine girl.

p.42   Bohemians: a term denoting those who lead an unconventional life, the expression was current in Paris before Henri Murger (1822–61) immortalised it with his *Scènes de la vie de Bohème* in 1849.

p.42   George the Fourth: King of England (1762–1830; reigned 1820–30); his reputation for decadent excess implies that he was a bad companion for Trilby's father.

p.42   the Montagnards Écossais: the Scottish Highlanders.

p.42   Rue du Paradis Poissonnière: 'the street of paradise and the fishwife', now the rue Paradis in the 10ème. Du Maurier lived there with his mother in 1856.

p.42   *à la grâce de Dieu!*: by God's grace!

² **p.42   blanchisseuse de fin**: a washerwoman for fine linen.

p.43   was *en pension*: was boarding with.

p.43 Madame Doche: Charlotte Marie de Plunkett Doche (1821–1900); a French actress of Irish descent, she played the part of Marguerite Gautier in the original production of 1852.

p.43 *entr'actes*: interludes.

p.44 Albion: Roman name for Britain.

Part Second

p.46 Dieu! qu'il fait . . .: Charles d'Orléans (1394–1465), Chanson, 6.

> God! He does wells to watch her,
> Everyone is willing to hire her.
> For the virtues which she contains
> Everyone is willing to praise her.

p.46 *au sixième*: in the sixth arrondissement.

p.46 Rue Tire-Liard: another invention; 'tire' is to pull or draw, and a 'liard' was an old French coin of negligible value.

p.46 'Ils safent tous . . . grand'chose!': 'They all know how to play the piano a bit but not very much!'

p.46 Leipsic: or Leipzig, a German city and important cultural centre; the Conservatoire was founded in 1843 by Felix Mendelssohn Bartholdy (1809–47).

p.47 *pis-aller*: a last resort.

p.48 Impasse des Ramoneurs: 'the cul-de-sac of the chimney sweeps'; apparently another invented street.

p.48 Gymnase: Théâtre de Gymnase, Boulevard Bonne Nouvelle, in the 10ème.

p.48 *une jeune femme du monde*: a young woman of the world, a young woman of society.

p.48 Mimi la Salope: see note for p. 25, 'la betite Honorine'; 'salope' means slut.

p.49 *tout ce qu'il y a de plus canaille*: the worst of the rabble.

p.49 Béranger: Pierre-Jean de Béranger (1780—1857), French writer of songs and propagator of the Napoleonic myth; 'Grandmother tell us about him' is from his 'Les Souvenirs du Peuple'.

p.49 rapins: art students.

p.49 Brasserie des Porcherons in the Rue du Crapaud-volant: there was a famous brasserie of this name in rue St Lazare in the 9ème, whose proprietor was Ramponneau, and which disappeared in 1851; the (invented) street name means 'flying toad'.

p.50 shawm: reed wind instrument.

p.50 David and Saul in one!: second and first of the Israelite kings respectively.

p.50 Rose of Sharon: Song of Solomon 2: 1.

p.50 *beauté du diable, beauté damnée*: beauty of the devil, a damned beauty.

p.50 Niobe: the mother in classical legend who angered Apollo and Diana by boasting of her children, who were then killed. Niobe turned to stone from grief.

p.52 *premier déjeuner*: breakfast.

p.54 French of Stratford-atte-Bowe: a reference to the Prioress from Geoffrey Chaucer's 'Prologue' to *The Canterbury Tales*. Lamont objected to the criticism of his French, and Du Maurier admitted that he had exaggerated.

p.54 *tâchant de se nettoyer!*: trying to clean himself.

p.54 *faute de mieux*: for want of an alternative.

p.54 'Demang mattang, à votre sairveece!': 'Tomorrow morning, if you please!'

p.54 'Gott in Himmel!': 'God in Heaven!'

p.55 You filthy black Hebrew sweep!': not in *Harper's*.

p.55 'Donnerwetter!': 'Good Heavens!'

p.55 *verfluchter kerl*: accursed fool.

p.55 crémerie Souchet, in the Rue Clopin-Clopant: the Café (or dairy) Souchet in 'hobbling-along street'; the rue Clopin was in the 5ème until 1928 and is now the rue Cardinal le Moine. Armstrong says that the group often ate at a 'crémerie'.

p.55 as naked as your hand!: not in *Harper's*.

p.55 'Fous afez du chacrin, matemoiselle?': 'Are you in pain, mademoiselle?'

p.57 'Recartez-moi pien tans le planc tes yeux': 'Look hard into the whites of my eyes.'

p.57 'Oh! presque plus du tout, monsieur – c'est le ciel': 'Oh! hardly at all, sir – it's heavenly.'

p.57 Düsseldorf: a German city on the Rhine. From the 1830s to the 1860s the Düsseldorf Academy (whose style was characterised by hard lines and noble subject matter) attracted art students from Europe and from the United States.

p.57 'Vive la Prusse! me v'là guérie!': 'Long live Prussia! See, I'm cured!'

p.57 au sixième au-dessus le l'entresol: in the sixth arrondissment, on the mezzanine.

p.57 'wunderschön!': 'beautiful!'

p.58 'voce sulle labbre! ... c'est un cri du coeur!': 'a voice on your lips ... it's a cry from the heart!'

p.58 Café de la Rotonde, in the Palais Royal: this was a little pavilion like a temple with columns built in 1793, which disappeared in 1885. The Palais Royal was built in the 1630s by Cardinal Richelieu (1585–1642) and became a royal palace after Richelieu's death. The palace area housed a theatre, shops and formal gardens.

p.58 basso profondo. Tiefstimme: deep bass. Deep voiced.

p.58 Café Larsouille in the Rue Flamberge-au-Vent: untraced; 'flamberge au vent' is a satirical expression meaning with a drawn sword.

p.58 Panthéon: built between 1758 and 1789 in fulfilment of a vow made by Louis XV, the Panthéon is dedicated to the patron saint of Paris, Ste Geneviève. It stands on high ground and is dominated by a huge dome. In the 1850s the official name would have been Ste Geneviève, not the Panthéon.

p.58 St Sulpice: an older church which was substantially altered in the seventeenth century, St Sulpice is one of the most impressive churches of Paris.

p.58 All Saints' Day: November 1.

p.58 Stradivarius: a violin by the famous Italian craftsman Antonio Stradivarius (c1644–c1737).

p.58 Vaterland: Fatherland, which is how it appears in *Harper's*.

p.58 Votre coeur est un luth ...: unidentified.

> Your heart is like a strung lute!
> As soon as one touches it, it resounds ...

p.60 'Messieurs les étutiants ...': 'Les Étudiants' by Frédéric Soulié.

p.60 mesmerised: Friedrich Anton Mesmer (1733–1815), an Austrian doctor, developed a system of putting his patients into a hypnotic state.

p.61 'Parbleu! . . . de moins!': 'Indeed! I do know Svengali!' 'What do you think of him?' 'When he's dead, that will be one scoundrel fewer in the world!'

p.61 **Rue Notre Dame des Potirons St Michel**: presumably a made-up name; 'Potirons' means pumpkins. Gleyre's studio was in the rue de Vaugirard.

p.61 **Augean sweepings**: the cleaning of the Augean stables was one of the mythic labours of Hercules.

p.61 *mobilier*: furniture.

p.61 *des charges*: sketches.

p.61 **bell-wether**: the leading sheep of a flock wears a bell to direct the others.

p.62 *bienvenue*: welcome, reception.

p.62 *blague et bagout Parisien*: Parisian banter.

p.63 **Ollendorff**: *Heinrich Godefroy Ollendorff*. A new method of learning to read, write and speak a language in six months, adapted to the French, 1843 with a ninth edition in 1861.

p.64 **Judee**: Saturday rather than Sunday is the Jewish day of rest.

p.64 **Colonne Vendôme**: a stone column in the Place de Vendôme decorated with a spiral of bronze made from canon captured by Napoleon I at the Battle of Austerlitz (2 December 1805) and with bas reliefs showing scenes from his victories. The column was pulled down during the Paris Commune of 1871 and re-erected.

p.66 'Dites donc . . . à l'échelle?': 'Tell us then, Englishman'. 'What?' 'Do you have a sister?' 'Yes.' 'Does she look like you?' 'No.' 'That's a great pity! Does she say her prayers when going to bed at night?' . . . 'Shall we put the Englishman on the ladder?' Such initiation ceremonies were common practice in Parisian studios.

p.68 **Babas, Madeleines, and Savarins**: various kinds of sponge cakes, some of them steeped in syrup or rum.

p.68 **sous**: the smallest French coin.

p.68 **a song about a gay cavalier**: Edward Poynter actually sang this song.

p.68 *'je ne sais quoi!'*: 'some special quality!'

p.68 **'n'est-ce pas, vous autres?'**: 'isn't it, you others?'

p.69 **'Nous vous en prions tous'**: 'We're all begging you.'

p.69 'Ah! voilà ... Très fin!' 'Ah! that's really well done!' 'Amazing!' 'Really fine!'

p.69 **The fox and the crow**: one of the fables of Aesop. The crow carries off a piece of cheese and flies into a tree to eat it. The fox stands under the tree and flatters the crow by praising his fine singing voice. In order to demonstrate the voice the crow opens his mouth and the cheese drops down to the fox. This is an excellent parallel for what is happening to Little Billee.

p.71 '**C'est un rude ... coco-là**'!: 'He's a tough cookie [rabbit], the English fellow! At least he knows how to spell properly when he's painting, that chap!' (This is an ironic commentary on Little Billee's French.)

p.72 *locataires*: lodgers.

p.72 *ragots, cancans, et potins d'atelier*: gossip, scandal and tittle-tattle from the studios.

p.72 **Rue des Cloîtres Ste Pétronille**: 'the street of the monastery of Saint Pétronille'; unidentified.

p.72 **Fontainebleau or Barbizon**: towns south-east of Paris in the Forest of Fontainebleau. Fontainebleau has a royal castle rebuilt by Francis I in the sixteenth century; Barbizon was popular with nine-teenth-century landscape painters (see note for p. 89).

p.72 *ma tante*: pawnbroker.

p.73 *persona gratissima*: persona grata means one who is acceptable or accredited; here it means that Trilby is exceptionally welcome.

p.73 *concierge*: door-keeper in a Paris apartment block.

p.73 **Christie's**: the London fine art auctioneers.

p.73 *bonne camaraderie voilà tout*: it was all just good companion-ship there.

p.73 **Ces animaux vivaient ...**: Jean de La Fontaine (1621–95), 'La Querelle des Chiens et des Chats, et celle des Chats et des Souris', *Fables*, XII, 8.

> These animals lived together like cousins;
> Their relations, so gentle, almost fraternal,
> Were a lesson to all their neighbours.

This was a favourite quotation with Du Maurier, who applied it to the Rossetti circle in October 1863.

p.75 '**Found drowned**': this is the title of a well-known painting of a drowned girl by George Frederic Watts (1817–1904). It was painted between 1848 and 1850 but not exhibited until 1881. Taffy's 'realist' work presumably relates to one of the corpses in the Morgue.

p.77 **Gérôme:** Jean-Léon Gérôme, French painter (1824–1904).

p.77 **Calypso:** nymph in Homer's *Odyssey*; she kept Odysseus on her island for seven years.

p.77 **Coventry, like Lady Godiva:** Coventry is a city in Warwickshire and Lady Godiva or Godgifu (c1040–1080) was the wife of Leofric, Earl of Mercia (d. 1057). According to legend, she rode naked round the market place in order to persuade her husband to reduce the local taxes. Peeping Tom, the one person who looked at her, was struck blind.

p.77 **Don Juan:** the legendary rake, subject of several works, including a poem by Byron (published 1819–24) and an opera, *Don Giovanni* of 1787, by Wolfgang Amadeus Mozart (1756–91).

p.78 **'It was poor Trilby's ... As for Trilby':** this passage was added in the book edition.

p.78 **Sir Galahad:** the blameless knight of King Arthur's court, Sir Galahad achieved the quest for the Holy Grail.

p.78 **Silenus:** Phrygian god, father of the satyrs and nurse of Bacchus. In paintings, Silenus is often shown as a drunkard.

p.78 **Jove:** the chief of the gods in Greek legend.

p.78 **Quixotise:** a reference to the novel *Don Quixote* of 1605 and 1615 by Miguel de Cervantes (1547–1616) in which Don Quixote is a burlesque figure of chivalry.

p.78 **Phryne:** Greek courtesan, model for Praxiteles' statues of Venus. J.-L. Gérôme's 'Phryne before her Judges' of 1861 (Kunsthalle, Hamburg), which Du Maurier may have had in mind here, is a famous painting of the period, illustrating Phryne's strategy when accused of impiety. She showed the judges her naked body and was acquitted.

p.78 **never bared herself ... paint her legs!:** added in the book edition.

p.78 **Ilyssus:** or Ilissos, a figure of a river god from the Elgin Marbles. Du Maurier once showed the Ilyssus in a *Punch* cartoon, where a pretentious woman speaks of the beauty of the head of the (headless) statue ('Distinguished Amateurs: The Art Critic', 13 March 1880).

p.78 **Bains Henri Quatre:** unidentified, but presumably one of the temporary bathing places of which Du Maurier writes in *Peter Ibbetson* and *The Martian* (1897): 'delightful summer baths in the Seine, that are so majestically called "Schools of Natation" (*Peter Ibbetson*, Part First).

p.78   *à la hussarde*: like a hussar. In *Peter Ibbetson* and *The Martian* Du Maurier explains that this was one of many ways of diving into the river.

p.78   Bains Deligny: now at 25 Quai Anatole France in the 7ème.

p.78   'Sac à papier! ... contre moi!': 'By Jove! [Paper bag, a slang expression] What a strapping fellow this Englishman is, eh!' 'Have you seen a body like it?' 'And his arms!' 'And his legs, too, by Jupiter!' 'By Jove! I'd sooner be angry with him than he be angry with me!'

p.78   *Omne ignotum pro magnifico!*: Tacitus (*c*55–*c*117), *Agricola*, XXX, ('Now the boundary of Britain is revealed and) everything unknown is held to be glorious.'

p.79   Venus Aphrodite (alias Aselgeia): Venus is the Roman name for the goddess, Aphrodite the Greek. Aselgeia is Greek for licentiousness and lust. Du Maurier once wrote about Aselgeia at some length in a letter to Henry James.

p.80   Miss Pinkerton's academy: a reference to *Vanity Fair* (1848) by Thackeray, which opens with a scene outside the academy.

p.80   Up he shot ... Mr Ilyssus either: added in the book edition.

p.80   *beaux habits de Pâques*: their best clothes for church at Easter.

p.81   Meudon: town on the Seine with a château badly damaged by the Prussians in 1870; it was a popular home for painters and sculptors in the nineteenth century.

p.81   *garde champêtre's*: the gamekeeper's.

p.81   *mirlitons*: reed pipes.

p.81   *la loge*: the lodge

p.81   *et vera incessu patuit dea!*: Virgil, *Aeneid*, I, 405: 'by her gait you know the goddess.'

p.81   Kate Vaughan: Catherine Candelon, comedy actress (*c*1852–1903); she was one of the Gaiety Theatre quartet from 1876 to 1883.

p.81   Nelly Farren: or Nellie; another popular actress from the Gaiety Theatre. She was famous for playing boys' parts.

p.81   'dongsong le konkong': dancing the can-can; added in book edition.

p.81 *pas seul*: a dance for one performer.

p.82 'Voilà l'espayce . . . swee!': 'That's the kind of man I am!'

p.83 'Quel bonheur! . . . brave garçon!': 'What good fortune! He's been saved, dear doctor, listen! He's saying his prayers in English, the dear boy!'

p.83 Green herbs . . .: another passage from Thackeray's 'Ballad of the Bouillabaisse'.

p.83 'Ah! . . . très bien!': 'Ah, but it's very good of him, the brave young man, to give thanks to heaven like that, now that the danger has passed!'

p.85 *hein?*: eh?

p.85 mahlstick: or maulstick, a stick with a soft leather ball at the top, held by painters in the left hand in order to support the right.

p.85 'Prinzessen, Comtessen, Serene English Altessen': 'Princesses, Countesses, Serene English Highnesses'.

p.85 *'küchen'*: 'cakes'.

p.85 *'e da capo!'*: 'and back to the beginning again!'

p.86 *Figaro*: a satirical paper founded in 1826, now one of the most important French newspapers.

p.86 Dummkopf!: blockhead!

p.86 canaille: rabble.

Part Third

p.89 Par deçà . . .: Charles d'Orléans, Chanson, 6.

> Neither here nor beyond the sea
> Will you encounter a lady or girl
> Who is so perfect in all respects –
> It's a dream to think of her:
> Heavens! He does well to look upon her!

p.89 Rousseau, Millet, Corot, Daubigny: all French landscape painters; Théodore Rousseau (1812–67); Jean François Millet (1814–75); Jean-Baptiste Corot (1796–1875); Charles-François Daubigny (1817–78).

p.89 Luxembourg Gardens: the Luxembourg Palace was built in the early seventeenth century by Marie de Medici (1573–1642), widow of Henry IV (1553–1610). The formal gardens are particularly popular with Parisian children.

p.92 Ingres's famous figure: 'La Source' (the fountain) of 1856 by Jean-Dominique Ingres is now in the Louvre. As Du Maurier says, it shows a naked girl with an earthenware pitcher of water on her left shoulder, and the novelist seems to have had it in mind when he entitled Little Billee's painting 'The Pitcher goes to the Well'. In *Harper's* the pitcher in Ingres' painting is inaccurately described as 'a stone pitcher'.

p.92 'Qu'est-ce qu'il a donc, ce Litrebili?': 'What's wrong with Little Billee?'

p.94 'L'Enfance de Psyché': 'The childhood of Psyche'; in classical mythology Psyche was the young girl with whom the god of love, Cupid, became enamoured.

p.94 *La source aux larmes*?: the fountain of tears?

p.94 So the pitcher went to the well once more: added in book edition.

p.96 several other people besides ...: apart from Gérôme, these artists are apparently fictitious, although Philippe-Augustin Hennequin (1762–1833) was a painter of an earlier date.

p.99 'Les Noces du Toréador': 'the bullfighter's wedding'.

p.99 'à ce soir donc ... de Dew!': 'until this evening, then, a thousand confounded thunderbolts, by God!'

p.100 *blanchisserie de fin*: laundry for fine linen.

p.101 Buckner: Richard Buckner, (1812–83), painter of fashionable portraits.

p.101 Album beauties: *The Book of Beauty* and the *Court Album* were among the journals and albums of the 1840s and 1850s which featured engravings of the fashionable beauties of the period.

p.101 Musidoras and Medoras!: appropriately exotic names for fantasy portaits of young women.

p.101 Sir Edward Burne-Jones: painter of medieval and mythical subjects. Burne-Jones was made a baronet in 1894 and Du Maurier accordingly changed the reference in *Harper's* from 'Mr Burne-Jones'.

p.101 Rossetti: Gabriel Charles Dante Rossetti (1828–82), known as Dante Gabriel Rossetti, painter and poet, founder member of the Pre-Raphaelite Brotherhood in 1848. Burne-Jones, Millais and Rossetti were all personally known to Du Maurier.

p.103 Gavarni: the working name of Guillaume Sulpice Chevalier (1804–66), the French draughtsman and caricaturist.

p.103   gendarme: policeman.

p.103   *dragon de la garde*: guardsman.

p.103   **Ellen Terry**: actress (1847–1928). When Du Maurier was writing she was working at the Lyceum Theatre with Henry Irving (1838–1905).

p.104   'Sacrement!': 'By heaven!'

p.104   *'fotre betit fin planc'*: 'votre petit vin blanc', 'your little white wine'.

p.104   **Heinrich Heine**: German Jewish lyric poet (1797–1856).

p.104   **Countess Hahn-Hahn**: Ida, Countess von Hahn-Hahn (1805–80) was a popular German novelist who wrote what have been described as 'aristocratic bodice-rippers'. Like Du Maurier, she had only one eye. In *Harper's*, Du Maurier referred to her as the Countess Varnhagen. Rachel Varnhagen von Ense (1771–1833) was a German Jewish literary hostess whose parties were famous. Heine knew both of them, and, as a Jewess, Countess Varnhagen might have been more appropriate here. However, the reference to eyesight clearly indicates that Du Maurier had the Countess Hahn-Hahn in mind, and was simply correcting a mistake.

p.104   **Mathilde**: Heine married his mistress 'Mathilde' in 1851.

p.104   *süssen fussen*: 'sweet feet', 'beautiful feet'.

p.104   **the École de Medecine**: the School of Medicine in the 6ème.

p.104   **carabins**: medical students.

p.105   **Chopin's funeral march**: Frederic Chopin wrote two funeral marches, but this must be the one published in 1840 as the slow movement of the Sonata for piano no. 2, op. 35.

p.107   **Mr Sandow**: Eugene Sandow (1867–1925) was a Russo-German exponent of physical culture. His name was used for a type of strong man and applied to exercise machines.

p.107   *mémoires pour servir*: to serve as reminiscences.

p.107   *pour le bon motif!*: with good cause.

p.107   **Pygmalion**: a mythic king of Cyprus who carved a statue of Venus, and then implored the goddess to let him have a wife as beautiful as the statue. The living statue was called Galatea. Ovid, *Metamorphosis*, Book 10, 243–97.

p.107   **Parc Monceau**: one of the most attractive parks in Paris, off the Boulevard de Courcelles in the 8ème. It was fashionable during the Second Empire.

p.107 'La belle aux pieds . . . rose!': 'The beautiful girl with alabaster feet and two pink toenails!'

p.107 Vincent: unidentified, although Armstrong, in his *Memoir* (p. 183), writes of a friendship with an American medical student. Oculists had unpleasant associations for Du Maurier, who lost the sight of his left eye in 1857.

p.108 the Halle: Les Halles, the food market (later for vegetables only) of Paris, in the 1er. During Du Maurier's time at Gleyre's atelier, the market was being greatly extended.

p.108 the Greek: Alecco (Alexander) Ionides (1840–98), third son of Alexander Constantine Ionides (1810–90), a Greek merchant who had settled in London and been naturalised as British in 1837. The Ionides family, generous patrons of art, were particularly kind to Du Maurier when he came to London in the 1860s.

p.108 *bonhomie*: good-nature.

p.109 Carnegie: unidentified.

p.109 Balliol: Balliol College, Oxford.

p.109 the band in the Luxembourg Gardens: the bandstand is in the north east corner.

p.109 Antony: based upon Edouard Hunziker (1827–1901), a Swiss painter with whom Du Maurier shared a studio in Düsseldorf.

p.109 *le roi des truands*: the vagabond king.

p.109 François Villon: French poet (1431–c1489); he led a riotous life and narrowly escaped hanging for theft.

p.109 *à cause de ses gentillesses*: because of his good nature.

p.111 rue du Ghette: unidentified; the Jewish quarter was le Marais and Strasbourg St Denis, but the ghetto had disappeared by Du Maurier's day.

p.111 *vogue la galère!*: set sail again!

p.111 *e poi, da capo!*: then go back to the beginning again!

p.112 *le bon temps où l'on était si malheureux!*: the lovely days when one was so wretchedly poor!

p.112 The aimless jest . . .: unidentified.

p.112   Crusaders: those who undertook the Christian expeditions in the eleventh to thirteenth centuries to recover the Holy Land.

p.112   Lorrimer: drawn from Edward John Poynter, academic painter and later President of the Royal Academy. Poynter was a student at Gleyre's atelier from 1856 to 1859.

p.113   Phidias: the greatest sculptor of ancient Greece (d. *c*431 BC).

p.113   Academician: an elected member of the Royal Academy of Arts in London.

p.113   Rudyard Kipling: poet and writer of fiction (1865–1936). At the time when Du Maurier was at work on *Trilby*, Kipling was best known for his short stories of British life in India. He was a nephew of Du Maurier's friends Edward Burne Jones and Edward Poynter.

p.113   Dante's *Inferno*: the first book of Dante's *Divine Comedy*, which recounts Dante's journey to hell.

p.113   Signor Tosti: Francesco Paolo Tosti (1846–1916), singing master and composer, particularly associated with popular songs. He was in England from 1875 to 1880, and was music master to the royal family.

p.113   Shoo, fly! ...: a song written by Billy Reeves and Frank Campbell (1869), made famous by 'Bryant's Minstrels'.

p.109–114   Then there was the yellow-haired Antony ... Not even Taffy's and the Laird's: This entire passage was altered for the book edition after James Whistler had threatened legal action, claiming, with justification, that the original character, Joe Sibley, 'the idle apprentice', was based upon himself. The illustration showing Joe Sibley was suppressed, but another, 'Taffy à l'échelle', continued to show Whistler clearly, and a third illustration, 'All as it used to be', with Whistler easily recognisable in the background, appeared in most editions. The original version of the Joe Sibley passage can be found in the appendix.

p.114   Oh, Orestes! Oh, Pylades!: Orestes, the son of Agamemnon and Clytemnestra, killed his mother to revenge her murder of his father. Pylades, his first cousin on his father's side and his closest friend, helped Orestes in his revenge and later married his sister, Electra. Their friendship became proverbial.

p.114   'wait till you get to forty year!': W. M. Thackeray, 'The Age of Wisdom', *Rebecca and Rowena* (1850).

p.114   History goes on repeating itself: this has been said by many people, but the original source is probably the Greek historian Thucydides (*c*460–*c*400 BC), *History*, 1, 2.

p.114 may too cecee ay nee eecee nee lâh!: But all of this is neither here nor there!

p.114 Dodor: drawn from Du Maurier's younger brother (Alexander) Eugène 'Gyggy' (1836–90).

p.114 *les plus mauvais garnements*: the worst rascals.

p.115 Nous allons ... d'une pipe!: We are going to have a really good time, by Jove!

p.115 *sous-officier*: non-commissioned officer.

p.115 *en maître d'école*: as if they were all dancing masters.

p.116 Pont de la Concorde: bridge leading from the Place de la Concorde.

p.116 Rue de Lille: runs parallel to the Seine on the south side from close to the Pont de la Concorde.

p.116 Rohan-Chabot, Montmorency, La Rochefoucauld-Liancourt, La Tour d'Auvergne: all names of aristocratic French families. Du Maurier claimed descent from the Rohans, and the hero of his last novel, *The Martian*, is a member of the family. The Hôtel de Rohan-Chabot was at 35 Boulevard des Invalides; built in 1782 it passed to the Rohan-Chabot family only in 1872. The Hôtel de la Rochefoucauld-Liancourt is at 14–18 rue de Seine. The Hôtel de La Tour d'Auvergne is at 28 and 28A rue St Dominique in the 7ème; it was owned originally by the de La Tour d'Auvergne family but from 1820 to 1929 belonged to the de la Rochefoucaulds. Du Maurier stayed in the humbler Villa Montmorency at Auteuil in 1877 and was in the habit of having his hired coach announced after parties as 'The Duke de Montmorency's carriage'.

p.116 Froissart: Jean Froissart (*c*1337–1410), author of the *Chroniques*, which recount the events of the period from 1325 to 1400.

p.116 Saint Simon: Louis de Rouvroy, Duke de Saint-Simon (1675–1755), author of the *Mémoires*, which cover the period 1691–1723.

p.116 Brantôme: Pierre de Bourdeille, seigneur de Brantôme (1535–1614), author of *The Lives of the Great Captains and Ladies of Society*.

p.116 'Parbleu! ... connu, farceur!': 'Good Heavens, of course I know what it is; are you pulling my leg?'

p.116 6th of March 1834: this was Du Maurier's own date of birth.

p.118 **Suisse**: porter of an aristocratic house. Such men were originally from Switzerland and still retained the name.

p.120 *'Parbleu! si je la connais!'*: 'Good Heavens, yes, I know her!'

p.120 **"patronne"**: woman in charge, mistress.

p.120 **Roncesvaulx**: in producing some fantastic aristocratic names (very much in the manner of Thackeray) Du Maurier includes the name of the battle (Roncevaux) of 778 where Charlemagne's paladin, Roland, was said to have died heroically while holding up the Moorish advance.

p.120 **'l'enfant dit vrai!'**: 'the boy is telling the truth.'

p.120 **Rigolot de Lafarce**: an invented name which means something like 'practical joke'.

p.121 **Passefil**: a joke name meaning 'pass the thread'.

p.121 **Boulevard des Capucines**: runs through the Place de l'Opéra in the 2ème.

p.121 **English chapel in the rue Marboeuf**: established in 1868 in the rue Marbœuf in the 8ème.

p.121 **the final *bonne bouche***: to keep the most delicious mouthful until last.

p.122 **Pour y danser . . .**: Frédéric Soulié, 'Les Étudiants'.

> To dance the can-can
> Or the 'Robert Macaire' there
> Forever and ever and ever
> Night and day
> and Youp! Youp! Youp!
> Tra la la la . . . la la la!

Robert Macaire was a popular criminal character in the play of the same name. The part was first played by the French actor Frédérick Lemaître (1800–76).

p.122 **West Riding**: the western part of Yorkshire.

p.122 **Homeric feast**: a reference to the feasts described by Homer in the *Iliad* and the *Odyssey*.

p.123 **Rue St Honoré**: runs between the Palais Royal and les Halles, in the 1er.

p.123 *ratafia de cassis, and anisette*: blackcurrant and aniseed liqueurs.

p.123 *rillettes de Tours*: potted minced pork.

p.123 *fromage d'Italie*: meat loaf made of minced calves' or pigs' liver.

p.123 *saucissons*: sausages.

p.123 *charcutiers*: pork-butchers.

p.125 **Roucouly**: 'roucouler' means to bill and coo, but Du Maurier seems to have been thinking of the Italian baritone Giorgio Ronconi (1810–90), who was working in Paris and London from the 1840s. He was particularly attached to the Théâtre Italien.

p.125 **Opéra Comique**: rue Favart, in the 2ème.

p.125 **Adam**: Adolphe Adam, French composer (1803–56), best known for the music for the ballet *Giselle*. The *Noël* for solo voice was published in 1851 and dedicated to Jules Lefort, whom the English edition describes as having sung the work.

p.125 *réveillon*: Midnight party on Christmas Eve.

p.125 **Parthenaic**: in the Greek style, like the Parthenon.

p.125 *attendrissement*: a sense of tender sympathy or pity.

p.125 **Minuit, Chrétiens . . .:**

> It is midnight Christians! It is the sacred time
> When God came down among us as Man!

p.126 **Peuple, debout . . .:**

> Rise, people, sing of your deliverance!
> Noel, Noel! Behold the redeemer!

p.127 **Allons Gycère . . .:** unidentified.

> Come on Gycère!
> Turn my glass red
> With the juice for which my heart is always yearning . . .
> And then come to the table,
> My lovely maid of Bacchus!
> Let's get drunk, tippling together is a good way to meet! . . .

p.128 *patronne*: landlady.

p.128 *bien malade ce matin*: had a monstrous hangover that morning.

p.128 **Pharisee**: member of an ancient Jewish sect known for their strict observance of the law.

Part Fourth

p.129 **Félicité passée ...:** song with words by Jean Bertaut (1552–1611) and music by J. B. Weekerlin (1821–1910).

> Happiness which has passed,
> Which can no longer return,
> Torments my thoughts –
> If only in losing my happiness I could also have lost my memory of it!

p.129 **Mid-day had struck ...:** the events of Christmas Day in *Trilby* are closely based upon the Christmas of 1856, with two important differences. No women were present on the original occasion, and the scene was not the studio (into which they had yet to move) but Lamont's lodgings. See *Thomas Armstrong: a Memoir*, p. 152, for more details.

p.129 **Madame Vinard:** Monsieur and Madame Vinard were drawn from the Vinots, who were porters at no. 53 rue Notre Dame des Champs.

p.129 **Chemin de Fer du Nord:** the railway of the north. The Gare du Nord was and is the Paris terminus.

p.130 *la permission de dix heures:* they had only been able to obtain permission to stay out until 10 o'clock.

p.130 **Juno ... Diana ... Hebe:** Juno was the wife of Jupiter in classical mythology, Diana the goddess of chastity and hunting, and Hebe the goddess of youth, usually shown pouring nectar for Jupiter.

p.130 *tutoyé'd en bon camarade:* addressed familiarly, like a close friend.

p.131 **Harvey sauce:** Peter Harvey, the landlord of the Black Boy at Bedfont in Middlesex, invented a famous thin sauce for fish, game and steaks.

p.131 **John Leech:** draughtsman and satirist (1817–64); he was Du Maurier's friend and predecessor on *Punch*, and an artist whom the younger cartoonist much admired.

p.131 **veeverler companyee!:** vive la compagnie, long life to everyone.

p.131 **Hi diddle dee for the Lowlands low:** 'The Golden Vanity', traditional ballad.

p.131 **Old Joe ...:** 'Old Joe, or, 'Somebody in de House wid Dinah', a popular negro melody, one version published in 1846.

p.131 **Le Sire de Framboisy:** 'Le Sire de Franchoisy' or 'A jeune Femme, jeune Mari' is described as an old song from Savoy. It appears in a publication of $c1841$, but may have been printed before that. The words are by E. Bourget and the music by Laurent de Rillé. The song tells of an older husband who spends seven and a half years at war and returns to find his wife at a ball in Paris. He takes her back to his castle and kills her. The concluding moral is 'for a young wife a young husband is needed'. It was regarded as an anti-imperialist song, possibly because of the difference in age between Napoleon III and his wife. Du Maurier used to sing it in his London lodgings in the early 1860s.

p.132 **Hallelujah Chorus**: from the oratorio *Messiah* of 1741 by George Frederick Handel (1685–1759). Edward Poynter sang it while he worked.

p.132 **Plaisir d'amour ...**: 'Plaisir d'Amour' by Jean-Pierre Claris de Florian (1775–94); the music is by Jean Paul Martini (1741–1816).

> The pleasure of love lasts only a moment
> The pleasure of love lasts only a moment
> The pain of love lasts all life long.

p.132 *le vin a quat' sous!*: a popular drinking song with words by de Clairville (Louis-François Nicolaie, 1811–79) and Vanderbuch, and music by Eugène Déjzet (1844–74), celebrating the pleasures of cheap wine which costs four sous. The opening lines are:

> Fi! de ces vins d'Espagne,
> Ils ne sont pas faits pour nous.

'Be blowed to the Spanish wines, they are not for us.'
This was another of the songs which Du Maurier often sang.

p.132 **Of this 'ere song ...**: 'Bucks a-Hunting go', a traditional song from the North Midlands, printed versions are known from $c.1780$.

p.132 **'My Sister Dear' out of *Masaniello***: the opera *La Muette de Portici* of 1818 by Daniel François Esprit Auber (1782–1871) is referred to here as *Masaniello*. In the opera the song is 'Pourquoi pleurer?' (Why cry?). It was interpolated from Auber's *Le Concert à la Cour* (1824) in nineteenth-century performances in Britain and America. Armstrong recalls that it was a favourite with the Paris group.

p.132 **'Il est gentil ... confession!'**: 'He's simply too nice this officer of the guard. My God, how well he can sing! And English too, it seems. They're terribly well brought up these Englishmen – all as nice as the others! And as for Little Billee, he could go up to heaven without confession.'

p.134 **'Mais comme che ... craindre!'**: 'But since I never bathe, I've nothing to fear!'

p.134   sword dance: traditional Scottish dance over two crossed swords.

p.135   cuirassier: horse soldier who wears body armour on duty.

p.135   *sergent-de-ville*: policeman.

p.135   *rassemblement*: gathering.

p.136   *fin-de-siècle*: end of the century, used of the 1890s when Du Maurier was writing *Trilby*.

p.136   Derby: annual horse race on Epsom Downs in Surrey.

p.136   Punch: comic magazine, founded in 1841. Du Maurier worked there from 1860 until his death, joining the permanent staff in 1864.

p.136   *trinquéd*: chinked glasses with them.

p.138   *caryhattide*: caryatid, a sculpted female figure used as a pillar.

p.138   Quoi de plus ... 'Vin a quatre sous':

> What could be nicer
> Than a few drops –
> A few drops of wine for four sous.

p.138   Rue de la Chaussée d'Antin: near the Boulevard des Capucines in the 9ème.

p.138   *tisane de chiendent*: an infusion made from couch grass.

p.139   'au moins il a *bon coeur*': ' at least he has a good heart'.

p.140   'Credieu! ... tante Kolb!': 'Good God! you had a jolly good time last night! What a party that was, eh? I bet it was more fun than my Aunt Kolb's!'

p.141   On New Year's Day ...: this scene is closely modelled on the appeal made to Marguerite Gautier by Armand Duval's father in *La Dame aux Camélias* by Alexandre Dumas the younger.

p.148   remise: hired carriage. Armstrong says (p. 120) that a ' "Voiture de Remise" did not ply for hire on the cab ranks, and had a higher tariff than those that did'.

p.151   the quick disenchantment, the lifelong regret: a rough translation of the song 'Plaisir d'Amour'.

p.156   throw stones: a reference to the story of Christ and the woman taken in adultery, John 8, 2–11.

p.158   Vibraye: now a small town near the Forest of Vibraye; the 'small stream' is the Braye.

p.158   La Sarthe: a province of Northern France, with its capital at Le Mans. Du Maurier's own family came from this area.

p.158   'The Pitcher Goes to the Well': 'The pitcher goes so often to the well that it is broken at last' – fourteenth-century proverb.

p.160   piping times of peace: Shakespeare, *Richard III*, I. i. 24.

p.161   A lightsome eye . . .: unidentified.

p.161   Mars: the Roman god of war.

p.161   grigs: lively young men; merry as a grig means merry as a grasshopper.

p.161   napoleons: gold coins worth twenty francs.

p.161   *de bas en haut*: from top to bottom, in every respect.

p.161   tempi: speeds.

p.161   Boulogne: then a village west of Paris.

p.161   Luxembourg Gallery: during the period of *Trilby*, the picture gallery of the Luxembourg Palace was dedicated to works by living artists.

p.163   a cordon bleu: originally referred to the blue ribbon worn by the Knights Grand Cross of the Holy Ghost; now means a first-rate cook.

p.163   Pazienza!: Have patience!

p.163   porte cochère: carriage gate.

p.164   Royal Academy in Trafalgar Square: the Royal Academy was housed in the eastern part of the present National Gallery building from 1837 to 1868.

p.166   National Gallery: the National Gallery was founded in 1824, and moved to its present site in Trafalgar Square in 1838. Little Billee's painting, like other nineteenth-century works by British artists, would have moved to the new Tate Gallery in 1897.

p.166   wounded thing with an angry cry: Tennyson, Maud, I, x, 363: 'A wounded thing with a rancorous cry'.

p.166   the Pope's choir: the singers in the Pope's choir were traditionally castrati; Du Maurier's 'cracked soprano', having been castrated, still could not sing in tune. It is worth noting that the practice died out only in the nineteenth century. There were castrati singing in the Vatican in Du Maurier's lifetime.

p.166   Santley – Sims Reeves – Lablache!: Sir Charles Santley, baritone

(1834–1922); John Sims Reeves, tenor (1818–1900); Louis Lablache, Franco-Italian bass and teacher of bel canto (1794–1858). Queen Victoria was one of his pupils.

p.167   Stamboul: Istanbul.

p.167   pasha: a Turkish military commander or governor.

p.167   she was sweet . . .: another reference to 'Ben Bolt'.

Part Fifth

p.170   Then the mortal coldness . . .: Byron, 'Stanzas for Music' ('There's not a joy the world can give').

p.171   Passage Choiseul, or the Passage des Panoramas: the former runs between the rue des Petits Champs and the rue St Augustin, the latter between the rue St Marc and the Boulevard Montmartre; both are in the 2ème.

p.171   Panatella: a long slender cigar, tapering at the sealed end.

p.171   *Galignani's Messenger*: a journal, published by the Anglo-Italian firm of booksellers and publishers. Between 1804 and 1886 they were at rue Vivienne in the 2ème, and they are still at 224 rue de Rivoli.

p.171   Cercle Anglais: the English group.

p.171   Rue Sainte-n'y Touche: 'Sainte n'y touche' means a hypocrite, a woman who pretends to be purer than she is; the invented street name is appropriate here.

p.171   Antwerp: Du Maurier left Paris for Antwerp in the summer of 1857 and entered the Antwerp Academy of Fine Arts, which had a reputation as an inexpensive and sound institution. He lost the sight of his eye a few months later.

p.171   Kermesse: annual carnival.

p.173   pifferari: pipers.

p.173   Munich: the focal point of German painting in the second half of the nineteenth century.

p.173   *au grand sérieux*: very seriously.

p.174   the fishmonger's shop: Frederick Walker's 'A Fishmonger's Shop', painted and exhibited in 1872, was considered by some to be his finest work in watercolour.

p.175   *Que la terre leur soit légère!*: may the earth lie lightly on them.

p.175   Wanderjahr: year of wandering, from the German practice of travelling to perfect a skill after apprenticeship.

p.175 **Fitzroy Square**: south of Euston Road and Regent's Park.

p.176 **Collard and Collard**: makers of pianos. Founded in the eighteenth century, the company was taken over by Chappells in 1929.

p.176 **Eros**: Greek god of love.

p.176 **'dans le pays du tendre!'**: in the land of love!

p.176 **viol, viola, viola d'amore, viol di gamba, violino mio**: a bowed string instrument with frets; the alto member of the violin family; eighteenth-century viola with sympathetic (resonating) strings; bass viol, my violin.

p.177 **Aeolian harp**: stringed instrument producing musical sounds on exposure to the wind.

p.177 *de par le monde*: in the whole wide world.

p.177 **A dirty bit . . .**: Charles Stuart Calverley (1831–84), 'Precious Stones, in *Complete Works* (1901), p. 81.

p.178 *de pair à pair*: on an equal footing.

p.178 **osseous**: bony.

p.178 **Duchess of Towers**: heroine of du Maurier's novel *Peter Ibbetson*.

p.180 **Waterloo**: battle in which Wellington defeated Napoleon, 1815.

p.180 **Piccadilly**: fashionable street in the West End of London.

p.180 **Cavendish Square**: north of Oxford Street.

p.180 **Upper Conduit Street**: off Regent Street.

p.180 **Whitechapel, the Minories, the Docks, Ratcliffe Highway, Rotherhithe**: all in the unfashionable East End of London. The Minories runs from Whitechapel to the Tower of London; the Highway, which is close to Ratcliffe Orchard, Ratcliffe Cross Street and Ratcliffe Steps, runs along the north bank of the Thames in Stepney. Du Maurier was familiar with Rotherhithe (on the south bank) in 1860, when James Whistler was working there. Armstrong recalled that Du Maurier sang in a public house there.

p.181 **Mr Barkis**: from Dickens's *David Copperfield* (1850), where he declares himself 'willing' to marry David's nurse, Clara Pegotty.

p.182 **Kathleen Mavourneen**: Julia Crawford, 'Kathleen Mavourneen', 1835: music by Frederick Nicholls Crouch (1808–96) of 1840. One of the most popular drawing-room ballads.

p.182   'Earts o' hoak: 'Heart of Oak' by David Garrick (1717–79), 1759.

p.185   locomotor ataxia: unsteadiness in the use of the limbs.

p.185   Franco-Italian pothouse near Leicester Square: possibly Bertolini's.

p.188   Like Mars, A-smokin' . . .: unidentified.

p.188   Sir Louis Cornelys: Arthur Lewis of the drapery firm of Lewis and Allenby of Regent Street. Lewis's Saturday night musical parties were famous, first in Jermyn Street and then, after 1863, at Moray Lodge on Campden Hill (Mechelen Lodge in *Trilby*). Lewis's choir were known as the Moray Minstrels.

p.188   a Greek matron: Euterpe Sgouta (1816–92), wife of Alexander Constantine Ionides and mother of Du Maurier's friend Alecco.

p.190   Signor Giuglini: Antonio Giuglini (1827–65) first appeared in London in 1857. Du Maurier heard him sing in June 1860 and was not impressed.

p.190   Adelina Patti: Italian diva of bel canto (1843–1919), who eventually settled in Britain.

p.190   'Miserere': the 'Miserere' comes in Act IV, Scene 1, of Verdi's *Il Trovatore* (1853).

p.190   Mendelssohn's letters: the letters of Felix Mendelssohn began to appear from the 1860s. An English translation by Lady Wallace came out in 1862. Felix Moscheles published an edition of Mendelssohn's letters to the Moscheles family in 1888.

p.190   Prime Minister: at this date presumably Henry John Temple, 3rd Viscount Palmerston (1784–1865).

p.190   Joachim: Joseph Joachim, Hungarian violinist (1831–1907). Du Maurier, after hearing him play in March 1867, thought him the greatest of violinists.

p.190   Madame Schumann: Clara Schumann (née Wieck) (1819–96), one of the greatest pianists of her day. Mixed bills like this were not uncommon, with talented instrumentalists acting as curtain raisers to great singers.

p.190   Sebastian Bach: one of Joachim's specialities was the D minor Chaconne for unaccompanied violin by Bach.

p.191   Zola: Emile Zola, French novelist (1840–1902). Something of an anachronism as his first important novel, *Thérèse Raquin*, did not appear until 1867.

p.191 Guy de Maupassant: French short story writer and novelist (1850–93). Du Maurier, who did not approve of the sexual outspokenness of much of Maupassant's work, discussed the subject with Henry James. He met Maupassant through James in 1886. Another anachronism, which the narrator admits two paragraphs later.

p.191 Pierre Loti: Julian Viaud, French writer (1850–1923), popular for his exotic subject matter. Pierre Loti's work would certainly not have been under discussion in the 1860s, as the narrator goes on to admit.

p.191 Feydeau: Georges Feydeau, French dramatist, famous for his farces (1862–1921).

p.191 Miss Austen: Jane Austen (1775–1817).

p.192 Glorioli: unidentified. Felix Moscheles also records his presence at Arthur Lewis's concerts, but this is presumably either a pseudonym or a representative example of an esteemed singer.

p.194 Bonjour Suzon ... Bonjour Suzon: Alfred de Musset, 'Chanson', 1844.

> Good day, Suzon, my flower of the woods!
> Are you always the most beautiful of all?
> I've come back, as you can see,
> From a long journey through Italy!
> I've made a tour of Paradise
> I've written some lines – I've had some love affairs ...
> But that doesn't matter to you!
> I'm outside your house:
> Open your door!
> Good day Suzon!
>
> I saw you in the lilac time,
> Your heart had just burst out with joy
> And you said: 'I don't want,
> I don't want to be loved again.'
> What have you done since I left?
> He who leaves too early returns too late.
> But what does that matter to me?
> I'm passing by your house:
> Open your door!
> Good day Suzon!

p.194 Monsieur Jourdain: the ridiculous parvenu in Molière's play *Le Bourgeois Gentilhomme*.

p.194 Sephardim: Spanish or Portuguese Jews.

p.195 'soi-disant dix-neuvième siècle': so-called nineteenth century.

p.195 *la rossignolle*: the nightingale.

p.195 'et vous m'en direz des nouvelles!': 'then you will tell me something new!'

p.195 'Ça n'est pas dans mes cordes!': 'it's not in my line!'

p.195 'le beau rire! . . . Mon ami': 'Ah her laugh! to be able to make you laugh when your eyes are full of tears – that's what beats me! My friend . . .'

p.195 'je sais ce que je vaux, moi!': 'I know what I am worth!'

p.195 'J'en suis fou! hélas!': 'I'm maddened by it'.

p.195 'une fameuse crapule (sauf vot' respect)': 'an infamous blackguard, begging your pardon'.

p.197 'belle comme un ange . . . un pot': 'as beautiful as an angel – but as stupid as a pot'.

p.197 **Paganini:** Nicolo Paganini, Italian violinist and composer (1782–1840).

p.197 **Herr Kreutzer:** there was a composer called Conrad Kreutzer (1780–1849), but Du Maurier was probably using the name at random.

p.197 **Vinter Balace:** the royal winter palace at St Petersburg.

p.197 **Trury Lane:** Drury Lane, one of the leading London theatres; it is near Covent Garden.

p.197 **Chullien:** Louis Antoine Jullien (1812–60), conductor and impresario who put on promenade concerts in London.

p.198 **God Save the Queen:** British national anthem, first performed in 1744. The authorship of both words and music is disputed.

p.198 **Pop goes the Weasel:** tune from an old English dance, probably first published under this title in 1853.

p.198 **Old Hummums:** originally a Turkish Bath, set up in Covent Garden in 1631, but by this date a hotel.

p.199 **Jakes Talboys:** in *Harper's* the character was called Macey Sparks, and was a 'Rabelaisian' Royal Academician rather than a doctor. He was easily recognised as the painter Henry Stacy Marks (1829–98) and the paragraph was extensively changed. See appendix for the original version.

p.199 **the Great Western Station:** Paddington Station.

p.199 *Silas Marner:* by George Eliot (1819–80), published 1861.

p.199 **Darwin's *Origin of Species*:** *On the Origin of Species by Means* *of Natural Selection* by Charles Darwin (1809–82) was published in 1859.

p.202   Of this 'ere song . . .: 'Bucks a-Hunting go'; see also p. 132.

p.204   *pour si peu*: so easily.

p.204   She comes – she's here . . .: Thackeray, 'At the Church Gate', *Pendennis* (1850).

p.205   'Break, break, break': Tennyson, published 1842.

p.205   Roll on . . .: Byron, *Childe Harold*, IV, 179.

p.205   'And on thy ribs . . .: Tennyson, 'The Sailor Boy', 1861.

p.206   Ulysses: hero of Homer's *Odyssey*. He filled the ears of his sailors with wax so that they would not be lured onto the rocks by the sea nymphs. On his return to Ithaca after twenty years away his dog recognised him.

p.207   Leave thou thy sister . . .: Tennyson, *In Memoriam*, XXXIII, 5.

p.208   Judea: part of Palestine. Little Billee is referring to the flood and Noah's ark; see *Genesis*, 7–8.

p.208   Jonah: Old Testament prophet, swallowed by a whale after a shipwreck; see *Book of Jonah*.

p.208   Joshua: war leader of the Israelites. When he was fighting the Amorites, Joshua asked God to make the sun stand still until the Israelites had avenged themselves. The sun remained at its zenith for 'about a whole day', *Joshua*, 10, 12–14.

p.208   Little Red Riding-hood, Jack and the Beanstalk, and Morgiana and the Forty Thieves: all figures from popular children's stories and pantomimes. 'Little Red Riding Hood' was translated from the French of Charles Perrault (1628–1703), Jack and the Beanstalk is based on a worldwide myth, and Morgiana and the forty thieves appear in the oriental tale of Aladdin, often included in *The Arabian Nights*.

p.208   that's another pair of sleeves: 'c'est une autre paire de manches'; French saying meaning that is quite another thing.

p.209   *la maladie du siècle*: the malaise of the century.

p.210   Jephthah: Old Testament figure who swore to kill the next living thing that he saw if he was victorious in battle; it was his daughter coming out to meet him (*Judges*, 11: 30 ff).

p.210   Shylock: Jewish merchant in Shakespeare's *Merchant of Venice*. His daughter Jessica left him for her Christian lover, Lorenzo.

p.210 Her Majesty's commission: the document authorising a man to take up a position as an officer in the British Army.

p.210 butchers and bakers and candlestick-makers: from the nursery jingle 'Rub-a-dub-dub, three men in a tub'.

p.211 tinker, tailor . . .: an amended version of the old rhyme for counting cherry stones.

p.211 *ab ovo usque ad malum*: 'from the beginning to the end', from the Roman practice of eating eggs at the beginning of meals and fruit at the end, Horace, *Satires*, III, 6. 'Malum', which means both evil and fruit, allows for a punning interpretation of the expression.

p.211 chiaro-oscuro: treatment of light and shade in painting.

p.212 le Dieu des bonnes gens!: 'the God of right-thinking people!' This is the title of a poem by Béranger of 1817 in which he opposes a comfortable idea of God to the concept of a God of wrath.

p.212 *bâton de maréchal*: Field Marshall's baton or insignia of office: in French an expression meaning the ultimate goal.

p.215 Oh! could I feel . . .: Byron, 'Stanzas for Music' (There's not a joy the world can give); 'or be what [not as] I have been' in the original.

p.215 Lucifer, son of the morning: Satan.

p.215 loved a dog: Byron's beloved Newfoundland dog, Boatswain, is buried at Newstead Abbey.

p.215 Humpty Dumpty: nursery rhyme. Humpty Dumpty fell off a wall and 'All the King's horses and all the King's men/ Couldn't put Humpty together again'.

p.215 When Greeks joined . . .: Nathaniel Lee (*c*1653–*c*1692), *The Rival Queens*, IV, ii.

p.215 Apelles: court painter to Philip and Alexander of Macedon (active late fourth century BC).

p.215 'Who shall put forth . . .: Shelley, 'Time', 1821. The quotation should end with a question mark and not with an exclamation.

p.218 *en évidence*: on public display.

p.218 Positivist: follower of the secular religion founded by Auguste Comte (1798–1857) which placed a man in the centre of the universe and dispensed with God. It was a 'Unitarian' (a Christian who does not accept the concept of the Trinity) in *Harper's*.

p.218 *un ménage bourgeois . . . ni mauvais*: a middle-class marriage, neither beautiful nor ugly, neither good nor bad.

p.218 *Ce que c'est que de nous!*: that's what's become of us!

Part Sixth

p.219 **Vraiment . . .**: Victor Hugo, 'La Guitare', 1837.

> Truly, next to her, the queen looked only ugly
> When, towards evening
> She passed over the bridge to Toledo
> Wearing a black bodice!
> A necklace from the days of Charlemagne
> Adorned her neck . . .
> 'The wind which comes from the mountains
> Will drive me to madness!'
>
> Villagers, sing and dance: night has come . . .
> One day Sabine
> Gave everything – her dovelike beauty,
> And her love –
> For a ring from the Count of Saldagne,
> For a jewel . . .
> 'The wind which comes from the mountains
> Has driven me to madness!'

Harper's has another quotation here, 'Vi ravviso, o luoghi ameni!' from Count Rodolfo's aria in Act I, scene 1, of *La Sonnambula* by Vincenzo Bellini (1801–35).

p.219 **cinq ans après**: five years later, taken from *Vingt Ans Après*, the title of Dumas' sequel to *The Three Musketeers*. Du Maurier uses the full Dumas title as a heading on p. 333.

p.219 **Porthos and Athos**: two of the three musketeers. Porthos is large and strong, Athos a dissembling aristocrat.

p.219 **'assommer un homme . . . de poing'**: knock a man down with a punch.

p.219 **ongbongpwang**: 'embonpoint', stoutness.

p.219 **D'Artagnan**: the 'fourth' musketeer; the Gascon D'Artagnan joins forces with the other three.

p.219 **Quentin Durward**: a novel (1823) by Sir Walter Scott (1771–1832). The only oil painting of Du Maurier's student days was of a scene from Scott's *Rob Roy* (1817).

p.219 **Ah, wasna he a Roguey . . .**: 'The Piper of Dundee', a Jacobite song probably sung to a traditional pipe tune, and made popular in the eighteenth century by Hamilton Bangour.

The piper came to our town, to our town, to our town,
The piper came to our town, and he played bonnilie.

p.220 **tout ce qu'il . . . historique!**: all most historical.

p.222 **Cirque des Bashibazoucks**: the stadium is apparently invented; a bashibazouck (literally, one whose head is turned) was an irregular Turkish soldier. Bashibazoucks became notorious for brutality.

p.222 *comme autrefois*: as in the past.

p.222 **Rue de la Paix**: runs north from the Place Vendôme to the Opéra in the 2ème.

p.222 *rhum de la Jamaïque*: Jamaican rum.

p.223 *gardien de la paix*: policeman.

p.223 **'une bien jolie Morgue, ma foi!'**: 'a very beautiful morgue, I declare!'

p.163 **'Messieurs devraient . . . très bien!'**: 'You gentlemen ought to go and see it – it's very fine!'

p.223 **La Sainte Chapelle**: thirteenth-century royal chapel on the Ile de la Cité.

p.223 **equestrian statue of Henry IV**: on the western end of the Ile de la Cité, beside the Pont Neuf.

p.223 *C'est toujours ça!*: that's something!

p.223 **'Faustine'**: a poem by Charles Algernon Swinburne (1837–1909), first published in *The Spectator* (31 May 1862) and later republished in *Poems and Ballads, First Series* (1866). *The Spectator* was a weekly radical periodical started in 1828.

p.225 **Howard of Norfolk**: probably not a reference to a specific Duke of Norfolk. The first Howard took the title in 1483.

p.225 **'fote de myoo!'**: 'faute de mieux', 'as nothing better presents itself'.

p.225 **Baron Haussmann**: Eugene Georges Haussman (1809–91), famous for his rebuilding of Paris during the Second Empire. Du Maurier very much disliked the changes.

p.225 **À louer . . . à coucher**: To let. A studio and a bedroom.

p.225 **'Ah! Mais quel . . . la semaine dernière!'**: 'Ah! but what a joy to see you again! And how well you all look! and M. Littlebillee, how he has grown!' etc. etc. 'But before everything else you must have a little drop to drink – quick, Vinard! The cassis liqueur which M. Durien sent us last week!' Du Maurier revisited the Vinots in 1867.

p.225   loge: the concierge's lodge.

p.225   *Le Retour ... ans après!*: The return of the three Englishmen, five years later!

p.226   Rue Taitbout: near the Boulevard des Italiens in the 9ème.

p.226   charbonnier: coal merchant.

p.226   Rue de la Canicule: 'street of the dog days'; apparently invented.

p.226   'un bon mariage; bien solide!': 'a good marriage; very substantial!'

p.226   'perdu par les femmes! ... par exemple!': 'ruined by women! such an attractive boy, you understand! Upon my word, it didn't bring him any luck!'

p.226   'A dix-huit ans, pensez donc!': 'At eighteen, just think of it!'

p.226   'messieurs savaient ça?': 'do the gentlemen know that?'

p.226   'que voulez-vous!': 'what can you expect!'

p.226   'Car il pleuvait averse!': 'because there was a downpour!'

p.226   'the douaniers': 'customs officers'.

p.226   'douzième chasseurs-à-pied': 'the twelfth division of the light infantry'.

p.226   'sapper-pumpers, en grande tenue': 'the firemen [sapeurs pompiers] in full dress'.

p.226   'q'c'était beau! ... j'croix bien!': 'how lovely it was! My God, how lovely it was! how I cried to see it! didn't I, Vinard?' 'Indeed yes, my love! depend upon it!'

p.226   'comme il est idiot, ce Vinard': 'what a fool he is, this Vinard'.

p.226   *magasin de bric-à-brac*: a curio shop.

p.226   'vous verrez ça!': 'you must see it!'

p.230   Pauvre Trilby . . .:

> Poor Trilby – so beautiful, so good and so dear!
> I am her foot. Let whoever wishes look at it.
> Which dear friend was it who, loving her in days past,
> Set here this charming memento of her (and of his sincere love)

Which a whim inspired
And which a breath will carry away!

I was a twin: what has become of my brother?
Alas! Alas! Love led us astray
Eternity will unite us, I hope;
And we will be a pair as we were before
At the foot of a chaste bed where none will trouble
Trilby, who will sleep.

O dear friend, what are you going to do without us?
The door is closed where Trilby used to live.
Heaven is far away . . . and on earth
(Yes it was sweet for us and will be easy for her)
No one will ever find our equals
However hard he searches!

p.231 'Vous avez vu . . . n'est-ce pas?': 'You have seen it, haven't you, gentlemen? Trilby's foot? it is very pretty! M. Durien had the glass put over it, after you had gone; and M. Guinot composed the *Epitaph*. Poor Trilby! what can have become of her! what a good girl she was, eh? and so beautiful! and so full of life she was, so full of life, so full of life! And how well she loved you all – and especially Mr Little Billee – was it not so?'

p.231 'Voyez cette pendule!': 'See this clock!'

p.231 Louis Onze . . . Madame le Pompadour: Louis XI (1423–83); Antoinette Poisson, Marquise de Pompadour (1721–64), mistress of Louis XV (1710–74).

p.231 'Combiang?' . . . 'véritable occasion': 'How much?' . . . 'It is a hundred and fifty francs, sir – it is very cheap at the price – a real bargain.'

p.231 'trois cents francs': 'three hundred francs'.

p.231 'Et voici . . . avec': 'And here are the shoes to go with it.'

p.231 'le piay . . . Je prong!': 'Trilby's foot – on the wall, you know – with the glass and everything else – cut the wall – you understand? . . . How much?' . . . 'it is a bit difficult, you know – cutting a wall like that! I will ask the landlord if you like, and it could perhaps be arranged, if it is made of wood! only it will mean . . .' 'I'll take it!'

p.232 fauns and hamadryads!: classical rural deities with horns and goat feet and nymphs who lived in trees.

p.232 Pavillon de Flore: a summer-house dedicated to Flora, the classical goddess of flowers.

p.233 Polichinelle: Punch.

p.233 Rosa Bonheur's 'Labourage Nivernais', Hébert's 'Malaria', Couture's 'Decadent Romans': 'Labourage Nivernais' (Ploughing in the Nevers region) established the reputation of Marie Rosalie (Rosa) Bonheur (1822–99) and is now in the castle at Fontainebleau; Thomas Armstrong was commissioned to copy it in the Luxembourg Gallery. 'Malaria' by Ernest Hébert (1817–1908) is now in the Musée Hébert in Paris. 'Romains de la Décadence' by Ernest Couture (1815–79) is in the Louvre.

p.234 Ledoyen's: a restaurant in the Champs Elysées.

p.234 Lutetia: the Roman name for Paris.

p.234 *beati possidentes*!: blessed are they who have property! a play on the words of the sermon on the mount (Matthew, 6: 9).

p.234 Hampstead Heath: an area of open land in the north of London. Du Maurier lived in Hampstead and walked daily on the Heath. The fair on Easter Monday is famous.

p.234 *l'irrésistible*: the irresistible.

p.236 the Empress: the Empress Eugénie (1826–1920), wife of Napoleon III.

p.237 Second Empire: Reign of Napoleon III (1808–73; reigned 1852–70).

p.237 Albert Hall: built in South Kensington (1867–71) as a memorial to Queen Victoria's consort, Prince Albert of Saxe-Coburg-Gotha (1819–61).

p.237 *estrade*: rostrum.

p.237 Martin: John Martin (1789–1854), painter of huge canvasses and apocalyptic landscapes.

p.237 an august British personage ... broad blue ribbon: the Prince of Wales, later Edward VII (1841–1910). The ribbon is the sash of the Order of the Garter, instituted in the fourteenth century.

p.238 'Nussbaum' of Schumann: 'Es grünet ein Nussbaum vor dem Haus', a nut tree grows in front of my house; song from *Myrten* (1840), by Robert Schumann (1810–56) to words by Julius Mosen.

p.238 'Malbrouck s'en va-t'en guerre': 'Marlborough's off to war', an old French song, apparently referring to the campaigns of the first Duke of Marlborough but bearing little relation to the facts. In the song Marlborough dies in battle, which was not the case.

p.238 'un impromptu de Chopin, sans paroles': Du Maurier presumably means the same impromptu played by Svengali on p. 13. Pauline

Viardot (1821–1910), who 'sang' Chopin mazurkas in this way, must be an important model for Trilby.

p.240   Ellen Terry as the priestess of Artemis: Ellen Terry played the part of Camma in Tennyson's play *The Cup* at the Lyceum Theatre in 1881.

p.240   *gaucherie*: awkwardness.

p.242   Au clair de la lune . . .: traditional French nursery song.

> In the moonlight
> My friend Pierrot
> Lend me your pen
> To write a word.
> My candle has gone out . . .
> I have no other light!
> Open the door for me
> For the love of God!

p.242   Catalanis, Jenny Linds, Grisis: Angelica Catalani, Italian diva (1780–1849); Jenny (Johanna Maria) Lind, Swedish soprano (1820–87); Giulia Grisi (1811–69), Italian diva.

p.242   Pierrot and Columbine: figures from the Italian commedia del arte or the French pantomime. Pierrot is shown with a white face and a white baggy suit, and Columbine is the lover of Harlequin.

p.243   Marguerite . . . Faust!: Marguerite is betrayed by the scholar Faust in Goethe's play of 1808, but Du Maurier probably had in mind the opera of 1859 by Charles François Gounod (1818–93).

p.243   *débonnaire*: good-natured.

p.245   Vivarelli: apparently an invention.

p.245   Mädchen . . . Fräulein: German terms for a young girl and a young woman.

p.245   *verlobte*: a girl just engaged.

p.246   Elysium: the classical paradise.

p.246   Ida: the mountain near Troy in Homer's *Iliad*.

p.246   'Chanson de Printemps' by Gounod: 'Spring Song' by Gounod, an 1860 setting of a poem by E. Tourneux, which was then arranged as a song without words in 1866. Gounod, who is described as being in the audience, had died while Du Maurier was writing the novel.

p.247   Ne sais quand reviendra! . . . Il reviendra-z à Pâques. . . . Ou . . . à la Trinité!: I do not know when he will come back . . . He will come back at Easter or at Trinity.

p.247   La Trinité se passe ... Malbrouck ne revient pas!: Trinity passed, Marlborough did not return.

p.249   Madame à sa tour ... :

> His lady climbs her tower,
> As high as she can climb
> She sees afar her page
> All dressed in black!
> My good page, my good page
> What news do you bring?

p.249   Sarah Jennings: the wife of the first Duke of Marlborough (1660–1744).

p.249   Aux nouvelles ... :

> When you hear the news I bring
> Your lovely eyes will weep!
> Change out of your pink dresses
> And your satin brocade
> Marlborough is dead
> Milord Marlborough is dead and buried!

p.250   We won't go home till morning ... : the music was associated with 'Malbrouck' from the eighteenth century, but may date from much earlier. The song 'We won't go home till morning', to the same tune, appeared in England and America in the mid-nineteenth century.

p.253   *pianissimo*: very softly.

p.253   Berlioz: Hector Berlioz, French composer (1803–69). Berlioz was the music critic of the *Journal des Débats*, but *La Lyre Éolienne* is fictitious.

p.254   Théophile Gautier: French poet, novelist and critic (1811–72); his account of Trilby is also fictitious.

p.254   Herr Blagner: Richard Wagner, German composer and poet (1813–83). This passage is based partly upon Wagner's battles with the popular writers of opera, such as the Italian composers Vincenzo Bellini (1801–35) and Gaetano Donizetti (1797–1848) and the German/French composer Jacques Offenbach (1819–80). Wagner, with his father-in-law Franz Liszt (1811–86), was also part of a progressive German movement, in opposition to the traditional practice of Schumann, Johannes Brahms (1833–97) and others.

p.254   *café chantant*: café with a cabaret singer.

p.257   by hopeless fancy feigned ... : Tennyson, 'Tears, idle tears', *The Princess*, IV, 37–8, published 1847.

p.260 *Il y en a toujours un autre!*: There's always someone else involved!

Part Seventh

p.262 **The moon has made thy lips pale . . .**: Shelley, 'The cold earth slept beneath', IV, 1.

p.262 **As when we dwell . . .**: Tennyson, *Lancelot and Elaine*, 1859, line 1020.

p.263 **'Marriage of Cana' and the 'Woman at the Well', and Vandyck's man with the glove, and the little Princess of Velasquez, and Lisa Gioconda's smile**: 'The Marriage Feast at Cana' is by Veronese. The 'Woman at the Well' is something of a mystery; such titles usually refer to representations of Christ with the Woman of Sumeria, but there is no obvious work of this kind in the Louvre. Du Maurier may have been thinking of the famous 'Concert Champêtre' of Titian, on the left of which a woman draws water from a fountain. 'The Man with a Glove' is by Titian and not Van Dyck. The Velasquez is a portrait of the Infanta Marie Marguerite (1651–73), daughter of Philip IV of Spain. Lisa Gioconda is the sitter in Leonardo's 'Mona Lisa'.

p.263 *coûte que coûte!*: cost what it may!

p.263 **Pré Catalan**: a park within the Bois de Boulogne, named after a captain of the local hunt.

p.263 **Crystal Palace**: originally erected in Hyde Park for the Great Exhibition of 1851, the Crystal Palace was later moved to South London. It was destroyed by fire in 1936.

p.264 *dégringolé!*: tumbled down, slipped down.

p.264 **'très joli garçon . . . fait bien!'**: 'he was a handsome boy, well turned out and very well bred. The Rigolets are a very old family – from Poitou, I think – Lafarce and all that, very fine indeed!'

p.264 **Compiègne**: a town north of Paris, with a royal palace loved by Napoleon III.

p.265 **'le joli petit peintre . . . copain Dodor!'**: 'the nice little English painter called Little Billee who couldn't stand on his own feet, and who used to weep tears of brotherly love in the arms of my mate Dodor!'

p.265 **'ce que je donnerais . . . c'est impayable!'**: 'what I'd have given to see that. . . . One of my guardsmen – on all fours – in the street – with a hat in his mouth – oh, it's priceless!'

p.265 **'très bien pensant . . . et à Rome'**: 'very right-thinking, and very well taught at Frohsdorf and at Rome'. Frohsdorf is an Austrian castle which became the residence of the Count de Chambord (1820–83), who represented the 'legitimate' Bourbon claim to the throne of France.

p.265 'Un très brave homme, à ce qu'on dit!': 'A very fine man, from what they say!'

p.265 'Il ne fait pas gras . . . assure!': 'He doesn't eat meat with us at the moment, I promise you!'

p.267 '*particeps delicti*': 'his companion in crime'.

p.267 '*mais bien pour ses beaux yeux!*: 'but for the sake of his pretty face!'

p.268 un '*huit-ressorts*': a carriage with eight springs.

p.271 *Par nobile fratrum*: A noble pair of brothers; Horace, *Satires*, II, Satire 3, 243.

p.272 *en perspective*: in expectation.

p.272 *ingénue*: unsophisticated girl.

p.272 'Les Cloches du Monastère: the bells of the monastery. Louis James Alfred Lefébure Wély (1817–69) was the organist of the Madeleine until 1858 and then took up the same post at St Sulpice. His compositions were usually ecclesiastical and choral works or piano pieces.

p.272 Noah Claypole in *Oliver Twist*: the unpleasant fellow apprentice of the hero in Dickens's novel of 1838.

p.274 Venus Anadyomene: Venus rising from the waves.

p.274 *blanche comme neige . . . dans le coeur*: white as snow, with a volcano in her heart.

p.274 Rue de la Souricière St Denis: 'street of the snare or police trap of St Denis'; an invented name.

p.274 a 'Hari-Kari in Yokohama': a common corruption of Hara Kiri, suicide by disembowelment as practised among the upper classes in Japan. Yokohama is the principal Pacific port in Japan.

p.274 'verfluchter Schweinhund': accursed filthy fellow.

p.275 'Lâche . . . mes témoins!': 'Great big coward! I'll give you my seconds!' Svengali, who is threatening to fight a duel with Taffy, says that he will send his emissaries, his seconds.

p.277 'C'est une affaire . . . et autre part!': 'It's an affair which will be sorted out in a different way and in a different place!'

p.281 Stereoscopic Company in Regent Street: a photographic company, founded in 1854, which, by this date, specialised in small 'carte de visite' photographs. Du Maurier had one of himself taken there.

p.282   **an Oriental Israelite Hebrew Jew**: added in book edition.

p.282   **Front-de-Boeuf**: an unpleasant Norman noble in Scott's *Ivanhoe* (1819).

p.282   **ruffians that treated Jews like dogs**: added in book edition.

p.283   **'Home, Sweet Home'**: one of the most popular of all Victorian ballads, the music by Henry R. Bishop (1786–1855) and the words by John Howard Payne (1791–1852).

p.283   **'ne me battez pas ... ce que je peux!'**: 'don't hit me, my friend, I'm doing all I can!'

p.287   **'Mais chantez donc ... connais ça!'**: 'Well, sing then, Madame – for the love of God, begin then – begin!' ... 'Sing? But why do you want me to sing? And sing what?' 'But "Ben Bolt", of course, good heavens – sing!' 'Ah – "Ben Bolt", yes – I know that.'

p.287   **'Comment diable' ... 'chantez!'**: 'How the devil do you expect me to sing with all this crowd, all these confounded musicians!' 'But, my God, Madame – what's wrong with you?' 'I'd rather sing without all this devilish music, good Lord! I'd rather sing by myself!' 'Without music then – but sing – sing!'

p.287   **'Qu'est-ce que ... peur de vous?'**: 'What's wrong with all of you? You're a heap of rotten old potatoes! Do you think we're afraid of you?'

p.289   **'qu'est-ce qu'elle ... devenue folle!'**: what's wrong with your wife? ... she's gone mad!'

p.292   **Haymarket**: runs south from Piccadilly Circus.

p.292   **'On va vous y conduire' ... 'Qu'est-ce qu'il a?'**: 'We're going to drive you there.' ... 'Yes, that's it ... but Svengali – where is he?' 'Ah, Madame, he is very ill.' 'What's wrong with him?'

p.293   **Jermyn Street**: runs west from the Haymarket.

p.294   **'J'aime tant ça – c'est le ciel!'**: 'I love all that, it's heavenly!'

p.296   **Place Notre Dame des Victoires**: in the 2ème near the Bourse.

p.298   **Rue des Saints Pères**: in the St Germain quarter, in the 6ème.

p.298   **Elberfeld in Prussia**: there is apparently no Elberfeld in Prussia, but there is a town of that name near Wuppertal in what is now Nord Rhein Westphalia.

p.300 **'Dors, ma mignonne!'**: 'Now sleep my little darling!'

p.304 **All three, perhaps**: added in book edition.

p.304 **Circe**: in Homer's *Odyssey*, the enchantress Circe turns men into wild animals.

p.307 **Dr Jakes Talboys**: Jacob Wilcox in *Harper's*.

p.307 **'Je voudrais bien ... dérange pas'.**: 'I would very much like to speak to the landlady, if I'm not disturbing her'.

Part Eighth

p.310 **'La vie est vaine ... Et puis – bonsoir**: Léon Monte-Naken (b. 1859), 'Peu de Chose'.

> Life is futile
> A little love
> A little hatred
> And then – good day!
>
> Life is short
> A little hope,
> A few dreams
> And then – goodnight

Du Maurier's own translation appears on p. 356.

p.310 **'Ah, pauvrette ... ange du Paradis!'**: 'Ah poor little girl, the poor little girl – ah, sir! – I loved her so much, I loved her so much! There aren't many like her, O God of wretchedness. She's an angel from Heaven.'

p.311 **Trilby vue à travers quatre tempéraments!**: Trilby viewed in four different attitudes.

p.315 **homme d'affaires**: business manager.

p.316 **congé**: dismissal.

p.318 **Tam o' Shanter**: a round woven cap; the name comes from a poem by Robert Burns (1759–96).

p.318 **demoiselle de comptoir**: barmaid.

p.319 **Dr Cummings**: John Cumming, Scottish Divine (1807–81), who published works including *The Great Tribulation or Things Coming on the Earth* (1859) and *The Sounding of the last Trumpet* (1867).

p.320 **Pilgrim's Progress**: an allegory of the Christian life by John Bunyan (1628–88).

p.320 John Leech's *Pictures of Life and Character*: published 1854, with later volumes in 1857, 1860, 1863 and 1869.

p.321 'Après tout . . . ma foi!': 'After all, it's not too bad to die. I've seen many who have gone that way. At the end of the ditch there's a drop, believe me!'

p.321 *casseur de pierres*: stone breaker, a road worker.

p.321 Impasse des Taupes St Germain: unidentified; it means 'Mole Cul-de-Sac'.

p.321 *Il y aura amnistie générale!*: there will be a general amnesty!

p.322 Invalide: pensioned soldier from the Invalides.

p.322 Vieille Garde: the old guard, Napoleon's finest troops.

p.322 Parlez-nous de lui grandmère!: Grandmother tell us about him; Béranger, 'Les Souvenirs du Peuple'.

p.322 *blagué*'d: teased.

p.322 'C'est égal, voyez-vous!': 'It's the same thing, you see!'

p.324 Palm Sunday: the Sunday before Easter, when Christ's entry into Jerusalem is celebrated.

p.324 St Philippe du Roule: in the 8ème, between the Boulevard Haussmann and the Champs Élysées.

p.324 'who – who was Mathieu's mistress . . . Ste Maritorne la Pocharde': added in the book edition. 'Maritorne' means a slut, and is the name of the servant girl in *Don Quixote*; 'pocharde' means a drunken woman.

p.326 Catherine the Great . . . Madame Rachael or George Sand: all women known to have had lovers. Catherine II, Empress of Russia (1729–96); Elizabeth Rachel Félix, French actress (1821–58), George Sand, French novelist (1804–76).

p.326 the Atonement and the Incarnation: expiation of human sin and assumption of human form by Christ.

p.327 *Ce serait trop bête!*: that would be too wicked!

p.332 'Encore une fois? . . . donne-moi le ton!': 'Once again? Very well, I would certainly like to. With a pure voice, like that? And then sink down to the middle register. And not too quick at the beginning! Give the beat clearly, Svengali – so that I can see it well – for it's night already! That's it! Come on Gecko, give me my note!'

p.332 '**Gott im Himmel! wieder zurück!**': 'God in Heaven! Back again!'

p.333 '**Cạ y est-il . . . bon soir!**': 'Is that right, was it right this time, Svengali? Ah! Much better at the end! That's not too bad! And now, my friend, I'm tired – good night!'

p.333 caravansérai: originally an eastern inn with an inner court for caravans; here the courtyard of a hotel.

p.335 *ex pede Herculem*: from his foot you can tell Hercules; i.e. you can tell the whole from a small part.

p.335 Viscount of Bragelonne – *bon chien chasse de race!*: a dog of good pedigree; the Viscount of Bragelonne is the eponymous hero of a novel of 1850 by Dumas the elder.

p.335 Wilfred of Ivanhoe . . . Edgar, the Lord of Ravenswood: the dispossessed heroes of two of Scott's novels, *Ivanhoe* and *The Bride of Lammermoor* (1819).

p.335 Colonel Newcome: the father of the hero of Thackeray's novel *The Newcomes* (1855), a particular favourite with Du Maurier.

p.336 *Tout vient à point, à qui sait attendre!*: All things come to him who waits.

p.340 A.R.A.: Associate member of the Royal Academy.

p.341 '*Que le bon dieu les bénisse! . . . braves gens*': 'May God bless them! They were such fine fellows.'

p.341 *parlez-moi de ça!*: tell me about that!

p.341 the Salon, the Louvre, the porcelain manufactory at Sèvres, the Gobelins, the Hôtel Cluny, the Invalides: the Parisian annual exhibition of new painting; the Louvre; the Royal porcelain factory at Sèvres, between Paris and Versailles; the tapestry factory in south-east Paris in the 13ème; the museum of medieval antiquities in a fourteenth-century monastic building in the rue du Sommerard in the 6ème; the home for old soldiers, originally built in the seventeenth century, where Napoleon's ashes were placed in 1840.

p.341 the Variétés: home of vaudeville and operetta, in the Boulevard Montmartre in the 11ème.

p.341 Madame Chaumont: Céline Chaumont, French actress (1848–1926), who appeared at the Variétés in the 1870s.

p.341 the Français: there have been several Parisian theatres called the Français, but none was apparently operating in the 1870s. Du

Maurier probably meant the Comédie, where Bernhardt, Coquelin and Delaunay were all working at the time.

p.341 Sarah Bernhardt and Coquelin and Delaunay: Henriette Rosine Bernard, Sarah Bernhardt (1844–1923), was the greatest actress of her generation; Benoit Constant Coquelin (1841–1909) acted in French classic comedy; Louis Arsène Delaunay (1826–1903) played many classic roles.

p.341 Lassalle: Jean-Louis Lassalle, French baritone (c1845–1909); he was based at the Paris Opéra in the 1870s.

p.341 *sur le pouce*: to eat a snack.

p.341 Durand's: no. 2 Place de la Madeleine.

p.341 Café des Ambassadeurs: in the Champs Élysées.

p.341 Mouches d'Espagne and Madame Cantharidi: The name Cantharidi is the biological term for a Spanish fly, which is also the name of the theatre. There was a Théâtre de Folies Espagnole at 57 rue Taitbout, in the 9ème.

p.341 'Petits Bonheurs de Contrebande': little pleasures of smuggling.

p.343 *La Revanche*: The Revenge.

p.343 Victors or vanquished . . . laugh the same!: unidentified.

p.343 V'là une jolie p'tite Anglaise ... celui-là!': 'There's a pretty little English girl who isn't prudish, at any rate! And the great ox with the eyes like loto balls – he's her husband, no doubt! He doesn't look very happy, does he!'

p.344 *obbligato*: literally, 'necessary'; an obbligato instrument has an important, semi-solo role.

p.344 Café Anglais: 13 Boulevard des Italiens, in the 2ème.

p.344 le premier violon ... cheveux blancs: the first violin, the one with white hair.

p.344 chambertin: Burgundy wine.

p.345 'Ah! c'était un ange! un ange du Paradis!': 'Ah, she was an angel, an angel from Heaven!'

p.345 artichokes à la Barigoule: artichokes stuffed and fried in oil.

p.345 *toujours souffrante!*: always in pain.

p.347 V'là mon mari ...: unidentified; the song is repeated on p. 356.

> There's my husband watching!
> Take care – don't tickle me!

p.347 *'quant à ça*: 'as regards her'.

p.348 *'en veux-tu en voilà!'* 'you want some? there you are!'

p.350 *'Bel ucel di Dio! ... de la voir!'*: 'God's beautiful bird ... it was enough to make you weep for love just to see her!'

p.352 *à se boucher les oreilles!*: to make you stop your ears!

p.352 *ce pauvre Litrebili, ce qu'il a perdu!*: poor Little Billee, think what he lost!

p.352 *un écho, un simulacre ... pas autre chose!*: an echo, an image, a sham, nothing else!

p.352 *chaconne*: originally a dance, often for the end of a ballet.

p.352 *il s'en moque pas mal, ce fameux violon!*: he doesn't acquit himself badly, this famous violin!

p.353 *demantibulate*: dislocate her jaw.

p.353 Gott sei dank! Ich habe *geliebt und gelebet!*: God be praised! I have loved and lived! 'Ich habe gelebt und geliebet' was a well-known song by Maude Valerie White (*c.*1885).

p.353 'O Dieu de Misère, ayez pitié de nous': 'God of wretchedness, have pity on us'.

p.355 'si bon et sympathique accueil': 'for such fine hospitality'.

p.355 'Ah, bon ... n'est-ce pas': 'Ah good – I know him well. You know he plays the violin at the Mouches d'Espagne. He's had his dinner, is that right sir? "Little Joys of Smuggling", eh? ... don't worry! we will take care of him! He plays terribly well, sir, doesn't he?'

p.355 'Où restez-vous' ... 'au cinquième': 'Where are you staying, Gecko?' 'Forty eight rue des Pousse-Cailloux, in the 5ème'.

p.355 'Oui, oui ... *j'y reste* ...': Yes, yes, it's the garret where Trilby used to live – I've been there for twelve years – there I live, and there I will stay.'

p.356 'Merci, m'sieur ... monsieur et dame!': 'Thank you, sir! It's on the other side of the river, near the Sorbonne. Do you know it? We'll take care of the old fellow. Relax, don't worry! Forty eight, let's go. Goodnight, monsieur and madame!'

p.356 *Où peut-on ... sa famille?*: Where could one be happier than in the bosom of one's family? From the Quartet from the opera *Lucille* (1769) by André Grétry (1741–1813).

p.356 A little work ...: Du Maurier's translation of Léon Monte-Naken's 'Peu de Chose'; lines from this poem are quoted on his grave in Hampstead.

DU MAURIER AND HIS CRITICS

By literary critical or academic standards, *Trilby* has never been regarded as a novel of the first rank. It has, however, continued to be widely read and to attract attention, either as a runaway best-seller or as an archetypal and mythic work. The name of the novel's villain, Svengali, is a generally accepted term for a teacher or father-figure who attempts to gain an unholy possession of his pupil's mind. This, together with the Trilby hat, has helped to ensure the book's immortality.

Early reviews

Trilby was serialised before appearing in a book edition and reviewers delayed writing until the work was complete. By this time two things were clear: the novel was remarkably popular and it was a *roman à clef*. James Whistler's threatened lawsuit only increased *Trilby*'s fame. Under such circumstances, reviewers behaved predictably. Most condemned the book as shallow or meretricious and some seized the opportunity to indulge in spiteful gossip. Others, such as the writer in *The New York Review of Books* for October 1895, merely printed a summary of the story of *Trilby*, in this case entitled 'The Book of the Month'.

One of the few serious reviews came from the critic of the *Athenaeum* (29 September 1894). The review quickly established some of the novel's antecedents:

> The manner and the mannerisms of the elder Dumas, of Dickens, and of Thackeray are imitated on nearly every page, and there are numerous references to their characters. . . . the story is told with never-failing enthusiasm, with the good humour of a Gallic Pendennis which nothing can destroy – not even the parenthetic outbursts against snobbery, censoriousness, prudery, and truculent criticism. If anything wearies, it is the eternal superlative in which Mr Du Maurier's thoughts are expressed. He scorns comparison which admits of calculated degrees (p. 418).

Like several modern writers on Du Maurier, the *Athenaeum* reviewer admitted to a preference for the earlier novel, *Peter Ibbetson*.

The *Athenaeum*'s comparison of Du Maurier's style with Thackeray's narrative manner is repeated in several other reviews. The elder novelist's frequent interjection of his own views was clearly echoed in *Trilby*, and Du Maurier never denied that Thackeray was his master. Even so, he must have winced at the *Pall Mall Gazette*'s unflattering title 'Thackeray for the Kitchen' (5 October 1894), which prefaced a stinging personal attack from a magazine which vociferously supported Whistler.

In strict evangelical circles *Trilby* was regarded as a potentially corrupting work, and even in more liberal families it was often kept away from young girls. The critic of the *Westminster Review*, Mary G. Husband, took a great deal of space to say very little about the novel. Instead, she welcomed the opportunity to launch an attack on the book's anti-clericalism and apparent defence of sexual freedom, a line much followed in the United States.

George Bernard Shaw, '*Trilby*: an Entertainment in four acts based by Paul Potter on Du Maurier's Novel', *Saturday Review* 80 (9 November 1895), 617–18, reprinted in *Our Theatres in the Nineties* (1932), I, 238–42.

The opening of the *Trilby* play by Paul Potter in October 1895 stimulated reviews which often cast an eye back over the novel. One of these came from George Bernard Shaw in the *Saturday Review* for 9 November 1895. Shaw said that he had read *Trilby* with pleasure and, on the evidence of Little Billee's anti-clerical harangue, he decided that Du Maurier was a man after his own heart, 'the pleasantest of freethinkers and the most charming of artists'.

> It is no mere novel with illustrations, it is a homogeneous work of art in which the master, like a composer who sets his own poem to music, shews us his people by the art of the draughtsman, and tells us their story by the art of the fabulist . . . (p. 617)

Shaw criticised Du Maurier for his characterisation. Each character, he believed, was drawn 'to please the author'. The novelist did not tell the truth about Taffy, Trilby was unreal, 'a man's dream', and Svengali a melodrama villain, 'a poor egotistical wretch' whose nose readers would want, like Taffy, to pull. The artist in Shaw recognised the divided personality in Svengali, at once the villain and 'the luckless artist-cad' (p. 617).

Henry James, 'George Du Maurier', *Harper's New Monthly Magazine* XXV (September 1897), 594–609.

The most perceptive early critic of *Trilby* was, not surprisingly, Du Maurier's close friend the novelist Henry James. In letters to Du Maurier and in published accounts of their relationship, James stressed the mystery of *Trilby*'s fame, acknowledging the novel's abundant charm, but failing to comprehend the precise quality which resulted in the *Trilby* boom. James, the younger and undoubtedly the greater novelist, was not destined to achieve such a success himself. He perceptively remarked that the structure of all three Du Maurier novels was essentially the same. Each had an autobiographical opening which led into the supernatural complications. Why then did the public single out *Trilby* from the others? James was unable to find an answer.

In the article which he wrote in *Harper's New Monthly Magazine* for September 1897, James noted that Du Maurier had always been a story teller and that his friends were already accustomed to hearing his reminiscences of early life. For this reason his late career as a novelist did not come as a complete surprise to them. Writing of the genesis of the novels, James recalled two of Du Maurier's strongest characteristics. One was the Anglo-French flavour of his conversation and the other the passion for tall people, which is reflected in the characters of Trilby and Taffy. Searching for the 'keynote' of the novels, James feared that he might be insisting too strongly upon the 'personal explanation':

> I can only cling to it, assuredly, till a better is offered. The whole performance is a string of moods and feelings, of contacts and sights and sounds. It is the voice of an individual, and individuals move to the voice, and the triumph is that they all together produce an impression, the impression that completely predominates, of the lovable, the sociable, of inordinate beauty and yet of inordinate reality (p. 605).

James initially read *Trilby* in the unillustrated edition, feeling it:

a positive comfort to be left alone with the text; and quite in spite of my fully recognizing all that, in the particular conditions, was done for it by the pictures ... *Trilby*, at all events, becomes without the illustrations distinctly more serious; which is just, by-the-way, I know, what the author would not have particularly wished us to be able to say (p. 605).

Concluding his analysis of the novels, James turns to a discussion of the melancholy which characterised Du Maurier's writing:

We find ourselves constantly in contact with the beautiful unhappy young: a circumstance from which, for my own part, I extract an irresistible charm. They are happy, of course, at the start; there would else be no chance for the finer complication. He does with the lightest brush both sides of their consciousness; but I think I like best his touch for the pains and the penalties. His feeling for life and fate arrives at a bright, free, sensible, melancholy utterance; to which his imagination gives a lift by showing us most the portion of the perpetual sacrifice that is offered up in admirable forms, in beautiful young men and young women – most even, perhaps, in beautiful young men. Nothing could be more contagious – he had an unerring hand for it – than the tenderness with which he surrounds these prepossessing unfortunates. They are so satisfactorily handsome – I can't otherwise express it; so fair, so detailed, so faultless, and, except the little painter in *Trilby*, so humiliatingly high, that – well, that it's a joy to live with them and immensely improves the society in which we move. Splendid and stricken each one of them then, and stricken, with the exception again perhaps of Trilby, not only by the outward blow, but by fine tragic perceptions, on their own part, which make them still more appealing. Peter Ibbetson is stricken, and stricken in all her inches the lovely companion of his dreams. The victim of Trilby is stricken, and Trilby, the admirable, the absolutely felicitous, most of all herself (pp. 605–6).

T. Martin Wood, *George Du Maurier: the Satirist of the Victorians* (London 1913).

T. Martin Wood's *George Du Maurier* was the first book-length study of Du Maurier's work as a whole. Wood was concerned mainly with the drawings but his third chapter is a discussion of 'Du Maurier as Author'. Emphatically anti-Victorian, Wood rates Joe Sibley the true artist of the book, not Little Billee. For him, *Trilby* is spoiled by 'a note of smugness' most clearly

exemplified in Little Billee, 'the most insufferable picture of a
hero of a romance', compromising 'the effect of the charmingly
haunting presence of Trilby herself, and of the great-hearted
gentleman in Taffy' (pp. 95–6). Wood believes that Du Maurier
'had a curious skill in revealing states of mind of real psychological and pathological interest', but that he was led astray into
the mechanical account of 'the preposterous mesmerism' (p. 93).

Lionel Stevenson, 'George Du Maurier and the Romantic
Novel', *Essays by Divers Hands* XXX (London: 1960), 36–54.

The 1950s and 1960s brought a resurgence of interest in Du
Maurier. On 20 June 1957, Lionel Stevenson read a paper on
'George Du Maurier and the Romantic Novel' to the Royal
Society of Literature. Published three years later in *Essays by
Divers Hands*, the paper represented the first serious and
extended discussion of Du Maurier as a writer of fiction for half
a century. Stevenson begins with an acknowledgement of his
predecessor, Henry James, but his essay is concerned primarily
to set Du Maurier's novels in their historical context.

Stevenson associates the 'blend of realistic detail and visionary
mental states' (p. 42), characteristic of all three novels, with Du
Maurier's early experience of Pre-Raphaelitism, paradoxically
seeing the novelist's 'defiance of conventional prudery' (p. 43)
in relation to the themes of realist novelists such as George
Moore and Emile Zola. Parallels are drawn with other nineteenth-century novels featuring the figure of the Wandering Jew
or the artist teacher.

Stevenson astutely notes the divisions in Du Maurier's
responses. On the one hand, the novelist cannot help dwelling
on the rhapsodic Paterian moment, unable to 'omit any of these
moments of ecstatic sensuous gratification, whether or not they
contribute directly to the advancement of the action' (p. 44).
The constant attempt to 'convey the ecstacy of sensuous
response to beauty – whether in music, or in paintings, or in
poetry, or in splendid human bodies, or even in odours and
flavours' (p. 43), is likened in detail to the beliefs of the aesthetic
movement, of which Du Maurier was (as a cartoonist in *Punch*)
a particularly devastating critic. Stevenson was the first to notice
the parallel between Du Maurier's evocation of the taste of the
madeleine in *Trilby* and the famous passage in *A la recherche*

du temps perdu by Marcel Proust. Within the same book, however, Du Maurier was condemning aesthetes and glorifying physical prowess.

Stevenson shows how Du Maurier's 'eager probing of the subconscious mind' (p. 44), and his preoccupation with such themes as hypnotism, renders his novels, set in the 1830s, 1840s and 1850s, entirely appropriate for the decade in which they were written, the 1890s. If melodrama tempted Du Maurier 'far beyond the bounds of scientific possibility' (p. 46), the novels succeed, Stevenson suggests, because of the author's exceptional powers of memory and because 'their point of departure' lies in 'scientifically demonstrable phenomena' (p. 46).

Stevenson places Du Maurier within the tradition of romance literature popular in the 1880s and 1890s, describing the novels as 'masterpieces of romantic fiction':

> All attempts to differentiate romanticism in literature from its antitheses, whether classicism or realism, emphasize that the work of a romantic writer is saturated with his own personality, whereas the classic or the realistic writer is relatively impersonal and objective. Even though a novel is necessarily less subjective than a lyric poem or an informal essay, du Maurier demonstrates the extent to which it can be made a vehicle for expressing the author's individuality. His life-long popularity with everyone who ever knew him was due to his exceptional qualities of humour and kindliness, and above all to his unlimited zest. He relished every hour of his life to its full, and in his novels he was able to share this gusto with his readers. His friends read the books with special delight when they discovered that he wrote exactly as he talked. His digressive comments, his emotional versatility – abruptly shifting from humour to pathos, from satire to sympathy – gave the flavour of his personality to every page (pp. 53–4).

Edmund Wilson, 'The Jews', *A Piece of my Mind* (London: 1957), pp. 78–80.

In the year when Lionel Stevenson's paper was delivered, 1957, Edmund Wilson published an essay on 'The Jews' in his *A Piece of my Mind*. His pages on Du Maurier follow from an analysis of attitudes towards Judaism among certain New England writers, and he mentions *Trilby*, an 'odd non-American example of this tendency to credit the Jews with supernatural powers' (p.

78). After considering the striking contrast between the part-Jewish villain of *Peter Ibbetson* and the half-Jewish heroine of *The Martian*, Wilson turns to *Trilby*, where the 'conception of the Jew is developed in a major and a very strange way' (pp. 78–9). Svengali and Little Billee share a Jewish background, although in Little Billee's case this is no more than a faint hint: 'But the great Jewish character in *Trilby* is, of course, the German-Jewish Svengali' (p. 79).

Wilson's real concern is with the contradictions in the presentation of Svengali: 'dirty, insulting, boastful, mendacious, malicious, quarrelsome' (p. 79). Svengali is nevertheless able to achieve 'astounding effects' by turning Trilby 'into a simple automaton' (p. 79).

> But from whence does all this subtlety and innocence, this tenderness and joy and sorrow, arise in the Svengali we know? There is no explanation of this: the character, in human terms, is not in any deep sense created. What is really behind Svengali is the notion, again, that the Jew, even in his squalidest form, is a mouthpiece of our Judaico-Christian God, whose voice he has, in this case, transferred ventriloquially to the throat of Trilby. (pp. 79–80)

Edgar Rosenberg, 'The Jew as Degenerate and Artist: Du Maurier', in *From Shylock to Svengali: Jewish Stereotypes in English Fiction* (Stanford, CA: 1960), pp. 234–61.

Wilson's lead in analysing the role of the Jew in *Trilby* was followed by Edgar Rosenberg in his book *From Shylock to Svengali* of 1960. Rosenberg ranks Du Maurier as a populariser rather than a genuine artist, and complains of his 'nonchalant way of putting a novel together' (p. 242). The 'general breathlessness' of Du Maurier's 'gushy and exclamatory style', with its 'cloyingly sophomoric asides' (p. 236) offends him.

Rosenberg compares Svengali with the Jewish artists and heroes of George Eliot and Disraeli, and notes that, in English fiction of the period, the 'Jew-villain was generally the product of the sensation-novel, while the good Jew was appropriated by the domestic realists' (p. 242). Like Stevenson, Rosenberg relates Svengali to the myth of the Wandering Jew, from which he sees Du Maurier as increasingly diverging during the course of the novel:

It is a little unsettling to discover that the Wandering Jew is sufficiently domesticated by 1894 to get cash from his family, which consists of 'his old father and mother, his sisters, his cousins and his aunts'. He turns out, in fact, to be rather unpleasantly bourgeois for a sorcerer. (p. 243)

For Rosenberg, Du Maurier's Wandering Jew, while at times comic or parodic, is also possessed of 'some of the ghastly attributes which had been toned down' by earlier novelists:

> one is never quite certain how funny Du Maurier intends him to be or how funny he looks, because Du Maurier pulls all the stops. Every so often Du Maurier endeavors to define his perspective by noting that Svengali 'was almost droll in the intensity of his terrible realism': one suspects that he may be a good deal more droll than Du Maurier meant him to be. (p. 247)

Rosenberg goes far beyond Wilson, or any other critic of Du Maurier, in his attack on the novelist's presumed anti-Semitism. He draws attention to two scenes which 'help to point up Du Maurier's least defensible and most nearly hysterical attitude' (p. 255). The first is the passage in Part Second where Svengali looks into Trilby's mouth. Rosenberg shows, through analysis of language, that Svengali's pursuit of Trilby is presented as 'something physically obscene and shameful' (p. 255). The other episode is the scene in Part Seventh where Taffy finds Svengali bullying Little Billee and shakes him by the nose and slaps him, an incident which probably leads to Svengali's death.

Leonee Ormond, 'Trilby' and 'Joe Sibley', in George Du Maurier (London: 1969), pp. 431–79; Richard Kelly, 'Trilby', in George Du Maurier (Boston: 1983).

The first major biography of Du Maurier was published by the present author in 1969. Two chapters, 'Trilby' and 'Joe Sibley', describe the publishing history of the novel and consider its relation to the novelist's life and psychology. A possible connection is made with the sensation novels which Du Maurier had illustrated in the 1860s. Richard Kelly's George Du Maurier of 1983 includes a separate chapter on Trilby in which Kelly takes up the question of the musical background of the novel and considers Svengali as a demonic musician.

SUGGESTIONS FOR FURTHER READING

Thomas Armstrong, 'Reminiscences of George Du Maurier', in *Thomas Armstrong C.B.: A Memoir*, ed. L. M. Lamont, Martin Secker, 1912.

Daphne Du Maurier and Derek Pepys Whiteley, *The Young George Du Maurier: A Selection of his Letters*, Peter Davies, 1951.

L. N. Feipel, 'The American Issues of *Trilby*', *Colophon*, II, No. 4 (Autumn 1937), pp. 537–49.

J. L. and J. B. Gilder, *Trilbyana: The Rise and Progress of a Popular Novel*, New York, Critic Company, 1895.

Henry James, 'George Du Maurier', *Harper's Weekly Magazine*, XXV (September 1897), pp. 594–609.

Richard Kelly, *George Du Maurier*, Twayne, Boston, 1983.

Leonee Ormond, *George Du Maurier*, Routledge and Kegan Paul, 1969.

Edward L. Purcell, 'Trilby and Trilby-Mania: The Beginning of the Bestseller System', *Journal of Popular Culture* XI (Summer 1977), 62–76.

Lionel Stevenson, 'George Du Maurier and the Romantic Novel', *Essays by Divers Hands*, Oxford University Press, 1960, pp. 36–54.

T. M. Wood, *George Du Maurier: The Satirist of the Victorians*, Chatto and Windus, 1913.

TEXT SUMMARY

Part First
The three English artists – Taffy, the Man of Blood; Sandy, the Laird of Cockpen; and 'Little Billee' Bagot – are in their studio in Paris's Place St Anatole des Arts. The musical genius Svengali is playing their piano, accompanied by his violinist, Gecko, when Trilby O'Ferrall, an artists' model, enters, drawn there by the sound of music. She charms the company, singing the worst rendition of 'Ben Bolt' that any one of them has ever heard, and then leaves. Billee is smitten, and makes a sketch on the wall from memory of her beautiful left foot.

Two or three days later, Trilby calls again. Several friends are there, including Gontran 'l'Zouzou' and Jules Guinot, with whom Trilby exchanges some pleasantries about a party the night before. Billee's French being poor, he misconstrues the conversation, and when she has left he feels disappointed in her. The narrator defends her character, and tells us of her background.

Part Second
We learn more of Svengali, particularly of his treatment of 'Mimi la Salope', an artists' model whom he trained as a singer, worked too hard, became frustrated with, and finally threw out onto the street. Visiting Sandy to borrow money, he meets Trilby suffering from a painful neuralgia of the eyes, which he cures using hypnosis.

We see inside Monsieur Carrel's school, and hear how Billee and Taffy dealt with the ritual of '*l'échelle*'.

Trilby devotes more time to the three Englishmen and they all become fond of her. Little Billee is often pained by the idea that she models for the figure, and the narrator again defends her, and in doing so, nudity. They all take her brother Jeannot to the *garde champêtre's*, after which Sandy falls ill, and Trilby nurses him back to health. We learn that both Gecko and Svengali are in love with her in their own way.

Part Third
The three friends return from a short holiday to find that Trilby is modelling at Carrel's. Billee is so upset that he has to return to the seclusion of Fontainebleau to get over it. Taffy and the Laird begin to suspect that he loves Trilby, and that she loves him.

When she realises why Billee has left, Trilby is so upset that she has to go home. She stays there, too ashamed to see her friends, or even to leave her house for a few days, but Sandy reassures her and coaxes her back to the Place St Anatole des Arts. When Billee returns, the two are reconciled. Trilby resolves that she will work to improve herself over the next few months. The narrator takes advantage of this rather uneventful period in the story to introduce us to a few of the three friends' acquaintances.

Little Billee visits the Fête de St Cloud with Gontran and Dodor and learns of Gontran's noble family. A Christmas feast is planned at the studio.

Part Fourth

The Christmas feast. As Trilby is leaving, Billee proposes to her, and threatens to leave Paris for good if she refuses. Despite strong misgivings, she accepts. Later on, Billee gets very drunk, and staggers through Paris in the company of Gontran and Dodor. The next morning, when he has recovered, Billee finds that he has completely lost his faculty for recalling sensations and emotions at will.

On New Year's Day, Billee's mother and sister and his uncle Thomas, a clergyman, visit the studio. Billee has left Paris to avoid them. Mrs Bagot is distressed at the news of her son's engagement, and asks Taffy about Trilby's character. He is forced to admit that it would be an unfortunate match for Billee, and he and the Laird agree to try to stop it. Purely by chance, Trilby appears and promises Mrs Bagot that she will never see Billee again. Both Mrs Bagot and Billee's sister Blanche, who is waiting in the carriage outside, are impressed with her, but Mrs Bagot feels it her paramount duty to protect her son. Trilby meets Sandy outside, and tells him that she plans to leave Paris.

Billee returns to Paris, haggard and desperate. After a violent scene in which he accuses his friends of treachery, he collapses and becomes severely ill for several months, during which he is constantly attended by his mother and sister. In February, news arrives from the country that Jeannot has died and that Trilby has disappeared. Billee slowly recovers, but he finds that he has now lost his ability to feel love towards anyone. When he is well enough to travel, the Bagots return to England, taking Billee with them.

Over the next five years, Billee's reputation as an artist grows and grows, but his capacity for love does not return. After some time he feels he must leave the family house in Devonshire, to pursue his career in London.

Parth Fifth

Taffy and Sandy leave Paris and travel Europe for the next few years, after which they meet Billee in London. At a party they hear of 'La

Svengali', the protégée and wife of their old friend Svengali, and said to be by far the greatest singer alive.

Back in Devonshire, Billee becomes involved with a friend of his sister named Alice, but he is unsure whether he is doing the right thing. After a heated argument about religion with the girl's father, a parson, he decides to break it off.

Part Sixth
The three Englishmen visit Paris to hear La Svengali. They find Dodor working in a haberdasher's shop run by his father-in-law, Monsieur Passefil. Dodor comes to dine at their hotel, and when he leaves he invites them to dine with the Passefils the next night.

At the concert, they recognise La Svengali to be Trilby, her voice now magically transformed. They also see Gecko, who is playing first violin in the orchestra. Billee seems happy, but passes a bad night.

Part Seventh
Strolling about the Bois de Boulogne the next day, the three friends meet Gontran and his prospective wife, a wealthy American heiress named Lavinia Hunks. Afterwards the three friends argue about the morality of marrying for money and title.

In the Place de la Concorde, the three Englishmen are cut by Trilby and Svengali. They dine with the Passefils, and the next day prepare to leave Paris. In the hotel post-office Billee runs into Svengali who attacks him. Taffy breaks it up, pulling Svengali's nose and making a fool of him. The three Englishmen return to London, then Billee travels to Devonshire for Christmas, where he is again rather miserable. Taffy goes with him and stays nearby. When Mrs Bagot is told that they have seen Trilby once again she is very upset at recalling Billee's illness, and bitterly regrets her part in it.

After Christmas, Taffy and Billee go to London. They have not been there long before La Svengali comes to make her debut. At a rehearsal, Gecko stabs Svengali in the neck while defending Trilby. The concert is postponed for a week while Svengali recovers.

When the concert eventually takes place, Taffy, Sandy and Billee all go to it. Svengali is still not well, so the concert promoter conducts in his place. Svengali is given a box close to the stage. Trilby's opening song is to be 'Ben Bolt', but she repeatedly misses her cue to start, her eyes permanently fixed on Svengali. Eventually the conductor grows angry and orders her to sing. Trilby looks bewildered and gives a rendition quite as bad as her first in the Place St Anatole des Arts. The conductor appeals to Svengali, but discovers that the latter is dead in his box.

Billee takes the very confused Trilby back to his lodgings and sends for the doctor. She stays with him, but becomes very ill. She can remember exactly how she had become involved with Svengali, but not a single thing of her singing career. She recalls that he would send her to sleep whenever she felt uneasy, and she would wake up tired out. Despite the attention of several doctors, her health does not improve.

Part Eighth

Gecko is cleared of murder, but is given six months' hard labour for his attack. It soon becomes clear that Trilby has not long to live. She has many visitors and this keeps her happy. Mrs Bagot comes at Billee's request and stays to nurse Trilby. She asks Trilby about her faith, which is predictably unorthodox. Trilby tells the story of her greatest regret, which was to break a promise to Jeannot, and says that she has always repented of her sexual indiscretions while a model.

One Sunday afternoon, after Trilby has dictated her will, a large framed photograph of Svengali arrives, sent anonymously from 'the mysterious East'. Looking at it, Trilby falls under its spell. She becomes La Svengali long enough to sing one beautiful song, and then dies suddenly but peacefully.

Twenty years after, Taffy is in Paris with his wife, Billee's sister. Billee is dead, having fallen ill again at Trilby's death and never fully recovered. Sandy is in Scotland to be married. In the evening, the couple go to see a rather vulgar play recommended to them by Dodor, and Taffy recognises Gecko in the orchestra. They arrange to meet him after the concert.

Gecko tells them of Svengali's meticulous training of Trilby's voice, and the way he would cruelly overwork her. When Taffy quizzes him about Trilby's loss of memory and her last song, Gecko replies that there were 'two Trilbys', the one whom they all knew, and another who was entirely Svengali's creation, merely to earn him fame and to gratify his self-love. They say goodbye.

ACKNOWLEDGEMENTS

My chief debt is to Angus Wrenn, who helped me to translate the French passages and who traced many of the Parisian locations. Oliver Davies has made some truly remarkable discoveries about the many musical references in *Trilby*. Among others who have helped me track down some of the more elusive entries are Clive Bush, Anne Buddle, Hugh Cheape, Marie Denley, Christopher Elrington, Derek Glass, Diana Marshall, Eric Mottram, Richard Ormond, Constance Rahnen-Führer, Caroline Richmond, Judith Siford, Elspeth Wrenn, Shamoon Zamir, and, not for the first time, the French Department of King's College, London. My sincere thanks go to them all.